A Love by Any Measure

Killian McRae

Tulipe Noire Press

CALIFORNIA 2011

ALSO BY KILLIAN McRAE:

12.21.12

TALLIS

To Robin, Lisa, Michele, Jen, and Laura-

For words mean little, but actions do not. Thank you for your friendship.

In remembrance of Pa Short. If not for him, I would not have had clothes on my back, food on my plate, and love in my heart.

A Love by Any Measure

Killian McRae

Tulipe Noire Press
P.O. Box 815, Palo Alto, CA 94302
www.tulipenoirepress.com

First Print Edition, November 2011
First eBook Edition, November 2011

ISBN (print): 978-0-9839797-0-8
ISBN (electronic): 978-0-9839797-1-5

Chapters

I | The Arrangement

~Killarney, Ireland~

Fall 1866

"We have an understanding then."

Lord August Grayson sneered as his prideful, bemused eyes took in her frame from tip to toe. It might as well have been his hands that catalogued her every feature, so astute was his examination.

Maeve shuddered at the thought. *His hands.* With that to which she had just agreed, it wouldn't be long, she supposed, until it was those hands and not just his eyes that were exploring her on all sides and in all measures.

His attention turned back to her expression, no doubt noting the last threads of her hesitation dancing across her face in the form of a mouth slightly agape.

She took a quick, shallow breath, her gaze searching the floor for a divine sign, a reprieve waiting there for her and her father's precarious situation. She and Rory, while of meager means, did not consider themselves paupers. And they certainly didn't consider themselves beggars. But rent was due on their cottage, the cottage which sat on Grayson-deeded land, and there just wasn't money to pay.

Maeve wasn't sure what she had expected when setting out for the land-lord's middleman, the overseer of his estate who collected rents from the dozen or so tenants spread across the east shore of Middle Lake. At best, perhaps to buy some time—a month or two—until she could figure out something, *anything.*

When instead of the massive Irishman she sought, she crossed paths with the lord of the manor himself, she was befuddled. Stinging memories of August Grayson from ten years before remained, a mixed sack of pleasant afternoons weighted against the smoldering pain of the last moments they had spent together. They had been barely more than children then. Though she had heard several weeks prior of his return to Killarney, she had yet to catch more than a distant glimpse of him. That he should have grown to be so uncompromisingly handsome—a fine figure of a man who had never known hunger, with ebony hair and eyes greener than any Englishman had right to possess—smarted worse than his dominion over her. It would have been much easier to despise him properly if he had grown to be hefty, bald, and sickly.

Looking back up and trying to remain stoic, she could barely conceal the he unnerved her, how his return twisted her in knots. She simultaneously wanted to throw her arms around him, and to whack him with the riding crop that he rolled in his hands. But she wouldn't give him the honor of knowing he did anything to her. Ma had once said that the opposite of love wasn't hate, it was indifference. She would strive to be indifferent now, not to give him the honor of her kindness or her hate. She would not, *could* not, look him in the eye. She struggled to hold onto the last thing she had still in her control—her pride.

"I understand," Maeve returned, lifting her head ever so slightly to meet his gaze.

"Good," he answered. "See it through, and consider your rent paid."

Such emerald eyes were entrancing and seductive, but they could not outweigh the inhumanity of the compromise he had just offered. "I understand, but I will take no pleasure from it."

He marched to within inches of her quivering frame, his mouth so close to her ear that she actually heard him lick his lips.

"This isn't about your pleasure," he reminded her, a hint of both reprimand and excitement in his voice. He chuckled softly as he backed away, sensing the effect his proximity had. "You and your father can stay in your little cottage on my property as long as you present yourself to me when summoned. *Whenever*, without qualification. However, because I am a gracious, God-fearing man, you may reserve Sundays for your own affairs."

A disgusted scoff escaped Maeve's lips as he claimed the title of God-fearing. *Godless is more apt,* she thought.

At a distance better suited for gauging, his hungry gaze drank her in. Her attire certainly didn't flatter; the simple full length brown skirt and long-sleeved cotton shirt was likely as far from the glamour and glitter of British society as she could manage to achieve. Her hair was unkempt, though not messy, but it also wasn't neatly fashioned so as to enhance the soft curvature of her chin or the understated earthen tone of her eyes.

To a peasant, beauty was as much a disadvantage as not, and Maeve had learned early in life the danger being desirable held. It was for this reason she had shunned most suitors and allowed her reputation for being disinterested in marriage endure for so long. Not taking any efforts to appear more comely to the opposite sex helped as well. It was also the reason, however, that she was still unwed at the advanced age of twenty-two.

If anything could be garnered from her appearance, it was how badly off Maeve and her kin were. Not that the state of their poverty mattered to Grayson, Maeve knew. He only saw the Irish renting on his land as property, no better than livestock, animals to be used. And certainly, the way his eyes took measure of her now, she wouldn't have been surprised if he called out to his stable master to prepare the brand.

"I have agreed to your terms," the lass growled lowly. "I'll come tomorrow."

He smiled impishly as his mischievous eyes drew to her mouth.

"We will start slowly," he agreed, grinning. "Our first time together will last five seconds, ten the next, then twenty, and so on, doubling each time. As long as you hold up your end of our agreement, you have nothing to fear. Be warned, however, that I demand full compliance, and I've low tolerance for those who do not value my time. And we do not start tomorrow, Miss O'Connor."

She cast him a curious glare.

"We will start *now*, as a way to seal our deal in good faith."

Maeve sighed in reluctance, but she hadn't any choice. She unbuttoned the latch from her wool cloak, let it drop to the dirt floor, paced to the middle of the stable aisle, and closed her eyes. She had agreed to let him do whatever he wished, but she did not agree to reciprocate. He was sorely mistaken if he assumed any such intentions on her part, despite the fact that any of the other Killarney girls would have traded their best stockings for such a chance. Oh, he was handsome, she acknowledged, but the devil so often was when he came courting.

A low chuckle met her ears, and she again felt the heat of his breath on her neck.

"It almost seems an unfair tease," he whispered. "Five seconds is hardly enough time to do anything truly enjoyable. Still..."

In one brisk pull, the unsuspecting girl was pressed hard against his body, his mouth meeting hers. Maeve's eyes shot open as she felt his tongue slipping past her softening lips, before fluttering closed again. Her body betrayed her, heating over and giving into his insistence as he tasted her deeply, molding her to his embrace. Maeve's hands moved to touch his face just in the moment he pulled away.

He grinned at her as if he had caught her farce, her hands waving about in empty space where moments ago his face had been.

Anger surged through Maeve. She felt the fool, knowing she had wondered for years what it would be like to kiss August again. But they were no longer the youths they had been once. This man was no friend; he was her lord. She, however, was no lady. She quickly realized she needed to keep up her guard; his kiss might have set her pulse racing, but he would never hold her heart.

"See, Miss O'Connor?" he laughed. "What I do is for my pleasure, but I think you'll learn to like it a bit too… as time goes on."

Clenching teeth gave way to bitter words.

"I will never take pleasure from anything you offer," Maeve hissed. "If we should continue until we spend days on end together, I always at the mercy of your hand and lip, I will hold only contempt and disgust for you."

Maeve turned on her heel and charged out, quickly making her way down the stonewall path, en route to the meadow by Middle Lake. She arrived home to discover her father was still out. Maeve set about peeling potatoes, her mind reflecting on the abhorrent agreement.

To be Lord Grayson's plaything, loaned against the clock, with interest…

She worked out the numbers in her head, and even with her basic understanding of arithmetic, she figured out how quickly these episodes would add up.

Well, it would not need to continue forever, she consoled herself. Owen had promised that they could soon be wed. She just needed to endure until enough money had been saved, and then their vows could be made. Then, joined to a good man as wife, she and her da would be safe.

Safe from poverty.

Safe from hunger.

Safe from the likes of the despicable Lord Grayson.

2 | With Payment Due

"Maeve! Come down now or I swear to Saint Peter, I'm coming up!"

She groaned and rolled. The loft where she had her straw mattress wasn't entirely uncomfortable, but nor was it easy on the back. For one so young, it was a wonder she could feel so old.

Of course, dreams haunted by the remembrance of the kiss made the night hardly restful, and distinctly lacking in sleep.

Rory handed his daughter a cup of tea as she shimmied down the ladder, giving one last stretch when she reached the floor. She took it wordlessly, though she gave him a quick nod to convey her thanks.

"Going to field?" she asked as they sat at the table and began dividing between them the soda bread and eggs Rory had prepared.

"Mm-hmm."

Rory O'Connor was a man of great action and few words. Often, his offerings were limited to a bare minimum, and consequently Maeve had learned to keep to the point and save socializing for those more appreciative of conversation.

Like stones.

It was in the morning that she most missed her mother. Rory had never been unkind, but after his Sine's death a few years prior, he wasn't warm to many. She wondered if perhaps she had imagined having been closer with him when her mother was alive. Perhaps Rory saw the relationship he had with his daughter only as an extension of what he had with his wife. Or maybe Rory pulled back his affections, fearing Maeve's eventual marriage would be losing another woman he loved, leaving him even more broken than he now was.

Though, maybe not. After all, he had made no secret of how thrilled he was when Owen Murphy had asked for his daughter's hand. After they had announced their intent to wed following mass one Sunday, he used some of their limited funds to order a round of pints at the pub and toast to Owen's relieving their—and Maeve wondered if he meant his—burden.

In the meantime, he and Maeve made do as best they could.

"Will you be back for supper?"

Rory scooped up some egg on his bread and stuffed it in his mouth. "Suppose I might go to the pub a bit."

Maeve rolled her eyes in frustration. "Da, however are you to get better if you stay out all hours of the night boozing?"

"Owen's right next to me the whole time, Maeve."

With the taste of August still on her lips, her insides squirmed at the mention of her husband-to-be.

"I can picture the wedding now. My drunken father will present me to my drunken husband, and the priest will invite all to make hopeful wagers on who will fall down first. Who needs communion wine when there's the Jolly Root Pub?"

"Don't get smart, Maeve O'Connor. Neither one of us is set drunk. Only… warmed."

"Warm as a hot day in Aug…" The rebuke died on her tongue. When her father looked back up, confused, her brow furrowed, until, changing the subject, she was able to distract him. "Well, I suppose is doesn't hurt if you and Owen are becoming better acquainted. After all, he'll be your son-in-law soon."

Rory nodded offhandedly, as though acknowledging as much truth as "it might rain later." She knew that he was pleased by the upcoming union, but wondered if sometimes Rory had wished that Sine had left him with a son instead. If God was to give him but one child, what a shame that it should be a girl.

"Da?"

"Hm?"

She cocked her head to the side. "Do you ever wish I'd been a boy? Then I'd be able to go out and find work? A son would marry a good woman who'd keep house, and—"

"Shh-shh!" Rory's hand rose up, as though he could hush her with the power of his mind. "I've never vexed the Lord for sending us a daughter."

"But if you'd had a son, perhaps after I was born," she continued. "Mightn't you have…"

A look of great woe and sadness crossed the Irishman's face, a look Maeve saw him wear regularly following her mother's death. "We would have loved three sons, and four daughters, Maeve, but your mother just couldn't… Well, the Good Lord knows best his plan."

Maeve hushed and nibbled at her eggs, and Rory turned his attention back to his plate.

"Did you speak to Patrick?"

She almost choked as he asked after the middleman she had been dispatched to find the day before.

"No," she replied, gagging. "No…I was on…" she coughed "…my way to his cottage when I ran across Aug … Lord Grayson."

At the mention of the ungracious English lad who had wormed his way into their family only to spit in his daughter's face years ago, Rory cringed. "Don't suppose he was a sympathetic ear."

"No, he agreed to the extension," Maeve informed her father, then hesitantly added, "with certain … requirements."

Rory all but leapt up from his seat. "Bastard. What does he want? Bigger share of our crops? More livestock? Interest?"

Maeve rushed to calm her father before his outburst gave him a spell. "No, Da, nothing of the sort. He asked for an exchange of labor."

Rory's eyebrow crooked. "What type of…labor?"

Voicing the word in the same suggestive tone, Maeve's mind leapt to all the damage that could come from owing favors to an Englishman. Her reputation was untarnished. She was kind, charitable despite her humble state, and considered a fine beauty—all reasons the blacksmith had sought to court her. But Rory was a poor man, with no hope of changing that fact, and the only dowry Maeve could offer was her good name and good looks. No doubt her father didn't want one speck of dirt from Grayson muddying that.

"He's short staff, having just made home here. He wants me to help…" Maeve's eyes dashed around the room in search when she focused on their partially eaten breakfast. "…baking bread. Like Ma taught me!" she quickly supplemented to Rory's doubtful grimace. "He remembers Ma's bread and wants me to make it like she did. Ma's bread was famous, you remember? Of course, he asked that I give the recipe, but I refused. So I'm to bake bread at Shepherd's Bluff now and then, per his request."

Rory eyed his daughter suspiciously, then the bread on the table, then his daughter again. He hadn't known Maeve to be a liar before, and though odd, he wouldn't deny the truth of his deceased wife's culinary talents. Her bread was famous across County Kerry, and as a young man, August had been quite taken with it. Even Emmanuel Grayson, his father, was known to have enjoyed an offering sent home with August on occasion.

He accepted, but gave Maeve a strict warning: "When he asks it of you, you get straight there and straight back. Don't get yourself wrapped up in the affairs of the English. They're friends of no good fortune in the bye and by."

Maeve didn't question her father's cryptic remark, only agreed that she wouldn't tarry any longer than needed, glad to let go the topic. After all, she thought, it would be some number of visits before her payments to August would take longer than what would be expected for making bread.

"And one other thing, Maeve." She looked at him inquisitively. "If you're going to use his kitchen, maybe bake a few loaves for our table too."

Rory set to field with a pack of that famous bread tucked into his satchel while Maeve went about her chores, as always. Wash, more baking, cleaning away the ash in the fireplace, stacking the dishes in the cupboard. She paused when washing out the very mug she drank from that morning, her finger passing over a chip in the rim.

She remembered with a smile how that chip had gotten there ten years before.

August had mentioned that he had never drunk fresh, warm milk. In England, his milk was always fresh, but tepid or chilled. Sine had promptly sent Rory out to milk their cow, though so soon after its morning milking it hardly provided enough to fill the two matching, earthen mugs. She'd presented one to Maeve and one to August, along with a slice of freshly baked brown bread. August had gulped down the foamy offering and was upset when he found his mug so quickly drained. He had tipped it up high, trying to savor every last drop, and shook it. The resultant clink had sent Sine into a tizzy, thinking he had broken a tooth. When it turned out only the mug was chipped, she'd breathed a heavy sigh of relief.

It was fair to say that Sine O'Connor liked August Grayson then. He had been kind, though fiercely inquisitive, and she hadn't failed to notice the way he followed her daughter around like a puppy to its master. All this, despite the fact that he was two years Maeve's senior. Fair to say, however, that Maeve's interpretation of his behavior toward her had been quite different. August had been a pal at times, but other times he'd been a downright nuisance. Maeve grimaced still when passing the back field near the cattle's watering hole and remembering how August had snatched up one of the marsh frogs and chased her around. The event had ended abruptly when Maeve lost her footing and went crashing forward into the water and muck, covered tip to toe in vile, putrid filth.

Yet, that compared not a bit to the way she felt now, as if her soul had crashed into the watering hole and emerged soiled and grime-ridden. She felt pulled between two sins: if she did not go through with the arrangement, she kept her chastity intact for Owen but would lose their cottage, leaving her and Rory with no place to go. But a good daughter did what she could to take care of her widower father. Thou shall honor thy father and thy mother. How could she not agree?

To whom did she owe a greater allegiance, after all? Husband-to-be, or father? Father, for certain, and so she would go to August to make her next payment.

It felt like the sun was setting on more than just the day as afternoon dissolved into evening. She gathered her cloak tightly around her to ward off the chill. By the grace of God, she met no one on the road. She did not know how she would explain her outing if she had. All knew Maeve as a hearth-haunter and not one to go traipsing outside after dark. Rumors would abound.

Each step that carried her up the tree-lined drive to Shepherd's Bluff made her feet feel heavier and her head feel lighter. She approached the front door and found herself stalling, not knowing how to proceed. Was she to knock and wait, or simply go in? Though what she had told her father was true, and even Patty O'Keefe had mentioned Lord Grayson was short of staff, there were several servants who lived in the side quarters. Were they privy to this? Would she need to track them down and beg them to keep their lips sealed? Would they tarry off to tell Owen?

She pondered her options but was cut short by the ornately carved door swinging open, revealing Grayson. The firelight of her lantern flickered against his eyes, causing an entrancing clash of red on green. He was dressed in a nightshirt and woolen gray overthrow, and despite her best attempts to steel herself, she trembled upon her eyes meeting his.

"I saw you coming," he offered as she began to mouth the question, almost as if he had read her mind. "I saw your lantern's light from down the road. Am I mistaken, or did you trip coming up the pathway?"

Her cheeks flushed red as she followed him inside.

"I have a tendency to fall when you're concerned," she admitted shyly. "Perhaps you remember that one incident in particular?"

His lips curled into a knowing half-smile, an echo of the same grin he wore upon seeing a younger Maeve covered in muck. "Vividly."

He spoke no more as he led her up the stairs with only his lantern to light their way. His steps were feather light, as though he were sneaking about his own home. At the third door, they paused as he unhitched the catch and made a quick jerk of his head.

Her eyes were immediately drawn to the bed and to linens of pure white that would surely caress the skin like a milk bath. Across from the four-poster, a fire crackled and snapped on the hearth, two plush wingback chairs sat at angles in front. Grayson removed his cloak and sweater, tossing them over the back of the chair, took a seat in one, and indicated that Maeve should sit in the other. Already, beads of sweat dotted her brow, though she knew not if it was from her proximity to the hearth or to Grayson.

"I've been thinking about our agreement, and I need to make a few clarifications and alterations," he began as she perched on the edge of the chair across from him. She cocked her head to the side and let him continue. "For example, in these early days, when our time is so short, we need to agree from what point our clock starts. Simply sitting here as such is not satisfying the requirement on your end."

She had assumed as much. How ridiculous would it be for her to walk through the mists and cold to stay only ten seconds?

"So what would start us?"

"I will acknowledge the beginning of our time by stroking your cheek. You'll notice the ticking, no doubt, that is coming from the Comtoise clock. That will be your measure. Also, it seems my presence is necessary in town on Saturdays, so I will never require your time on that night."

Maeve tried not to dwell on the fact that they were negotiating how often she should be at his beck and call.

"I could see from your expression at the front door that you were uncertain how to proceed," he continued, taking her silence for agreement. "The thought has crossed your mind that the servants in the house might come to know of our arrangement, and how that would besmirch your name about town. I have no current interest in causing you harm in the eyes of all Killarney, and I likewise have no desire for them to be privy to our agreement. Let it stay our secret."

That she should share any secret with Grayson gave her an unnerving thrill, which she quickly shoved aside.

"My servants have been ordered to vacate this wing by eight every evening and not to return until six the following morning. When you arrive, do not knock, do not tarry. The kitchen door will always be unlocked. Enter and come immediately to this room and to no other room in the house. This is important. Do you understand, Miss O'Connor, never any other room?"

He leaned over in his chair ever so slightly, his nightshirt falling forward, providing Maeve with a clear view of his firm chest. Her breath caught, but she madly forced her eyes elsewhere.

"I understand, Lord Grayson," she returned somewhat airily. "I have a modification to make as well."

He sat back and gave a low chuckle.

"You are not in a position to negotiate," he said, a bit of taunt in his timbre. He eyed her from tip to toe, looking for jest. "Amuse me."

"Bread," she said simply. "Two loaves for each night you require me."

"Why on earth would you need bread?"

"I've told my father that our agreement is for me to bake your bread in exchange for rent," Maeve explained. "He has asked me to make a few extra loaves for our own table."

"And he believed you?"

The smirk across his face told Maeve how amused he was at her transparent deception. Saying it aloud, she realized how silly an attempt to cover up her true activities it really was.

"It seems outlandish," she admitted, allowing herself to smile for a moment before the crushing guilt overtook her, "but he's never had any reason to doubt me—until now."

It was clear from his countenance that Grayson found her dishonesty entertaining. The smirk that flitted across his face took her back a decade, to a time when their kinship had included summer secrets and stolen hours. He had worn that same expression then, a seal that their confidences would not be betrayed.

He leaned over so that a hand anchored on the armrest left and right, effectively caging her. He was intimately close, his head mere inches from hers, a hint of brandy floating in the air between them. Maeve's pulse tried to warn her that her body was again trying to overrule her better senses.

The corner of his mouth twitched again, his eyes focusing on her lips.

"Agreed." He pulled back, standing erect, before turning away. "You owe me ten seconds. Let's to it."

Maeve briskly bobbed her head. Crossing the room, he stopped in front of the clock and pointed at a spot on the floor.

"Stand here, if you please."

Maeve did not please, but of course she had no choice. She wondered how she would be able to make out the ticking of the clock above the overpowering cacophony of her pulse. Squaring herself in front of the clock as requested, she focused everything save the tick, tock, tick, tock out of her existence.

"One more thing, Miss O'Connor," he said. "We are here by agreement. I never want you to forget, you are standing in my room right now because you chose to be here."

As if this were my idea!, she thought. She opened her mouth to scream unholy words at him, as if he was the devil himself reminding her that the sin she was committing was not his doing. The moment her mouth opened, however, the back of his hand stroked gently down her cheek, causing her body—and her tongue—to freeze.

One… Two…

He leaned in closely as his lips brushed against her chin.

Three… Four…

His gentle hands cupped either side of her face and tilted her head to the right. His lips drew near, his eyes fixated on Maeve's mouth. The pathway he would take was made clear.

Five…

Grayson's lips met hers gently, then firmly. She melted against him, her body again overruling her conviction as she parted her lips, allowing him to mold them beneath his however he saw fit.

Six… Seven…

Her hands drew upward, wanting to cup his cheek or find anchor on his shoulders. They wanted to touch him, somehow, somewhere, but she would not let them. They lingered instead grasping fruitlessly in the air. He turned his head slightly and circled his arms around her, pulling Maeve hard against his chest.

Eight… Nine…

His tongue licked her bottom lip and then pushed through, tickling hers delicately. Maeve's hands took advantage of a wave of confusion running through her body, and her fingers threaded through his midnight black hair.

Ten.

He planted one more light kiss on her mouth and turned away, leaving Maeve breathless, flushed, and wanton.

"That's enough for tonight, Miss O'Connor."

He wouldn't turn to look at Maeve as she stood gasping for breath, her arms still held out before her. In the emptiness of his embrace, guilt enveloped her. This man was nothing to her, and yet he had the power to make her body betray the sanctity of her soul. He was a demon, a selfish, heartless, soulless cur who was abusing his power as the holder of her lease.

Maeve made a firm decision; this had been a mistake. She would not come to the manor again. She would not give Grayson the pleasure.

And she would deny him hers.

"Good evening, I said, Miss O'Connor," he growled out, peering out the window. The finality of his tone told Maeve he would offer no other opportunity to leave peaceably. She huffed across the room, snatched her cloak from the chair and lantern from the mantel, and stormed out and up the lane.

A half mile later, Maeve nearly slapped herself for her folly. She had neglected to obtain the bread. Rory would know that she had lied in the morning. Maybe she should tell him, anyway. He should know that she made her best effort, but the price Grayson had asked proved too high. He would forgive her, or he wouldn't, but Rory O'Connor would understand that Maeve's intent had at least been pure: she was doing it for him.

She settled into bed as rain drops began to pluck at the window. The ping of the water, of its splash and slosh, made her recall the feel of his lips sliding over hers and the gentleness of his hands on her cheek.

She cursed him from dusk till dawn, waiting for her morning of reckoning. Once, perhaps, they had been closer than peas in a pod, friends thicker than thieves. And now, he was so handsome, so powerful…so tempting. Could she ever learn to deny the want of him, the yearning to again be a friend, and perhaps more, in his eyes?

A small part of her wondered likewise if Owen Murphy's kisses would prove as incinerating. Could he, with one deep kiss, steal her breath the way that Grayson had? Even in her innocence, she already knew the answer.

Yet, she had been taken in by Grayson's affections before, only to be spurned. A lesson taught was a lesson learned, and she refused to be made a fool again. She knew precisely the cut of his cloak. Men like August Grayson thought of women like her no better than the sheep that roamed his pastures. What knew he of humility and poverty? What knew he of the true worth of an Irishman?

And what knew he of love?

3

The Irish Question

~Norwich, England~

1854

August knew he would get more than a tongue lashing from his father if he was caught out of bed this late, but he couldn't help his curiosity. His parent's guest, Sir Edmund Hobbs, was an infamous personage. Even a child such as August knew of his reputation as "The English Bulldog," though beyond that moniker, the young Master Grayson knew little.

Hobbs had dined with Lord and Lady Grayson, and if there was one thing August had understood without having to be told, it was how on edge his mother was over the possibility of losing her temper with their guest. It was one of the weaknesses she carried still from her roots in Ireland; she couldn't help but turn the brightest shade of red whenever someone—usually Emmanuel—got her ire up. Lately, she'd been wearing the shade as frequently as this season's hat.

August perched himself at the top of the stairs, concealed in shadows, so he could see into the sitting room and pick up threads of the adults' conversation. The flicker of fire from the hearth lighted his father's sullen features in a way that made August's heart beat faster in fear. His mother, Eliza, sat on the mauve sofa, the needlework in her lap the focus of her labor—a distraction, August understood—while Emmanuel leaned on the edge of the mantel.

Hobbs was situated in a chair nearby, his legs crossed, the smoke from his pipe clouding that side of the room in a haze.

"And now they have this—what was it?—Pope's Brass Band. The famine has left the whole lot of them with a gaunt look and a hunger that is from more than lack of potatoes, Emmanuel. I don't like it, not at all. It's inspired sympathy. Undue sympathy. The Irishman getting so much protection with these reforms does not bode well for England."

Emmanuel scoffed as he lit the end of his pipe, taking needy puffs before replying. "You mean that Independent Irish Party? I wouldn't bother to worry, Edmund. It's only proper that the whole lot of them should go about yipping, seeing as Parliament has given up so much to their cause these last few years. They're trying to take attention while they have a stage, not realizing the audience has already arisen and gone home."

To August's surprise, his mother ventured to comment, her muted Irish accent standing prominently against the rhythm of the men's conversation. "Isn't it the right of a man to try to improve his welfare by any means at his disposal, even an Irishman?"

Both his father and Hobbs chuckled, a reaction which drew Eliza away from her needlework.

"Well, a man, yes, I agree," Hobbs answered. "But one can hardly consider these Irish masses akin to decent society, Lady Grayson."

Eliza's back straightened. "I am Irish, Sir Hobbs."

He dismissed her comment with a wave of his hand through the smoke. "A diamond in the rough, you are. Of course I don't mean your folk when I speak of those flea-bitten fiends, madam. The peasants, the rabble—they are quite a different lot indeed. Barely human, lazy and stupid, and certainly not interested in improving anyone's welfare, even their own, if it means honest work and sober living."

The tension that followed was thicker than the smoke hanging in the air. Eliza's eyes burned into Hobbs. Emmanuel, perhaps wishing to supersede embarrassment on either side of this outcome, intervened.

"You must forgive my wife, Edmund. A woman's understanding of politics, it's rudimentary at best, and I fear Eliza's upbringing leads her to a mistaken assessment of her former countrymen."

Eliza all but jumped from her seat, stabbing the stitching in her hand with the needle. Dobbs arose as was proper in a lady's presence, though he seemed to be searching with his eyes for a hiding place should Lady Grayson front an attack.

Only her words presented arms. "Your pardon, Sir Hobbs, for my 'stupidity' on the matter. As my lazy nature has made me quite weary of speaking to English pokes who haven't even the spark of compassion the Lord God gave a tick mouse, I bid you a good evening."

With that, she turned and marched towards the stairs. August scrambled to his feet, barely making it to the safety of his room before his mother's footsteps passed by his door. The cadence, normally carrying on to the end of the hall where his parent's room lay, stopped in front of his door instead. When he chanced to crack the door, he saw there his mother, crumpled, crying silently, woe mad manifest.

"Mother?"

She caught sight of him and went still, her eyes wide. "August? Goodness, why are you up still, *mo chroí*?"

He opened the door further, creeping into the hall. When his mother opened her arms in invitation, he curled into her lap, as though he was still a tiny child, not the eleven-year-old he was.

Eliza's hand smoothed over his hair. "You don't think I'm stupid or lazy, do you, dear?"

His head shook vehemently. "No, and I'd pound anyone who dared say that of you."

This brought a smile to Eliza's teary face. "Yes, that's the Irish in you. Ready to fight, ready to stand."

"And ready to make a fool of his father as well, Liza?"

Neither Eliza nor August had heard Emmanuel climbing the stairs. His temper burned close to the surface, fuming over his countenance. He must have contained himself just long enough to see off his guest, but in the departure had amassed his anger.

"Emmanuel, I do apologize. It wasn't my intention to em—"

The Lord's hand took her scalp in its grasp, pulling her to stand as August fell from her lap and on to the floor.

"Do not be confused. I am an Englishman, and you are the wife of a Lord of Britannia, and our children are just as Eng—"

"Just as Irish as I am!" Eliza screeched.

She didn't have a chance to raise her arm in defense before Emmanuel's hand made contact with her face.

"Never," he growled at her, using a grip of her hair to fling her into the wall. "Never dare insult my children with that slur again. What to do with you, Liza? I've tried compassion. I've tried gifts. I've even tried overlooking your bizarre Fenian pride, and all you've tried in return is my patience. My children are not Irish! And neither are you."

Emmanuel's fearsome gaze turned next to August, shaking like a wee willow in the frame of his door, watching the scene with terror. Across the hall, a slow creak drew all their attention. Sleepy-eyed Caroline looked so small, so fragile, that before he knew what he was doing, August had cut an agile path around his father, grabbed his mother's hand, turned his five-year-old sister back around, and locked the three of them securely behind Caroline's heavy wooden door.

"Mother, are you hurt?" he whispered as Emmanuel continued to slur his mother's lineage in brash, haughty tones.

She shook her head, pulling a trembling Caroline into her chest, trying to stop tears that were threatening to break. "August, I'm so sorry you had to… It's just, when your father… The things he said, and that horrid man—"

"—and teaching our son that damned language of yours, that heathen tongue! Don't think I'll let you fill Caroline's head the way you did our boy! Our son, who will someday be a Lord! An English Lord!"

August put his hands over his mother's mouth, stopping her needless excuses. "Don't worry. It's plain to see who's being uncivilized now."

4 | *Our Daily Bread*

~Killarney, Ireland~

Fall 1866

"August!"

Jesus, Mary, and Joseph!"

Rory O'Connor leapt up in shock at Maeve's indecipherable scream and warily eyed his daughter above, as though he suspected the state of her sanity or sobriety. If there was one thing Maeve fell short on, it was drinking.

Her eyes were wide and her breath was wild. She panted and stared and stared and panted. When at last she realized she was in the familiar comfort of her own bed, her expression eased. Leaning over the edge of the loft, Maeve tried to asses her father's reaction.

"Was I…?" Her voice trailed off as she ran her fingers through her long, chestnut hair. "Was I…crying?"

Rory took a sip of his tea and smacked his lips. "A wee bit just now. Bad dream?"

Her smile threatened to belie the truth. The dream … flashing images of emerald eyes and firm red lips, a swish of ebony hair, the tracing of soft fingers over her cheek…

Maeve gave a quick, deceitful nod and came down the ladder.

"Know what I think?" Rory queried. "You caught a chill. It's not your way, going out after dark. Your constitution's not built for it. Weak lungs, just like your poor Ma."

Maeve smirked as she poured herself a cup of tea, relieved to have so convenient a diversion presented to her. "She had no problem yelling at you."

Rory erupted into laughter, and Maeve found herself smiling right along. He doubled over, smacking his knee before his peals transformed into a full-on coughing fit.

Maeve leaned over and examined her father closely, running her hand over his forehead and thinking him warm. "Perhaps I'm not the only one who caught a chill." Glancing out the window, she noted the overcast sky. "You should stay in today. The sheep won't die from one day's rest."

Rory cast her a downward glance as he threw his jacket over his shoulders.

"Sheep don't care. It's only we meek mortals that think all manner of life should halt when the rain falls."

"But you're just getting better," she argued, tugging on his jacket in a useless attempt to hold him back. "You spend the whole day out in the rain and you'll be down with consumption come morning."

Pushing his hat over his head, he made for the door. "I'll be fine. I'll just take them out for a few hours and be back. Make up some soup for your dear da tonight?"

The morning passed without much incident, and with nothing else of consequence demanding her attention, Maeve found herself seated in a chair by the fire, peeling potatoes and slicing onions. She groaned at the realization that there would be no bread; her rush to depart Shepherd's Bluff the night prior had seen to that. All their funds of late had gone in savings towards the rent. Grain prices were high these days, and the O'Connors hadn't been able to buy flour for weeks. As though the fact that she had failed to make Grayson keep his end of their arrangement, simplistic as it was, wasn't enough to irk her, Maeve also felt pangs of guilt. For the second time in as many days, she had crafted a lie and served it to her father. She played it over in her head, testing its veracity, and decided her story would sound plausible enough. She had tripped on the way home, she would say, and the bread had landed in some mud on the side of the path.

In the relative silence of the cottage, with only the sound of the occasional crack of a log on the fire and ping of steady falling rain on the roof,

Maeve's mind turned traitor and recalled images of the previous evening. Grayson was not only a selfish rogue for offering his trade-in-kind, he was a horrible wiffler as well. She hadn't been difficult and, in fact, felt she more than held up her end of their arrangement. Why, then, had he suddenly seemed so indifferent to her very presence? He may be a Lord, but he was not a gentleman, she concluded. He merely took his piece, then took his leave.

And worst of all, he had actually made her enjoy it.

Not his disdainful treatment of her afterwards, but the kiss. The kiss which now seemed etched in her mind like the smell of roses and feel of the sun in summer. The way his lips moved over hers, the way he tasted teasingly of brandy, the feel of his hand threading through her hair, pulling her closer, closer…

Maeve crossed herself thrice at the realization of how her breath and pulse were racing. God might forgive her, but only if she did not allow the devil's progeny to taint both her soul and her heart. How could she go again? She wouldn't. Instead, she would do what she should have at the onset: go find Owen and tell him that Grayson would file with the magistrate to revoke the lease, and that she and her da needed to move. Surely being formally engaged, the appearance of them living together before they wed would not be so scandalous. Not nearly as scandalous as the alternative, for certain.

A knocking on the door brought Maeve from her reverie.

Patrick O'Keefe, Grayson's middleman, stared out at her from under a broad-brimmed hat dripping with rain. A huge mass of a man replete with muscle and brawn, his patience with the O'Connors' tardiness was near an end. Compassion only went so far, and consternation tended to take reins from there. Whereas his size once had made Maeve cower, she now only found annoyance in Patrick's biweekly visit to collect the pittance of rent Maeve scrounged together per their compromised installment schedule.

"Maeve," he greeted cordially, though his expression evidenced intrigue.

She had no patience to pretend with him this day. "Patrick." He continued to stare silently, shifting his eyes to the fireplace suggestively. "Well, fine," she acquiesced with a huff. "Since you came all the way down, you might as well come in and dry a bit."

Patrick shook off his hat and jacket and loped through the room, negotiating the low roof and tightly packed furnishings to take a seat by the hearth. Maeve sat across from him and eyed him suspiciously as he lowered his side pack to the floor.

"I haven't the money, if that's what you're here for again."

He gave her a sideways smile. "No need. Grayson informed me that you had agreed to an exchange. He came to see me this morning and told me not to bother you about rent, then asked me to give you these."

Patrick leaned over to his sack and pulled out two perfect loaves of fresh soda bread with a folded scrap of paper tied by twine to one. Overcome with a combination of incredulity, disgust, and utter joy, Maeve eyed the loaves—and more so, the paper—as Patrick arched his body the distance between them, placing the lot in her hands. She quickly rose to put all three items out of sight. Let not Patrick O'Keefe think for one moment she was about to take out that note in front of him.

"Don't you want me to read it to you?" he asked curiously, confirming her suspicion.

Maeve vehemently shook her head. "I can read. Aug…" The name in the familiar died on her tongue. "Grayson taught me when we were children, and I've kept up the hobby."

Patrick leaned back in his chair and crossed his arms over his chest. "Tell me, why would the Lord of the Manor be so concerned about one of his tenants having bread?" he questioned in a tone that presented suspicion.

"As said he, we agreed to a work exchange," she answered stoically. "I make his bread, he forgives our rent."

"I take it that's what you were doing there last night?"

Her breath caught, but only for a moment. She feigned confusion instead, but her insincere, uncertain expression only drove Patrick on.

"Patty was up feeding the baby. She was certain she saw you coming down the lane and past our cottage. Said you looked in quite a huff."

Her sins were piling higher by the moment, compounded by each lie and half-truth. She wasn't certain Sunday was going to come quickly enough to save her soul as it was.

"As stated, a work exchange," Maeve retorted. "I bake Grayson's bread."

"So you're telling me that you, the same girl who refused to come to my and Patty's wedding because it would have meant being away from Middle Lake for a whole night, is traipsing a mile up the road after dark to satisfy Grayson's desire for…bread?" he asked, his head cocked to the side. She nodded, even as she told herself he wasn't buying it. "You know, Patty always tells me what good friends you are. She speaks so highly of you and Rory, tells me constantly how strong you were when your ma died, how you took over the household and kept Rory from going mad with grief. You're known about these parts as a woman of her word, pure as the day is long. Take my advice, Maeve, don't get taken in by Grayson. He's no good."

Reddened over in her fury, her words were barely restrained under an irate cloud of insult. "Whomever I choose to bake bread for is none of your concern, Patrick O'Keefe! If Lucifer himself should pay me an honest penny for a loaf, there's no need of you to take notice. Now, your piece is said and your task is finished, so I'll thank you to be on your way."

The words slapped him in the face as his eyes winced. Patrick threw back on his coat and took up his side pack, tossing it over his shoulder.

"I'm sorry," he apologized sincerely. The compassion evident in his eyes introduced a pang of guilt in her chest. "I'm sure you're just doing what's necessary. Like us all."

"That I am."

He smiled widely as he opened the door, tipping his hat back over the top of his head. "Of course."

He stepped out into the rain, but as she started to close the door, he turned and caught it with his hand.

"Oh, one other thing?"

"Aye?"

"Do let me know how you like the bread. I'm of the opinion that Patty's is one of the best in County Kerry, though I tend to play favorites."

Maeve was certain that she looked quite aghast—and guilty—as she pushed him out of the way and slammed the door closed. Patrick might not know exactly what was going on, but he certainly knew that the bread alibi was a lie.

The cottage was clean, but by the time Maeve had worked out her anger in laborious frustration, it was proper enough for a visit by the Queen. By mid-afternoon, the rain had tapered off, though the sky stayed dark and cloudy. Rory returned before dusk with nary a word, ate his soup with slices of Patty's bread, and went straight to bed.

This left Maeve in a precarious state. She couldn't take out her dwindling rage beating the rugs into submission; she wanted to keep the doors closed and let her da get some rest. With nothing else to distract her, she threw on her cloak, took the letter from where she had concealed it under her bed roll, and took off for the lakeshore.

The air was calming. She began to take some comfort in the realization that Patrick might not know anything for certain. After all, he had no proof, and Maeve had her good name to stand witness if anything should be accused in public. Yet she chastised herself for her stupidity; she shouldn't have gone to Shepherd's Bluff with a lamp. It drew attention, and the middle-man's cottage was too near the lane leading from the road. She resolved that when she should go next, the lamp should be left behind. She knew the road well enough, and moonlight and starlight could be her guide a good measure of the time.

As she lingered by the lakeshore, however, she saw suddenly how her own thoughts betrayed her heart and resolve. Hadn't she decided not to return? Hadn't she sworn to herself the previous evening to repent? The whole cavalcade had already caused her to lie to her father twice. In the wholeness of the universe, the Almighty could forgive a few fibs, but what of the other things that were sure to transpire with time? Would He forgive that as well?

Could she forgive herself?

If it wasn't so potentially tragic, she would have laughed. He sent bread. He sent her two loaves of bread. She kept telling herself there was nothing to it except for him seeing through his side of the bargain. Even a scoundrel could be a man of his word, no matter how devious the intent. So why should such a small gesture be so overwhelming?

With a sigh, Maeve took the paper from her pocket and opened it.

Tomorrow, at dusk.

As her fingers traced over the twist of each letter and her heart sped, it occurred to her. She was in worse straits than before. He was already doing it to her again: reeling her in, earning her kinship, using her as a comfort. And just as before, it was only a matter of time before he betrayed her.

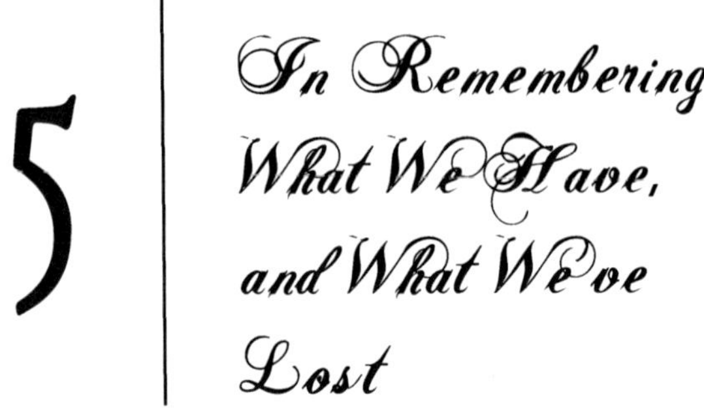

5
In Remembering
What We Have,
and What We've
Lost

~Killarney, Ireland~

1856

Such a sight young Maeve had never before witnessed.

There must have been twenty in all, an Englishman atop each. Certainly she had seen horses before, and had even been on the back of one a few times. The Boyles over the hill had one, and sometimes when she, Ma, and Da went into Killarney to attend mass, Billy Boyle would let her work the reins.

But in general, horses were work animals, and she hadn't seen anyone but August's father mounted right atop one laden with riding gear. She wondered if this was what the Knights of the Round Table had looked like when they rode off to Jerusalem. She had liked that part of the Tales of King Arthur most, and consequently August had read that passage to her several times over the summer.

August's favorite part, when Guinevere betrayed Arthur and rode off to be with Lancelot, was positively scandalous. Maeve had told him that Guinevere was a foolish woman of bad morals. August had argued that their marriage was doomed from the start. For one, Arthur became a king who was no longer worthy of obeisance, and Guinevere had been right to leave him. Secondly, Arthur needed an heir and Guinevere was unable to provide him one. On reflection, he couldn't understand why Arthur hadn't pitched her earlier. Then maybe he could have a queen who would have borne him a legitimate son before Mordrid had killed him.

Maeve had been confused. "I don't understand," she'd told August as they sat together in the hayloft over the stable. "I thought marrying meant they would have children. Why didn't Guinevere have a baby then, if that's what Arthur needed?"

"Perhaps they didn't do it enough," August returned with a slight blush on his cheeks.

But Maeve was more confused still. "Do what?"

August smirked. "It, Maeve."

She hadn't understood, but August was reluctant to offer any more explanation.

The riding party approached the dirt lane that connected the O'Connor cottage to Killarney. Further down shore sat the newly completed manor house where the Graysons resided. Most of the horseman continued on, seemingly pressed in their business. One, however, slowed near the O'Connors' gate. Maeve's mother and father walked out to meet him. They spoke in voices too low to hear from the cottage stoop where she sat, carding wool. At one point, there was a lull in their conversation as all turned to look to her. She blushed deeply as the Englishman gave a disappointed grimace her way.

Finally, the Englishman straightened on his steed and continued up the lane. Both Sine and Rory O'Connor's expressions spoke of anxious confusion. Sine exhaled and beckoned her daughter near with a wave.

Maeve set down the combs on top of the sack of wool and rubbed the oily residue from her hands onto her skirt as she walked over to her parents.

"When did you last see Master Grayson?" Sine asked her daughter.

Maeve fidgeted. August's formal title was detestable. Titles belonged to the English, and though August was English, she couldn't slight him that way in her own mind. To her he was simply August, a friend with whom she had spent the whole summer, running over hill and dale near Middle Lake.

"We were in the stable last night, reading until twilight," she answered in her matter-of-fact tone. "I came home right after dark. He said he was going to try to see his mother."

Sine scowled, her checks flushing red. She did not like the idea of Maeve getting, as the Yanks who came through town would say, "too big for her britches." After a summer of being Master Grayson's distraction from his mother's illness, Maeve's britches were beginning to look awfully taut. Firstly, she spent half her time cooped up with him in the hay loft of the stable, reading. The young Grayson had taken great delight and pride in teaching Maeve to read, but Maeve didn't see the lessons for what they were. Maeve thought August was doing her a kindness; Sine thought August held it as nothing more than teaching a puppy a fancy trick. Whenever they weren't running around the grounds around Shepherd's Bluff, they were to be found somewhere else together, whether seated at the only table in the modest O'Connor cottage, or with their knees covered in mud and muck at the lakeshore.

Then came the day when August's gaze fell upon her daughter with a new softness, a sense of reverence that she had understood at once with tempered fret. Her child wasn't even yet thirteen, but old enough to have caught the eye of someone of her own casting.

If not for the situation as it stood, Sine and half of Killarney would have thought it quite a scandal. Here was her daughter, of meager means and aspiration, running to and fro with the son of the landlord. Sine had very little problem with August himself; he was not entirely unpleasant a guest, and he rarely behaved in a manner that could be considered anything less than cordial. It wasn't clear that August's father was entirely aware of his son's daily regimen of general tomfoolery, but it was likely he had little ability to mind. Everyone knew why they were spending their summer at Middle Lake, except perhaps August.

Eliza Grayson had been brought back to Ireland to die.

Sine laid her hand gently on Maeve's shoulder.

"Darling, Lady Grayson…" she trailed off. Maeve's gaze grew heavy with concern. "Lady Grayson passed last night."

Maeve's hand flew over her mouth, stifling her gasp.

"August has gone missing. It seems he ran out of the house, and no one's seen him all day. Lord Grayson is very concerned. Do you know where he might have gone?"

Maeve shook her head as her attention was drawn to her father reemerging from their cottage, a rifle in hand. As a yeoman of the Grayson lands, he was allowed this privilege. Maeve wondered what would require such measure in the hills around Middle Lake.

"I best to be goin'," he said plainly as he loaded the ammunition. "The riders are going north towards town. We should check down in the abbey and lakeside."

Sine smoothed the palm of her hand over Maeve's cheek. "Stay inside. August may try to make his way here, after all. If he comes, you keep him safe until the Englishmen ride by again. Can you do that, sweet?"

Maeve nodded, still in shock. Sine leaned over, kissed her daughter's forehead, and departed.

Maeve was not without suspicion, however, as to August's probable whereabouts. They had dreamily talked of running away on several occasions. She wanted to go somewhere where she wouldn't be thought foolish simply because she was poor and a girl. August wanted to go anywhere where his father wouldn't find him. Maeve had suggested the mountains.

There was a stream that meandered through the woods in the hills. Billy Boyle's son, Jared, had told Maeve that if you followed the stream up the mountain, you would come to a pond where fairies danced at night. Maeve thought Jared was a right liar and didn't hesitate to tell him so. When Jared insisted, Maeve had lopped him square on the chin.

Nonetheless, August seemed intrigued when she passed along the tall tale. Not that he supposed there were fairies, but perhaps there were other wonders to behold. Maeve and he agreed that when they were older, they would follow that stream and find that pond, maybe even build a little cottage there. She didn't understand why, but Maeve liked the idea of sharing a cottage with August. True, sometimes he could be a downright spoiled brute, but most of the time he was sweet and sincere.

They were best friends, when it came down to it.

As the day carried on with only the occasional thundering of hooves over the road marking time, Maeve paced about her cottage in contemplation. As the sun began to set and twilight grew near, she grew more and more convinced that they would not find August. They didn't know where to look.

She threw on her cloak, said a quick prayer to Mother Mary for guidance, and grabbed one of her da's lanterns from the hook on the porch.

The woods and the hillside turned out to be terribly frightening at night, eerily basked only in the light of the moon and her lantern's humble flame. As she climbed higher into the hills, the trees became thicker and the lantern's light more valuable. After an hour or so of traipsing over fallen trees and scattered rocks, she heard the rushing of water.

The stream continued up hill as she occasionally called out fruitlessly. With every step she took, the terrain was less familiar, less distinguished. She began to wonder if she'd be able to find her way back down, and what would happen if she couldn't.

Maeve's mind wandered too much for her own good. The rain as of late had surged the flow of the waters for a short spell. Now it had receded and the soft, billowy banks were too slippery to cover in the dark. An unfocused mind led to a lazy eye; she did not land in the water, but she did slip on the muddy shore.

Maeve brushed herself off as best she could and let a few words slip from her mouth that were probably inadvisable for a girl of her tender years. No one would hear her, she thought dismissively.

Except for August, who was staring at her from just a few steps away.

His skin had been made pale by the coolness in the air, and even in the faint flicker of lantern light, it was obvious that he had been crying, though his face for the moment was dry. His tufts of ebony hair were chaotic, a few spots of mud dotted his temple and clothing, and his green eyes were utterly blood shot.

He looked at Maeve as though she were a specter, not sure whether to be afraid or intrigued.

"August!" She ran to him, the lantern left where it had fallen. The upward angle of the beaming shafts of light made each seem taller to the other. She threw her arms around him in the rush of her relief. It was the first that she had ever done so, and she was surprised at how comforting it felt to lean her head against his shoulder. She hoped for August to embrace her—to make any movement, to let her know that he was all right.

He did nothing, only stood stiff as stone and cold as coal, so Maeve pulled back and eyed him warily. The momentary thrill faded as soon as she remembered that from which he had fled.

"Oh, August," she sighed. "I'm so sorry. Your ma…"

"She called for me," August rebuked, though his voice became weaker and more cracked as he continued. "Before she… d…d…died. She called for me, but he wouldn't let me see her. He kept me from telling her I…loved her."

Maeve backed away in surprise. His face…she had never witnessed such horror, such anger, such bitter sadness as she did in August's present expression.

"I'm sure she knew," were the only words she could bring herself to say.

With August found, Maeve became suddenly aware of how cold it was getting. The wet mud covering her legs didn't help.

"Come, half of County Kerry is looking for you. Everyone's quite worried and—"

"Is my father?" His eyes were all at once frightened and full of hope.

"I don't know."

He chuckled ruefully. "Of course he isn't. He doesn't care. He doesn't love me the way your mother and father love you. You're so lucky. So very, very lucky."

Maeve knew Emmanuel Grayson was a strict disciplinarian, but she couldn't imagine a father not having his child's best at heart, even if all she had heard of him from August was cruelty. Maeve understood he was grieving, but she had been raised differently.

"You bite your tongue, August Grayson!" she spat out, pulling away and snatching the forsaken lantern from the ground. "The Bible says that you shall honor thy father and mother!"

Immediately, Maeve felt sorry, for August looked devastated by her rebuke. What he said next, however, overwhelmed her.

"I do honor thy mother and father," he nearly whispered, his eyes fixed on the ground. "And you."

August lifted his head to meet her watery eyes, his gaze never faltering. Maeve didn't know whether to back away or shorten the distance herself.

She chose to do neither and so stood planted in her spot.

"You cared enough to find me."

August's fingers brushed over her cheek as he hesitated before slowly closing the distance between them. Maeve trembled when his breath misted over her lips, and shook from head to toe when his lips ever so lightly touched hers.

She knew of kissing, for she had seen her parents and others give each other quick pecks. But she had never considered that she too might one day experience kissing, and never with August.

No words could she find. She didn't know what to do, or if she should do anything. What was he expecting? Was she supposed to kiss him back? Was she supposed to thank him?

No, it was best to say nothing at all. It was late and August was likely weary, she thought, having been away from home since morning. She herself could do with a cup of tea. Turning from his kiss, Maeve used the stream for guidance, making way down the hill.

When at last they emerged from the woods, a plume of smoke towered skyward from Shepherd's Bluff's chimney. August did not resist her coaxing, too tired from a day without food or shelter, as she led him to the front door without resistance.

Inside, the house was still and quiet. Maeve wondered if indeed anyone was at home. It didn't seem likely that everyone would have gone off in the search. Surely, one person stayed behind.

Just as this thought crossed her mind, a very woeful looking Emmanuel Grayson, rounded the corner from the foyer into the vestibule.

"August!"

The son, being so touched by the display of reverent and sincere relief on his father's face, of feeling of shared grief at the loss of a woman they both loved, ran into his embrace. Emmanuel's arms encircled August, rocking him side to side.

"I was so worried. I was beginning to think I had lost you both on the same day."

For the whole summer, Maeve couldn't recall having heard of August getting more than a passing snipe from Emmanuel Grayson. Now his actions spoke otherwise. August melted into his father's warmth, and Maeve hoped that this would finally prove to him that he was not only lovable, he was loved.

"No cause, sir," Maeve ventured, drawing Emmanuel's attention. "He's right dandy. Found him up in the mountains. Just a bit dirty and knackered, is all."

Immediately, Lord Grayson's face transfigured into a disgusted scowl as he barked at Maeve. "And what was your business with my son up there, Missy? Think you'd get a ransom for him? Or try to help him run away?"

"Father, Maeve was only—"

Perplexed, Maeve fell back a step. "No, sir. I just… Everyone was looking for him, and I thought…"

"Thought you'd take a chance on offing an Englishman? Or think you'd use his misery to gain a favor?"

"Father," August gasped. "Maeve's my friend. She'd never—"

"She'd do anything that she'd darn well fancy would work on you, boy! They're rapscallions, the lot of them. Always a plot, always thinking they'd be better off if we'd just give back 'their' land and leave. Always trying to trick us and take advantage of our good fortune."

Maeve wanted it clear that she was no such thing, and if anything, August was the mischievous and plotting one. The words left her mouth before she could think to recall them. "No, sir! In fact, he kissed me!"

Red stained August's cheek, complimenting Emmanuel's crimson flush.

"Kissed?" It sounded like an abomination on Emmanuel's lips. "Don't be so gullible, boy. She'll have you tricked six ways 'til Sunday if you give her a chance. These Irish…dirty, dishonest, barely human. Even your mother would…" He trailed off, the emotional reflection of the day's passing events echoing in his eyes. Finally, he hissed out, "Your mother left Ireland for good cause. She'd never want something so—" He vaguely motioned at Maeve, an expression of disgust, as though he had smelled something very unpleasant, marking his features. "—common. Here you are when still her body lays cold and forgotten upstairs, forsaking her."

August's face mired in confusion as he tried to make heads or tails of the statement. He looked to Maeve, her expression pleading, her eyes watering with tears, and back to his father, the man whose love he had wanted so long, and whose love he stood to lose in the same instant he had found it returned to him.

"You're right," he agreed, his lip curling in disgust. "Common. Well, lass, I'm back where I belong now. Away with you."

Maeve's heart broke into ten bits as she ran from the house. Her mother had been right: August didn't consider her a friend; she was a method of distraction that Emmanuel merely tolerated. Now that Eliza Grayson was dead, Emmanuel no longer required her "services."

It wasn't a week later, following the interment of poor Lady Grayson's body in the Irish soil, that the reclaimed son returned to Norwich with his father, perhaps never to return to Killarney, for all Maeve knew.

He left her with only her slighted heart and the bittersweet memory of a stolen first kiss.

6 | Sayeth the Lord

~Killarney, Ireland~

1866

During her life, Sine O'Connor had always held the belief that her daughter was too curious for her own good. Once, when she was eight, Maeve had heard from the boys in church that nuns were naked beneath their habits. Maeve had almost succeeded in raising Sister Mary Agnes' skirt in front of the whole congregation before Rory had intervened.

As Maeve marched the path from the O'Connor cottage to Shepherd's Bluff the following night, she cursed her own conflicting cause with every third step. Her only prayer and wish was that August's indifference would hold, and that he was not intending to check under her skirt. Anticipating the possibility, Maeve had made certain to put on her most restrictive underthings in layers. Just because she had to make herself available did not mean she had to make herself accessible.

She quietly closed the oak door behind her, repeating to herself her plan over and over: go to his room, thank him for the bread, serve her twenty seconds, and then tell him that she was through. It would buy a few days, at least, giving Maeve a chance to talk to Owen about her next course of action.

Grayson sat in his chair by the fire, again dressed in his bed clothes, his face buried in a book. The dancing firelight sparkled off the metallic rims of his reading glasses as Maeve sat wordlessly and waited. Several minutes passed with no movement except for the occasional turning of pages.

"If I'm going to make a fool of myself traipsing up here like a mad woman after dark, the least you can do is look at me when I sit down."

He kept his face turned downward, turned his eyes upward. Focused emerald eyes met hers with a certain degree of impatience and gaiety. The weight of his stare caused Maeve to shift around in the chair. He let out a small chuckle, removed his glasses, and bit down on the stem.

"If you insist," he acknowledged as he set the book on a nearby table. "Time runs away from me when I've found a passage that enraptures. Surely you understand. Have you been waiting long?"

"Have I been waiting?" she asked, gasping. "I've sat here patiently for three whole minutes, counting out the time on your precious clock over there. It seems an awful long time just to fulfill a twenty-second obligation. What could possibly be put into written words that you would find so engrossing?"

He ran the glasses' stem back and forth over his tongue, making butterflies flutter in her stomach for reasons she couldn't quite comprehend.

"You're quite right," he agreed. "At least as far as finding anything in this room more enrapturing than you. It's odd, Miss O'Connor. I remember you as pretty, but hardly beautiful. Time has done you good service."

"And turned you into a scallywag," she muttered under her breath, though she could not suppress the blush that broke across her face. She turned before he could notice, but heat radiated off her, making him smirk.

"You would find this one somewhat ironically apt: *The Tenant of Wildfell Hall*. But tell me then, what do you read?" he asked sincerely.

She answered him curtly. "I don't."

Grayson's expression transformed into shock and misunderstanding. "But… I taught you…" he uttered, astonished and perhaps slightly disappointed.

"I said don't, not can't," she snapped back. She turned her eyes from his and focused on the fire, desperate to break herself from the empathetic stare he suddenly fixed on her. "We don't own any books, Lord Grayson, except of course for The Book."

His back molded against the chair. "Ah, well, that's just a shame. Don't misunderstand, there are certain passages of the Bible I find thrilling. Why do you look at me so? Did I say something shocking?"

It seemed almost sacrilegious to her that he took a thrill from so reverent a source. Moreover, of course, she didn't believe him. "What passage?"

Maeve turned back, but Grayson was not in his chair. He had stood without her taking notice and was planted in front of the clock, eying her with devious intent etched into his features. Maeve's breath caught, but she kept it well hidden. He waited in a silence heavy with expectation, and then slowly raised his hand, pointing at the same spot he had her occupy on her previous visit. Maeve heeded the call, but kept her eyes fixed on the clicking second hand, not allowing herself an opportunity to lose her concentration by again being drawn into his needful gaze.

Without making any contact, Grayson circled her and leaned over her shoulder from behind, bringing his lips nearly flush with her ear, maintaining the slimmest of distances. He whispered softly, the heat of his breath sending a shiver into the pit of her stomach.

"'Blow upon my garden, that the spices thereof may flow out. Let my beloved come into his garden, and eat his pleasant fruits,'" he quoted conspiratorially.

August had instilled in her the ability to read, and only one book to practice the skill upon. She knew every Bible verse by heart.

"Song of Solomon."

She felt her breath stagger as he simultaneously cupped her cheek. It was the last graceful action he would allow. It was the last tenderness before he sprang.

He pressed his lips hard upon hers as he spun Maeve around and pushed her back against the wall, attacking her neck. For a moment, the thought crossed her mind that such action might leave marks that she would be hard pressed to explain, and in the next moment she couldn't have cared less. She even longed for him to do it, if that meant the pleasure coursing through her would continue. She knew she should have been counting the seconds, but Maeve found herself unable to concentrate as he brought his lips back to hers and pressed her into the wall with his hard body.

She found herself actually pulling him closer, if such a thing was possible. He yielded to the fervent clutching as best he could, his hand hooking under her thigh, over the cotton and wool layers of skirt, and pulling it up to hitch over his hip. Maeve's other leg instinctively wanted to follow, as even through four folds of material, she could feel Grayson's length press against her with one rough, upward jerk.

"Ungh."

Breath racing, Maeve realized embarrassingly that it was she moaning from frustration at the barriers between them. She saw Grayson smirk as he pulled his lips from their labor, his breath competing with her own. Maeve eyed him lustfully, but he brought himself no more against her.

Nor did he back away.

He stared at her, motionless, conflict warring behind his eyes. For a passing moment, it seemed as though he ached to say something, or perhaps to continue. Maeve then understood; twenty seconds had passed. Twenty seconds had passed, and he regretted the fact. Her eyes almost pleaded, wanting him to impart one kindness on her, or else throw words to the wayside and continue. She never anticipated desire to stir her the way it had. Now she understood why the newly wed were so oft in the pursuit of such stolen moments.

The thought of a fresh, blushing bride made Maeve recall her own situation. With a guilty twist, she cursed that she had allowed herself to be swept up in Grayson's snare. Determinedly, her eyes grew cold and her lips tightened in a spiteful sneer. Grayson took the shift in stride, growing stoic by comparison.

"You've fulfilled your obligation for the day," he panted as he lowered her leg to the floor and backed away. "You can go, and I'll not call you again until next week."

She paused, feeling suddenly forlorn. Tentatively and not fully understanding her whiplash desire to touch him, she took a few cautious steps in his direction.

"There's a sack of bread by the door," he continued with a quick jerk of his head. "Don't want Da suspicious now, do we?"

Mentioning Rory sobered her, froze her in place. She was falling into the trap again, not remembering that she was a meaningless object to him. Maeve could have been any tenant in dire straits. And for all she knew, his other tenants had similar arrangements with him. If he could broker such a deal with her, then why not others? Was she so unique?

Fearing her own befuddled thoughts, she crossed the room with determined steps. Maeve grabbed her cloak from the chair and turned toward the door, spying the small brown sack. As her hand reached out to grasp it, her wrist was encircled by his alabaster hand. He held her in place, eyes downcast. Maeve looked at him with beaming curiosity.

"We must tell no one of this," he reminded her, his voice soft, dare say she, compassionate? "No one, and we'll both be cursed souls if it should become known."

"I assure you, I would sooner throw myself from a cliff than have this arrangement known. Better I should make a deal with Lucifer himself than a bloodsucking English bloke."

"Lucifer? Surely my kiss cannot compare with hellfire, Maeve."

If only he knew…

A playfulness stretched across his eyes. A smile bloomed, but just as quickly, it was gone.

Maeve was surprised to hear her given name spoken from his lips.

"It was…well enough, under the circumstances," she bashfully admitted, once more averting her eyes so he couldn't see the depth of his effect on her. "But using the Bible to…seduce me. Well, that's positively devil-like in its device."

"I assure you, I've not even yet begun to seduce you."

To speak of hellfire and then feel it flood her senses as every reach of her body burned… Maeve felt a quiver in her stomach, an enigmatic desire to ponder if she might have an opportunity to have August proven right. Even his five-second kiss had unraveled her, after all. What possibilities would five minutes hold?

He eased his hold from her wrist and allowed her to open the door. She proceeded into the hall, feeling the presence of him following her at a distance. When she reached the front door, sack of bread in hand, she was startled when he spoke through the darkness, standing at the bottom of the stairs.

"Can I recommend a passage for your review before you depart?"

She said nothing, only half turned as she lingered in the doorway, the cool wind twisting her curls around her face.

"Genesis. In particular, the section where Eve sins and, by way of displeasing the Lord, is made to leave Paradise. Remember the price of bringing knowledge to the world."

"You needn't worry," she retorted. "Remember, Eve sinned only because she allowed herself to be seduced by the snake."

"The snake, Miss O'Connor?"

He caught her guilty as a goon, looking indicatively at a certain prominence that had yet to dissipate about his middle.

He chuckled. "The snake, indeed." A wink, followed by a nod, and he turned to ascend the stairs. Maeve crept away in the night, and only as she ripped a bite of bread and stuffed it in her mouth did she recall that she had meant to tell August goodbye.

Well, he had said it would be a week, and their next allotment put them at forty seconds. Surely no great misdeed could transpire in such a time. One more visit couldn't hurt.

7 | Divine Influence

The way Maeve eyed the confessional, anyone watching would have sworn she was walking to her death. The dark-stained, wooden booth was not so far from one of St. Mary's side doors leading outside. It wasn't uncommon that, whenever a girl or man of a certain reputation entered the confines of that box, one of the town gossips would linger nearby, pretending to be caught up in the reverie of the newly completed cathedral's glorious interior. In fact, they were stationed to overhear whatever sin from which the repentant was asking forgiveness.

Maeve had never been known as a sinner, so the gossips did not hover when she would make her occasional visits. Therefore, that she should hesitate now in such a fashion drew more than a few glances. Understanding at last what suspicions her display would likely spur, she gave herself a firm chastisement and marched the remaining distance, pulling the curtain quickly behind her.

The slice of wood over wood jolted her as Father Corbin slid the door of the window aside, leaving only the lattice barrier.

"In the name of the Father, and of the Son, and of the Holy Spirit. Forgive me father, for I have sinned. My last confession was a fortnight ago."

Recognizing Maeve's voice and expecting no great transgression, Corbin answered plainly, "Proceed."

"I have twice dishonored my father. I have taken the name of the Lord in vain thrice, and…" She winced. "…I have been inappropriate with a man."

Fearing all the depth of Hell Fire would encompass her after so scandalous an admission, the silence that met her was shocking. She could see Corbin's visage through the lattice, though shadowy in detail, and watched him take steady breaths. Every exhalation drew the knot in her stomach tighter.

At last, she wondered if perhaps he had not heard her at all. "Father?"

"It does not surprise me, Maeve."

"Father?"

He sighed heavily. "You are young; Owen is young. Love is new, and everything is exciting and novel. That you gave into some measure of temptation is only to be expected, not that that means it is anywhere near acceptable."

Owen? With utter disgust, her guilt was amplified by the fact that it would be the only possible assumption to make, that the other party to her sin would be her fiancé. Her mouth cracked, the correction creeping to the edge of her tongue, before she thought better of it and abstained.

She would admit to that particular lie during her next confession.

And when she foolishly heeded Grayson's call again, likely much more.

Corbin continued. "What you must remember is that there is no sin in the desire you feel. Once wed, these acts that God has made for us are a great blessing. Matrimony is no easy journey, and God's grace for a man and wife is the ability to join in the pleasure of their union. When you are wed. Until then, I caution you to keep your encounters with Owen limited, lest you be tempted. Remember that the Bible reads, 'lead us not into temptation.' It does not say, 'give us temptation and then help us to resist.' Do not allow opportunities to arise, and you'll not have the opportunity to fall. Tell me, though, to what extent have you sinned?" Silence forced him to clarify. "To help me determine your just penance."

She shifted uncomfortably, the heat of recollection crawling over her skin and scorching her memories. "We did not…consummate, Father. We only…kissed. Intensely."

"Kissed intensely?" he repeated back, as though it were a foreign word he was trying to decipher. "On the mouth?"

"Of course on the mouth." She was able to recall her senses before she added, for my part. "But *intensely*."

The last word colored uniquely the extent of the sin. Grayson's kisses, of course, were not merely on the cheek and lips, but up and down her neck as he gripped her hips, his breath on her ear, his hands tracing up slowly, until they reached…

She felt her breath catch in her throat and prayed that Father Corbin had not heard. If she had been with Owen in any intimate way, she might have felt disdainful of Corbin's advice. Alas, their infrequent contact had been restricted to pecks on the cheek and hand holding. But with Grayson, she had known it was wrong at the beginning, and hearing the sympathy and reprieve in Corbin's voice only emphasized that. She was such a fool.

And then she remembered why she had agreed to it.

Her father's face flashed in her mind, but not in the relatively good state of health which he now possessed, but in the sallow, pale recesses of despair and sickness into which he had fallen after Sine's death. He had been a shell of a man, a ghost lacking gaiety. Their home was almost like a part of their family, and Maeve suspected if they were forced away, it would be just like losing kin to Rory. And she and Owen had agreed, it would be a better thing once the children came along to be out in the fresh air of Middle Lake, not the hustle and bustle of Killarney.

Not to mention, she refused to give Grayson the pleasure of taking her home from her. Not after the way he had drawn her in once, only to spit her out when the winds shifted.

Corbin interrupted her thoughts with compassionate tones. "I would ask you to reflect on your faith and your dedication to the Lord. Be vigilant in your responsibilities. Make open your heart to His love, that He may fill you."

"To the Lord, Father?" she repeated. Had she really just heard him say that?

"Yes, Maeve. The Lord has built a home. He only longs for you to come into it and serve Him, that He may love you in return. Do not shun His offerings and He will keep you on the right path that you may walk it together."

Maeve had never been one to believe in signs. In a land of folklore and superstition, it was unique to her character. Still, the words coming from Father Corbin's mouth seemed too precisely tuned and surreptitiously selected, that she wondered at the coincidence and thought perhaps there was more to it than met the ear.

Maybe He had a plan for Maeve? Maybe it was her job to save August from his own misdeeds?

"But Father, if I open my heart, might not I be spurned when I err? If I serve him, what will I get in return?"

She could almost feel the smile in his voice. "The Lord's capacity for love is immeasurable. The Bible speaks often of the Lord's magnanimous nature and the doubling of blessings for the efforts of the faithful."

"Doubling?" That convinced her; surely something divine was at play.

"Yes. You see, when you decide to love someone, it is not merely a one-sided act. Your love is reflected back by the other in some measure. Therefore, your single effort has a double effect."

She pondered for a moment, carefully selecting her words that she might not give anything away. "But what effect can my…love have on the Lord? I am so simple a person, so meek and so powerless."

Corbin chuckled softly. "My dear, your humility shows me that your heart is capable of great love. The Lord wants to be loved, but remember, He makes it your choice. It is well within His power to demand your love, but He does not. He simply asks for your obedience, that you allow Him to show you the wonders He can bestow. That you allow Him to earn your love. The world and all creation are under His reign, but He made them all that He may find love."

Father Corbin mused a small space in the intervening silence before assigning Maeve what he felt was a proper penance. Crossing herself again, Maeve left the church and headed up the crowded Killarney streets.

Sunday was a day of rest by commandment, but in Killarney, it was anything but. Mornings were spent in church, either the Catholic St. Mary's for the Irish, or the Anglican St. Katherine's for the English. The French and Americans went to one or the other, if they went at all. It hadn't always been so. Even in the few years Maeve had to her credit, she had witnessed the change in town. Hardly the dark, dusty macabre silhouette of her youth on the tail end of the famine, the city had become a hub of commerce and thoroughfare. It was as if it had passed through a cruel, desolate winter, and now all the flowers and trees were springing back to life.

Which was an odd thought. After all, now in mid-October, there wasn't much blooming anywhere. But here in the market, life, wild and teeming, took root. She spotted the craftsmen's wares on display, a booth presided over proudly by Billy and Jared Boyle. Jared caught Maeve's eye as she passed and waved. To her right Patty and Patrick O'Keefe looked over the last autumnal vegetables. She quickened her steps, unsure if Patty was privy to Patrick's presumptions and hardly wishing to start a discussion regarding them in the market. As she strode past, cloak clutched tightly, she felt all the air whoosh from her lungs as steel-banded arms encircled her and picked her clear up off the ground, drawing a squeal and, in turn, all eyes in the marketplace.

"Don't panic, you banshee!" the familiar voice playfully reprimanded. "It's me."

"Owen!" she exclaimed as she caught her breath and he set her down. She had a good mind to slap him for scaring her so, but knew everyone nearby was watching, and withheld. "In the name of all that's holy, what are you doing?"

He shrugged nonchalantly, his blond locks scattering over his forehead and masking his blue eyes. "Not sure. Saw my girl and just got excited. Where're you off to, dearie? Thought you promised me a stroll after Mass?"

Feeling the weight of an accusatory stare from Patrick's direction, Maeve hooked her arm around Owen's and led him in a promenade, making sure to give a showplace, exuberant smile. It wasn't that she disliked Owen. On the contrary, she found his company quite enjoyable usually. She simply did not know if she yet liked him enough to be content in wedding him.

Maeve reminded herself that in her situation, she was lucky to have such an offer. As a blacksmith, Owen was a man of some affluence and respect. He had a kind heart and good humor about him that Maeve admired. Yes, she had been truly blessed.

They were to marry just as soon as Owen saved enough to support both his shop in the city and the rent on the cottage at Middle Lake. If she didn't lose it, first.

"You weren't at Mass today," Maeve commented matter-of-factly.

"Stopped in to see Katie this morning, stayed to help her. Poor waif is overwrought."

"Your cousin?" Owen nodded. "The one with the bakery?"

"Aye. Market days are an endurance for her. Actually, that was something I wanted to talk to you about."

"Me?" Maeve laughed. "Whatever for?"

Owen stopped her, circling in front and taking her hands into his. "You should have seen her running the range like a rabbit. An extra pair of hands'd do her a world of goodness, and look at these here..." Tenderly, he raised Maeve's hands to his lips and pressed a kiss to them. "Two of the finest hands in County Kerry."

The color drained from her face for a moment before it rushed back, causing Owen to fear her ill.

"Are you all right?"

Vaguely, she nodded. "Are you saying…I have employment?"

"Aye, Katie would like it if you could start next weekend. Of course, she'll let you out to go to mass. Knows your particular on that, and traffic lightens about then anyhow. So what say you?"

"We'll be able to wed sooner, and I can pay the rent to Grayson so I don't have to—" She stopped mid-sentence as Owen cocked an eyebrow. "—make excuses for why I can't pay," she quickly concluded.

Owen's look softened as he dropped her hands and drew the still slightly anxious Maeve into his arms, kissing her cheek quickly. For a moment, she thought she should pull away from such a blatant public display of affection. No doubt the gossips would have a fresh bag of seed to feed the other hens if they caught sight of this scandalous behavior. But as Maeve felt Owen's hold on her tighten, she melted into him, feeling the purity of his feelings wash over her.

He whispered into her ear. "It won't be long, I promise. Get Grayson or Patrick to give you one more extension, and then you can pay. Another fortnight, and you'll have the money they want out of you."

She lifted her arms and embraced him back, her truest way of showing her deepest thanks and appreciation. As she pulled away, a smile flitted across her face. She had promised her father bread, and now she would have an honest, forthright way to give it to him.

8 Let It Not be Forgotten

Miss O'Connor: I have need of your service. My bread basket is bare. Come tonight.

Thoroughly confused, Maeve read the note again and again. Did he actually intend for her to make bread? Or was this code, lest the note go astray? It had obviously escaped his recollection that a good number of the Irish could neither write nor read.

As she watched the sun sinking in the west, she again threw her cloak around her and crept off into the twilight, walking the familiar path toward Shepherd's Bluff. Fortunately, her father was once again detained by his social obligations at the pub. With any luck, she would serve her time and be in her bed before an inebriated Rory O'Connor made his way home.

Passing through the servant's entrance, she found herself in the deserted kitchen. Maeve remembered how August had once snuck her up to the attic this way so they could spend a rainy day together. The house had been new then, and the attic a vast complex of gables and arches, unhindered by any boxes or crates. Everything was new and untainted. The house. The attic. August. Maeve.

On the kitchen table set two perfectly-portioned loaves of bread, a cotton sack lying suggestively next to them. She sheathed them and, as instructed, did not tarry but made her way to Grayson's room, pausing only briefly by a mirror in the hall to straighten her hair. Her cheeks proved flushed, though she did not feel winded. The walk in the dark had been invigorating, but hardly taxing.

She removed her cloak and sat it, along with the sack, on the table, closing the door quietly behind. Pacing through the room with feather-light steps, she made hardly a sound. As before, Grayson sat in his chair by the fire, his eyes transfixed amid the pages of a book.

"You found the bread?" He did not look to her.

"Aye, thank you. I thought maybe you actually intended me to bake…"

His eyes turned up, though his head stayed inclined. His spectacles transformed him somehow, making him look much older than his twenty-four years.

"Why would you think that?"

"The note you sent."

He seemed confused for a moment, before realization dawned on his face. "Ah, yes, the note. I thought maybe if your father should see it, or even the courier… In any case, no, the last thing I desire for you to do right now is bake."

Maeve waited for him to make some indication, but he continued reading instead. She sat in the chair, staring blankly into the fire. She detested this game of his, perhaps meant to remind her that she was the servant here, and he would take her service only when he was good and ready.

"I almost didn't come," she blurted out, needing his attention.

And she received it. His fingers pinched the rim of his glasses and ripped them off as the book fell and he leaned forward.

"Why ever not? Are you…" August seemed at a loss for words. "Are you ending our agreement?"

She was positively thrown at the concern etched in his features. His eyes were keenly focused on her.

"I am not…" Grayson's tension eased, and he sat back. "Yet."

"Yet?" he repeated. "Whatever does that mean? Either our agreement is in place, or it isn't. There is no part way."

"August, I…"

Her voice faltered as his anger manifested, as though his hands had encircled her throat.

"I am Lord Grayson," he reprimanded. "Lord, Miss O'Connor, and you would do well to remember it."

Part of her wanted to slap August for speaking to her in such a tone, to strip off every air he had attached to himself with one fervent slam of her hand against his cheek. She could feel the fire of frustration building within, feel the burning in her face, and she knew she must have been as red as a rooster. It pleased him, her evident fury, which angered her further.

"You…" she growled.

His look grew expectant. "Yes, Miss O'Connor?" He was daring her with a devilish smile.

And yet, the other part of her knew that Grayson had it well within his power to cast her from her cottage if he so desired. The fact that he already had ability to evict her within a few days of making the decision to do so, and that he had not, had to mean something, she thought. True, she was offering him payment in the form of her presence, but what was the value of that? He was hardly aching for funds, so he must be receiving something from her. It couldn't simply be the company of a woman; surely a man of his stature would have access to… women of a certain sort, and ones that hardly had the time limitations that their arrangement precluded.

Maeve smoothed her skirt and kept her emotions at bay, trying to keep reason her guiding star. The words of Father Corbin echoed in her memory: *The Lord wants to be loved. It is well within his power to demand your love, but he does not. He simply asks for your obedience… That you allow him to earn your love...*

She could never love Grayson; she knew this to be fact. But maybe, if she played along with this charade in the remaining time, a little sliver of the boy who had once felt like family to her could be reclaimed.

"*Lord* Grayson," she continued, emphasizing her correction, "I have recently accepted a position in town. It isn't much, only two days a week, but the wages are sufficient enough that in a few weeks' time, I should be able to resume my payments to you. In a few months, I should be able to catch up completely. For now, I am obliged to remain in your service."

Grayson seemed disappointed. "Employment?" he queried. "Where?"

"A bakery. O'Toole's, to be precise."

He smirked. "Baking bread in lieu of the time in which you are…'baking bread.'"

She giggled. "Yes, that trick did not escape my notice. I wasn't looking for work, but my fiancé's cousin has a bakery, and she—"

His beautiful green eyes turned to brimstone. "Your what?"

Anxiety consumed her, though she knew not if it was because she feared Grayson's anger or regretted his lack of indifference. "My Owen, I mean, my fiancé, Owen Murphy. Well, that's just it. I am engaged."

He said nothing, but she noted the sudden paleness of his face. Without warning, Grayson was on his feet, taking off his robe and pitching it against the floor. A swirl of confusion left Maeve disoriented as he leaned over and gripped her by the wrist, dragging her behind him across the room, positioning her in front of the clock. Its steady tick tock clashed with the banging bodhran in her chest that was her heart.

"Forty seconds?"

A still confused Maeve nodded meekly.

"Good." He made a quick sweep of her cheek with his hand, his touch feather light.

Maeve's eyes fluttered at the warmth that radiated under the pulse of his fingertips. She could feel his breath on her lips as he leaned in closely, speaking in hushed tones.

"You and I reached an agreement," he began, so close she could feel his words as well as hear them. "My pleasure, your time. That is the only payment I will accept. You can leave the cottage if you wish, but payment by coin is no longer an option. This…" His hands ghosted over her frame and landed on her breasts. Despite the layers of clothing—four, to be precise—that she had put on as barrier, she quivered when his palms enveloped the peaks and pulled teasingly. "…is what I desire from you."

Her eyes opened to catch his. She couldn't recall seeing such wild demand before. In no uncertain terms, he was making it known that he would have her, as the time allowed him to possess her, and there could be no mistaking his intentions.

"I am to be wed," she countered, a hint of regret in her voice. "I will default on my payment then, if you will not take my shillings."

Grayson scoffed at her. "You may find, Miss O'Connor, that I can be a difficult creditor to outrun."

With his mouth, he attacked her neck, his lips working forcibly over the flesh. Maeve's hands were suddenly in his hair, weaving through the ebony locks and pulling him closer as he worked up her jaw before his lips crashed into hers.

She felt again the hardness of his attributes between them as he pressed her against the wall, and she wondered at the unfamiliar feeling it stirred within her. More than feverish, she felt aflame, as though fire danced on her brow and breasts. Gaining ever so slight a measure of flesh, he moved his efforts to the sliver of cleavage, his tongue quickly skimming the valley between the firm mounds.

"Mo Maeve," he muttered between his workings. "So…beautiful…"

His voice trailed off as he found a spot atop her right breast and suckled it, pulling the flesh between his teeth, biting. Though Maeve feared the pain, she was surprised when instead the teasing nip sent a heated chill about her, and the feeling manifested into a heavy sigh. Grayson's lips fluttered into a smile against her chest as he kissed the spot duly marked with his workings.

"So enticing," he uttered as he began to pull away. "I cannot wait for our interest to accrue in due time. Forty seconds passed much too quickly, and I fear you are left in quite a tizzy."

"Passed?" she gasped. "It's…it's over?"

Empty arms clutched the space left by his withdrawal. Maeve snapped back to the utter reality of the moment and looked down, taking in the oval red-blue patch of skin on her breast.

"Jesus, Mary, and Joseph!" she exclaimed. "How did you…? Why did you…?"

She looked accusingly at Grayson, but there found she no trace of regret or apology. Instead, he seemed whimsically proud.

"It will heal." Coughing, he continued on, taking on a formal tone. "Now, as to our arrangement, you will keep your end, or I will stick to the exit clause of mine."

"Our what?" Her breath still raced, and she wondered at his cool and collected countenance. How was he able to turn on and off so easily, while she was still stuck in the conflicted desires of thirty seconds before? "Yes, well, we shall see. When shall I come again? Or will you let me know?"

He rubbed his chin in contemplation. "Well, I cannot keep sending you notes. It was difficult enough today to find a courier whose discretion I could trust. I do believe you can see the top of the north wing attic from your hillside?"

Of course she could see it. No doubt he remembered the game they'd played that summer long ago. When at last they had departed each other's company for the night, August would climb up to the attic, lantern in hand, and Maeve would sit on her front porch with her father's lantern, and by way of a system of flashes, they would send messages back and forth.

"I expect the view is just the same now as it was then," she answered.

He nodded. "Yes, that will do. I will hang a lantern in that window. That will be your signal to come to Shepherd's Bluff."

His eyes glanced downward as he took in one more survey of his marking upon her, and his smile in its observation could only be called prideful.

"That is all for tonight. Good night."

She knew better this time than to expect his seeing her out. Instead, she made for the door. As she passed, he caught her by the arm and locked his eyes on her breasts.

"One request, Miss O'Connor?"

"Yes?"

His eyes shifted to her skirt. "Next time, wear something simpler."

9 Idle Gossip

Katie O'Toole possessed much too slender a frame and genteel a repose to throw about balls of dough as she did. Nonetheless, Maeve watched in awe as the petite woman slapped another heap into submission.

"Never be afraid to give it a good whacking," she advised in the back room of the bakery. "Remember, it feels no pain."

By this time, the daybreak crowd had already filtered in and out of the shop. They came now from catholic houses, as well as Protestant. Katie was spinning trying to keep up with expectations. For the Irish, she made brown or soda bread, for the English, white. For the French, she baked baguettes, and for the Americans, she simply gave whatever was left over. Katie's opinion of Americans was low, but she acknowledged that they at least has the good grace not to be English. And at least Yanks took what was available, while the English only complained no matter the selection.

"How long do you let it rise?" Maeve questioned as she saw Katie set the formed loaf aside and cover it with a cloth.

"Depends on the temperature. The warmer the air, the quicker the rise. You want it to about double, then stick it in the oven to bake. It's more about the size of it than the time."

A twinkle of bells in the front of the store alerted the women that the calm of the mid-morning lull was passing and the banking crowd was soon to arrive. Wiping her floured hands over her apron, Katie turned to Maeve.

"I'll bring up some loaves from the racks. Can you handle?"

Two English ladies, modest in the fashion befitting their station, stood at the counter chattering like little music boxes gone mad. Their expressions were mischievous and haughty, as though they were privy to some great secret and couldn't believe their luck at the lot of it.

"How can I help you?"

Their response to Maeve's inquiry was a snide glare.

The one to the right sneered as she overly enunciated the request in the Queen's proper English, as though speaking to a slow child. "Six baguettes and three white loaves, for Sir Edmund Gantry, charged to his account." She tossed a cotton sack on the counter with little concern where it landed.

A quick nod to acknowledge the order, and Maeve turned to the other maid with an inquisitive gaze.

"Nothing for me, thank you," the second woman returned, her voice kindly. Her companion gave her a little nudge as Maeve took the cotton sack. "Cecily, whatever did you do that for?"

"Oh, Margaret! 'Nothing for me, thank you,'" she mocked as Maeve pulled out the baguette basket and began to sort through. "So polite to the natives, are we?"

Maeve gnashed her teeth, wondering if Cecily really believed that a distance of five meters rendered her unable to hear. Still, she knew better than to raise ire against the English bit; having it out with a customer on her second day of employment wouldn't reflect well on her—or Owen. Instead, she kept her eyes trained on the loaves as Cecily continued.

"Oh, then again, your lady is half-native, isn't she?"

Margaret sounded almost admonished in her response. "Yes, Lord Grayson's mother was Irish. To the best of my knowledge, the pedigree has done Miss Caroline no ill."

Feeling a little jolt of surprise, Maeve stood erect and spun around. Her sudden movement drew curious glances from the English maids, but Maeve made quick her recovery.

"Sorry, miss. Was that five baguettes?"

Cecily scowled, her lip curling. "Six, and snap to." As she turned back around, Maeve heard the venomous voice continue. "My dear, the pedigree, as you so diplomatically put it, is the least to blame for poor Caroline Grayson's lack of decorum. She was practically an orphan, don't you know? Her mother died when she was a child, and they say that Emmanuel Grayson sent her off to live with her governess even before that. They say Caroline looks so much like her mother that he couldn't stand the sight of her. I heard she hadn't even seen her father or brother for ten years when the old frog croaked."

"But she's with him now," the kinder of the pair countered. "Miss Caroline told me herself that the first thing Lord Grayson did when their father died was come collect her. They've barely been separated since, and it pained him to leave her behind in England to come set up Shepherd's Bluff. Her arrival was quite the event. You should have seen Lord Grayson yesterday. He was positively alight with glee."

Despite herself, Maeve smirked. Until Cecily spoke again.

"Oh, Lord Grayson." From the tone, Maeve could imagine her swooning, even if her back was turned. "I would do nearly anything required to make him…alight with glee."

"Cecily!"

But she refused to be ashamed. "Come now, Margaret. He's handsome beyond all measure. Surely, sometime late at night, after your Mistress goes to bed, you could chance into his chambers to offer... to fluff his pillows."

Glancing back over her shoulder as she stuffed the rest of the bread into the sack, Maeve saw one girl looking wholly embarrassed as the other smiled wickedly.

"I would never," Margaret proclaimed in a low voice. "How profane. Besides, Lord Grayson orders all servants away from his and Miss Caroline's chambers after dark." Maeve set the bag on the counter as she took out the ledger to note the purchase. She was nearly blushing in a confusion of unease, but let her hair fall over her face to hide it. Meekly, she pushed the ledger forward. "Your signature, ma'am."

"You know what that means?" Margaret shrugged at Cecily's question. "It means he already has someone, and I bet—"

"You need to sign!"

It was fortunate that the outburst had the result of leading the English to want to move their conversation elsewhere. Cecily signed, and the women quickly made their way out the door.

A few hours passed until at last it was time for Maeve to make her way down the lakeshore toward home. On a good day, the distance took an hour to cross. Today, however, her feet dragged slowly as she tried to make sense of the anger—and dare she say, jealousy—that had wracked her.

Horse hooves clopping and a familiar voice drew her from her contemplating. She turned to find the smiling face of Jared Boyle beaming at her.

As he was heading her direction, he offered her a place on his cart, which she accepted gladly. Her feet had grown just as weary as her mind; she never would have imagined something as seemingly benign as working in a bakery could be so taxing. She grimaced when she thought of what poor Owen must feel like at the end of the day.

"How go things at O'Toole's?"

Maeve tilted her head in Jared's direction. "Does everybody know my every move?"

"It's Killarney," Jared answered with an eye roll. "You can't kick a stone without it being heard clear across town."

She sighed. That's what worried her. "The bakery is fine. Katie O'Toole is a good woman; it's very kind of her to offer me the work. The clientele, however…" Her voice trailed off, remembering the maids' conversation as she shifted uncomfortably on the seat.

"English mutts nipping at your skirts a bit?"

Her silence was confirmation. It wasn't in Maeve's nature to speak ill of… anyone.

A warm squeeze on her shoulder let her muscles relax a bit. "Don't let them get to you. Be patient. Everything will right itself soon enough."

His face looked oddly smug as he made the proclamation. Maeve wondered, but she let it fall by the wayside as they rounded the bend in the road and she saw the smoke rising from her own hearth. All else was forgotten in the warmth of coming home.

10 | The Voyeur

Killarney had changed little, yet presented itself as a tribute copy of smaller proportion to August's matured eyes. In his days of youth, Ireland had been exotic and formidable with its masses of people shifting about and the skeletal frame of St. Mary's Cathedral dominating the landscape like a leviathan. In the interim, funds had been raised and the edifice completed. As the carriage passed by its front steps, he could see women pulling their daughters in and out, lecturing them on the importance of mass, no doubt.

"You haven't said a word since Middle Lake, August."

"Hmm?"

Caroline's voice broke his reverie as the carriage bumped along the roughly cobbled streets leading to Burke & Woodrow, the Killarney office handling the legal and financial concerns of all Grayson holdings in County Kerry.

"What are you thinking of, dear brother?" she asked further, giving him a warm smile.

August leaned in, placing his leather-clad hands over the lace of her gloves. "I'm thinking how resilient they are. Think of all they survived, all they still endure. Makes me remember how fortunate we are, compared to them."

"I never considered you one for compassion," Caroline mused, turning over her hands and rubbing his fingers delicately. "May I tell you something? I think providence has brought you here."

"Providence had nothing to do with it."

"On the contrary. I'm a firm believer that the Lord makes paths for us to blaze, if we prove valiant enough, to compensate for those we were too weak to approach before. You couldn't help Mother, but you can help—"

"I'm here to develop the land our estate sits on, Caroline, and if it should help out the people here or not is none of my concern," he snapped. "It's just a consequence of business, not charity in the least."

Caroline eyed him inquisitively. "And yet, I notice the one cottage on which the mineral veins sit is still standing. Do not tell me you haven't a plan for compensating its occupants. You're negotiating with them, I'd gather, otherwise they'd have been gone by now. That is the one with the family in it you've spoken of, is it not? What was it, the O'Carrins?"

"O'Connors," August quickly corrected. "Rory and his daughter, Maeve."

At the mention of her name, he faltered and smiled, remembering their last interlude. Was that what he was doing with Maeve, negotiating? Even to himself, he acknowledged that he was becoming confused regarding his objectives with her. Through the years, idle curiosity had arisen, but he had realistically and fully expected her to have been wed when he arrived to Killarney. Upon learning that any man had yet to claim her, August couldn't help his fantasies of what it would be like to kiss her again after so long. But he knew the Irish temperament well enough to know Maeve would as soon give him a fist in the eye as anything if he dared approach her.

When she had shown up unexpectedly at his stable, he had already decided to send Patrick O'Keefe to offer Maeve and Rory compensation for the move, even a different cottage on his lands, if they wished. It was more than he was obligated to do, and certainly more than was fair given that their rent was late. But when Maeve sought him, offered her labor in place of payment until she could acquire the funds due, he couldn't help himself. Her skin had been flush from her walk, her eyes had looked at him so pleadingly, and her beauty as she stood before him… He was a right bastard for having taken advantage of her situation, knowing full well he was only putting off the inevitable. Come tide or teacups, he needed the O'Connors out of that cottage. But Maeve. Maeve! Her kisses made him forget himself, forget his aims, forget the convoluted mess awaiting in Norwich from which the was taking temporary refuge in Killarney.

Caroline's smug smile brought him back to the moment. They kept to silence some time before finally arriving outside the red brick building. A cacophony of carillon reverberations sounded as bell ringers across the city marked noon. Caroline waved goodbye as she continued on to the market.

Bustling clerks greeted August in the front office, but he passed them without acknowledgement, proceeding straight back to the door marked James Woodrow, Esq. He entered without knocking. Mr. Woodrow's eyes widened as he all but jumped from his chair.

"Lord Grayson, sir, a great pleasure to finally meet Emmanuel's progeny!"

His pudgy, pig-nose face and bald head blanched, then blushed over. The genuflection was embarrassing in its intensity. August said nothing, instead going to the table where the papers he had requested had been readied. He slipped off his gloves and began to rifle through the collection.

"Have you been able to determine if we have the mineral rights properly secured?"

Woodrow bumbled about. "It seems so, but I've had to write to London to verify the land deeds against the records. Your father met all his financial obligations, but it seems he never signed off on all the necessary documents. That can be easily rectified. Just a formality, really. I understand, though, that there are tenants on the land. Have you approached them about compensation? You don't need to offer them much, but they could put a damper on your plans if they decide to see out the terms of their tenancy, assuming they're fulfilling their rent requirements. I can inquire with your middleman after that later this week. I haven't had a chance to visit Middle Lake in some weeks to review his ledgers. Do you happen to know if these particular tenants are overdue?"

August's mind's eye flashed back to images of Maeve's swollen lips, of her chest heaving and her heavy breaths.

"They are keeping up their end," he returned, suppressing the licentious images of what he could do with Maeve's next payment. "Why? What remains of their lease?"

Woodrow rummaged through a stack of papers on his desk. "A little shy of two years," he answered, adjusting his glasses on the rim of his nose.

August clenched his teeth. That wouldn't work. He needed the land cleared by spring to start exploring the copper veins that ran underneath. He needed to start work on the processing facilities even sooner.

In short, now that he had entered this ridiculous, self-defeating arrangement he both regretted and relished, he was going to have to step up with Miss O'Connor to keep his timeline on track. He needed her out before the first frost set in. That allowed six, perhaps eight weeks. Maybe more bible verses were in order.

He reminded himself that so far, her reactions had been playing into a desirable outcome. Maeve resisted initially, but whenever she found herself in his arms, she lost control. The problem was, he was doing no better. Had he not sworn to press himself on her like a rogue, to make her disgusted with his brazenness? How could he do that when she was becoming so receptive, making him want to engage her even more for reasons that had nothing to do with his scheme? Certainly the initial kiss was meant only to sate his curiosity, but after that each had been undertaken with a firm purpose meant to deliver a specified result.

Hadn't it?

He bit his lip in contemplation.

"Sir?" Woodrow asked. "You inquired about some of the local businesses."

"What of it?"

"I have a portfolio here with possible acquisitions."

August held out his hand, into which Woodrow placed a set of papers bound in a leather satchel.

"You were certain to select only those which fit my specifications?"

He nodded heartily. "Yes, sir. Everyday goods and services. The 'meat and potatoes' of Killarney, as you put it. Can I ask why you are so concerned with existing enterprise, when with your resources you could easily open competitive establishments and drive the current ones out of business?"

"I do not do this for the money," he returned nonchalantly as he thumbed through the profiles of a dozen opportunities. "Though breaking even would be nice."

"As you wish, sir."

As he lifted the next page, the name written across the top gave him pause.

"What's your opinion on this one?" He handed the paper back over to Woodrow.

"Ah, yes, a good choice," Woodrow agreed. "Some of the best Irish bread on the island. People always need bread, good times or not. A fine product, but management is lacking. No doubt you could remedy that quickly enough."

"I'd like to see it," August announced as he took the paper back. "Is it far?"

Woodrow guffawed and stuttered. "No, just five blocks south. Do you mean now, sir? I haven't had opportunity to make an official inquiry. I don't think Miss O'Toole would be available on such short notice, and in any case, I can't leave my office at the moment."

August shook his head as he slipped on his gloves. "Nevertheless, I'll get a better idea of its viability from personal experience. Street?"

"Greenlawns."

"Good. I'll be back next week to examine my accounts. I'll let you know if I want to move forward on any of these by courier."

The bakery was easily found and nothing out of the ordinary. It wasn't on a main thoroughfare, but a steady stream of foot traffic on Greenlawns Court ensured an ample customer base. The building looked in good enough condition that few repairs were likely to be necessary. All in all, its potential seemed well-founded.

But August knew that was not why he wanted it, nor was it why he was going to have it.

Discreetly, he edged to the windows and peeked in, standing behind a man smoking a pipe and leaning against the glass of the shop.

Behind the counter, he spied Maeve smiling widely and talking with a gray-haired lady as she handed her a sack. When the old woman dropped her sack on the floor, Maeve all but leapt around to pick it up for her. It was evident from the frail figure of the matron that bending was difficult. She mouthed her thanks to Maeve and stroked her cheek. Maeve's angelic smile soon reflected in August's.

She was so beautiful when she was happy. In his presence, she had vacillated between irritation, annoyance, and lust. Lust looked good on her, but seeing her happiness was like a thick woolen blanket warming his soul. Maeve's hair was tied back, allowing August to focus on the supple curvature of her chin and the milky flesh of her neck. He would have to take more time to explore that flesh in detail as the mounting time frames allowed him to slow his attentions.

He snapped straight up when he realized the path of his thoughts. Wasn't he engaging in this undertaking in order to force Maeve not to want to continue? He did want to be rid of her, didn't he?

Maeve returned behind the counter, taking up a large wooden tray in her hands while shifting about. August pulled himself into the street a bit, keeping his view, and embarrassingly bumping into a dirty-faced Irishman in sooty clothes. The blond-haired, blue-eyed commoner tipped his cap apologetically.

"Pardon." August smiled and dipped his head respectfully.

"My fault entirely," the stranger returned, moving past.

As Maeve's eyes landed on this new arrival, a nervous giddiness overcame her features. She rushed forward as he picked her up and twirled her, before setting her down and taking her hand. Maeve turned to another shopgirl and mouthed something, and the girl gave her a go-ahead gesture.

August quickly swiveled away as Maeve and Blue Eyes left the bakery, hand in hand and looking quite content. He waited until they were a safe distance ahead, and then followed.

The couple settled on a bench on the edge of a public thoroughfare. They didn't notice August as he strolled behind them and leaned against a lamp post, his face turned, of course, in the opposite direction, but still keeping them well within earshot.

"Owen, what are you doing here?" Maeve started.

August's blood boiled. Of course, Owen, the fiancé.

"Jared stopped by to have his mare re-shoed. He mentioned you seemed weary," he answered in a compassionate tone. "Is it Rory?"

"Oh goodness, no!" she exclaimed. "At least, not directly. I don't know how else to say this. Truth is, we've run through all our reserves now, and Grayson's decided to charge interest."

August's teeth gnashed before the anger relented. Well, it was true, in a roundabout way.

"I think he'll have Patrick evict us," she continued.

"That's horrible!" Owen exclaimed. "Damn English! Your da is getting better, though. Maybe he can work?"

"Aye, that may well be," Maeve agreed, her voice sounding dismissive. August could almost see the sadness fill her brown eyes as she mournfully continued, "Or perhaps it's time to let go of our hopes for the cottage, and Da and I could move into town with you."

August gripped his arms in frustration, trying his best not to call out. Maeve live with this Irish cur? Sleep under the same roof—perchance, the same bed with the bastard?

Then again, why should it matter? Maeve was nothing to him. And, he reminded himself, her leaving had been the whole point. Yet the pang of unease wouldn't leave him. As August heard the blue-eyed man babble, he couldn't deny that his heart betrayed his intent while Owen continued to argue.

"Maeve, dearie, that would look bad," he told her gently. "What would everyone say if I had you living with me before we're wed? Come now, only two months, maybe three, and then we'll be together, just we two."

"And Da," Maeve added.

"Of course, and Rory," Owen agreed. "You'll be my sweet little wife, the queen of my castle. I'll make sure you keep your good name until then. If it's just a question of money, I could—"

"No!" Maeve interjected, cutting him short. For a moment, pride surged through August, and he felt relieved to see his Maeve keep her dignity with Owen wherein she could not with him.

His Maeve? Well, she had bound herself in an agreement to him. They had a contract, and he expected her to see out the terms. But hadn't he come up with the contract wanting her to break it? Wasn't that the whole point of this exercise?

"It's not about money," Maeve continued. "I think I can convince Grayson to show some flexibility. Besides, the more you save, the sooner we can wed."

"You really want to marry me badly, don't you?" Owen asked, the influence of a broad smile coming through in his timbre. "Falling in love with me now?"

August couldn't breathe as he waited for her answer.

"I think…" she stuttered. "I-I think I could. I will, in time. You are a good man. I hope I prove worthy."

There was guilt in her voice, and he knew he was responsible.

"Of course you are," Owen assured her. August chanced a glance over his shoulder to see him reaching timidly to stroke her cheek. Against his own volition, the imaginary tick-tock of a Comtoise clock started reverberating through him. "I have to get back to the shop."

August allowed the couple some number of paces before discreetly pulling himself away from the lamp post and following at an undetectable distance. At the corner, Owen gently leaned over and quickly kissed her cheek.

And then, it happened: a single, self-shattering declaration moved silently across his lips.

Mine.

August could take no more.

Woodrow's eyes flashed in panic when August burst into his office, the hard-set brow of determination etched in his features.

"O'Toole's," August proclaimed. "I want it."

II | At Her Hearth

The fever chased away restful sleep. Through the night, visions plagued him. He dreamed of a bride, fresh and fragrant and fine, and of her smile. He dreamed of standing before the congregation in the sight of the Heavenly Father as she took his name. He dreamed of pulling back her veil, and of the horror that followed as the crimson-lipped beauty mocked him.

"Oh, August, do you believe this will make you happy? Do you believe this is right? How utterly foolish."

The scene dissolved. He saw himself looking in the window of the cottage, a hearth alight with gentle flame. Maeve's form flickered, with a broad-shouldered man at her back, his arms wrapped tightly around her. As the figure pressed kisses down her neck, August pounded the glass, trying to get her attention. She seemed unable to hear, but the blond-haired Irishman saw August through the panes. Saw him, and laughed as he indulged in Maeve.

In the morning, August placed a lantern in the window the very moment he could escape attention, and waited.

He found himself pacing up and down the length of his bed chamber, staring at a clock with a steady tick, but whose hands seemed fixed. How could time pass so slowly? He wanted her here, wanted her now. He needed to reclaim his property, to reaffirm the contract. She was his, not Owen's, for as long as she stayed on his land. For as long as he could keep her on his land.

No, he needed her to leave.

He wanted her to stay.

His foolishness taunted him. What was he expecting this to become? Maeve was both Irish and poor. She could never be more than a plaything. As children, it hadn't mattered that they came from different societies. Ignorance had been bliss. But now he knew the ways of the world. Besides, what he may have once lackadaisically fantasized was impossible, and even if it wasn't, it wouldn't be fair to try to make Maeve legitimate in the eyes of English society. His father had tried and failed, and his dear mother's heart had never mended.

August affirmed his intentions. He would make her detest him so much that her hatred would poison him, too, and then all these inklings of…something…would sink back beneath the surface. She would marry her blacksmith and be happy.

Though by her own admission, she did not love Murphy. Perhaps her heart was set on another?

Twenty minutes later, August found himself staring at the modest, whitewashed cottage's fire-lit window across the meadow. He couldn't remember making the decision, or readying the mare. This was lunacy. Surely Rory would be at home, and how would he explain himself then? It was nearly nightfall; if he waited another hour, Maeve would make her way to him.

An hour, however, was simply too long.

He dismounted and approached the door, steeling himself for what he was contemplating. Would she see through this farce? Would she see that he found himself so desperate for her that after days without, he could not wait until evening to take her into his arms again?

Not based upon her crude glare which competed with the fire burning on the hearth as she opened the door.

"And here I thought Saint Patrick had driven all the snakes from Ireland," she muttered. August gave her a wry smile but said nothing. "What do you want?"

He looked down and saw the book Maeve was holding: the Bible, turned, it seemed, based on the small sliver of the text visible, to the Song of Solomon.

She saw his gaze tracking to the tome and quickly tossed it aside.

"As owner of this land, it is my right to inspect the property for upkeep. Is your father in?" He was careful to keep any indication of hope for a negative response out of his tone. Nevertheless, his eyes set past her, trying to search the interior. His dream had left him half-expecting to see that cursed Murphy.

"In town. At the pub, I'd reckon."

August concealed a devious smile as best he could, drew in a deep breath, and continued. "Pity, I would have liked to have seen him. Well, you'll do, I suppose. I wish to take a survey of your cottage."

"Oh really?" Maeve spat, cocking her hip and wrenching her fist into her waist. "At this time of day, no less?"

"Miss O'Connor, if I wished to inspect the property at midnight on Christmas Day, I have that privilege. Now, step aside and let me in."

Gnashing her teeth didn't make it any less true, so reluctantly Maeve deferred. August pulled off his riding gloves and set them and the crop next to the discarded book. The cottage was tiny, seeming far smaller than it had been to his adolescent eyes a decade ago. Besides the main room, there was only one other chamber, and a ladder leaned against one wall, leading up to what he remembered as Maeve's sleeping loft. He climbed up and found a spread of blankets pushed under the eaves of the low roof. Maeve must hardly have been able to sit up in so little a space, let alone find comfort, he thought.

"It's not quite as opulent as Shepherd's Bluff," she hissed from below, "but it does fine for us."

"Yes, everything seems in good condition," August agreed, coming back down the ladder and finding her red-faced and glassy-eyed, tracking his movements.

Her breath sped as he paced to within mere inches of her. She was obviously surprised, and she turned away to focus across the room but made no attempt to back away.

"You saw the lantern?"

"Yes."

"You had planned to come?"

"As agreed."

He grinned. "But, here I am." He raised his hand to her cheek, but did not yet touch, waiting for her permission. "If your father is out, I can spare another eighty seconds of time, I suppose."

Her brow furrowed in contemplation and with every moment, her breathing grew more unsteady.

"I suppose it would be better; smells like rain. How do we keep time? Our little mantle clock doesn't tick so loudly as that French contraption of yours."

"I will use your pounding heart as my pendulum, then," August assured her as his hand sought out the soft curvature of her cheek. She shuddered under his touch like a leaf in the wind, her eyes drawing closed and her body leaning into his. August pressed his lips fully on hers and sucked her bottom lip.

Mine.

He moved next to the softness of her neck just below her chin and gave it a bite.

Also mine.

He moved his lips around to her right ear and sucked the lobe into his mouth, dancing over it with the tip of his tongue.

You're all mine.

Maeve pulled her body closer as August embraced her and whispered softly into her ear.

"I saw you in town."

She gasped, trying to pull away, but he held her firm.

"I saw you with him, and I know what you asked him."

August gently pushed his tongue into her ear, causing her to quiver, her grip on his arms to tighten.

"I wonder if he'll ever kiss you this way?" he mused as he pulled himself back to her mouth and pushed his tongue past her lips. She yielded all too willingly.

"Will he be able to make your heart race this way?"

His hand drifted back around her front and cupped her right breast through the cotton folds of her blue dress. Her nipple perked instantly as he pinched the virgin flesh, making her moan.

"I doubt he'll ever do to you what I can, Maeve." August let his hand fall downward to the edge of her skirt, tracking lightly, reaching the apex of her femininity and trailing his hand over. He could feel her heated wetness even through the layers of material, and he had to use all his will power to deny himself the opportunity to explore flesh to flesh.

"He'll never make you respond like I do. Just remember that when you think about… making other arrangements."

With that, he backed away, hiding his own arousal from her as best he could. Gasping, Maeve was clearly on the edge of throwing herself back in to his arms—if August had wanted, he probably could have pushed her further. Had all of eighty seconds passed, after all? Unlikely. But this occasion wasn't about the time. Maeve needed to understand that August took business seriously, and he never had a partner in his transaction. He was a sole proprietor.

"'Til next time," he said as he replaced his gloves and took up the cherry riding crop. "Nearly three minutes. Won't that be…long. Just a petticoat, if you can find a way. My respects to your father."

Maeve nodded, her face flushed and her chest heaving.

August closed the door and threw himself onto his horse, galloping away as quickly as possible before he could change his mind and throw time frames out the window. He chided himself in reminder that Maeve wasn't the goal, the cottage was. Besides, knowing Maeve's prejudices, he suspected she would find a way to imbue herself again with the disgust she obviously held when her body wasn't manipulated into overlooking it. Just because he was tricking it into deceiving her opinions of him with sensations never felt before, didn't mean he was a changed man in her eyes. He would never take residence in her heart.

Nor should he, he reminded himself. He would return to England eventually, and no matter how August tried to dismiss the reasons why, his chest seized with self-contempt when he imagined once again winning Maeve's friendship, only to abandon her the way he had before.

He could not break her twice. He could not hurt her that way again.

He could not hurt that way again.

12 | Scoring Time

Like a true apostate, Maeve threw her Bible in the corner with as much might as she could muster, and felt right silly soon after. It was no fault of the Good Book that she had been staring at the same page for fifteen minutes, reading and rereading, taking nary a word from it. It was not the book's fault that she could not soothe the burning sensation boiling on her body in all the places he had touched the previous night.

"Oh! Bring yourself to your senses, Maeve!" she yelled out to the empty cottage, realizing her hand was tracing delicate lines over her cheek bones, trying to replicate the titillation Grayson had caused.

She needed a distraction and a swift kick in the shins to drag her back to her senses. She would not let Grayson's touch be construed as something other than what it was. And what was it really, but his self-satisfying manipulation of her for his pleasure?

His pleasure.

"Jesus, Mary, and Joseph, you've got to stop thinking about him, silly girl! Think about Owen instead!"

Though he had rejected her plea to move in with him, looking back she realized it had been a silly idea. Engaged or no, a firm date wasn't even fixed. What sort of scandal would ensue if she had pressed the issue? Owen had seen it for what it was. He cared enough to tell her no, to protect the good name she seemed so determined lately to sully.

That's what a real man did: protected his woman. Grayson was a little boy, playing a game with a borrowed toy.

But Maeve wasn't exactly not enjoying being played with.

Guilt was too often brushed aside as something undesirable, as something to be rid of at the first opportunity. Maeve knew better than that. Guilt was an opportunity for the improvement of the soul, and she needed a good dose of it. What better a place to find it than exposing herself to the only one who seemed to know of the arrangement?

The note she left for her da said she'd be at the O'Keefes. Maeve grimaced as she left, catching sight of the lantern burning in the window at Shepherd's Bluff.

She knocked three times on Patty and Patrick's door and heard a scattering of foot steps behind. Patty opened it after a few moments, bobbing up and down with baby Mary on her shoulder.

"Maeve?" she asked, a little taken aback. "Good heavens, you look all flustered. Is something wrong?"

Aye, something's rightly wrong. "May I talk to you?"

Patty smiled sweetly, but her eyes belied the otherwise warm welcome as they scanned Maeve from tip to toe, almost as if she could see the blight upon her through her dress.

"Of course," she sighed, opening the door further and allowing Maeve to step in from the cold drizzle coming down outside.

The middleman's cabin was hardly bigger than the O'Connor cottage, but it did have the luxury of two fireplaces and two bed chambers. Being an only child, Maeve had never minded that her bed lay in a cramped sleeping loft, but she could imagine in a house full of children, the additional space would be most welcomed. Patty had claimed from the age of fourteen that she would have ten young before she turned thirty. She had married Patrick right after her eighteenth birthday, and Mary was born a year later. As her gently-rounded belly evidenced, she was on schedule to fulfill her wish.

"Would you like a cup of tea?"

Maeve nodded wordlessly and sat at the table. Patty handed little Mary Bernice off to her guest as she poured the hot water from the kettle and into the pot, adding a spoonful of leaves. Mary reached to pull down Maeve's curls, her chubby little cherub hands surprisingly strong despite a mere six months of life. Maeve kissed each of her angelic knuckles, dreaming of having her own *leanbh* not so far off in the future, a little girl perhaps with dark hair and bright green eyes.

Green eyes? She admonished the thought.

"She likes you," Patty concluded as she set a mug of tea down on the table and took a seat. "And that is no small thing. She shrieks to high heaven whenever Grayson tries to hold her, though she snuggles right to her da like a sweet babe."

"Grayson?" Maeve asked, taken aback. "He comes to see her?"

"Well, not her specifically." Patty smiled, pulling a sip from her mug and licking her lips after. "He comes to see Patrick, needing something or other. And Patrick, of course, passes along news he picks up as he's about. Gets an ear full every round he makes, he does, especially the days he passes the Sharons. Aye, those days it wouldn't matter how many ears Patrick had, Brocc would fill them all."

Maeve nodded her understanding. Mrs. Sharon was well known as the prominent gossip of Middle Lake, but her daughter, Brocc, was an artesian of the craft, having had quite a history of not only spreading scandalous truths with great enthusiasm, but also of inventing to supplement where truth proved bland.

"I can imagine," Maeve whispered, carefully taking a draft off her mug while bracing Mary in her lap with her other arm.

Then the thought occurred to her: what if the dispelling of gossip was not one way? What if Patrick gave as well as received? Was he spreading word about what he suspected? But then Patrick had never said exactly what he had suspected, only that he knew something was going on. Perhaps that made it worse. Perhaps he had supposed Maeve was engaged in some lurid love affair with the lord of the manor. Was that so far from what it was, truth be told?

No, not at all. The motivations might be different, but the results were the same. With every moment she spent in his arms, the closer she came to losing her innocence. Their next encounter would span three traitorous minutes. Three minutes! Her mind couldn't even comprehend what a man could do to a woman with so much time at his disposal. Maeve was hardly well versed in the physical aspects of a relationship to have a clue.

But Patty was, and if asked, would she tell?

"Patty," she began hesitantly, "I know we haven't talked like old times for a while. I'm not complaining to make you feel bad, but as you are the closest friend I have, can I ask you about…something?"

She rolled her eyes and smiled expectantly. "I was wondering if that's why you came! Aye, we don't get to visit much these days, but you can talk to me, sure as rain. After all, with your wedding coming up, you'll want to be sure to be ready, won't you?"

"My wedding?" Maeve suddenly understood with a lurch of her stomach. But that also meant Patrick likely hadn't said anything about her and Grayson. "Of course, my wedding. Yes, normally a girl learns these things from her ma, but in my case…"

Patty grabbed her hand up and patted it lovingly. "We all miss your ma. Sine was a good woman. So how much do you know? Maybe that's a good place to start."

"Well, I know the basics, I suppose," Maeve shyly admitted, a blush overcoming her face. "After all, you don't live around sheep for so many years and not catch a glance of them in spring. But I imagine it's a little different for people."

"Ain't that the Lord's truth!" Patty laughed heartily and little Mary giggled in response. "Have you kissed him yet?"

Maeve blushed even further, answering her question as forthrightly as any words could.

"You will, and often. And then you'll find your hands want to touch him just about everywhere."

That Maeve knew, remembering when her hands seemed to have a mind of their own, reaching out to grab August any place they could find harbor.

"But then you begin to feel…almost animal like, if you're doing things right. Owen will know what to do. You'll feel like you're catching fire, and your whole body will be driving you to get as close to him as possible. I don't know how to explain anymore to you than that. It's not as though there's a set order to it. But when you lay in the arms of the man you love and you give your whole body to him, it's divinity. You'll never feel anything in the whole world that rivals that moment. Oh dear, look at the angel! She fell asleep right in your arms."

Mary was indeed asleep, her little chubby cheeks vibrating softly as she breathed in and out. Children are such funny creatures, bouncing like frogs one moment and dead asleep the next, Maeve thought. Patty stood up to take her and set her down in a blanket-filled basket on the floor across the room, not far from the gently crackling fire. Maeve sat back in her chair, nursing the mug in the divine tranquility that looking at a sleeping babe gives.

"Oh, and you shouldn't let the pain of the first time upset you," Patty added matter-of-factly.

Maeve's head bolted upright. "Pain? What pain?"

"You've always been so easily shook. Don't worry. It lasts a few moments, and only the first time. And then, well, then things after are really, really pleasant."

Maeve tried to wet her tongue, but found her mouth had gone oddly dry. She swigged the tea instead, so that she could talk in more than a croak. "And how long does it all… take?"

Patty took this question quite seriously. Her brow furrowed and she mouthed numbers as she counted out silently on her fingers.

"I guess it can take a good while, or be very quick. Depends."

Maeve felt as though she should have been shocked by her candor, but then again, Patty O'Keefe was never one to shy on anything. It was one of the things Maeve loved most about her, even if at the moment it was making her a wee bit skittish.

"Right after we were married, it was quick- a few minutes, maybe?- but we'd do it three or four times a day," Patty continued. "Over time and since Mary it's been less, but it lasts longer. Of course Patrick and I are so much more occupied and weary than we used to be. Saints preserve us, look at the way you're fretting. You're getting yourself so anxious, and the wedding isn't anytime soon. The way you're sweating you would think that you're going to be lying in his bed tonight!"

An irrepressible, nervous giggle leapt forth before Maeve could contain it. She bit her bottom lip in order to stifle the outburst.

They rambled on for some time as Patty asked about Owen, having never met him but in passing, though Patrick apparently had. Maeve told her all she knew about him—he was the eldest of three children, but his brother had left for America three years prior; his mother and father still lived in Cork with his sister; he was an apprentice to the master furrier of Killarney; and he rented a small flat near the cemetery on the edge of the city. They had met at the market early the previous spring, and he had asked to walk with her that very afternoon. They had strolled together nearly each Saturday afternoon since, talking about nothing in particular, and Maeve not having any idea of his motivations. In late August, he had come out to Middle Lake and stated quite frankly that he would like to meet Rory and ask his permission to wed as soon as his circumstances allowed. Rory was only too happy to grant his blessing.

"Do you love him?" Patty asked pointedly. The display of shock in Maeve's eyes must have provided her an answer. "All right, then. Do you think you could love him?"

"Owen is a good man, and I would be a fool not to love him someday."

Though Patrick and Patty had fallen head over heels with each other as soon as they started courting, love before marriage was a luxury few could afford.

Maeve looked out the window and noticed darkness had fallen. Then she turned to the mantle, noting the hour. Her heart leapt.

"Oh! I have to go! I'll be in for a tongue-lashing if I tarry any longer! Thanks for tea. My greetings to Patrick."

Maeve rushed. As she turned around to close the door, however, a certain sadness in Patty's expression caught her by surprise. Maeve hesitated, a hand lingering on the knob, and waited.

"Patty, where's Patrick this late?"

It was just a guess, but proved a good one. Patty gave a little jerk of her head.

"Out," she stated simply and with a finality that told Maeve not to inquire any further.

"Everything will be fine. I don't think Patrick would do anything…wrong."

With an air of disbelief, she sighed. "I hope you're right. Soon you'll be in love too, and you'll know the torture of having a husband who loves you too much. But he thinks he's doing rightly by us, so I hold my tongue."

A sense of foreboding overcame her and she shuddered, though if from the discomfort of the words unspoken between them or from the chill of the night air, Maeve knew not.

"Well, good night."

The middleman's cottage was only a brief walk from the main house, but Maeve ran the distance as though there were wolves at her back. She stole into Grayson's room just a few minutes later, breathless and beet red. He sat in his chair reading once again, this time wrapped in a wool blanket. Glancing momentarily at Maeve over the top of his book, he returned his attention to it without pause.

"Do you believe entombing yourself in a winter cloak meets my request for 'simpler,' Miss O'Connor?"

Her chest heaved as she sat and she saw Grayson trying to focus his gaze without appearing to be looking at the movement. He was failing. Finally, he gave up his pursuit of the written word and closed the book, leaving it on the seat of the chair as he rose. From a cabinet, he withdrew a glass and tumbler filled with something red. Having dispensed some of the drink, he presented it to Maeve with a half-smile. She took the offering and sniffed; it was sweet and pungent and bitter all at once. But it was wet and her mouth was dry, so she tipped back the whole of it in one gulp.

"I considered a petticoat," she finally gasped out as the wash in her throat simultaneously burned and soothed, "but I don't own one worthy of your eyes trained on London finery. Besides, I've come up straight from Patty's, and I didn't think showing up to your middleman's cabin in my undergarments would be wise."

He chuckled slightly. "I'm not certain Patrick would have been totally disapproving, if you had blushed over the way you are now. And I haven't even laid a hand on you yet."

She handed the glass back to him with a snide glare. "You think your touch does anything to me?"

It was a stupid, rhetorical question with a self-evident answer. Patty was right. When he touched her, something else took over. He knew it too, and just to prove his point, he approached and lowered his hand toward her cheek. Maeve's reaction betrayed her words as her breath hitched, her eyes fluttered shut, and her face leaned forward, trying to reach.

No touch.

When she opened her eyes, he was looking at her smugly.

"I don't know what you think of me, but you hunger for this almost as much as I do."

He paced back across the room and set the glass on the far table next to a sack Maeve knew instinctively held two loaves of bread.

The turn of phrase caught her attention. "I do not," she contested, before his comment fully struck her. "You…hunger for it?"

His composure slipped. In the recesses of her mind, a little bit of her swooned. This wasn't just a casual contract for him—he anticipated their meetings. Maeve could see the conflict in his countenance. He was trying to determine whether he should retract the statement, or let it survive.

Finally, he stood in front of her chair and relaxed his body, talking in soft, cracking tones when at last he spoke.

"I want you in my arms and in my bed. I want you to be… But we…"

She had seen this look before. It was the expression someone wore when they'd just emerged from a long stay in the confessional, one which the roosted chickens would later balk about. August broke off, his face contorting. Maeve almost rose from her seat in her instinct to comfort him, to throw her arms around him and whisper soothing things in his ear. But she kept back, reminding herself that she mustn't allow this to become anything beyond a contractual relationship.

"*We* have an agreement."

The words sobered them both. Grayson composed himself and addressed her once more, his tone all business. "One-hundred-sixty seconds, if you're still intending to proceed?"

"Aye, well I am here, aren't I?" Maeve spat back ambiguously. "But do you really expect me to stare at your clock and count that high while you're distracting me so?"

He laughed and his eyes shone in a way that twisted Maeve's insides anew.

"No," he answered. "I think I'll get more out of our time if your attentions lie elsewhere. Have you ever seen an hour glass?"

She nodded and internally scoffed, "*My goodness, we're not that far removed from civilized society!*"

"I have one on this table that's modified a bit."

Maeve eyes fell upon a foot-high hourglass piece, oddly capped with a small bell. The bell's pulley was attached to a string that led into the inner chamber of the hourglass and was fixed therein to a small metal hoop.

"This piece is scored to measure thirty second intervals," he explained, pointing at the etchings on the side of the glass. "I've poured sand enough for three minutes. As it falls, it pulls down the metal hoop. When all the sand has emptied, the string pulls just enough to ring the bell. Very simple and very effective. I'm releasing the plug now and giving you twenty seconds to come to me."

His body pivoted as Maeve leapt from her chair. She wasn't sure if the buffer time had elapsed or not when she flew into his arms, pressing her lips to his. Stroking the cheek wasn't an option tonight. Maeve had been turning yesterday's encounter over in her head as he spoke, and she was not interested in starting from scratch. Grayson stumbled, then righted himself as his arms wrapped around her and drew her in.

You'll feel like you're catching fire, and your whole body will be driving you to get as close to him as possible…

Yes, fire was the right word. Maeve ached to be flush against him. Again, her leg rose instinctively, trying to hook around him. Grayson sensed it against his side and moved his hand to the underside of Maeve's knee while never breaking their kiss. He drove her to symmetry, as his other hand reached down to find the other leg and pull her up to straddle his waist. They faltered, trying to find balance.

"The bed," he practically growled.

Was he asking permission? Maeve nodded, and before she could understand what was happening, she was splayed flat, looking at the ceiling.

"Next time, we start here," he declared.

August presented a hard, demanding kiss and slid her head and body back to meet the pillows. His mouth sought out her neck and Maeve twisted his ebony hair through her fingers. From the corner of her eye, she glanced at the hour glass.

She was of the opinion that the sand was falling much too quickly.

Maeve's breath doubled. His mouth left a wet trail across her chest as his right hand traveled up her torso, leaving a path of incomplete sensation, and arrived at the neckline of her dress. His green eyes looked up from his pursuits long enough to catch Maeve's hungry gaze as he pulled down the bodice to free her right breast.

She gasped, but the momentary shock quickly passed when Grayson's mouth found its goal and his teeth and his tongue danced around a quickly hardening peak. The movements sent shivers spiraling through her body.

And then, you'll find your hands want to touch him just about everywhere…

Maeve drifted her fingertips down his back and practically clawed into it. She wanted him, needed him to feel something from her in reflection. He shifted his hands and freed the other breast, turning his mouth to it as his fingers then pinched the freshly abandoned one.

A moan escaped her lips and she called out without thinking. "August…"

She froze, as did he.

Then he went wild.

The invocation released a flood gate. August bit down hard, and though it hurt her for a moment, it felt divine the next. Maeve became aware of a wetness below that accompanied a dull ache building in the pit of her stomach. Something primal was driving her—she felt like she needed to be touched *there.*

But denial was a way of life, and she instead focused on August's pursuits as he drew himself back up to meet her lips with his again, his tongue shooting into her mouth and dancing about. Though the action was unexpectedly hostile in its intensity, Maeve liked it enough to try doing the same back. Their tongues played against each other, as below the shaft of his manhood pressed against her knickers. He had pushed her skirt up over her waist without her noticing.

What was she doing? Maeve didn't understand her impulses, but her hips were pushing, rocking forward, trying to meet thrusts that were making her dizzy with need. She hoped he didn't laugh at her. She felt both compelled and humiliated.

As she felt his body shift and his hand slip under the waistline of her knickers, his fingers pushed into the wetness below, and every rational thought Maeve had ever had was gone. She gasped as he pulled back, revealing a self-satisfied smile.

"You hunger for it as much as I do. Admit it. Tell me… Tell me it's not just me."

There was no point in denying him. Maeve couldn't in the state she was in, but she couldn't concentrate long enough to form words either.

"Yes…" her raspy voice admitted.

"Maeve," he gasped, pressing his lips hard to hers, his fingers stroking her below.

The twinkling ding of a bell stilled them both.

August's head fell to her shoulder and his fingers lingered inside her. Maeve swore she heard him mutter something obscene under his breath before concluding, "Time is always my enemy."

Maeve could hardly catch her breath, even as the pulsation below began to die. Despite her fervent attempt to suppress it, her hips swung forward, inducing the friction of his fingers against the wetness again.

His eyes shot up, the amazement and—she hoped it was delight—sharpening into a feral stare. He pumped his fingers twice more, soliciting a gasp and moan.

"Do you even know why I'm doing this to you?" His eyes blazed heatedly at her. "Do you know what will happen if I do this?"

She shook her head and rocked her hips forward once more as he applied pressure back, also twittering his thumb above and making her stomach pull into an unresolved knot.

"I don't know, but it feels good. Why, August? What happens?"

He stroked her a few more times, then stopped. Maeve felt a wave building inside—as though she might explode. If only he'd continue.

He bit his bottom lip and withdrew his hand, slowly dragging his fingertips up to her navel. It left her with a bitter chill as the heat subsided and the sweat covering her began to evaporate. Maeve grimaced, thinking she would probably catch her death walking home.

"What happens?" He laughed bitterly as the wall of his status re-erected itself, leaving Maeve feeling lowered and inferior. "A little knowledge is a dangerous thing, and I'll not let you discover this without a proper space of time. Besides," he added, rising from the bed and leaving her with a feeling of complete exposure and unease—perhaps even shame, "I'll remind you that what we do is for my pleasure, not yours. You will only gain that knowledge if it pleases me to make it so."

Maeve sat up and looked at him, perplexed. "But, August, I…"

"Playtime is over, Miss O'Connor. That…" He preceded her in confusion, but didn't leave her behind for long. "You are to address me properly. In the heat of the moment, it pleased me that you should be so informal. Not now."

Her head lowered in shame, having given in to the fantasy for a moment that he was acting from more than just an arrangement of convenience. But it was just a fantasy, she reminded herself. Even if it had been something more, they could never be.

And of course, there was Owen.

"Yes, of course," she whispered abashedly. "My apologies, Lord Grayson. I didn't mean to… I only thought…"

"This is nothing to me," he boldly stated, motioning vaguely to the bed where she lay. "You mean nothing to me, Maeve. I was…confused in the heat of the moment, is all. Best that you go now."

"But you said you hungered for it, and made me admit... Oh, I see." She felt stupid in her gullibility, but was quick to learn when she'd been fooled. "It was part of the game to you."

His eyebrow crooked as he turned back to her. "Is it not to you?" he questioned indifferently.

Indifferently. How simple indifference had seemed at the start of this all, but now the mask of stoicism grew too difficult to don. She rose reluctantly, adjusting the knickers around her waist before rethreading her buttons.

The uncharacteristic boldness shocked her. More than boldness—it was a compulsion. Passing him standing at the end of the bed, Maeve propped herself up on the tips of her toes and placed a gentle, chaste kiss on his cheek. "Good night, Lord Grayson."

His eyes slammed shut. He clicked his tongue against the roof of his mouth and said once more in a low, pleading tone, "Go."

She wasn't about to chance raising his ire. Maeve had witnessed tonight all too well how his emotions could reverse so quickly.

She took the sack of bread, threw her cloak over her shoulders, and dashed out of the house before he could see the tears streaking down her cheeks.

13 | A Little Knowledge

Maeve's kiss did more to August than she could have possibly imagined. She thought he had not seen her begin to cry as she left. He had. What she had not seen was August's own tears, and his breaking of the brandy jar against the fireplace mantel as he collapsed on the floor.

How could he allow this to happen? And why had he denied himself? She had been ready and wanton in his arms. If he had wanted, he could have had her. He could be lying in post-rapture bliss this very moment—or even taking her a second time. It was his every fantasy come to fruition, his wildest hopes made flesh. What had stopped him?

But he knew all too well, realized it with painful clarity, that compassion for the potential consequences had outweighed his selfish desire for her body. If he truly was the bastard she believed him to be, it would have been simple enough. He had seen the fire burning in her eyes. He could have had her at that moment in any way and every way he wanted. And oh, how he wanted that. Laying with Maeve O'Connor was not without risk, however. If he should leave her with child, or if her blacksmith or father ever learned of her being spoiled…

He trembled to think of what her life would be like. It was difficult now as it was, and that was the consequence of poverty. If he should add to that a level of depravity in the eyes of her kin? It would ruin Maeve.

Though he thought the contract a well-engineered plan, he would admit a part of him now hoped she would not so quickly default on her obligations, for both their sakes. He also had a feeling a small part of Maeve was more than willing to continue paying indefinitely.

The following afternoon, August sat in the library, contemplating if he should account to Maeve for his misdeeds, while appearing outwardly to be reviewing surveys of the back pastures. When then the head of staff, Mrs. Compton, informed him that Patrick O'Keefe was waiting in the foyer, he was more than a little taken aback.

"Show him in."

She nodded, and a few moments later the behemoth Irishman was standing in front of his desk, veritably shooting daggers.

August tried to look disinterested. The truth was, Patrick gave him quite a fright. The physical mass he represented alone was enough to make one happy to get a grin if not a fist. However, there was something off in his standard demeanor. Patrick may have been as large as a bear, but he was generally as cordial as a field mouse. Not today. Today he was a raging bull tied down with ropes, and August no doubt of the object of his ire.

"What business have you, Mr. O'Keefe?" He kept his gaze low, only raising his eyes once to acknowledge Patrick's presence.

"Maeve O'Connor was over to see Patty last night," he said, obviously trying hard to restrain his voice from any tones too loud or ungracious.

August fixed his eyes more firmly on the surveys before him, even as he shuffled them a bit, and perhaps cued Patrick to his jumping nerves.

"Really?" he simply stated. "I hope Mrs. O'Keefe enjoyed her visit."

"Mrs. O'Keefe was answering questions that Maeve has no place asking," he spat back, making it clear that August's undivided attention was required. He set down the papers and invited Patrick to sit. Patrick hesitantly took a seat opposite and kept his threatening gaze fixed. "Maeve O'Connor is a good woman who has suffered poverty all her life. She is engaged to a man who can give her some comfort and a sound life for her and Rory. What do you think you're doing to her, then?"

Impulsively, August felt his hackles rise. When threatened, it was his father's nature he embraced. The fact that the man sitting in front of him could easily have pressed him into paste was irrelevant. No one questioned August's motives or dared dictate how he should conduct himself with tenants.

"I'm not quite sure what you're insinuating, but let me remind you of this: you are my employee. As my employee, you receive a monthly stipend and home without charge on my property. For a man with a wife, young child, and another on the way, you would do well to be most cautious in how you choose your words. However, let me assure you that Miss O'Connor's arrangement with me is of her own free will, and that I will respect her decision should she choose to discontinue. I would even consider taking her back to Norwich as a member of my staff, if I thought she'd ever consider the offer."

"Consider the offer?" Patrick gasped. "The O'Connors have lived on Middle Lake for four generations. That cottage is where Maeve was born. That cottage is where she held Sine's hand as she lay dying. What do you think you could ever do that would make her want to leave?"

Ravish her from tip to toe and make her scream out my name in ecstasy, August mused.

"I'm confused. I thought she was engaged to the blacksmith in town," August pondered. "Wouldn't she be expected to live with her husband once she weds?"

"For a few years, but Maeve and Owen want to raise their children on Middle Lake," Patrick answered. "He's been saving up money to pay the rent on both places. Otherwise they'd have been married by now."

The conflict of emotions he was feeling brought the taste of bile to August's tongue. Now August understood why Maeve had been so intent on retaining the lease. It wasn't because of her father's health, though that was certainly a consideration at the moment. What she was really after was securing the long term ability to move back to her family home and raise her children there.

In his mind, the image formed: little children gathered around Maeve's chair, listening to her stories, as Owen Murphy sat across the way, smoking a pipe and grinning. Patrick was right, Maeve deserved that prosperity. Why couldn't he just let her go? Why torment her like this?

Because that future did not include him.

"Lord Grayson?"

Patrick was looking at him askew, and August realized his attention had drifted off. Quickly, he glanced at the mantle clock, wondering if it were too early to place a lantern in the attic window.

"She wants to raise her family here? On my land?"

"No, they want to raise their family here, *on Middle Lake*." Patrick tilted his head in a curious fashion, and August suspected from his tone that there was more to his statement than the mere words therein. However, having entertained this intrusion into his day and feeling that his implied message had been sufficiently conveyed, August arose from his chair.

"I understand your concern, Mr. O'Keefe, but I consider the matter closed. I am required elsewhere. Please show yourself out."

Running from the potential confrontation may have made him seem cowardly, but August didn't like the direction his instincts were taking him, telling him to promise to keep Maeve's honor intact. Why should he promise any such thing? And further, how had Patrick O'Keefe come to suspect the truth? August had always credited him with exceptional intuitiveness—it was, after all, one of the reasons he had appointed him middleman. Patrick was not particularly emotional, but evidence had proven he was not the type of man to evict tenants ruthlessly or overlook the occasional tardiness of rent. He was precisely the combination of firm hand and local credibility that August needed acting on his behalf.

He half-wished in this particular case Patrick had acted in opposition to character. If he had thrown out the O'Connors when their rent was first late, or kept to the customary practice of collecting annual rents rather than larding it out monthly, as he had done, August never would be contemplating doing the things he was to an innocent, untouched woman like Maeve. There would never have been a chance for any of these adolescent attractions to blossom.

Confusion was fast becoming a bosom chum. August needed to retreat, to consider in a clear frame of mind what was going on about him. He walked to the garden, where Caroline sat on a stone bench, reading.

"News from home?" August asked, making his presence known.

Caroline jolted and clutched a letter, the focus of her attention, to her chest, her cheeks flushing red as though caught doing something she shouldn't.

"August! You gave me a fright!" she gasped, moving the sheets of paper around her back.

Now his curiosity was piqued, and Lord Grayson gave way to the menacing big brother. "What do you have there, sister?" He squirreled around her in an attempt to grab the document from her dainty little hands.

Caroline squealed and took flight. Even as demure and petite as she was, she could move sprightly enough. "That's none of your affair."

She took off along the hedge rows, but August gave chase. He caught up with her at the edge of the lawns and grabbed her around the waist, causing both to tumble to the ground. In the ensuing jostle, August at last snatched the parchment. He sprang to his feet, held the paper aloft, and began reading aloud what was certain to be no more than a gossipy drudge from Caroline's familiars back in Norwich or London.

"'Dear Miss Grayson, you'll forgive if I should seem forward or unconventional in my addressing this inquiry to you so soon after our introduction, but I would very much like to beg permission to call upon you at Shepherd's Bluff.' Caroline—what…? Who?"

She snatched the letter back vehemently, her face flushing even brighter red, a trait inherited from their fair-faced mother, and spat back her reply.

"A gentleman whom I chanced upon in the market and is no further your concern than that."

"No further my concern?" August realized his words were somewhat bitter in tone, but did so hope that Caroline was not attempting to keep secrets. The sentiment made those he was keeping become more palpable in their unspoken discourse. "It is most certainly my concern. If someone intends to court my little sister, it is my duty to weed out the insurrection. So let's start with the basics. British or Irish?"

Caroline looked up from a now quiet repose. "American."

Well, that was unexpected, and it left August with little power to coerce or punish within his capacity as a British lord. "What is he doing in Killarney?"

"I do not know. Our conversation in the market place did not lend itself to that subject."

August grew more curious. "And to what did your conversation lend itself?"

"Death, brother," she answered solemnly, beginning to make her way to the house. "We spoke of death."

"And he was so inspired by your morbid elocutions that now he wants to call upon you?" This man reeked of suspicion even by so few of these known characteristics. "His name?"

"Captain Jefferson Schand."

"Captain?"

She nodded, "Of the Confederate States of America."

"Caroline!" August rebuked. "A disgraced soldier? Sincerely?"

She shook her head violently in an attempt to eschew his conclusion. "Oh, he isn't as you would suppose. He is a gentle man of great compassion and understanding. When I told you we spoke of death, I did not mean to say that we spoke broadly of dying. We spoke specifically about the deaths of our parents, and the plight of the Irish in the Americas and here in Ireland. His intentions, dear brother, seem not that unlike your own."

His head snapped in her direction. "What know you of my intentions?"

An understanding smile was her only reply. "Please, let's have him to tea?" Caroline begged, clasping her hands before her. "I would very much like for you to meet him."

She batted her green puppy dog eyes, melting him in the way that always she could. How she looked so like their mother.

"Well, all right then. Let me meet this Captain Schand and make out his intentions for my little sister," he said as her face exploded into a smile. "Send word for him to join us Friday afternoon."

Caroline rose on her toes and kissed his cheek. August knew she would immediately employ her quill and ink and pen a reply. Caroline was more than an appropriate age to receive suitors if she wished, but only with proper etiquette observed. He would not tolerate the besmirching of her character by salacious rumors borne of Caroline's misunderstood sense of abandon once she got an idea in her head.

He sat himself next to the fountain's edge and watched the wind blowing through the trees. By this time in the fall, most of the leaves had turned. His eyes were drawn to those blushing red, the crimson tone reminding him so of Maeve's flush as she lay across his bed the previous night.

"What happens?"

What was happening? He couldn't help but wonder if her question, though direct to the moment, didn't speak of a larger inquiry. More than any other woman he had held in his arms, Maeve felt fitted to him, both in body and in spirit. She wasn't like the fainting, weepy, status-obsessed females of Norwich. She was sincere, caring, self-sacrificing, and unapologetically blunt. He knew she must have been in utter confusion over his treatment of her, hot as Hades one moment, colder than winter the next. In truth, he didn't really understand himself why he acted so passionately, for ill or for will, in her presence. What would happen now? They couldn't continue in this in-between much longer. Already he knew he was approaching a tenuous place with her. It would break his heart when it ended, but he could always run away from the consequences. Maeve was stuck, woefully at his mercy.

One thing August knew for certain: he mustn't allow Maeve to fall in love with him. He feared, however, that if he let his guard down, she would do just that. But oh, how lovely endearments from her lips would be. She had a spark he had recognized even in their youth. Now as a woman, that spark blazed.

He wasn't truly evil if, even kept in secret, he was so concerned for her welfare, was he? He had hurt her so terribly the night before, and guilt nagged him with need to compensate his offense. A gift. Yes, a gift was in order. But any bauble he may give her would be worn as clearly as a brand against her flesh. Surely there was something he could offer her that was discreet enough to remain hidden, yet sincere enough to be treasured.

Then, it came to him. Apparently, she needed a proper petticoat. Every fine lady in London or Norwich had a dozen; Maeve O'Connor should have at least one. Perhaps he could sneak away one of Caroline's to give to her. But then Caroline was so petite, a petticoat of hers would likely rip in two if Maeve tried to shimmy into it. The image of this coursed through his mind's eye: Maeve's breasts pulled by the lace of the bodice, nearly bursting the seams, begging for him to unlace her.

Goodness, no, that would not do. August took a few breaths and focused on a frog swimming about in the fountain. The image was enough to distract his licentious train of thought and dissuade the arousal that had begun to stir below.

Perhaps while he was in Killarney he could stop into a shop and purchase a petticoat for her. But that could set rumors running. If Maeve's good name was to be protected, wouldn't he be undermining his own efforts?

Then it occurred to him what to do. August quickly climbed the servant's stairs to the third floor attic. Following his mother's death, his father had attempted to wipe away all evidence of her memory, even going as far as placing Caroline in the custodianship of her governess outside Norwich so he wouldn't have to look into the echo of Eliza's eyes. All that Lady Grayson had brought over from England that summer remained in storage above, and her size was about the same as that of Maeve's.

August spotted the collection by a far ventilation window. The outer edges of the cedar chest had darkened to a grimy brown after years of neglect, but he opened it to find the items inside still in good condition, and other than being seeped in the cedar scent, fresh. He rummaged through sheets and lace work and quilting to find what he sought: a singular ivory silk petticoat with fine lace trim.

It should have seemed wrong, giving away his departed mother's things, but nothing about it felt inappropriate. And if Maeve hesitated in accepting, he could call it a wedding present. On her wedding day at least, she should feel beautiful, he'd explain. Women felt beautiful in silk, and the material would slide delicately along her…

Her whatever wouldn't matter, he reminded himself. She'd belong to someone else then.

At eight-thirty, August placed the lantern in the window and retired to his room with the sack of bread concealed beneath his robe. Not that Caroline ever emerged from her quarters this late. She'd be sitting by her fireplace reading, if not in bed. He set the bread on the table by the door, placed the folded, silky petticoat on the bed, and took up his place by the fire. His poetic mood was filled by *Don Juan.* As the Comtoise clock struck nine, August trained his ears on detecting her footfalls.

Five minutes later, Maeve still had not arrived. Perhaps she had been scared off?

Ten minutes more, and the clock struck a single soft ding for nine-fifteen. With a panic, he concluded she wasn't coming.

August began to pace the room, considering the possibility that Maeve had fallen down on her way up the road and was lying, bruised, bloody, and helpless. Perhaps she had chanced upon some vagabond walking the lane who saw her as a quick opportunity.

Or maybe she had just plain decided to stop coming.

August was turning the handle to his door before he even realized he had arisen. The need to strike off into the night and assure she was unharmed was a compulsion.

But as he struggled to get his arm through the twisted sleeve of his overcoat as he opened his chamber door, two brown eyes stared quixotically back at him.

"Maeve?"

She wet her lips before speaking softly. "I ... made an agreement with you and I shall hold to it, even if it is all a matter of business…to you."

The air rushed from her lungs as August pulled her through the door and into his embrace. Her body was stiff and unyielding, shock holding her still, but August didn't care for the moment. His was an expression of pure relief that she was safe. He kissed her forehead softly and rocked her gently back and forth.

"Is this time?" she muttered, her face buried in his shoulder.

He released her immediately and caught her caustic gaze.

"Most certainly not," he answered. "I only… When you were delayed…I began to wonder if… I thought perhaps you… Maeve?"

"I am certain I am fine, Lord Grayson," she answered, curiosity coloring her words. August turned and closed the door as Maeve crossed the room and threw her cloak over the chair. When he turned back, he nearly fainted; Maeve stood silent and unmoving, dressed only in a cotton camisole and knickers.

He had never supposed she would actually be so bold, nor had he thought a woman could appear so desirable in the pantaloons so reminiscent of boy's clothing. August had seen English ladies attempt it, and the result was always comical. Maeve's pale Gaelic skin, deep brown eyes, and curled brown locks, however, made her nearly irresistible.

"I'll admit you've utterly surprised me. You look…" He swallowed. Hard. "…different."

She seemed confused, examining the lines of her figure, looking for a flaw. "Isn't this what you wanted?"

Wanted, yes. Expected, no. "What convinced you to do it?"

She settled into the chair. "I can't rightly say. I just… If you don't like it, fine. I'll—"

"No!"

As Maeve rose and attempted to gather her cloak back around, August grew anxious. He could not see her leave so soon, especially not with what he was planning.

Maeve froze, staring at him.

"I like this," August added, vaguely motioning to the entirety of her body. "I like it very much, in fact. I just can't believe you did it. For me."

She actually blushed. "I would not chance your further ire. Nor your rejection. I am… flattered?…that you even consider me…desirable."

If only Maeve knew how tempting she really was to him. And not just her body.

It was hard to tell who was the more surprised, then, when August hesitantly replied, "You have no conception of how much I desire you."

At once, he felt his insides quiver, the seeping suspicion that he had hinted at something which, even to himself, was revelation, making him shiver.

Maeve blinked twice, and August breathed a sigh of relief when she seemed to take no notice of it. Her eyes froze when she glanced at the bed, focusing intently on the petticoat. Without saying another word, Maeve paced the length of the room and held up the silky garment as though it were sacred.

August saw her slowly pull it to her frame, testing it against her curves.

"Is this for me?"

August drew close behind her, skirting his fingers inches above her skin, his breath speeding.

"If you like it," he answered, kissing the nape of her neck ever so lightly, so that she might not have even noticed. But Maeve certainly did notice, and she momentarily melted as she tilted her head to the side, giving August a wider patch of skin to utilize. Then she recalled her senses and snapped away, tossing the petticoat on the bed. She shut her eyes, sat on the bed, and stiffened.

"The hour is already late, Lord Grayson," she hissed. "I wouldn't want to overstay my welcome or overstep my place."

Her words were full of venom, and August regretfully recalled the cruel lecture he had given her the night before. He might well need such a lecture himself tonight as pangs of unease filled him, his mind beginning to question how much he bought into his own philosophy. It wasn't Maeve's fault she was born poor and he had the blessings of being born of the aristocracy. It wasn't Maeve's fault that she was born Irish. It wasn't even her fault that she was born beautiful and entrancing.

"Eh, you're doing the damned thing again!" she snapped.

But for her lack of respect, Maeve was wholly to blame. "Doing what?"

Her eyes opened, her glare full of fire. "The same thing you did when we were younger. You know something I don't know, and you're right happy about the fact. That smile you wear is unmistakable."

He cocked his head and grinned. "I never did such a thing."

"Did, too." Was she actually smiling? "Like when you knew why Guinevere wasn't having children. You wouldn't tell me what s… Why you thought what you thought, and now I know what you knew and I didn't."

"And you noticed this supposedly knowing smile back then?" He vaguely motioned to his face.

"Aye."

"Same one I'm making now?"

Her voice trembled in time with her body as he stepped her way. "Aye." She paused, musing over what she just said. "What is it that you know now?"

August didn't answer, but instead removed his robe and tossed it next to her cloak on the chair. He stood before her in only his undergarments, and already the thought of what he was about to try was causing his arousal to become visible beneath the cotton shield.

He made his way to the far table and to the graduated hour glass.

"Goodness, five and a half minutes already?" he asked coyly as he situated the plug and slowly filled the sand to the appropriate mark. That knowing grin widened when he considered that their next occasion would make the specialized time piece with a maximum ten-minute capacity insufficient. August turned back to her and brought his mouth right up to, but not touching, her ear, so that the heat of his breath could dance over the sensitive skin.

"I apologize, Miss O'Connor," he started in a low, husky voice. "I forget sometimes that you have never felt a man's touch. I forget that while your kisses light primal fires in me, the sensation to you is very new and disorienting. I should tell you how sorry I am that I caused your body to escalate so quickly into what it might not have been ready to interpret."

August lead down to her, his hands ghosting over her frame but never, never touching. Maeve began to tremble more with each word, her composure easing with every additional utterance.

"I should not have thrown up the fact that we both had the misfortune to be born into stations of life neither of us would have otherwise desired as a wall between us. I should not have been so dismissive of your willingness to enter our agreement."

He lowered his jaw and spoke into the valley between her breasts. Beneath the thin cotton covering, August saw her peaks pebble as his heated gasps called them to attention. Her breathing picked up pace, and the fact was making him anxious and eager.

"As I told you the first night, you are free to end our contract at any point you desire, knowing the consequences. You are still here tonight, and so you desire to be with me, and I am pleased by that fact alone."

She grimaced but kept her eyes closed. August could tell she was fighting a longing to lean into him as his mouth found hers, but still did not make contact.

"You know why I'm here," she whimpered. "So that I have a home to go to when you're done using me. I am here for your pleasure, Lord Grayson, not my own. You made that perfectly clear."

"True," he agreed, ever so delicately blowing on Maeve's lips. They parted as though expecting a deeper answer, but he withdrew. "But that's only because you don't know what pleasure is, Maeve. If you knew what your body was capable of, if you knew the things I can help make your body do, of the feelings I can create for it, around it, inside of it… That's the reason for this 'knowing' smile. Because I do know what I can do to you. And I do know that what pleases a man most is giving a woman that…pleasure."

August turned back to the table and removed the catch holding the sand at bay, letting it fall into the bottom chamber in a slow and steady stream.

"What would please me tonight is to share that knowledge with you." His fingers reached the cotton folds of her knickers and he was delighted to find her wetness already soaking through. "Now," he pushed his finger over the apex of her legs and clutched her, causing her eyes to shoot open and her breath to go staccato, "lay back, and let me show you what happens…" He slid his hands under the waist of her knickers and into the moist heat beyond, making one quick twirl into her with his fingers and causing her knees to tremble. "…when I keep doing this."

Maeve gasped. She fell back fully without hesitation as August eased her knickers down over her hips and past her ankles, tossing them unceremoniously on the floor. He pushed her back so that she rested comfortably and pulled her legs open slightly. Mysteriously, she surrendered herself completely to the action.

August inverted his right hand to a better angle and pushed two fingers into her. Even the first stroke shook her frame, and she threw her arms to the side, fisting the quilt in her hands. He established a steady rhythm of pull and push, arching slightly on the outbound, stimulating the bundle of nerves within her, certain she had never had a clue that they existed. Her breaths grew staggered and crisp as delicious, meager ahhs rose from the base of her throat.

Much to his chagrin, half the sand allotted for their subscribed time had fallen away.

Without disrupting his hand's labor, he pulled his body alongside hers and licked the rim of her ear. "This is about where we left off before." He unclenched his hand and moved the thumb over the pearl of her pleasure, echoing the rhythm he had already established, then speeding it. Her essence flowed freely, covering her thighs and his hand. Her whole body gave a tremendous pulse as she felt the tensing of her muscles in response to his efforts.

Every little push made into her was reverberating up her torso, causing her breasts to heave. August's mouth wanted them, wanted to taste them. He undid the ribbon that laced the front panels of her camisole and peeled it aside. Her stiff-peaked mounds were revealed as his lips surrounded them, taking one of her nipples between his teeth and nipping.

"Oh, Grayson…" she moaned. He could tell his efforts were being properly appreciated.

August looked up at her, catching her smoldering brown eyes. "August."

"Au…gust," she repeated, her breath so ferociously humming in and out that stringing two syllables in one gasp became impossible. "What…is… this…?"

He hushed her by pressing his lips to her mouth, sucking her bottom lip as he quickly pulled away, allowing her the air she needed. The air she would need soon to gasp in pleasure.

"Trust your body," he told her. *Trust me.* "It knows what to do. Let it go. Don't hold back."

The bell of the timer rang. August ignored it, and Maeve didn't hear it over her own racing breath. His hand manipulated her every nerve, leaving her body dancing on the edge of climax, her hips instinctively rocking against the sensations and inducing further friction.

August felt his own hips involuntarily shifting, trying to align his arousal. His control was slipping, his reluctance to take her lessening with each moment.

"Maeve, let go."

Her body began to answer the request. August felt her tighten, and her segmented whimpers began to bleed over into each other, graduating into a sustained ecstasy-driven moan.

"Yes, that's it," he coaxed, quickening both pace and pressure. "Give in."

Her hand rose from the bed, and she placed it on his cheek. Her body was so consumed with achieving its first release, however, that she didn't notice August's confused expression. Her hand quickly fell, skirting along his chest and falling into his lap, right where his erection was pushing against the restraint of his undergarments.

"August!" she screamed loudly. Her face contorted in a most alluring way. She licked her lips, and the image of her glistening wet tongue running over her reddened, swollen bottom lip nearly undid him. "Oh, my… August… Ungh…"

A hard pinch of her nipple tipped the scale, sending Maeve reeling on the crest of her climax. Her moans echoed around the bed chamber, drowning out the sound of both the clock and the crackling fire. He slowed his workings gradually as the tightness that had squeezed them so delightfully washed away, leaving Maeve gasping and flushed.

"That's what happens when I do that," he teased, drawing a trail of her wetness down the inside of her thigh. "And ecstasy looks so beautiful on you."

She rolled her head, her eyes meeting his. She was overwhelmed, and he was over-proud. Maeve's lips quivered, and for a moment, it looked as though she were trying to say something.

"Yes?" August asked.

She whispered in a raspy yet confused tone. "…for…your…pleasure?"

August leaned in and kissed her neck tenderly, the movement surprising even him, though he felt the truth of his words as he spoke. "Feeling you experience your first delivery against my hand was very pleasurable," he assured her. August moved his mouth underneath her ear and lightly bit, being careful in his stance so as to not press the stiff manifestation of his desire into her side.

More startling to them both was Maeve's sudden boldness as her fingers ghosted over his cheek before trailing over the length of his arm, over his hip, and brushing purposefully over his erection.

Her eyes met August's; desire, reproach, curiosity and embarrassment competed for control in her gaze. Not wanting her to feel any shame for her inquisitiveness, his hand covered hers, not moving her away but letting her know it was permissible to explore him.

"Does it hurt?"

Her words were so simple, so evidencing of her innocence. And in some way, his nakedness to her at the moment. Not of his body, but of his soul.

"Not hurt," he answered. "A dull ache. Like being hungry when you've just sat at a table watching another feast. It's…hungry."

She nodded slowly, her eyes falling to have a glance at its outline through the cloth of his undergarments. "And it hungers for…what I just had," she concluded. "Will that happen to you too?"

"Yes, a little differently. You needn't…" He stilled her hand, aware that her stroking was again playing havoc with his ability to withhold himself. "You must stop. There isn't any need tonight to… If you keep doing that I'm going… Maeve, please, I… Oh…"

August's whole body twitched as her feather touch turned to uncertain, inconsistent strokes. She had no idea what she was doing. Despite the fact that such ignorance may have been laughable with any other woman, that it was Maeve now learning how to arouse and titillate a man first hand, as it were, was only more exciting to him. In his state, even with the irregular rhythm, he wasn't going to last long against her efforts.

"Maeve, please," he begged. "Please, this is a bad idea. If you…"

"Trust me, August," she mirrored back, a playful smile on her face. "What I do is entirely for your pleasure."

He felt his body surrender to her siren call. August bit his bottom lip and tried to pull free from his undergarment his hardened cock. When it sprang free, Maeve's pace slowed again, as she took in the feeling of him in her hand, flesh to flesh.

He was rising to his breaking point. The combination of her hands, her flared hair, her post-orgasmic grin, the flush of her face, her deep brown eyes.

Just her presence.

"Oh, Maeve, almost…" His breaths were deep, hefting. His stomach began to clench, and his voice was becoming rough and gravely. "Oh, you're… Uhh…"

It was happening. He took one more deep breath, his hips working his cock in her grasp, his heavy eyes focused into her intense gaze, the friction taking him…

"August!?"

Knock. Knock. Knock.

They both all but fell off the bed.

"August?" Caroline's insistent voice came again from the other side of the door. "August, is something wrong? I heard a noise."

Maeve sat straight upright, ashen-faced. Before August could advise her otherwise, she had grabbed her knickers off the floor, her cloak from the chair, and the petticoat from the bed, and dove into the wardrobe, slamming the doors shut behind her.

"A moment, Caroline!" August cried, running to his chair and throwing his robe around himself. He opened the wardrobe to find Maeve pulling her knickers back up in the cramped, overcrowded space.

"Two minutes," he whispered. She gave him a surely, you jest smirk. "It's just my sister. She's usually asleep this late. I'll get rid of her."

Closing the wardrobe, he rushed to the door, throwing it open to find Caroline, dressed in a full body bolt of white cloth, complete with a sleeping hat, candlestick in hand.

"Caroline?"

She attempted to glance into the room over his shoulder. "Is everything all right? I thought I heard shouting."

"Shouting?" August laughed, but clearly was not fooling her. "Oh, yes. I banged my foot into the bed post. I must have called out without realizing. I'm sorry if I woke you."

"Bed post?" she questioned, uncertainty, and perhaps doubt, still evident in her voice. "Are you hurt?"

"Nothing with which to be concerned," he assured her, placing his arm on her shoulders and beginning to suggestively pull her back towards her room. "It was nothing, and I swear to do my utmost not to be such a clumsy oaf in the future. Go back to sleep."

At his back, August heard the catch of a door unhinge and saw, from the corner of his eye, Maeve's silhouette lithely tip-toeing toward the stairs, the bread sack and her cloak thrown over her arms. Wisely, she had her shoes in hand, and thus stepped silently. Still, as a precaution, August raised the volume of his voice as he continued.

"I was thinking about your caller, Caroline. Why don't you suggest that he stay Friday evening with us?" *Perhaps he'll keep you distracted.* "After all, I'll be going into town on Saturday morning to meet with Woodrow, and taking him back would be no bother."

"Are you certain?" she jubilantly asked, turning around. He quickly spun her back to her door, opening the entrance and pushing her in.

"Yes, dear heart, I'm quite certain."

"Oh, thank you! I'll write him first thing in the morrow," she said, her face absolutely beaming with joy.

Caroline's head curved around the door frame as the foyer door shut loudly. "Was that the front door?"

Quickly moving to dissuade her and pushing her back into her room, August gave the first excuse he could conjure. "Probably one of the servants forgot to close it fully. I'll just go have a look and be sure. Good night, dear."

With a quick peck on her cheek, he forcefully closed her chamber door behind her and raced down the staircase. Maeve was already half way across the front yard to the gate when he caught up with her.

"Maeve, wait!"

She turned, vibrant anger emanating from her face. "I can't believe the position I let you get me into."

"I…let you?" August repeated back at her. "Time had expired. Your necessity was filled, and what you chose to do beyond that was just that. Your choice."

"I didn't hear the bell," she retorted in disbelief.

"I'd wager not, over your caterwauling, which nearly got us discovered, by the way." He motioned vaguely to the house behind him as a playful smile danced across his face.

She clicked her tongue. "But you did hear it, didn't you? And you didn't stop…whatever it was you were doing."

"Did you want me to stop?"

A curious look overcame her; contemplation, confusion, and concurrence screwing her face into a reluctant admission by expression.

"Maeve, I can't stop."

August couldn't resist. When he pulled her close and pressed his lips to hers, Maeve resisted, but only for a moment. Then she melted into his embrace. It was short lived. As soon as she felt the response of his male body against her, she pulled away, slapping August full force across the face.

"What are you playing at?"

"There's something happening here. I know you feel it too. Please, Maeve. Let's not deny it any longer. Tell me."

She shook her head tersely. "No. I… I'm engaged. Don't you see? That was providence just now. Providence pushed your sister to knock on your door. If she hadn't, we may have…"

"Your purity is still intact," he assured her, kissing her nose. "I vow I will not steal your innocence from you." He smiled deviously at her. "Unless you request it of me."

"I shall not," she assured him. "That was wrong. I should not have… Oh! My knickers are to remain on from now on, and you'll simply have to find your pleasure around them."

She turned to leave, but August grabbed her arm and spun her around.

"Will you please come again tomorrow?"

"Wha…?" She hesitated, her body softening as she pulled herself away again. "Aye," she agreed, throwing her cloak around her shoulders. "But I'm sincere about the knickers."

He couldn't resist the flush in her cheeks and the way the tepid moonlight bounced off her brown curls. Without breaching her skin, he pulled her again and gently grasped her knickers beneath the concealment of her cloak, feeling her folds beneath the cotton.

"And should I try the other thing again, with them on?" he asked suggestively.

"Aye," she agreed as her breath hitched. "Aye, that you may do twice if you desire."

August let her go. She made quick her escape through the gate and up the pathway. He turned and grimaced as he walked back up the yard. From the corner of his eye, August saw the light of the middleman's cottage flash. Looking back, the curtain swung in the window.

"Damn it all to hell." Clenching his jaw in frustration, August supposed he had more or less been caught by his middleman with his hand in the cookie jar. "Well, Friday's tea should prove most interesting."

14

Searching for that which has been lost

"Maeve O'Connor! What in the name of Saint Peter do you think you're doing?"

Maeve had, on occasion, witnessed others on the receiving end of Patty's foul dispositions, but this was the first it had ever been turned at her. And she was in no mood. Jared was due back from town at any moment, hopefully with news as to her father's whereabouts. Her insides writhed as she sat wordlessly in the chair, not sure Patty intended for her to answer. Then again, she wasn't precisely sure what she was asking after.

"I thought you were asking all those questions because you were going to try to do something with Owen, not so you could be bedded by August Grayson!"

Maeve gasped and threw her hand over her mouth. "How did you find out?"

A smug expression overcame Patty's features as she wagged her finger in reprimand. "Ah, so you admit it! Not that you could deny it after we saw the two of you outside our cottage. For heaven's sake, laying with Grayson? Your ma would turn over in her grave."

Maeve scoffed. "I haven't laid with him!"

Patty narrowed her eyes intensely. "But you want to. I can see it plainly in your eyes. "

"I…do…not… I would…never… How… could…? Psha!"

Such a stutter was as good as a confirmation. "Come to your senses!" she exclaimed. "You fool! Do you know how hard it was to talk Patrick down? He almost bolted out and broke Grayson's neck! If anyone were ever to find out about this, word would get back to Owen quicker than whiskey to a sailor. Do you think he'd marry you then? Really, my husband should not have more concern for your good name than you do. Why would you subject yourself to this?"

Maeve felt all of two thumbs tall and made of mud. Quite sure all the color had drained from her face, her words died on dry lips. In a bitter, hostile turn, she reflected the venom right back.

"Why not ask Patrick?" she spat. "Quick to take a shilling but shill the lassie, is he? You know what kind of vicious money grabber he can be come rent's day. Further, why not ask him what he did with the ewe he took from us? And then ask him why I had to make an offer of my body to Grayson so we wouldn't be evicted?"

If the fire on the hearth had suddenly died away, the cottage could have been warmed by the flames burning in Patty's cheeks alone. She gnashed her teeth almost to mush.

"How dare you!" she hissed, her hands fisted in anger and tugging at the sides of her dress. "What would we do with your bloody ewe?"

Maeve stood fast and faced her down with all the veracity one could muster against a mad Irishwoman. Her anger drove her feet to move swiftly, crossing the room and taking a firm stance just a few steps away.

"I don't rightly know! Maybe he had his way with it, seeing as he's busy sticking himself into other places he doesn't belong!"

And so, as day turned to night and still her father had not come, Maeve hadn't anyone else to whom she could turn. She didn't know what August's reaction would be, especially given the state she was in as she threw open the doors of Shepherd's Bluff just past sunset. He had told her to always come straight to his room. The fire crackled and the clock ticked its customary cadence, but the master proved absent. She stood a few minutes in the solitary chamber, contemplating her next move. Would she dare go in search of him throughout the house?

Yes, she would. Matters were too grave and time was short. Maeve needed to act.

She ventured forth, driven by determination and desperation. Quietly at first, and then in ever growing volume, Maeve called his name from corner to cove. She passed slowly by each door, trying to discern if there was evidence of any human inhabitant in the room beyond.

Across the landing in the adjacent bank of doors, one opened. In anticipation of seeing August, of running into his arms and begging his assistance, Maeve swung about. Familiar green eyes stared back, but the petite, fair-skinned beauty was not August.

Maeve was momentarily frozen in fear. Her eyes set about gauging the distance to the front door when the lady spoke.

"Do you need something?" Her tone was sweet and tender and somehow sounded motherly despite her youth. "Is something wrong?"

Maeve wet her palate and attempted to sound coherent and proper. "Yes. I'm looking for Aug... Lord Grayson. I need help."

The lady smiled warmly as she made her way from behind her door, standing in a night gown that was more of a white sheet with arms, and a frilly sleeping cap. In her hand she held a candle lantern, and the flickering against her complexion made Maeve think so of August's beauty.

"Help with what?"

Poor Maeve drew breath to begin dispensing her woe, but the light creaking of footfalls up the back hall drew both of their attention. August strode quickly into their company, his gaze fixed somewhat frighteningly, somewhat excitedly, on both women before him.

"I see you've met Maeve O'Connor, Sister," he stated as he reached the top of the staircase, sounding dismissive of her name. Maeve has suspected, but would admit that her imagination had been mocking her. "Though as to what she is doing here at this hour is beyond me."

"Lord Grayson, I apologize for so rudely barging in, but I'm in dire straits. Dire straits, indeed, and I haven't anywhere else to turn."

He scratched his chin and nodded, keeping his eyes fixed to the floor and avoiding her gaze. "Is this inquiry of an official matter?"

His eyes caught Maeve's for a second, and she gave a little gasp. Caroline did not seem to notice, thankfully.

"It's about my father."

He looked reassuringly at Caroline. "Go back to bed, dear. I'll take Miss O'Connor to the library. I'm sure she's quite sorry to have disturbed you."

"I am, Miss Grayson," Maeve said, playing along.

"Think nothing of it," Caroline returned, reaching out to rub Maeve's arm gently. "After so many years, it was a pleasure to finally meet the infamous Maeve. I hope your troubles are quickly resolved. Good night."

Maeve returned a good night before following August down. They rounded the banister post and moved through a dim corridor with walls covered in lavish paintings. August neither spoke to nor acknowledged Maeve in word, though a certain sense of gravity began to manifest between their bodies when at last they reached a set of double doors. Maeve ventured inside at his gesture, beginning to fear that his silence perhaps implied anger. He followed her in, closing the doors behind.

In an instant, She found herself thrown against the wall, August's hungry mouth pressing hard against hers. All fears were abated and even her urgency was temporarily pushed aside as she attempted to make reason of what was happening. His moves were desperate, hurried, and dare she say, even sincere and passionate. But the worries which had driven her to act so brazenly quickly brought her back to the moment.

"August, please…"

He drew back, his eyes meeting hers, his expression one of frustration.

"What's happened?" he quietly asked. "Are you hurt? Did Patrick do or say something to you?"

Maeve's head cocked to the side as she tried to decipher his immediate assumption. "Patrick? No, nothing. But my da, he's missing. He went out yesterday afternoon and never came home. I've been all over Middle Lake today. Jared Boyle searched all over town and couldn't find hide nor hair of him."

August looked both confused and conflicted. "Maybe he found a place to sleep for the night."

"No, Da is always home by dawn. Please, August, I know it's none of your concern, but I just need…"

Maeve shivered as he reached for her, cupping her cheek in his hand and kissing her forehead gently. "Don't worry. We'll find him."

He pulled her by the hand back through the double doors and up the corridor.

"Caroline?" he called from the base of the stairs.

Her door opened again without delay and she stood looking down, her eyes narrowing on August's hand around Maeve's. Instinctively, Maeve withdrew and rung her hands in nervous deflection.

"Miss O'Connor's father is missing. We'll go on horseback and start looking. Wake up the staff and have them organize a search party."

Maeve sputtered. "The staff? Surely—"

His insistent gaze cut her off. "We will find him, but we shouldn't fail to make use of all the resources at our disposal. Caroline?"

She nodded and dashed up the far second floor corridor and back towards the servants' quarters. August took Maeve's hand again and led her out the front door.

"Perhaps we should ask Patrick's help?" she timidly suggested, seeing the light of the middleman's cottage across the grounds. Even if Patty was upset with her, surely they wouldn't carry that grudge over to the detriment of Rory's welfare.

"I think it best if we avoid the O'Keefes for the time being," August said, pulling her toward the stables. "They are not likely to be very pleased at seeing us together again so soon."

Her insides twisted. So August too had learned of the witnesses to their parting the evening previous. They reached the stable and August began dressing two horses, one of which Maeve recognized as Gwen, August's mare.

"August, I cannot."

"Of course you can. Arthur's easy-going." He smiled wryly as he finished off the bindings of the saddle on the stallion's back and threw a saddle blanket over Gwen's. "He doesn't buck too much."

Maeve let out an exasperated sigh; he didn't understand what she was trying shamefully to admit. "No, I mean I don't know how to ride a horse."

An incredulous glance met eyes that tried to look away. The saddle blanket was abandoned as August mounted his mare and offered out a hand.

"Then you'll just have to be with me."

Reluctantly, Maeve extended a hand, and August pulled her effortlessly onto the mare's back, positioning her in front, his right arm hooking around and anchoring her. As he directed Gwen from the stable, his chin came to rest on her shoulder as he whispered in her ear. Don't worry. We'll find him. Where should we start?"

Despite the dire situation, his warm breath sent shivers through her entire being. Maeve's left arm hooked over his, under the pretense, she told herself, of keeping herself from falling off.

"Let's pass the lake again, then make our way into the mountains. Perhaps someone along the way has caught sight of him."

Maeve hoped her fears were foolish and August was right. There weren't many cottages in the mountains, but a few misers kept shabby residences away from the valley and the city. Though not social creatures, surely they would offer Rory O'Connor a warm spot of ground if he should stumble upon them intoxicated.

Gwen strode effortlessly across the stretches of field as though she carried a sack of feathers. August pulled Maeve closer when jolts or jarring threatened to shift her away. Every so often, his lips ghosted across her cheek or neck. If she hadn't known better, she would have sworn he had orchestrated her father's disappearance purposefully to get her in this position. Guilt and exhilaration battled for mastery of her senses at the self-acknowledgement of how much she was enjoying the closeness the situation provided.

The lakeshore was empty, and they passed the O'Connor cottage again to find it vacant as well. In the meadow, the lamp light of several of the servants of Shepherd's Bluff crisscrossed, looking wherever a patch of ground was concealed in tall grasses. Maeve and August stopped only long enough to learn that the others had found no trace of Rory. Under the blessed light of the full moon on an unusually cloudless night, Gwen whisked them away from the valley and up in to the forested hills, where the occupants of three cottages reported no sign of him. When the trees became too thick for the mare to maneuver, they dismounted.

"Will we be able to find our way back?" August asked hesitantly, securing the leather binds around a tree.

Maeve scoffed, feeling a rush of superiority in this particular venue. "I know these woods better than you know your house. I could walk through here blindfolded and touch nary a thing."

"Make your way up here often, do you?"

Her cheeks flooded red. "At one time, I came her often." She was able to stop herself from saying, *"in order to relive that day."*

"I suppose I'm left with no choice but to trust you," he said offhandedly, and added with a teasing smile, "though wouldn't this be a keen way to do away with me."

He followed wordlessly as she led him down one of the lightly-treaded trails running along the stream. Every minute or two, a call of "Da" or "Mr. O'Connor" would carry on the breeze, but not once was there a response. As they wound up the hillside, Torc Falls revealed itself as a sliver of silver through the trees.

August froze in place, forcing Maeve to double back after a minute or so when she realized the she was alone.

His eyes were fixed upon the falls. The moonlight filtered through the trees, creating the illusion of a thousand fairies dancing in the water. The sound was gentle, as it hadn't rained since several days before. Maeve allowed the silence to endure, waiting for him to make spoken that which she was certain he was thinking.

"This is the place, isn't it?"

An echo of the pain of that horrid day ten years ago stood like a phantom between them.

"Aye."

In a moment, his mood changed as a childish grin overcame his features and he turned his hand around, lifting it to Maeve's cheek.

"Why did you let me kiss you?"

Blushing cheeks were poorly disguised by dismissive words. "Oh, come along. I was shy of thirteen. How could I have had understanding of such things?"

"And I hadn't hardly more years to my tally than you," he countered, flexing his thumb. "I repeat: why did you let me kiss you?"

She shrugged her shoulders and hid her eyes. "You seemed sad. I imagined what it would have been like to lose my ma." The words died in the air. No, she told herself, this wasn't about Sine, this was about August. "You just seemed so frustrated all the time. So when you went missing, I followed your trail and found you here at last, and you were so glum and alone and lost…"

"I was lost."

"I know. Everyone spent hours looking for you. Your father was in such a state. Da said there were rumors he was saying we had stolen you and were holding you for ransom. Anyhow, when I found you here by the waterfall, I just wanted to comfort you."

"I was so weak then." He seemed to be speaking more to himself than to Maeve. "I was powerless to help her. Powerless the stand up against my father. All I could see in his eyes was his disappointment. And then, when she did die, a miracle happened: he cared about me. But he hated Ireland, hated the Irish, somehow blamed the whole country for her death, as much as her life. When he treated you so… Maeve, I…"

Those words hung in the air as he turned his gaze to her, trying to will her to understand what she felt might be an apology for the shame and castigation suffered when they returned to Shepherd's Bluff that night years before.

"It was so long ago." It was her best attempt at letting him know she didn't hold fault with him for Emmanuel's words. As to his own, Maeve came to know later how that pain of losing a mother could twist good judgment. She had forgiven August his transgressions in absentia. "I don't know why. It just seemed…right." With a hastened sigh, she turned away. "Mercy, it was only a little kiss. Nothing to make much ado about."

"Please don't say that."

"What?"

"That it was nothing," he clarified, beginning to close the distance between them, pulling her hand up against his cheek and leaning into it. "In that moment, it was everything to me."

There was no space between them, not between their bodies, nor between their hearts. He kissed her the same way as all those years ago: warmly, swiftly, and chastely. His hands laced through her hair as he followed with a similarly styled kiss on her forehead.

"If only you knew the thoughts that ran through my head that night," he muttered, laying little kisses on the corners of her mouth. "If only you knew how often I still think of that night."

She turned a gentle gaze to his, the heat of desire rising up through her again. Maeve planted her lips firmly on his, working against them with unyielding motions. "Tell me now?"

He answered with an even tighter embrace, running his hands down her back and pulling her hips into his frame.

"I thought…if I wasn't Lord Grayson's heir, and you weren't my father's poor tenant, you'd be exactly the girl I would—"

"Maeve!"

The voice was weak and battered, but unmistakably Rory's.

They found him after a minute's search, lying a few steps off the path, his right leg half buried in leaves and earth. Maeve threw herself on the ground beside him as August took off his coat and covered Rory's chilled body.

"Da?" Maeve asked worriedly. "Are you hurt?"

When August tried to pull Rory's foot from the hole in which it was lodged, Rory let out a cry, forcing August to release it.

"I think his ankle is broken," he declared, though the amount of blood visible seemed an odd accompaniment to such an injury. He ran his hand over Rory's forehead. "He's burning up. We have to get him out of here and in bed or the fever will do him in."

"What happened?" Maeve begged, examining the trapped appendage and trying to figure a way to free it. August snaked his arm around Rory's shoulders and slowly sat him up before pulling him to a straight stand a moment later. The angle allowed the leg to slip free, and Rory pulled it up as though he were a wounded hound.

"My hat blew off so I went a chasing it and fell into this hole," he explained meekly. "Thanks be to Heaven for your help, Lord Grayson. I won't be forgetting it."

"Your hat?" Maeve sounded incredulous. "Way up here in the woods? Jesus, Mary, and Joseph! Just how drunk were you?"

"None of that, Maeve O'Connor! You're still not too old for me to take over my knee, you know."

August said nothing, though Maeve noticed his bashful smile. Rory was not an overly large man, but he held dominance over August enough to cause significant strain under the weight. Maeve took up her da's other arm and hooked it over her shoulder, relieving August of the sole stress as they dragged him back over the paths they had traversed, toward Gwen. Every so often, Rory let out a groan or a cry, causing August to move more swiftly while muttering something reassuring in his ear.

When at last they reached the mare again, August heaved Rory over the saddle, leaning the Irishman's body onto Gwen's back. They walked down from the woods, emerging on the outskirts of the back pastures. In the valley below the rolling hills, Shepherd's Bluff stood like a testament of opulence, and the tiny dot of the O'Connor cottage looked like a pebble in the field. Maeve turned towards the pebble, but August coaxed Gwen in the opposite direction.

"Where are you going?" he asked amusedly, flashing his warm smile and soft eyes.

Maeve answered hesitantly. "You said yourself we need to get him rested up. So let's take him back to the cottage. I'll get a fire going straight away and boil some water."

"That will take at least thirty minutes," he kindly rebuked. "If 'as soon as possible' is to be properly heeded, and as we are equidistant between my house and your cottage, then we will take him to the house, where I'm sure Caroline has preemptively readied a pot of tea."

"Are you suggesting I let you whisk him off, leave my father alone, tossing in fever and pain all night?"

August clicked his tongue and took up her hand as Rory slept through the gentle rock of the mare's gait.

"Not at all. You're coming too. We have plenty of space and I will entertain no argument to the contrary. Rory will need you there. And I…" He seemed to search for the right words, finally deciding upon, "…I would not be opposed to your presence as well."

Maeve nodded and acquiesced, his hand tightening around hers. Maeve knew not why the small gesture moved her so, but a sense of relief and comfort overcame her. She beckoned to his side. August reacted just the way she had hoped, lapping his arm over her shoulder and pulling her in. While she had grown expectant of the quiver of anticipation his touch brought, now it was tempered by the warmth she also felt.

"What were you about to say? Before Da called out?"

"Was I to say something?" His tone was sarcastic, suddenly distant.

A disappointed smirk erupted across Maeve's face. She pulled away from him, and he made no attempt to prevent or reclaim her. "I suppose not. My error."

"No, the error was mine. I never should have…" *everything*, he thought. "I sometimes forget myself in your presence. My apologies if I seemed to imply there was ever something… Well, what was, was and what is, is. Your father was always kind to me. Please allow me to honor that kindness by seeing to his convalescence."

How could she deny such compassion, even if not meant for her?

"Of course. Honor my father, honor me."

15 | The Clock Pauses

Three knocks in rapid succession on the door of the stock room of the Jolly Root Pub, then two more paced at length. Just as had been agreed.

Their leader rose and crossed the room, opening the door cautiously, his pistol in his hand and at the ready. Precautions were wise. One never knew who among them could truly be trusted and who, if offered money or otherwise discovered by the Brits, would turn traitor.

When the Woodsman entered, however, the leader relaxed and sheathed his weapon.

"You're late," he accused the Woodsman. "I thought O'Connor was coming with you."

The Woodsman scowled. "He's been delayed."

"Delayed?" Rory O'Connor wasn't the latent type. "By whom?"

The Woodsman shuffled in and closed the door behind him. "Not whom. What. And the what is a bullet."

Without another word, he tossed the Confederate-issue pistol on the table in front of where O'Keefe sat, arms crossed.

"Son of a bitch," Patrick growled. "Well, let it never be said that Rory wasn't willing to put himself on the line for the Brotherhood." He picked up a half-filled glass of watered-down whiskey and raised it. "To Rory O'Connor, best of us all. *Slainte!*"

Caroline met them at the door, a lantern hanging from her hand and a heavy shawl drawn over her shoulders. Under the moonlit sky, August had traversed the distance to Killarney and back in the space of two hours, bringing Dr. Johnson despite his fervent protests.

"How is he?" August asked as they passed over the threshold.

She led them up the stairs by the light of her lantern. "Whimpering a bit, and his fever seems to be getting worse. Maeve's not left his side."

August smiled. Of course Maeve wouldn't have.

They opened the door to find a flushed and sweaty Rory O'Connor, eyes open, watery and fixated on the ceiling. Maeve had pulled a chair to his side and held his hand, speaking lowly in the gentlest of soothing tones.

"… Owen, says he to me, 'Maeve, there isn't enough cloth in all of Ireland…' Oh, Lord Grayson."

August lingered in the doorway, giving her a weak smile but simultaneously feeling her discomfort at being caught mentioning her fiancé.

Dr. Johnson, an aged, plump Welshman, no longer possessing a full head of hair, took to Mr. O'Connor's side with a swiftness that belied his stout frame.

"Child, if you will please let me examine him in private."

Maeve looked to her father, asking for his leave with her eyes. He nodded meekly and she kissed the backside of his hand before going. Caroline and August followed her out, Caroline coiling an arm around Maeve's shoulders and drawing her near.

"You're being a darling to him."

August was slightly taken aback by the familiarity with which she spoke, as though they were childhood chums suddenly reunited. While Maeve and

August were, in fact that, Caroline had never been permitted an opportunity to visit Ireland in her youth. Yet here was his baby sister, seemingly bosom friends with his secret lover. It could either bode well for him, or be the beginning of Maeve's descent into social ruination, depending on how Caroline warmed to her and what she should come to learn of the arrangement.

Maeve looked to Caroline with a gratitude that was nearly palpable. "Thank you for staying with us, and for being so welcoming."

Caroline excused herself, claiming she was tired. When August heard her door close in the distance, he looked to Maeve with full sympathetic awe. She was clearly unnerved. She fidgeted and bit on her lip tensely, shifting her eyes back between the floor and August's gaze.

"Thank you."

The weak utterance sounded more like an inquiry on her lips, and it was then that August noticed the subtle shake of her body.

"Why are you trembling, Maeve?"

She shrugged. "Oh, I didn't realize… It's just… what to do."

"You've said thank you, and if it is of comfort to you, you're more than welcomed."

"No, not that." Her eyes rolled and her cheeks filled in red. "What I mean to say is … the doctor. I didn't know that's where you had gone off to. I… That is, Da and I cannot afford… I'm already indebted to you for the rent, and the doctor bill…"

His stomach turned when he carried out her thought. Maeve had found a way to "pay" her rent, and now she must be wondering if she would have to present an offer for Dr. Johnson's services. The thought was disgusting and abhorrent. August tried to tell himself that it was the modicum of morality he must have somewhere peeking its head, not that he would be insanely jealous knowing Maeve had been touched by someone else. He was already trying to rationalize not stalking down Murphy daily.

"I will pay doctor," he assured her. "I had no expectation of your paying, in any way."

"I like hearing you say that." His head cocked to the side in confusion. "My name."

A tiny thrill went through him as he reached out and stroked her cheek.

"As do I," he assured, laughing softly. "Maeve."

As she leaned into his hand, he was reminded of the truth: something had irrevocably shifted between them. At least he felt so, and he was fairly certain that she did as well. In the woods, he had all but admitted that his vague childhood memories of her had created the image of his ideal woman against which every female who had traipsed into his existence had since been measured. How would Maeve have reacted? Her eyes were bright and welcoming in the moonlight, but August began to realize that it may very well be due to the fact that she saw him only as the landlord and master that made her so eager to appease. Perhaps he was confusing her physical desire for him – which he would admit was an illness to have befallen others – with a deeper stirring of emotions.

"Do I still… owe you time… while Da's…?"

The sincerity in her eyes brought a chuckle from August, and she relaxed a little in the wake of his joviality.

"No," he answered. "I could not ask you to do such a thing when your father lies ill just a few doors down from my room."

Her entire frame relaxed and her hand slid over his, an expression of utter gratitude coloring her features. Without thinking to do otherwise, August smiled brightly in return, taking her hand to his lips and delicately kissing the flesh of her wrist.

Neither seemed ready to acknowledge it, but it was there.

August was quick to break the tension. "If you'll allow me to say though, I didn't think you were so displeased with my actions the other night," he teased, meaning nothing more than jest, but consequently having inspired in her some degree of shock.

She pulled back. "It's not that at all," she whispered. "It is that… my time has come upon me, and I wouldn't think such actions would be…"

"Oh. No need, I understand. But know this: I will demand no time from you, regardless, while you are our guest. I am not that much of a tyrant."

Her gaze admonished him. "You are not a tyrant at all. You only think that 'Lord Grayson' ought to be, but I suspect the boy who spent a day shearing sheep with Da, despite how much he hated it, is there somewhere still. He was noble and self-sacrificing, and I think Lord Grayson could learn a thing or two from my August."

Coldness overcame him as he dropped her hand, and though they were standing mere inches apart, August ran half a world away in a blink of an eye.

"If only you knew, Maeve. If only."

She made to embrace him, to regain and affirm the ground she thought they'd gained. August allowed a moment's indulgence before pushing her gently away. Her confused and hurt expression made him feel the same.

"This house by day has a dozen hungry eyes matched to forked tongues. While you are here, we must take special care not to let our… kinship be misconstrued by the gossips. I don't want something getting back to your fiancé. You… are still planning on wedding him, are you not?"

The business-like manner of his words sobered her.

"Of course," she answered, matching the matter-of-factness of his tone. "So how do I treat you while I am here? Lord Grayson in repetition grates my nerves."

"Around Caroline, you may still call me August. Otherwise, the formal title is advised, especially at tea later."

"Tea?" she gasped. "What tea?"

He looked at the ceiling as though the answer was there. "It was Caroline's idea. She'll be there, of course. And Patrick and Patty, as well. Oh, and some Yankee, so that ought to give us a good deal of discussion. Just think of it as a garden party. Now," August opened the door to the room which would be hers until fate took her elsewhere, "I'll go inquire after the doctor. I'm certain your father only has a minor injury and a bit of exposure. A week or two in bed and I'm certain he'll be as healthy as a horse. You should try to sleep."

She gave in without much resistance, spent beyond her ability to deny it. As she entered, her eyes went straight to the bed, carved ornately of oak and fitted with linens worthy of royalty. August's mind suddenly filled with visions of what Maeve would look like sprawled on those linens, stripped down to the flesh, as he tasted her every asset. Tonight, however, he would be content to know that she slept in comfort beneath his own roof and not on the flimsy palette of her sleeping loft in the cottage a mile away.

Returning to Rory's room, August found the doctor emerging.

"Lord Grayson," he replied stoically. "I think the young lady's father will be fine in a few weeks." He noticed then that he was wiping his hands on a kerchief, leaving the cloth streaked with crimson. "The fever should pass with rest, comfort, and proper diet. He is a little delirious at the moment, but that too should pass. Luckily, the shot passed right through without breaking any bones. There shouldn't be any permanent damage."

"Shot? I'm sorry, but you must be mistaken. Mr. O'Connor wasn't shot. His leg stuck in a hole and he twisted his ankle. Perhaps he was punctured by a stick in his fall?"

Dr. Johnson shook his head. "I think I know the difference between a stick and a bullet, Lord Grayson. He's asleep now, and best to leave him until morning if he'll deign to rest that long. I'll show myself out. Good night."

As August undressed and crawled under his own bedding a short time later, he focused on the ticking of the Comtoise clock, its steady rhythm creating the tempo at which he let the day's events parade out across his consciousness. Maeve needed help and she ran to him. When he had seen her talking to Caroline, he thought her desire had driven her to Shepherd's Bluff early. He wanted to answer it fully, or as fully as she would let him without removing her knickers. But when he learned of the situation, his impulses switched in a moment from wanting to hold her to needing to help her.

Then, by the waterfall, she had looked for a moment as though…

Nothing can ever come of loving Maeve O'Connor, he sternly lectured himself. Nothing, but heartbreak and despair. He would ruin her, just as his father had ruined his mother.

And then, there was Norwich.

Yes, Norwich. Even if he should be able to move Heaven and Earth and find a way to be with Maeve, Norwich was immutable. He shuddered at the recollection of what awaited his return. Not wanting to allow his mind to wander up that tangential road, August forced his eyes closed and drifted off into visions of a lovely Irish gal standing by a cascading waterfall in moonlight, dressed in a gown of pure white.

16 | Taking Tea

Maeve did not join for breakfast, taking to Rory's side instead. August requested the cook prepare a tray to send up. He spent a large part of the day in his library reviewing correspondences and trying not to think about the lovely Irish girl whose presence suddenly made her so accessible. In the early afternoon, Caroline asked if she and Maeve might take the carriage down to the O'Connor cottage. If they were to be guests while Rory convalesced, she said, they would need some things from home – clothes, for example.

The idea of Maeve wearing her meager attire to tea disheartened him. It was not that he viewed it as unpleasant, or her unworthy of company. On the contrary, the fact that Maeve's beauty could still shine so brightly despite the lack of opulent Parisian fineries was one of her finest attributes. She was deserving of such fineries, nonetheless, and thus August again found himself ascending the stairs to peruse his mother's things in the attic. He found some dresses there still hung in an old wardrobe.

If there was one credit August could allow his father, it was that he had never withheld from making certain that Lady Grayson's dresses were at the very height of fashion. Of course, how could Emmanuel live down any public slight that suggested he might be stingy. August reveled in the memory of how keenly attired Eliza had always been. Though the style may now be somewhat outdated, he selected a light blue walking suit and hat from the collection. Not wanting to face the retorts that he knew would certainly come at the presentation of this gift, August hastened to Maeve's room and left the garments on her bed. Almost as an afterthought, he retrieved the silk petticoat from where he had hidden it in his wardrobe after Maeve left it behind in her mad escape prior, and set it beside the suit.

Rory's condition was… perplexing, but the time to ask the old man about his injuries would come later. A letter was due Norwich, and so August returned to the library and scribbled out his obligatory weekly missive bound for the Grayson estate, Meadowlark. A member of his staff arrived at the library door promptly at four o'clock to inform him that tea was ready in the garden, and that the O'Keefes had already been seated.

"And my sister?" August asked. Caroline was usually the first at the table.

"She has been trapped behind doors since returning with that girl," his housekeeper answered somewhat bitterly.

"Miss O'Connor," August corrected. "Her name is Miss Maeve O'Connor, and she is my guest."

The servant blushed and gaped, before clearing his throat and nodding. "Of course, sir. Miss O'Connor."

The Norwich letter was signed off with due civility, and August sealed the envelope properly before taking his leave to the garden.

Patty and Patrick sat, speaking in low whispers, Patrick running his finger tenderly up and down the back of Patty's hand. He appeared so much more approachable to August now than he had at their last meeting, a placid smile emanating from ear to ear. Patty reflected much the same. The love the two shared had impressed August from the moment he had met Patrick's other half three months prior. They could hardly pass a moment together without making contact with each other in some way or another.

"Mrs. O'Keefe, you're positively radiant," August declared as he approached them from behind and, by way of such, made his presence known. "I take it you are well?"

Her smile melted into an indifferent straight line, and in a tone that was neither rude nor kind she replied, "I am, Lord Grayson. Thank you."

August sat across from them at a table heavily laden with jams, jellies, biscuits, and sandwiches as he nodded his greetings to Patrick, who dipped his head quickly in response. Silence followed as Patrick's eyes grew hungrier with each passing second.

"Please, do not wait," August suggested finally. Patrick seemed confused at the change of etiquette, clearly not Grayson's normal style. "Caroline's guest is yet due to arrive, and my house guest will be along shortly. I will wait."

Just at that moment, one of the servants announced formally, "Captain Jefferson Schand."

Schand descended from the back stairs with a gait brimming of confidence and poise. Walking swiftly, he nonetheless had a grace that was nearly artistic. Ruby-red locks nearly shoulder length and a mustache slightly overgrown the length of his beard must have been the American fashion. His attire was adapted to the Irish mode; though a nice suit he wore this day; he was clearly a man setting about a courtship. Yet August could picture him dressed in a soldier's uniform, saber in hand and orders on his lips.

August rose, meeting Schand on the pathway to the garden table.

"Captain Schand, August Grayson." August motioned to those seated behind, who rose at the gesture. "My middleman, Mr. Patrick O'Keefe and his wife, Patty. Miss Grayson is attending to our house guest and will be along shortly."

A quick, knowing glance passed between Patrick and Captain Schand. An observer might have claimed the gentlemen flushed red at the sight of each other.

With invitation to the table, they all assumed a seat.

"Captain, Caroline has told me so little of you. May I ask what brings you to Killarney, all the way from the Americas?"

His Dixie drawl was one with which August was not familiar, the twists and tones even more foreign in the land of Eire than August's British flavor.

"Well now, I've always been partial to the islands," he began, his words fully annunciated and slowly dictated, making August believe Schand to be a man of some learning. Fools rushed to disclose every measure of their being, but the wise man dotted the conversation with only enough of himself to remain relevant.

"My own ancestors emerged from Cornwall, but my mama came from Scot roots. When the war ended, a gentleman in Atlanta told me of reformation efforts being undertaken in Killarney and I decided to cast in my lot."

"So you work then?" August hoped it didn't sound too rude or accusatory, but he needed to be sure Caroline's potential suitor could provide for her.

Schand nodded. "Foreman at the North Mines. It's tough and grueling work, but the men are hardworking and dedicated to a fault."

A foreman was hardly an earl or a duke, but it was a position of some responsibility, though it was true that Schand seemed to August somewhat short in tooth. If he'd achieved the rank of captain at so few years – he couldn't be more than thirty – it boded well for his long term prospects. His pedigree, of course, was one which Emmanuel hardly would have approved, but that fact only seemed to Captain Schand's credit.

"I often find that men who take up positions of power are neglectful to rise to the opportunity presented them," August commented, getting a curious look in exchange from his guests. "That is, if one believes in providence, Captain, then one must believe that the Lord God in his infinite wisdom places a man in a position to effect change as a test of his very valor. We all know these stories of men whom – due only to their inherited station – were assumed representative of their class' shortcomings. Yet when given opportunity to prove otherwise, they became an inspiration to all, regardless of lineage. We must never forget that it was a simple carpenter who was King, and the King who fell down to kiss his feet."

"Are you the King or the carpenter in this scenario, brother?"

Caroline made her way down the pathway, dressed in a pale yellow walking suit and frilly lace-trimmed hat. The gentlemen rose respectfully. Captain Schand, not as well versed on codes of comportment, hastened to her, however, placing a kiss upon her hand in a bold Yankee manner.

"My dear woman, you are positively beauty personified by the grace of God and painted on this earthly canvas by the brush strokes of angels."

Caroline blushed fervently and nearly stumbled in her attempts to remain proper. "You are too kind, Captain Schand. I am so pleased that you were able to join us today."

Not to be displaced, August too approached Caroline and kissed her cheek. Indeed, in the presence of Schand, she seemed to glow. August thought, perhaps, their meeting in the marketplace had been much more impressive than he was first led to believe.

"Where is Maeve?" August whispered in Caroline's ear as the others sat back down.

"She is nervous about the suit," she whispered back as she rose on the tips of her toes to return the kiss, "though a lovelier specimen of eighteen-forties fashion I have not seen. She is coming directly. Look yonder."

Maeve was transformed. Surely, it was Aphrodite herself walking up the pathway in slow, measured steps. Caroline had no doubt spent a large part of the day coiffing the unbridled tresses into submission, and they were bunched atop her head in a configuration of twists and pulls that would have left a sculptor dizzy. After a good nights' rest and a milk bath (August had Caroline order the staff to provide her one), her skin was soft and begging to be touched, though the restrictive cut of the suit did not offer much campus for such endeavors. August suppressed every urge to cross the lines of propriety and expectation, to take this beauty into his arms and worship her properly. As it was, he stifled his impacted breath and gave her a respectful bow as he approached, keeping an honorable distance despite the drive of temptation, and with full recognition that Patrick O'Keffe's face was fast approaching the color of mulberries.

"Miss O'Connor, I'm told by the staff that your father's fever has broken. Wonderful that he's recovering so quickly."

"Thanks to your hospitality, Lord Grayson," she returned, putting emphasis on the title.

"Captain Schand," August said, turning back to the table, "may I present Miss Maeve O'Connor, my tenant and temporary house guest."

A startled look came over Patty's face and August could almost see the wheels of her mind twisting in contemplation as to why Maeve was staying at Shepherd's Bluff.

"Miss O'Connor's father went missing last night and I was able to help in locating him," August explained, cutting off the accusations that were all but being spoken from Patty's countenance. "We found him in the hills, somewhat injured but none the worse for wear. He's resting upstairs."

"The woods?" Patrick asked. "Is that where he –"

He cut himself off as simultaneously Jefferson's expression flashed. August made an effort to move the conversation to more temperate subjects instead, and due to the ladies' desire not to speak of unpleasant things, was successful in doing so.

The rest of tea was spent in mostly idle chatter, with a little business discussed by Patrick and August regarding irrigating the back pastures and turning the field to crops. Despite initial hesitation, August found Schand a most enjoyable conversationalist. Caroline was all but sold on him, that was sure. Maeve quickly relaxed into pleasant discourse, despite her initial discomfort upon arriving.

In the by, as the men waxed on as to the nature of sovereignty, August overheard low chattering between Patty and Maeve and realized that they were conversing in Irish. Knowing their intent was to keep him in the dark, he smiled inwardly at the vainness of the effort.

"Seems you took no lesson from my warning yesterday. Fine, then. What are you really doing here?"

"It's exactly like he said. Nothing more, nothing less."

"Aye? And where did that pretty little dress come from? Find it up on the hillside too?"

"I don't know where it came from. It was on my bed when I returned."

Speaking in Irish, her voice took on a more natural rhythm to match her accent.

"You're in love with him."

Maeve nearly spit out the tea she was sipping. "I'm engaged."

"Not denying it then, are you?"

Maeve chanced a look at August, mid-word with Patrick. Their eyes met for a moment before, flushed, Maeve hurriedly looked elsewhere. "It would be impossible, Patty. Like wishing for the stars in the sky."

Tea being concluded, Captain Schand asked permission to escort Caroline on a walk of the grounds and down by the lake, a request with which she was all too happy to oblige and to which August conceded, provided that Caroline's maid chaperoned. Patrick concurred with August's plan for the back pasture and said he would start drawing up irrigation plans, and then he and Patty made their way back to the middleman's cottage to relieve Mary Bernice's minder.

Thus, Maeve and August found themselves alone at the table.

"I suppose I should check on Da."

"May I join you?"

His compassion made her smile. "Of course. Thank you."

As Maeve and August passed the library doors, August took a quick survey of the hall to be certain they were out of anyone's witness, and pulled Maeve inside. As the doors shut with a ruckus behind her, August pushed her up against them, pinning her in place. He held her at arm's length, though it was clear to Maeve he was struggling with his own temptation to close the distance between them. Much as she found herself struggling to do the same.

"Is it so wrong to wish for the stars from the sky, Maeve?" he asked as he smoothed her hair and cupped her cheek. His eyes focused on her lips, drawing himself near as he dared without making contact. "I swear, if I could reach them for you…"

"You speak Irish!" she whispered in dread realization. "You understood everything we said, didn't you?"

He nodded, licking his lips, getting closer, closer.

"I don't… I know I can't … This just… We simply can't."

Was he trying to convince her, or himself?

"I know, I know. And no, there's nothing wrong with wishing for the stars, but it's only a fool who expects to catch them."

"I want you laid across my bed." He pressed her body fully into the door with his own, letting her feel his arousal against her. "What are you doing to me? Why is it that I want you so – more than any woman I have ever known? Why can't time diminish this pull?"

She slipped from under his restraint and opened the door, effectively ending the conquest.

"You know exactly why," she whispered. "You can't have me, not in the way you want. And you feel powerless at being unable to keep the women you love in your life."

She turned to leave, but August took her hand to hold her back a moment still. "I don't love you."

Her eyes fluttered shut, the bitterness of his words a dull sting to her heart. Trying to conceal the wound, she made her tone as dismissive as his. "You don't love me as much as I don't love you. And it needs to stay that way."

"Yes, you have much more serious difficulties to worry over."

Maeve paused and turned her head over her shoulder. "I would hardly call having a fiancé a difficulty."

"That's not what I mean." When she didn't respond, he elaborated. "If Rory's willing to tell you, ask who shot him."

17 | Shepherd's Bluff

"Shot? Saints preserve us, Maeve. I haven't a clue what you're talking about."

That was all her da was going to say on the matter. Some said, "as stubborn as a mule," but Maeve had never met a mule who could out-stubborn Rory O'Connor.

The suggestion of foul play from August vexed her, however, and for certain, more had happened than her da was going to admit. She could tell from the stiffening of his expression, the snap of his chin into rigidity, and how he folded his arms across his chest like a petulant child that there was more to it. His energy was sucked dry; he spent nearly all the day and well into the next sleeping. Maeve would take time to sit by him, but mostly left him to rest. She also saw August steal in to his room here and there, but given the way he emerged with grinding teeth and a crease between his eyes led her to believe that he made no better with her da than did she.

Maeve woke with a start before dawn on Saturday morning. No matter the circumstances, she was due to be at the bakery, but couldn't deduce how she would get there. Gone was the option to hop on the back of Jared Boyle's cart as he drove his goods into town for market. Walking from the cottage was not impossible, but now she was a mile further out and would no doubt be late if she went on foot.

As Maeve took proper shop clothes from the sack stuffed at the cottage the day before, she was surprised to hear footsteps outside the door. Cracking it open, she saw August walking past, dressed to go into town. At the top of the stairs stood Captain Schand and Caroline, who was bidding her farewells. By overhearing their conversation, it became clear the gentlemen were indeed heading into Killarney. When Maeve asked if she might join them, August looked – as much as he was able under the oddly suspicious gaze of Captain Schand – pleased with the prospect.

She spent most of the ride staring out the open window. Occasionally, the weight of eyes upon her grew heavy, and Maeve would catch August looking in her direction. Their eyes would meet briefly, making her blush fervently. She only prayed Captain Schand took no notice.

The day otherwise passed much as usual; a shift in the bakery, broken in half by a midday stroll with Owen. The only difference came after the bakery closing, when August was there to chaperon her back to Middle Lake. Owen, upon learning of the arrangement, was not pleased with his fiancé staying at Shepherd's Bluff, but relented in his objection. As Maeve reminded him, since her da was also there, nothing prone to start malicious gossip could be occurring.

Secretly, she found herself wishing that something improper would occur.

Life at Shepherd's Bluff quickly developed a rhythm, much to her surprise. Rory's state prevented him from getting up and down the stairs easily, so he agreed to let August move him to the servants' quarters. Maeve remained upstairs in a bedroom next to August's, a placement she was quite certain was not accidental, though August made no attempt to take advantage of her proximity.

Miss Grayson, or Caroline in the familiar as she demanded to be called, became Maeve's companion. Despite the differences in upbringing and station, the two grew instantly inseparable. Maeve sensed that perhaps Caroline's life in England had been one of loneliness, that she was somehow attempting to make up for years of such an existence. Caroline, having known something of the mischievous Irish girl whom her brother had spoken of through the years, saw Maeve as a mythic creature brought to life.

After breakfast and a morning walk down to the lake, sometimes accompanied by August, Caroline would retreat to her room and August, to his library. Often, the temptation to sneak in was daunting. As staff were always likely to be about, she kept away at the fear of being discovered in a compromised position should such temptation manifest.

In the evenings, Rory would sit with the others in the parlor after supper, sometimes spinning old Irish tales that delighted both August and Caroline to no end. Caroline was apt to take a book or collection of poetry from the library and recite a short concert, acting out Canterbury Tales with such witticism she had them busting their stitches.

But at night, Maeve remained sleepless for hours, kept awake by the steady ticking of August's clock in the adjacent room. Her thoughts returned to moments spent in front of that clock. The absence of August's touch only made her yearn for it the more. Sometimes, when he came a little too close in passing, or lightly brushed her hand with his finger while handing something across the table, the proximity would have too noticeable an effect. August, however, remained true to his word, and never pressed her to act.

But when another Friday night came, she heard the clock again.

Tick. Tock. Tick. Tock.

Maeve knew the rhythm of the house – the adagio that was the night. Caroline would be asleep at this hour, and the servants and Rory were slumbering in the far wing. Still, she could not convince herself to be so bold as to go to him. What would he think if she burst into his room, demanding that he take the time he was owed? She thought instead of all the things she still needed to talk about with Owen. The tediousness of such matters quickly made her find sleep.

In the dream that followed, she found herself chained to the very clock which teased her waking hours. August sat by the fire in his usual chair, wearing nothing more than a smile. Maeve was clad only in a corset, which nearly fell off her from the pull of his lusty stare alone.

"Are you ready to play, May?" he snickered, his body shimmering like a mirage. When he spoke, the words echoed about the room.

"Aye, if it suits you."

He stood and approached, running one finger lightly over her cheek when they stood face to face. Maeve turned and took the finger into her mouth, pulling it hard over her tongue, drawing a moan and a plotting smile from August.

"Such intelligence for so virtuous a girl. Are you sure you've never... Ah, Maeve, you..."

She suckled the finger slowly, turning her lips over the tip.

"Never yet," she purred as his wet finger traced a line down her throat. "I want you to be..."

His length pressed against her as he drew himself near.

"Say it." His hot breath sent shivers down her frame like raindrops. Below, Maeve felt a slight nudge of pressure as he teased her entrance.

"You know already, August. You've always known how much I..."

Her lips parted to offer a confirming declaration, but her focus shifted to the door as a malevolent figure, bathed in shadow, burst in. The room was dark, and Maeve could not see his face. The silhouette of the gun, however, was all too clear.

Two shots fired in rapid succession. August collapsed to the floor dead, and Maeve toppled over him, suffering the same fate.

The scream pierced through the darkness as Maeve clutched her chest, trying to find where the shot had landed. August appeared at her side in a moment, wrapping her in his arms and smoothing her hair as she cried and trembled.

"Maeve, it's only a dream. Calm down, don't cry… Just a nightmare…"

"He shot us!" she exclaimed in a near frenzy, hands flailing.

August clutched her wrists tightly to calm the shaking, drawing her hands to his mouth and brushing his lips across her fingers. "No one is going to shoot you. You're safe here. As long as you're in my home, no harm will come to you."

With the moonlight streaming from the windows, the sincerity in his eyes shone, a slightly pacifying smile gracing his countenance. She steadied her breathing.

"Sleep, Maeve. All will prove right in the morning."

Her bashful gaze met his. She could nary believe the thought she was entertaining. Then again, he would surely say no.

"Will you stay with me?" She swallowed her pride. "Please, when we used to lay together in the hay loft years ago, you always made me feel so … at ease."

Suddenly, August's face looked pained and contemplative. "Maeve, I ... I don't know if.... Everyone's away now, but if..."

She flashed him a pleading pout, and instantly saw his resolve melt. Silently, he drew himself around, leaning his back against the headboard. An arm encircled her, and Maeve leaned her head against his chest, hearing the steady drum beat of his heart playing like a lullaby.

"You named your horses Gwen and Arthur?"

"You approve?"

She nodded.

"Yes, well, what can I say?" he continued. "I've thought often about Arthur and Guinevere, wondering if they were to blame for their woes, or if it was all outside their control."

"If their lives were not in their own hands, then whose?" Maeve pondered.

August shrugged. "Destiny? Fate? What could they do, given the times? Divorce? As unacceptable then as it is now. They had their roles to play, and they played them until their hearts would allow it no more. So, Arthur yields and Guinevere and Lancelot run off together."

Maeve added, "To live their lives in sin."

August tilted her chin up. "To live their lives in bliss," he countered. "Where did the greater sin lie? In the lovers? They asked for no one's acceptance, just that they be left to love. No, I believe the greater sin was expecting Arthur and Guinevere to remain loyal to their vows, which were taken to satisfy the crown, not their hearts. In the shadow of that, how can we call the rectifying of that wrong, a sin?"

A chill crept up her spine. She tucked her head into his shoulder and closed her eyes."It's only a story, August."

A great sigh made his chest fall, after which his body eased down. He kissed the crown of her head. "I suppose it was, Maeve. I suppose it was."

When Maeve awoke in the morning, August was gone. But on the table next to the bed was a vase of pale yellow roses – likely the last of the season – and a note.

I think that counts towards time.

Frowning, she sighed and was filled with confusion. He hadn't even touched her, except to put his arm around her. Could he really have taken pleasure in nothing more than her presence?

Caroline and Maeve strolled by the lake one evening when Captain Schand had come for a visit. They had insisted on her presence, for propriety's sake, but with every bat of Caroline's eyelashes or blush of Captain Schand's, Maeve felt her presence ever more superfluous. Excusing herself, she feigned fatigue and turned back to the house. From the corner of her eye, she caught their kiss.

Love was blooming there, amid the dying leaves of autumn and the fading light of day. It gave her a queer, jealous pang in her heart.

Soon, the week's end again arrived. This time, Maeve found herself alone in the coach with August. They sat in silence as he seemed deep in contemplation and Maeve was reluctant to disturb him. Surely, Lord Grayson had many affairs on which to dote.

A short distance from town, his mouth contorted into a mischievous, knowing grin, forcing a smile onto Maeve's face in reflection, though for reasons she did not quite understand.

"Can I ask you a question, Maeve? What's wrong with the bakery?"

The inquiry threw her. To be sure, the business was sound enough, if somewhat inconsistent. Few city-dwellers had kitchens or hearths that would allow them to bake their own bread. Still, she had been considering the matter as of late when she saw Katey scowling over receipts at the end of the day.

"Our clientele is changing," Maeve finally offered, "and we don't change with it. Our Irish bread is the best in Killarney, County Kerry even, but

Killarney is being run over by Americans, Frenchmen, and the English. They don't care for our bread, and we don't bake nearly enough varieties to change that. We keep our current customers for sure, but we don't pull in many of the newcomers. Crusty ryes, fruited wet bread, that sour tack that the Yanks like so much... We need to make those too. At least..." She hesitated in realization of the exceedingly long length of her reply, "...I am of that opinion."

His devious smile grew ten-fold as the coach pulled to a stop outside the bakery. "That's exactly what I needed to hear. This shall be perfection. Quickly, then."

He hopped down from the coach platform and offered a hand. Maeve felt a near Judas as she strode into the shop at six in the morning, dressed in a suit clearly too well tailored and cut for someone of her station. For reasons only known to him, August had insisted that she wear this particular suit this morning. The pale yellow material perfectly accentuated her eyes, he had said. Now she wished she had thrown on the same shop clothes as each weekend. The other workers, six total, were staring at her loathsomely, and as August followed her into the shop, something he had never done, she read the unspoken accusation in each of their glares.

"Ah, Mr. Woodrow," August called to a pudgy man with bloodshot eyes and a forehead as grimy as it was flawed, standing in the far corner. Either he had been up all night, or he was simply unacquainted with consciousness this early in the day. "Is everything in place?"

Woodrow nodded slowly, though his disorientation was evident. "Yes, Lord Grayson. I was explaining about the change in ownership."

"Change in ownership?" Maeve muttered through her confusion. Was this the cause of August's contemplation? He had bought the bakery and was looking for business advice from someone with an inside perspective?

Only, what possible reason would he have to buy the bakery? Katey had day-dreamed of selling, but she didn't seem that determined to…

No, he wouldn't have...

Woodrow nodded, thumbing through a collection of papers in his grip. "Yes, Miss. Lord Grayson has been the owner as of Thursday."

"Yes, and may I make an announcement, please," August beckoned to the room. "Ladies, gentlemen, please allow me to be frank. This bakery was once renown as the best of Killarney, I'm told. But in recent years a sagging clientele and increased competition from the new arrivals in town has taken toll. To survive, there needs be a shift in strategy."

August, whether with purpose or unconsciously, reached out to Maeve, laying his hand on her shoulder and bringing her forward.

God, no. Please, no, she thought.

"When one steers a ship in a new direction, it is best to have a wise and intelligent captain at the helm."

Internally, she cowered. They're going to see right through this.

"And to that end, I have compensated Miss O'Toole, and have decided to turn over management to..." – *his kept woman* – "Miss Maeve O'Connor."

Acidic scowls and accusatory eyes burned her as Maeve smoldered and her sins bubbled to the surface for all to see. She had decided that she would not lose ground if ever the accusation was made in public; she had vowed to herself to stand by her decision and deal with the consequences they entailed. However, she hardly wished to have the banner thrown upon her by the show of such favoritism. She had to flee, to escape the stifling air of the shop with the ovens baking full blast. Perhaps she could crawl inside one now for a preview of what awaited her in the hereafter.

Maeve turned to August with a hardened expression and clenched teeth. "We need to talk."

"Of course, Miss O'Connor," he answered, almost giddy with his own doing and clearly not seeing the reality that was laid before him – their secret was suspected, if not confirmed. "We can speak in your office, if you like."

Maeve's expression must have given away her confusion.

"Your office, Miss O'Connor," he confirmed. "As manager, you have an office and apartment on the second floor. You'll have to share it with some of the paper work and supplies. It's stocked near half up with surplus bags of flour I was able to secure. You are content sharing your apartment, aren't you?"

She had a feeling he didn't mean with the flour. How bold he had gotten. Or desperate that she should be branded a harlot by the end of the day.

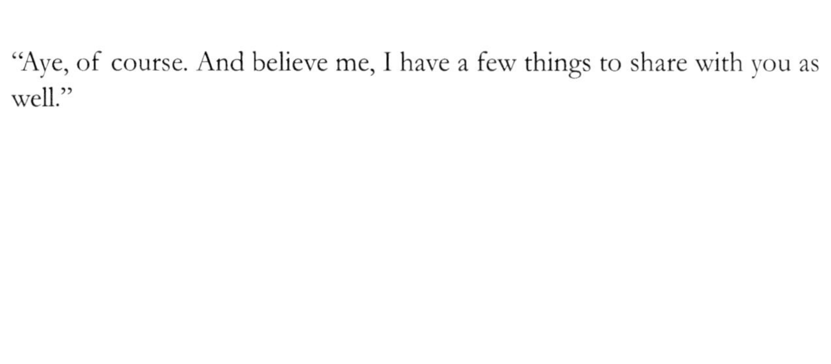

"Aye, of course. And believe me, I have a few things to share with you as well."

18 | Dissolution

Accusatory, hostile glares traced her every step. Two options lay before her: be apologetic and claim this was only business and nothing was going on between them – an effort which Maeve knew would fail, as the truth of her conflict would be evident on her face; or she could bluff and take on an air of authority. In this second scenario, the other workers would at least had a fear of losing their position for saying anything, if they believed she was indeed Grayson's girl.

"We open in thirty minutes, and I don't see a single loaf in the window," she barked with false confidence. "Hop to it, eh?"

Maeve drew her eyes to the most fidgety of the shop girls, Clara, whom she knew would be all too eager to please and not dare speak a cross word. With a flex of her arm and pointing of a finger, Clara's petite frame practically sprang to the back room. As Maeve turned to exit the shop to follow August, a cacophony of banging pans near the ovens arose and baked loaves were shoved in to the display glass.

The stairs to the manager's apartment lay behind a cast iron gate on the side of the building. Maeve waited for August to exit and lead to the quarters that must have been Katey's until very recently. August's green eyes twinkled in fervent delight. He still had not understood exactly what he had wrought, making her believe that his intentions had been benevolent despite the dreadful consequences they were likely to bring.

Maeve passed through the door. He followed and waited to be lauded and thanked for his keen plan and humble generosity.

"How could you be so daft?!" Her arms flew up as her balled fist walloped his chest.

He attempted to stutter a response, but she cut him to the quick.

"What did you expect they would think? I've been only a shop girl, and that only for a short time. And then some bloody Englishman sweeps into town, puts me up at his place, buys the bakery, and makes me manager?"

"I…?"

"Don't you see what this does? Brand me a whore, is what. And for what? Just to have a place where you could continue this arrangement in private with me now that your sister and middleman are privy? Has a fortnight without driven you to insanity?"

Without courage, or perhaps, will to look at her, August shook his head wildly and sat on a stout wooden stool next to the door.

"I never .... It wasn't my intention....." He paused, collecting his thoughts before finally making a better retort. "Oh, Maeve, I didn't think. I... I ... I was only thinking about... you. This wasn't what I meant to happen."

She scoffed with a cackling grunt. "Aye? And just what did you intend to accomplish by this maneuver then?"

"Your freedom."

August finally chanced an upward glance on the heel of his sincere admission. Maeve shrank back, perplexed.

"You are asked far beyond what should be of someone who's already given so much. You went as far as to broker a deal with me that nearly cost you your chastity. I don't want you to have to choose between having a home and having a choice. And if it's just a question of money –"

"I never asked you for money. I never asked you for … this."

He gave a weak half-smile. "I know. You'd rather rent your innocence to me than sacrifice your pride for a penny. If I could have simply given you money, I would have. But I could, at least, have seen the ramifications of that action. Instead, I decided to create an opportunity for you to earn your security. I thought, if I gave you the bakery..."

Maeve's frame eased a little as she began to understand. Crossing the room, she kept her body turned away, yet laid a hand tenderly on his shoulder. She was surprised to feel a twinge of sadness.

"And you would... What about our contract? I still want the cottage, even if I'm living in town. What would I need to do? Would you have to come to town, or would I have come to...?"

"You'd still do that? Just to keep the cottage? Even with this apartment, you'd do anything to still have... the cottage?"

He turned toward her and gazed hopefully into her eyes, as though his very ability to breathe depended on the answer to his query. "Would you not want to be with me, Maeve?"

Brown eyes darted wildly around the room, looking to focus on anything but the optimism etched in his every feature. Yes, she'd want to be with him, but what did it matter? In the end, there was no way of being with August, there was only being under him. If there was a sliver of possibility, a minute modicum of chance that they might ever be together, she'd throw herself at it full force. But wishing simply couldn't make it so.

"I am engaged to be wed, August," she finally returned. "What I want is irrelevant. But I will do what I need, and I need my home."

"As do I," he whispered in shame.

Maeve looked at him sideways, blinking rapidly three times. "I don't follow."

"Your cottage sits on a wealth of copper. I have the mineral rights by virtue of it being on Grayson land, but as long as you occupy the cottage and adhere to the terms of your lease, I cannot access it. My retrieving the land is… not negotiable. "

August had heard stories of the temper of the Irish, of the way their faces could, in the span of a few moments, shade into a red that put the sun to shame, but he had never witnessed such a fervent and sudden spike of ire until this moment, looking at Maeve.

"You…? What? Why? So, this… this arrangement? I thought you were taking pity on me, on us. But you were after ... our home? And all that… All the things we did. And now that you've relieved whatever smidgen of guilt you have for doing it, you're passing off the bakery on me? You're getting rid of me and Da and getting our home just for money? Why not just keep me at Shepherd's Bluff as your chambermaid, August? Then you can have my cottage *and* my keep."

"Maeve! Please, you don't understand! I want to…"

Jumping up abruptly, he began to pace the meager length of the room, running his fingers through his hair.

"Having you... in my house, so near..." He stopped before her, reaching out with shaky hands as if to embrace her. "Pacing next to your door each night, convincing myself not to go in. You don't understand how many times I wanted to just... take you into my bed... and .... and..."

"And what, August?"

Maeve's breath raced her heart for speed. Her head was spinning as his finger made the lightest contact. She leaned into it, longing to close the difference between them.

August shifted his stance, laying his forehead against hers and closing his eyes.

"I can't do that to you. And I can't keep myself from you. I need the distance, for your welfare and mine."

For a moment, the pain of his desire, of the sincerity in his eyes, tugged at her heart. Everything seemed possible and impossible, intimately close and leagues away.

"Besides," he said after a few still, quiet moments, "you shouldn't have to marry Murphy just so you can have food on the table or a roof over your head. That would make you a whore far more than anything I have done."

The rage returned in an instant as Maeve twisted around and crossed the room to search for something, anything that she could chuck at him. A random loaf pan was the first thing that went flying. It missed its mark, but her anger had not.

"You think I'm marrying Owen just so I don't starve?" Maeve shrieked, knowing full well at this volume that those below were almost certainly privy to the discussion. For the moment, she didn't care. "You really think I am such a simple creature that I would marry someone just to be fed? You think I wouldn't lower to begging first? Or worse?"

She could see that he was afloat in confusion again, struck speechless by the instant reversal in her composure.

"Why else would you marry him?" he whispered, more to himself than her.

"Because I want it all, August!"

Dumfounded, he repeated the word as though foreign to him. "All?"

She sighed heavily. "Yes, all. A happy home with a loving husband and messy-haired little children at my heels. A hearth and a chair by the fireplace where I can sit with a few books and teach my daughters to read. I want my sons to bring home their best girls. I want to sit around a table with my family in the evening. I want a man who will stand by my side in the eyes of God and acknowledge me as his without shame or hesitation."

His reaction was as swift as it was shocking.

August was before Maeve with two large steps, a hand on each of her arms, holding her framed to his burning gaze. He backed her against the ceiling-high stack of flour on the opposite wall, pinning her mercilessly, rendering her unable – or unwilling – to move.

"Maeve, oh, Maeve!"

August lowered his head, his mouth brushing lightly against hers in a teasing simulation of a kiss. When he spoke again, she felt his words on her lips.

"I want that too, more than anything. I just simply… can't give it to you. This, Maeve…" His arm swept a wide path through the air, indicating their surroundings. "This is the best I can do."

His voice was both desperate and angry, sad and sadistic. She wondered if he was reconfirming the reality to her, or only to himself.

Maeve slipped from his hold and backed slightly towards the door. With his hopeful stare, he was begging, pleading with her.

"I know," she returned softly. "That's why I'm marrying Owen."

As when the Lord had made known their nakedness to Adam and Eve, so both Maeve and August saw the inescapable truth of their lives.

There was a burden of gravity upon them, and she knew he felt it as much as she. August had not considered fully the implications of his actions, but it was too late to reverse the course. Maeve must keep in good standing, and that meant making clear to him both in action and in word that no matter what each felt for the other, the true essence of the world would not forgive and make whole their hearts in the face of such obstacles.

"By breaking the agreement now, will you take back the bakery?"

"Of course not," he gasped. "It was a gift."

"And the cottage? Is there no way? Even if I were to continue the contract? Or even if I offered you money?"

"I don't need money. What will rent taken of one little cottage do?" His voice broke, shameful it its tone. "I need the land."

Of course, she thought. The tiny sum she could offer would pale in comparison to the profit of a copper mine.

"But I wish…" Again, he spoke in a tone that betrayed his self-seeking motivation. "I wish you would continue. Perhaps I cannot give you all Maeve, but I can give you some. We don't even need to keep time, and you could see me only when you desired. Please, Maeve, please. Just…"

"You wanted to give me my freedom," she interrupted, her expression taut. "It is a wonderful gift, and I thank you sincerely for it. But if I keep to our arrangement, even with modified terms, then you've taken it back in the same breath. Keep me to the contract, and you will have made me your whore."

He began to slowly, then more quickly, then frantically shake his head in denial. "Please, Maeve," he begged, taking her hands into his, falling to his knees. A shudder wracked him as he pressed her knuckles to his forehead. "Please, don't."

"August, we must." Maeve tried to keep stern, but felt on the edge of tears. She pulled her hands back from his and took on as stoic a demeanor as she could muster. "Lord Grayson, I dissolve our contract. If you have nothing further about the bakery to discuss, then please leave. I have work to do."

A specter of a man who had kissed her just minutes before reemerged onto the Killarney street. As she followed him, Maeve saw the hungry eyes of the workers peering through the glass, waiting for some fodder for gossip to add to their suspicions. Several jabbed each other's ribs, pointing at August suggestively. In a moment, Maeve knew the scene was playing to her advantage. They no longer assumed that she was his mistress, but rather saw him as a man who had attempted an unsuccessful conquest. He was leaving dejected, and she was emerging purified.

"Lord Grayson," Maeve called over her shoulder as August began to walk towards his waiting coach. He spun around with a cloak of hope falling over him. "I trust I can count on you to keep my father as your guest until I'm able to collect him?"

Again, he became crestfallen, the whole of his features clouding over. "Of course, Miss O'Connor. You… He is always welcomed to Shepherd's Bluff."

She bowed her head in thanks as she turned to re-enter the shop. After a few formal orders to the workers to shore up her place as their superior – whether deserved or not – Maeve stole away to the small, dark storage room at the back of the shop.

At which point she could hold back no more. Closing the door behind her, she fell back against the wall, sliding down into a heap of tears and disheartened gasps, ruining her new dress.

"I can't give it to you…"

"No, August," Maeve spoke into the darkness. "You could. You just wouldn't."

19 | Betrothed

Even the cold, crisp air couldn't dampen Owen's spirits. The wait was over. Today, he would make Maeve his.

As he reached into his jacket pocket, the chilled metal of the ring met his finger. He slipped it carefully over his pinkie and hoped that the remaining blocks until Greenlawns Court would prove enough time to heat the band of gold. Likewise he hoped that this would recall Maeve from the grasp of despair into which she had mysteriously fallen.

Two months ago, she'd given Owen quite a surprise. He had found her flustered and trying to hide her tears. When pressed to explain, she informed him that Grayson had given her management and quarter at the bakery in exchange for the cottage. The tears, she said, were bittersweet. Owen had held her close and tried to comfort her, feeling the same combination of grief and relief as she.

Later, Owen came back to the bakery to check on her and found her in the apartment, sitting silently in the dark, calm and serene. And very, very drunk.

A quick peck on the cheek – all he usually allowed himself, as was proper – had quickly escalated under her persuasion as Maeve pushed him down and kissed him into dizziness. His hands overrode his head for a good part of ten minutes, even at one point succeeding in undoing the buttons of her shirt and the lacing of her corset.

But when he saw his flower bare-chested, Owen had sobered. Maeve apologized the next day, realizing her wrong. They had agreed that, for the sake of both their good names, they must not be alone again until their wedding night. Their determination was aided by Rory's arrival from Shepherd's Bluff a few days later, brought by Jared Boyle. With the apartment no longer a den of temptation away from peering eyes, Maeve and Owen had succeeded in keeping chaste.

There was little Owen knew about Grayson outside of gossip, which claimed he was the second coming of his father. He had made a quick play in early autumn, buying up an impressive number of businesses in town. Yet he did not take any actions to exploit the muscle of his estate. Rather, Grayson acted contrastively to the manner of his station, seeking to restore and improve. Grayson had given Maeve free reign over the bakery, only writing to learn of its status through post, never inspecting in person, though he made regular Saturday rounds to his other holdings and potential investments. He'd even bought interest in the smithy shop where Owen apprenticed. His not-too-small first orders had finally given Owen the last funds needed to wed his beloved Maeve. Grayson seemed, to Owen's observations, a good man.

Which made Owen feel a shameful schemer, knowing what loomed on the horizon.

The O'Connor cottage had been brought down in the night, and it was reported that Grayson was busily developing his mineral rights where once it stood. Maeve nearly doubled over at the news, as though she had lost a member of her family. For two days, she neither ate nor slept.

Afterward, she was left changed, though not in a way that others noticed. But Owen knew her well enough. She gave an outward representation of contentment, always with a smile and pleasant in demeanor. Yet she was never really happy – she simply went through the deceptive motions.

As Owen turned into the renamed Killarney Bread & Baked Goods, it was Clara Grady who greeted him at the counter. Her placid smile and chipper spirit always made one grin. Today was no different, and combined with the anticipation born by the ring in his pocket, Owen grinned like a child skipping church.

"Mr. Murphy," she greeted with a slight bow of her head and twinkle of her eye. "Good afternoon. How are you today?"

"Right fine, Miss Grady. Where's Maeve?"

Her smile straightened to a perfect grimace. "Mass, sir."

"Again?"

She attended nearly every day of the week now. To pray for their future, she claimed.

"I heard the bells a few minutes ago, and her father went with her this time," Clara continued. "They should be back soon. A good thing, too, as we just got a curious order I know she'll be interested to hear."

The excitement brimming in Clara's eyes became palatable, forcing Owen finally to ask.

"Five cakes for the engagement party of Miss Caroline Grayson and Captain Jefferson Schand!"

The news hit him like a bullet at close range. Jefferson was engaged to a Grayson? He knew he had been courting her, but thought it a calculated move, not so unlike Rory O'Connor's. Or was the Yank still playing the game?

The door of the bakery opened behind and the voice of his angel filled the room as she walked in off the street. Owen spun around to meet her curious eyes, seeing him in her shop on a late Thursday afternoon.

"I wasn't expecting you until Saturday," she stated as she laid her bag behind the counter. "Is something wrong?"

His smile stretched from Cork to Dublin, and immediately she became suspicious. Owen saw a half grin tick up on her face.

"What are you up to, Owen Murphy?"

He pulled her by the hand and off to the side where they wouldn't be in direct earshot. So close to closing time, there was only one customer in the bakery. The sun was getting low in the sky, and Clara was folding up her apron to store in the back room.

"Maeve, we're ready," he said simply as he took her hands and kissed her knuckles.

She looked at him with a smile, but clearly didn't understand to what he was referring. Pulling his hand back, Owen fumbled through his pocket and pulled out the golden band. He held it up in front of him as realization overtook her.

Clara squealed, and Rory gave a hearty laugh.

"Well, do it proper, boy-a," Rory chuckled, giving Owen a rough push on the shoulder, forcing him to the floor.

Owen took a deep breath to calm his jumping nerves, and took Maeve's hand in his own as he slipped the band over her slender finger.

"Miss O'Connor, I made a vow before God and man that I intended to take you as my wife. With this ring, I pledge to take you as my bride, if you'll have me."

It seemed a silly formality; they had been engaged for months. Yet Owen was soon glad of the coaxing Rory had given as he saw Maeve break into tears, her free hand flying over her mouth. She did not speak a word, however.

Owen let out a manly sigh. "This is usually the part where the girl says yes and lets the poor man kiss her."

With a giggle, her head began to nod vigorously. "Of course, Owen. Yes, of course."

She was in his arms and on his lips without another moment's hesitation. Both Clara and Rory rushed forward to congratulate them, and even the round, little woman loading the last loaves of the day into her sack was beaming.

"A blessing to you both," she offered as she took her leave.

Owen nodded before pulling Maeve closer and kissing her full on the mouth. This wasn't the first time he had made the attempt to partake of her lips, but it was perhaps – with exception of her first night away from her cottage – the most receptive she had been. She met the kiss fully, throwing her arms around his neck and pulling herself up the difference of their heights. Heaven help him, but Owen couldn't deny himself a moment's pause when he felt the heat of her feminine frame push into him. His arms wrapped around her and pulled her tighter still. For a moment she froze, and then her tongue very quickly and delicately made contact with his. Rory's booming voice from behind halted his temptation from carrying any further.

"Blessed be, you two, show a little respect to your old man standing here," his hearty baritone declared. He put an arm around them both as Maeve was kissed roughly on the cheek and Owen was shaken vigorously. "Now, when will it be? The sooner the two of you are wed, the quicker I can be expecting wee Owens and Maeves."

"Da, you're going to trample that cart with your poor horse!" Maeve laughed.

Owen blushed, but secretly considered the same.

"Well, why wait? All matters with the church have been cleared."

Rory's enthusiasm rivaled Owen's in intensity. He looked to Maeve, and saw a sudden strike of hurt flash through her eyes, but disappear quickly when Rory's eyes caught hers.

She sighed. "Well, I suppose there's no reason to wait."

Rory and Clara pulled off to the side in the talk of what needed to be done, Clara mentioning that a simple dress would suffice for the church.

Owen laid his head to rest on Maeve's shoulder. She returned the warmth and put her arms around his waist. Then, he felt her go stiff in his arms and heard a small gasp escape her mouth as the door to the bakery opened.

"I'm sorry. I didn't intend to interrupt."

The English lilt was unmistakable. The man whom Owen had seen at a distance around town and once or twice speaking with the master smithy stood with his hat in hand and a question on his lips. Owen glanced to Maeve, who seemed petrified, her eyes locked into Grayson's with a certain sense of desperation and fear.

Grasping her hand, Owen hoped to give her strength in the presence of the man who had ordered her homestead destroyed and who now held the lease over her livelihood. Of course, she was a little taken aback. After a moment, however, she eased in her stance a precious little and uttered a response.

"Of course you're not, Lord Grayson." Her voice was shaky, and her smile a thin attempt to gloss over the anger she was certain to be feeling. "In fact, your timing is perfect. Won't you please come in?"

Grayson entered fully, his eyes darting from face to face in an attempt to read the mood of the now silent room. Owen prayed that Grayson might judge the steadfast hold on Maeve as his effort to keep distance between them. All Killarney had been privy to the rumors that had flown about town two months before, but Maeve had assured Owen that Grayson had made no attempt against her. And in retrospect, he had helped the O'Connors, and by extension, Owen, quite a deal.

No matter the Brotherhood's long term goal, he could not see the harm in telling Grayson their news.

"If you would offer a congratulation to my blushing bride," Owen said with a smile.

Grayson's eyes fixed on Maeve, who was now indeed blushing.

"You are wed?" he asked hesitantly.

"Not yet. Soon."

"Well, then..." he stumbled. Finally, he took up Owen's hand and shook it vigorously. "Congratulations to you both. Many blessings. Clearly this is not the time for business, I see. I'll come back tomorrow."

Owen felt bad. Even English as he was, as lord he could have easily exploited any number of devices to push the O'Connors from their cottage. He had given her the bakery, however, and thereby a livelihood. As Grayson turned to leave, Owen called him back.

"Lord Grayson, perhaps you'll join us at the pub… to celebrate?"

He looked surprised, then turned to Maeve. She nodded her consent.

"I suppose I could join you for a pint," he answered uncertainly, looking to the floor at no spot in particular. "As an engagement present, however, would you allow me to pay?"

"Aye, well, if the English won't give us back our land, perhaps we'll settle tonight for their hospitality at the pub. Booze makes brothers like no mothers ever do."

Clara told the others to go along, that she would finish up the shop for the day and close down. A few minutes later, they emerged from Greenlawns Court en route to the Jolly Root Pub. Rory and Grayson made small talk behind Maeve and Owen as they strode arm in arm. Owen looked to his soon-to-be bride all flushed in the cool winter air and lifted her hand to his mouth, kissing the chilled skin with warm lips.

"I love you, Maeve."

Though he hoped she would say the same in return, he took comfort in the fullness of her smiling grin, and the twinkle of her deep brown eyes.

20 | Time Catches Up

Maeve bounced down the street, leading August to wonder if his memories had been glossed over by an unrequited heart. Perhaps she did care for this blacksmith after all. If Murphy made her happy, then so be it; August would yield. It had been foolish to suppose anything would or could come about between them.

Maeve let out a long sigh as they turned up a street filling with evening strollers. What did she think of his joining them? Judging by the way Maeve's eyes had bulged from her head, she was the most startled by the invite. Since leaving the bakery, however, she had put on a very impressive show of indifference. He couldn't help but notice, somewhat arrogantly, how many times she glanced back over her shoulder to catch him in the corner of her eye.

"Lord Grayson," Maeve finally said, falling a behind to take up step next to him. "You'll forgive my rudeness. I'm certain you didn't come to the bakery in an attempt to get invited to the pub. Was there something you needed?"

You.

"Yes, actually. Caroline asked me to ensure that you were personally invited to the wedding."

"Wedding?"

The news seemed to take her off guard, and he realized that having the order for Caroline's cake sent to the bakery hadn't gotten to her yet.

"Last evening, with my blessing, Captain Schand proposed, and Caroline joyfully accepted."

He tried to gauge her reaction, but saw only confusion in her expression. "They haven't known each other long. Whatever will be said in England of such whirlwind courtship?"

"What can I say? Perhaps when they realized how much they meant to each other, propriety didn't matter anymore." Oh, how the flush that filled her face brought back memories, but a public street with Maeve's fiancé nearby was hardly the place to make a scene, so August adopted a more formal tone and continued. "She wanted me to inquire if you could come to tea tomorrow. We miss you at Shepherd's Bluff, Miss O'Connor."

At the pub doors, Maeve motioned for Owen and Rory to continue inside, which they did without delay. The wind gave a sudden push of bitter chill.

"Yes, I miss it as well," she said nonchalantly.

"Do you? Do you miss anything else?"

Silence said as much as any words may have conveyed.

"Inviting you to the wedding is not the only reason I came, though a convenient excuse."

"Oh?"

August took advantage of their momentary isolation to pull Maeve aside from the light cast off by the flickering lamp and into the shadows. His words were sincere, but somehow distant. "I wanted to make sure you're well. I've been thinking of you and ..."

His words tapered off as a couple strolled by too closely.

"And…?"

For the briefest of moments, August's face screwed in conflict. He hardly knew himself, it seemed, what he wanted, or if he really wanted anything. Finally, he began to stutter quietly, his eyes focusing on a shilling he rubbed between two fingers and the black leather of his riding gloves. "The shop, to see if the facilities are being kept in wise order."

A momentary sense of crestfallen haze overcame her. "Of course. Later. I think we should join the others, don't you?"

Pulling back the handle and opening the door, Maeve rushed for the shelter and warmth of the pub. August was not accustomed to a wholesome lady deigning to be seen in such an establishment. Certainly, those of English society would be quiet shocked. He reminded himself yet again, however, that Maeve was no lady. Not in the noble sense of the word, that was. Yet her determination and perseverance proved her possessing of a nobility no other he had met could ever equal. She was walking into a marriage of convenience with her head held high and her shoulders squared. She had given the blacksmith her word, intending fully to make good on it no matter the taxation to her own dreams and soul. She was, in many aspects, the ideal woman bound by an honor and duty that Emmanuel had always ventured to seek for August.

The realization that one other held attributes exact in nature slapped him with sudden shock.

Inside, Rory, Owen, and a few others August vaguely recognized were seated around several small, circular tables, already with pints set before them. Maeve had meandered over to another table where a few other townswomen sat – perhaps Maeve knew them as customers, August thought, as her rather stilted posture told him she was not entirely at ease or comfort with their company.

Owen caught eye of August and waved him over to the only remaining empty chair.

"I'm disappointed, Mr. Murphy," August opened as he sat himself down. "Would you forgo my hospitality so quickly? I offered to treat a round for everyone."

"Aye, but no one said it had to be the first." He laughed as he motioned to the barkeep to bring another pint for the Brit. "Pick up the third or fourth, if you can hold your liquor that long."

Seated at a table with four Irishmen, drinking a toast to an engagement, August instantly felt a part of his mother's homeland as he never had before. It may not have been acceptable to Emmanuel's class, but his son was determined to be a proper Irishman for one night. One night to pretend, to imagine that life had come to him differently. That in a life such as this, he might have had Maeve…

Casting off the coat of nobility, he heartily grabbed the pint of frothy brew set before him and hoisted it high. "If we are to be friends tonight gentlemen, then let us be true friends. I am Gus, not Lord Grayson, and to your engagement, Mr. Murphy! *Sláinte!*"

With a chipper smile, they all rang in unison, *"Sláinte!"*, and raised their glasses in kind.

Then it was a race to finish. Whiskey was generally August's drink of choice, and he would occasionally partake of other spirits in his travels across Europe, but the bitterness of the Irish ale hit him hard. It simultaneously burned the throat while tickling the tongue. As he set down the stein on the table, August worked every muscle of his face into submission and demanded that it not belie the fact that his eyes were watering and his throat was afire. These gentle blokes, however, could see right through the ruse, and August soon found the pointing and raucous wailing was directed at him. He jolted as Rory O'Connor's flat hand made contact.

"A very fine downing of a pint for a first try there, boy-o," he howled through his chuckling.

"Mary, set up our dear English friend here again!"

His shout drew the further stares of many others at nearby tables. With speed that would have challenged Hermes himself, their empty vessels were replaced with ones dangerously full. This time, it was another at the table who took up the toast.

"We drink to Owen Murphy." He gestured upward with the brew. "May you love as long as you live, and live as long as you love, sleep in bed with the woman of your dreams, and dream the woman of your sleep into bed!"

It was rather a vulgar comment, August thought, but was taken in good humor by the others, so he made no indication of his surprise. Instead, he stole a look deftly across the expanse of the room to where Maeve sat, each woman beside her also hoisting a pint, though their words at that distance failed to reach over the hum of conversations filling the room. Maeve was veritably beaming and radiant, and August thought with some disappointment of how she once looked at him with such a glow. The fervent smiling made her cheeks blossom into pink roses, transporting him to the memory of her stretched across his bed as he led her body down a path to near ultimate fulfillment.

Her eyes dashed suddenly across the room. He saw her shudder and transform from darling pink to fiery red. His breath stopped before he realized that someone was speaking to his right.

"Did you hear me?"

August blinked a few times and recalled the air to his lungs. "Sorry, no. What?"

He followed the path of August's abandoned fascination and saw there one of Maeve's mates staring licentiously across the room. With a nod and a grin, the Irishman waved and the blond-headed beauty shied her eyes away.

"I said," he ventured, turning his attention back, "why do you stay in Ireland? Not many of the lords do so."

The ale he again nursed shot out his nose before he could stop it, bringing a hearty laugh all round.

"My interests lie here for now," he answered shortly. "Also, I wanted to see the land my mother called home."

"Your mother?" Owen asked with an airy tone. "She's Irish?"

"Was Irish," August corrected. "She died. Many years ago."

Owen wasn't from Killarney, it seemed, or surely he would have known this. The blacksmith's face remained in stern contemplation, before burgeoning into an all-encompassing smile. "Then you really are our brother! Barkeep! This man's a true Irishman! Don't insult him with ale! Bring whiskey!"

"Jesus, Mary, and Joseph, they're calling out for whiskey," Brocc Sharon laughed, crooning her neck back to get a full glance at Owen's table across the pub. "I hope you weren't planning on bedding him tonight, Maeve. Oh, he'll be stiff all right. Stiff drunk."

Brocc made little effort to cover the fact that she was well acquainted with a man's body. Many men's bodies, from what those who stationed themselves outside the confessional said. Maeve set down the emptied ale glass on the table and sighed.

"I'm not bedding him at all until our wedding night like a proper lass," she rebuked with a double-edged smile. "And if whiskey is my love's choice, let it be mine as well! Barkeep! Whiskey!"

It would be the death of her, she knew. While no stranger to the occasional sip of brew, the hard stuff was likely to set her calling out for her long dead ma afore morning. Maeve didn't care. She knew it would set her a bit at ease, as well. As she looked in Owen's direction, it disturbed her to no end that August seemed just at home with the brood as he had once with her in private.

It made her feel unequivocally common, as well as more than a bit wary. It was as though the two planes of her existence were running straight forward like goats in a tussle. Maeve knew the alcohol being downed on the other end might very well loosen lips she'd rather stayed tight. She'd prefer to be numb herself if that did happen.

"He's a lovely little ram, isn't he?"

Brocc's eyes were sizing up August as though she were thinking of making a cloak of him.

Maeve clicked her tongue in disagreement. "A horrid ferocious lion, him. I am living in town instead of Middle Lake because of Grayson."

Brocc gave a mocking laugh. "Why wouldn't you want to be here? After all, this is where Owen is. Wouldn't a lass in love want to be near her beloved? Unless..."

She gave a quick look back over at the far table at an inconvenient moment and caught August and Maeve exchanging glances. From Maeve's end, the stare was full of heat and loathing, but on August's side, the look could only be described as crestfallen and forlorn. It left Brocc all too certain of her conclusion.

"You fancy Grayson!" she squealed, half-hidden behind her mug of ale.

"Curses, no, I don't fancy August," Maeve vehemently denied as she took from the barmaid a glass of golden whiskey.

Brocc still eyed her suspiciously as Maeve thought back on what she had said. *Damn, I used his given name.* She could see the anticipation building in Brocc's bold brownies, eying Maeve like a hungry man to a sack of potatoes.

From the backside of the pub came salvation: a fiddler rosining up his bow.

"There's talk about town regarding your sister marrying a Yank," the man sitting next to August, whose name he had learned was Eric, said in an all too casual tone.

August suppressed his anger, remembering that a Killarney pub was hardly an appropriate place to expect proper social decorum. He polished off the last shot and let out a growl as the alcohol burned his throat.

In as gentlemanly a tone as he could manage, August answered. "Yes, my sister has recently announced her engagement to Captain Schand. They are to be married in March in Norwich."

Owen's voice was slurring, and no wonder of it. He had downed four shots of whiskey in the time it had taken August to finish off two. His eyes, too, became glassy as he leaned forward and put his hand on August's shoulder, before it trailed down and dropped to his side.

"Dat's wonderful news, Gus," he said sloppily. "Aye, marriage is always... always... always... great news. I am so happy for she... for her.... for them. Maybe, you....? Ha, you're a man with... well, everything we Irish let you take from us, and that's a good plenty.... You should get married too."

As he was clearly drunk – August never thought he would find the likes of a man who could not hold well his liquor in the whole of Ireland – he took no offense. Instead, August waved his hand dismissively.

"One needs to find the right match," he offered with a smile, casting a quick glance over to the captivating brunette in the far corner of the room. "And one should never marry in less than ideal circumstances, if one has such options." He took a moment to reflect on his own words before muttering, "Shouldn't, anyway."

Owen held up his hand as though some truth had just dawned on him. But then, the scratch of a fiddle pulled everyone's attentions to the back of the pub where the musician started a lively reel. When they turned back to the table, Maeve was standing beside Owen, staring at him intently.

Her mere presence made August's breath catch and his mouth widen into a warm grin.

"Dance with me."

It was a firm command directed at her fiancé. Owen's face grew to a full grimace as he looked proudly to each of the men in turn.

"Gladly, *mo chroi.*"

Maeve's head was a wee bit hazy, but Owen's was thoroughly spun. She led him by the hand to the back of the pub, each step in full swing and sway. With a lively two step, they circled. A few hollers grabbed her attention and Maeve saw Brocc atop a table, lifting her skirts half way over her head. A good many lads circled, cheering her on. As Owen swung Maeve to face that direction, she saw August, now seated alone. Again, their eyes met, but this time she was not so easily able to remove her stare. His lips curled in a half smirk and Maeve stumbled.

"Whoa, there," Owen laughed, bracing her around the hip and pulling her up. "It won't do for us both to be drunk off our arses. That's a man's work."

She kissed his cheek softly and slowly, knowing full well August watched with scorn. "Well, find me a man to do the work, and I'll not tarry," she teased.

Owen bellowed in laughter as he sloppily pressed his lips to her cheek. From the corner of her eye, Maeve saw August shift uncomfortably in his chair. Good, she thought, let him squirm. In fact...

Maeve didn't know if it was her drunken stupor or her need to set August's mind straight, but suddenly kissing Owen Murphy in as scandalous a fashion as possible became the best idea she had ever had. She pressed her lips gently at first, then coaxed his open. For a moment, Owen seemed resistant, then either by will or by spirits, his lips parted and he returned the kiss. His feet planted firmly on the floor as he deepened the kiss, circling his arms around her and pulling her body flush to his. Within moments, every physical boundary achievable by the clothed and standing was crossed as hoots and hollers arose in every direction. Owen's mouth moved against Maeve's, tasting of whiskey, but no less than her own, she supposed. He pulled back a moment, his eyes full of lust and need. She thought he might pull her out of the pub right then to take her in the alley. His hand raised slowly to brush her cheek and he smiled coyly.

Then he was flat on the ground, passed out cold.

Eric and Seamus rushed forth with a mighty chuckle, picking up the drunken Irishman from the floor. Rory emerged as well, hooking his arm under Owen's and pulling him over himself with Seamus' help.

"Owen never could put up a fight against whiskey," Rory laughed.

"Yeah, and after a kiss like that, there wasn't likely much blood left in his head!" A chorus of laughter followed Eric's jib.

Maeve was overwhelmed, fretting that she had been too scandalous, and there with her da in earshot. He seemed to pick up on her discomfort, however, and squashed it.

"Don't you worry, just pub talk, and I've heard plenty. Seamus and I will take him home and take care of 'til morning. You go home. I'm sure Eric won't mind walking you back."

"Actually, Mr. O'Connor, I'll be happy to escort her."

His voice was soft as rain and as gentle as the mountain breeze. August stepped forward and offered Maeve his arm. Her da eyed him suspiciously, as did Seamus and Eric.

"My horse is tied up in a public stable near the bakery, and I must pass that way anyhow. It wouldn't at all be inconvenient to walk her back and be certain that she arrives home safely, if you will give me leave."

Rory hesitated, suspiciously eying the Englishman, then gave a wary but assenting nod. "Aye, go quickly and make sure you lock the gate behind you, Maeve. Thank you, Grayson, for your hospitality. I'm afraid Owen took of it a little too much."

The last thing Maeve saw before emerging back on the street was Brocc kissing on some lad in the corner. Rory, Owen, and Seamus headed left, and August and Maeve departed right.

Maeve focused all her might on not stumbling. She wasn't as gone as Owen, but she would surely be feeling the echoes of the alcohol in the morning.

"Your fiancé enjoys his whiskey," August said matter-of-factly, breaking the silence at last.

"Aye, it'll make us a well matched couple," she retorted with a bit of a rogue tone.

"Is that what you want, then? Is that part of it 'all' – a drinking partner?"

She threw him a scalding look as she planted herself firmly and refused to take another step. The bakery was within sight now, and the view of her own stoop lent itself to her boldness, knowing she could make a dash for it if things got too heated.

"I thought I was perfectly clear about what I wanted, Lord Grayson. And you were perfectly clear that you didn't want to give it to me."

"I said I couldn't, not that I didn't want to," he corrected with such soft-spoken sincerity that she was momentarily speechless.

As she leaned forward to poke him in the chest, her footing was lost, and August caught her in his embrace before she could fall to the street. His eyes locked unto her even more, his face mere inches away as he held her firmly to keep her from slipping.

"Maeve..." His focus shifted to her lips. "Maeve, I've wanted to..."

"...see the books. Yes, I recall."

He appeared crestfallen as she drew away in a blur, forcing herself to remain in control. She would not be seduced by his sweet gaze or his alluring voice. Maeve would keep her dignity here, where she had failed with him before.

"Wait, please. We need to talk, and not about the books."

She quickened her pace all the more, the gate now just a few steps off.

"Maeve, I've missed you so much. Middle Lake is barren without you."

The small gesture did the trick. Although she did not turn, her hand stopped upon the gate and she stood motionless.

"My cottage is gone, August. The only place I ever called home is gone."

It came across as an accusation, leaving August scrambling to respond.

"I am sorry, but I needed the land. I had hoped that perhaps... someday... You..." He cast his eyes downward.

"I had hoped for certain somedays, too, August."

As moonlight broke through the cloud cover above and lit the street, Maeve hoped it didn't illuminate the tears threatening to break. In her chest, a swirl of every emotion she had ever felt in his presence overwhelmed her – hate, desperation, longing, confusion, compassion, dominance, love…

"What do you expect from me?" she began as her tone turned bitter. "You bring me to town, set me up at the bakery, and I somehow manage to take the powder keg you created and defuse it. I was able abate gossip and still keep Owen unaware. Two months have passed, and I was finally beginning to convince myself that it was all a dream. Now you show up here tonight of all nights and make me remember that what I had with you ... You remind me that you and I..."

August had managed to close the distance between them. Standing now just an arm's length from her, he held out his hand and tried to touch her. She pulled away just enough to deny him access.

"No, don't," she demanded, opening the gate. "You can't use me anymore. You've destroyed my home; there's nothing left for you to barter. I'm marrying Owen Murphy and you and I will never speak unless it's directly regarding the bakery. Just accept it."

"No."

Unfettered, he took another step toward her, bringing his lips ever so closely to hers. Walking backward, Maeve climbed a few more steps to reestablish the space between them.

"I'm getting the dream. The one you didn't want to give me, so please, just leave."

He erased the distance again, causing Maeve to start their slow tandem ascension of the stairs.

"I fully intended to stay away, and I didn't come here with any plots in mind. But now, in this moonlight, and maybe with a little help of the whiskey... Maeve, Lord help me, how could I let such a beautiful creature go?"

"I'm more than a pretty face. I'm to be someone's wife, and eventually a mother."

The image ransacked her mind before she could stop it: a Christmas tree tall as the ceiling, three children gathered around her lap with their new clothes perfectly pressed, their eyes full of delight and anticipation as each tore at a pretty-papered package. As day passed to night, her eyes looking lovingly out as August pulled her into their private chamber, kissing gently down her jaw to her neck, pushing her trembling frame away before slowly removing her night coat...

They had reached the stoop outside her door. She used her whole body to try and wedge the oaken frame open. The first volley only brought a moan of resistance from the wood. Without turning, but in a voice mixed heavily with desperation and resignation, she begged, "Please leave."

"Only if you tell me you love him."

She was done for.

"Love will grow," Maeve said over her shoulder. "It needs only time. I will love Owen someday, as he loves me now. Besides, who marries for love?"

He winced. It was obvious he had no intention of leaving until his piece – whatever that maybe – was said. Maeve turned around slowly, dropping her arms in surrender and pressing her back against the door. She needed to get in, needed to leave him outside. If he saw in, anything she was about to tell him would be all too obvious a lie.

"So you admit you do not love him."

"How could I deny it? I barely know him."

August's head cocked to the side. "Do you know him any less than you know me?"

"No."

"Not much to build a future on, Miss O'Connor."

Her cheeks must have burned as she felt the heat tickle her nerves. "What I am building a future on is his good name and mine. A good name, I'll remind you, that you nearly succeeded in dragging through the mud."

The words bore no fruit in repelling him. Instead, his form pressed into hers, backing Maeve against the door, leaving no route of escape except inward, against that very door that would not budge.

"And what of our prospects? Can you take no future from that?"

She scoffed, feeling every Judas nerve calling to seek out his lips, his eyes trying to draw her further into his web.

"You are English. What worth are you in Ireland?"

"You are Irish, what worth are you in England?"

August angled his chin and leaned in, seeking her kiss. In a last ditch effort to deny her desire, Maeve tried to pull back from him, but there was nowhere to go. Instead, her head slammed back, and their combined weights finally forced the door to yield. The wood upon wood friction made a terrible cry as Maeve fell inward, landing hard on the floorboards, August's body landing right atop hers. His head picked up, looking not at her, but across the room with wonder the likes of a child.

Silence.

Except for the steady tick of one previously-owned Comtoise clock, the very one August had cast off at auction only a few weeks before.

"Maeve, my clock?"

"Yes, our clock."

21 | A Moment Stolen

Wherein so bitter August had found the constant tick of the clock that he had sold it off, now each moment it measured was a victory for his heart.

Maeve's arms encircled his neck and pulled him closer as his lips took from hers every portion of warmth they were able to offer.

"How?" he asked breathlessly, flashing his eyes to the clock and back again to her flushed visage. Even with a manager's salary, the purchase of such an opulent item would be nearly impossible.

"I'm afraid you'll discover when you go over the books."

His lips returned to hers but were left unsatisfied. August simply couldn't kiss her hard or fast enough to be convinced that she understood his rapture.

"August, the door..."

It was quite chilly and the air was causing the flat – and Maeve – to lose heat. August nodded, begrudgingly withdrew, and rose to his feet. The heavy door refused to completely close until he used the weight of his whole body to press it into place. When at last he succeeded, he found her spot on the floor empty.

His eyes searched the room. Across the way, Maeve's silhouette ghosted through the darkness. Soon, a soft glow filled the room, throwing amber highlights about. August smiled coyly as he slipped off his overcoat and let it fall to the floor. Maeve had abandoned her cloak as well.

"I'm drunk," she said through a half-smirk.

"Me too."

Her eyes turned devilishly delighted as he reached her, pulling her back to him. She set the lamp on top of the nearby mantle and twisted her fingers through his hair.

"Last time I was drunk I tried to seduce Owen, but he was too good a man to take advantage of me."

He placed light, wet kisses along her neck just where her hair cascaded behind.

"Good thing I'm an English bastard with no morals."

Maeve tilted her head back, exposing her throat, and August tasted every inch, using his arms to pull her closer all the while. Her hands reached up to his dress coat and tugged at the sleeves. He was all too happy to oblige her and removed the needless garment, surrendering it to a pile on the floor that was soon joined by his shirt and vest, her blouse, and then her skirt. The sight of the petticoat and camisole he had gifted her underneath sent his spirit soaring.

Their hands acted only as utilities of undressing, but even now as they both stood only in their undergarments, August was surprised when Maeve's fingers began skirting down his sides, over his hip, and reached around to grab the hem of his drawers, tugging at them.

"Maeve...." he hissed through gritted teeth. "Are you certain?"

"I'm standing in front of our clock, August," she answered as she began to slip the cotton fabric down, revealing his hardened manhood without the further hindrance of cloth. "What I do here is for your pleasure."

The drawers fell to the floor and Maeve's hands circled forward, both beginning to stroke the exposed and ready instrument. His eyes rolled back. He had touched her from nearly head to toe, but had recalled the only instance of her soft hand upon him so intimately with longing since it had happened. Still, a bit of his gentlemanly upbringing would not allow her to press forward unwarned.

"Maeve, the first time for a woman... There can be pain. It may hurt... And, I don't ... Oh, Maeve, yes ... Are you certain that... Ungh, May..."

The anticipation August had felt since first they struck their deal in the stable was coming to a head. Maeve's hands had grown so strong from working dough in the bakery – a consequence he had never considered when giving her the position, but one he was surely benefiting from now. Her fingers united in their grip and worked the embrace of her hands up and down his shaft. His release would not be long in coming, and he wasn't sure what her reaction would be. Even now, his mind raced to know how she had figured out how to do what she was so masterfully doing.

As though his eyes had put into words this very query, she looked up at his ever-contorting features. "Brocc talks."

He nodded, understanding that the girl's reputation must have been well earned. Maeve loosed her left hand as her right journeyed lower, cupping the sac beneath and nearly undoing his control.

With breaths heated and fast, he growled, "Maeve... Please, you're going to make me.... Oh, my.... May... I'm .... Imma...."

With the force of a raging river, he arrived. As her hand took the evidence of his climax, she didn't seem the least bit surprised, only somewhat intrigued and entertained.

"Did I make such a mess?" she laughed as she wiped her hand across her cotton camisole.

August smirked down at her. She was not disturbed at all, and that fact relieved his tension. This, paired with the physical relaxation that was now cascading over his body, and August drew face to face with her yet again, before leading her towards the floor.

Maeve's joviality gave way to a renewed hue of lust. She bit her bottom lip as. August's hands rose first to her arms and clasped for a moment the tender, soft flesh. Then he moved his attentions around front and began unlacing the camisole's ribbons. Maeve said nothing, using only her eyes and the twitching of her mouth to make him aware of her acceptance. The lacing undone, August pulled back the camisole and took in the miraculous sight of her naked breasts.

Slowly, tenderly, he palmed one, then the other, making light circular motions over the hardening peaks. Maeve gasped as her back arched. August felt more than impulse; he felt it vital to his mortal existence to draw her to him. His hands abandoned their labors and wrapped around her back in an effort to close the remaining distance. Her soft form slammed into his as their lips found each other's in the new proximity. Be it instinct or good fortune, Maeve crumbled in his arms, and soon he found himself covering her body with his own.

Tick, tock, tick, tock...

His tongue explored the taste of her chin, her ear, her lips. Again, the strength of an otherwise so gentle set of hands laid claim to his hips, pulling him down on her. He had already resurfaced from his release, sensing an opportunity for another so close. Only one piece of clothing remained between them, and one irrevocable decision to be made.

But the decision had been made, and the consequences be damned. It had been made long ago on a late summer's day, when a pretty Irish lass had found a confused and lost English boy, running away from the crushing reality of his own immovable fate. It had been affirmed when that boy returned to her shores, a man, to run away once again, and certified the moment she committed herself to five seconds at his side despite obligations that would have her do otherwise.

August pulled back and stroked her cheek slowly, his eyes falling to her swollen lips. He would afford her this last opportunity to decline, he thought. After that, he wasn't sure he would retain enough control to be able to stop. She answered with a kiss so pure he knew she shared his desire. Pulling himself back, August sat back on the balls of his feet and bent down to slip his hands under the hem of her petticoat.

Achingly slowly, he pulled the garment down the length of her strong, slender legs and past her ankles, the fabric catching on her smallest toe as he pulled it away. Completely undressed before him, August saw her whole body trembling under his stare. If she felt an anxiety at their compromised state, there was no indication of it. Rather, she seemed to quiver in anticipation. For a few moments, he relished the angelic vision before him. Her pale ivory skin glowed under the lamp light that fell down over them both. He could see the glisten of sweat upon her chest and brow, and the glint of wetness below that taunted him.

Maeve held her arms out and curled her hands, gesturing him to come. He lowered over her again and felt himself align perfectly with her entrance. He distracted her from the initial entry with a heart-stopping kiss as he pushed himself in halfway. The instinctual reluctance began to ease as her body recognized the natural consummation of the lover and his mate. August pulled back, and then again pushed forward, still locked in a kiss that had become more important than the need for transient elements like air. This was the air, the water, the fire.

As he sank completely into her, Maeve gave a yelp. His concerned gaze shot to her face, evaluating her expression. She smiled after a few moments' pause and raised her hips in invitation. Their bodies flowed like water, slipping over each other, under, through, around... together. As his rhythm established itself, Maeve's gestures and reactions mirrored his, complementing his sex. Their kisses were hard and deep, leaving both dizzy. August became so enraptured with the feeling of multiple sensations that he didn't notice when their bodies exchanged positions. Maeve straddled him, allowing him deeper access and freeing his hands to explore the swell of her breasts, to feel the flex and release of her muscles as he pulled her body back and forth over him, to place his hands on her hips and lead her in a meter that pulled every essence of pleasure forth from the farthest reaches of their bodies and souls.

August worked her sense of push and pull at a quickening pace, her overflowing wetness making his efforts easily rewarded. A gentle moan brought his attention from the apex of their joining to her face. Had he hurt her? Another moan, this one deeper and louder, soon followed and was accompanied by a tightening of her walls around him.

He realized that she was beginning to break her zenith. It excited him beyond measure. August doubled the pace by insistence of his grip upon the curvature of her hips. The increase in the friction matriculated in the impending release of his own climax. He became vaguely conscious that Maeve was saying something... actual words, and focused only long enough to learn that she was in fact invoking his name.

"August!" she called feverishly.

"Maeve!" he growled, his stomach clenching. August called out to her in Irish through the wave of pleasure breaking from every corner of his being. "*Mo shearc, mo Maeve.* You're so … beautiful. "

Her hands leaned forward and steadied her body on his chest as her noises manifested as screams of his name. Maeve's body shuddered and collapsed just as August felt himself release into her. Her hair stuck to his sweat-gleaming front as her head found relief on his shoulder, their bodies still maintaining connection. He kissed her forehead before falling silent. When she shivered, he feared for her comfort. Gingerly, August maneuvered the sated creature into his arms and carried her to her bed. Once she was situated under her blankets, Maeve reached up without speaking, inviting August into her embrace.

Eventually, she rolled off and lay at his side. August turned on his side too, their eyes locking and each smiling through post-coital bliss. Maeve began to drift off to sleep, her eyes still flickering open every few minutes to look at his. Though weary, August forced himself to remain awake, frightened that Puck would find them in their slumber and enchant their hearts away from each other.

August slid his hand down to take hers in turn and felt his fingertips graze over the ring - the sole piece of foreign attire left on her body. He recalled the words of the man whom had made binding his contract by way of this ring just a short time ago, said through a drunken stupor. Yet, even this near stranger could look at August in a moment and see that he was incomplete. August needed his complement, his other half.

No, more than half. He had been empty before – a mere container for the flesh and bone of which his parents' tragic coupling had resulted. Maeve made him whole. This ring upon her finger threatened to take her away, however. He would be left again without purpose or pride. He would be a fallow field.

"May?" he whispered softly.

Her eyelids, heavy with the effects of whiskey and weariness, flickered open, the wetness of her eyes twinkling under the lamp light. She smiled in the way that only a satisfied woman could.

"August?" Her eyes closed again.

"Don't marry him."

She propped herself up on one elbow and looked aghast. "What do you mean? Everyone is expecting... If you think I can...."

He stopped her words with a kiss planted firmly on her soft lips, threading his fingers through her hair and pulling her to him. Maeve rolled over on her back and he followed, feeling the stirring of desire take hold again. Maeve's body reawakened too, her legs wrapping around him and pulling herself to meet his interests.

"Don't marry him," August said as he slipped into her once again. "You can't marry him."

He thrust harder and harder, building them both again to a rapid climax.

"Don't you see, May?"

She began to twitch and quiver on edge of release. He sped up, willing her body to echo his desire reaching fruition.

Maeve pulsed beneath him, her heart pounding. He had lost his grasp on reason, his caution in giving everything he could to her, though the danger of their act was well known to them both.

"See what?" she gasped.

"I love you," he cried as he felt himself give over to her once more. "Lord help me, May, I love you too much to let you go."

22 | Misnomer

~Boston, MA~
September 1872

The girl's eyes sparkled across the cobble-stoned street as she leaned over the side of the bench precariously. She sought permission from her watcher, who quickly nodded approval. She snatched up one golden-orange fallen leaf forcefully and stuffed it into pockets already overflowing with a collection of autumnal foliage. A gust of cool air shot through their clothing, making all out on the street in the evening shiver. The woman wondered how the child remained unaffected; only a loose ebony curl or two danced behind her before falling limply back against her shoulder.

"Gettin' late, Maeve."

"Aye."

"She'll be catching her death o' cold if you don't get her in."

Tara's accent was so much more pronounced, Maeve thought, than her own. While Maeve had attempted – though perhaps not as successfully as hoped – to craft her speech with less Irish flavor, Killarney still echoed in her words. Tara, however, was hopeless, not trying to sound either British or American, choosing instead to let her pride be paraded in every twill and tweet.

"She's a hardy one," Maeve argued. "Reminds me of my ma that way. She could stand naked and wet to the wind on Christmas morning and think herself overdressed for comfort. And if I told her a bit of anything contrary, she'd have me tongue-lashed from tip to tail."

Tara finished stuffing some parsnips into her bag and taking a few onions back from Maeve's in exchange. An old woman, she was Maeve's neighbor and friend, but never hesitated in saying an iron word or two when she thought it proper.

"This is no place for you, and not for her either." She motioned to the child, who had now taken to skipping pebbles across the walk before scurrying to fetch them back.

Maeve sighed fully. Attempting to come across as completely sincere, she somewhat failed at the words. "This is as close to home as she's ever felt. She barely remembers the old house anymore. Every so often, I think she's going to ask me something about it, but she quiets, like she's trying to figure out if it was a dream. Then she goes about her business again."

A silence fell for several minutes as they both focused intently on the way the child fingered the pebbles about in her hand.

Finally, Tara spoke. "She'd do well in school. A real keen eye, that one. And studious. Look at the way she flips those over and over so she doesn't miss a single detail. Very determined little sprite, she is. She looks at the stones likes she could pound them into something useful."

Maeve smiled warmly. "Much like her father that way."

Tara leaned back a bit, a knowing smile on her face. "Certainly not like you. Not to begrudge, but she has a certain… spark of rebellion?... in her. Yes, a wee Fenian, that one."

Maeve didn't respond. Tara knew she didn't like to speak about the past too much. She kept the warmth of it around her like a blanket and the cold of it slung over her shoulder like a sack of potatoes.

But in the moment, the similarity, the way the child played – simultaneously carefree and yet completely consumed by her work – was so very much a reflection of her parentage that she couldn't deny a momentary recollection. "So much her father's child, in both brand and banter, as my da would have said."

Immediately, Maeve bit her tongue, fearing that revealing the secret carried in the child's name was dangerous. Before Tara could even have a chance to question it, if she had noticed, Maeve thought it wise to take her leave.

"You're right. Gettin' late. We better be off. Night, Tara. Come along, sweet!"

The child turned and her blue eyes shone with the brilliance of a thousand stars. She skipped the distance between and threw her tiny frame against the firm-set Tara, gripping her midsection.

"Good night, Miss O'Terri!" Augusta chirped in her delicate childish way.

Tara leaned over and kissed the angel girl on the forehead as she ran a thumb over her cheek.

"Good night, dear heart. You take care of your Ma now, and make sure she gets home safely. Will you do that, Miss Murphy?"

Augusta squealed at being addressed so formally. "Of course, Miss O'Terri. She's safe with me!"

23 | *Forged*

~Killarney, Ireland~
December 1866

If Owen noticed the red flush of her cheeks, or the way she fidgeted as they stood before the congregation three weeks from the intended date of their union, making the very hour known and public, he gave no outward sign of it.

It was a mere formality, one which the church required. She would have thought nothing of it had she not carried with her the guilt of having been bedded by another two nights before.

Maeve and August had awoken in each other's arms, not certain what to say. One grace of the Almighty was that her da had not come home that night. In the heat of their union, August had declared that he loved her. Maeve suspected he told the truth, though while he had shown kindness and even compassion, August had never made any indication that his feelings for her ran so deeply.

And also, they had been drunk.

Wisely, Maeve had managed to bite her tongue and say nothing of her intentions or her own confused feelings. After the second time they had laid together, she melted into his embrace and allowed herself to enjoy the warmth of his body against hers, the feel of his chest rising and falling. It would not happen again; even in the moment she knew the encounter had been a mistake, an unalterable blemish that would forever stain her soul. Still, she couldn't ignore the look of utter sincerity on his face as he had made his declaration.

I love you too much to let you go…

The next morning, Maeve rose early and spoke none to August. She made her way below to the bakery while he dressed. He must have left discretely, for no one mentioned seeing him and he was not present when she returned after the morning rush. Despite how perfectly he felt when he was near her, with her, in her, it didn't change facts. No matter what they felt, they couldn't let what had happened between them be known in public.

It was only further evidence that what she did feel for August was misguided. She could never be anything of significance to him. Never. The sooner she accepted that and moved on – with Owen – the better. Besides, Owen loved her, that was for certain. He was a good man with a good heart and a good name. He was perfect for her, a man of whom Rory approved, and whom Sine, if she had still been alive, would have wanted for her daughter.

As thoughts of August tugged at her heart, Maeve knew she must not allow herself to be led astray by her own wild fantasies. She must… *must* resign herself to her fate as Owen's bride. Owen would be the father of her children. Someday, hopefully years away, Owen would lay beside her in a cold and earthen grave.

She had to find a way to undo what she had done, or at the very least, lay the foundation for her new life with Owen as quickly as possible, to affirm the path she would walk with him. She would do so, and do it by giving herself to him completely.

After mass, Maeve led Owen back to her flat. Rory had set out to Middle Lake for a visit to Billy Boyle's and would be gone the night. Every step felt like twenty, however, as though she were walking to a fate worse than death and trying to stay the road between. That she should be so nervous about the decision she had made perplexed her. It wasn't as though what she was about to attempt was something she hadn't done before.

Anymore, anyhow.

As she closed the door behind them, Maeve turned to Owen and reached to take his coat. Easing it off his shoulders, she laid it over the back of a chair near the fireplace. As her eyes scanned the floor before the hearth, she quivered at the recollection of what had happened there just two nights prior.

"Glad to be done with it finally?"

"Eh?"

All the color left Maeve's face as she turned back to Owen. She inwardly chastised herself for her reaction. There was no way Owen could know what she had done with August.

"Oh, the announcement of the date?" He nodded. "Yes, the sooner I am your wife, the better, in my opinion."

His smile faltered as he moved around the confines of her modest flat, the cloak of shame overcoming his face. "I'm so sorry about your cottage. I had hoped there was something I could have done, but that scoundrel just moved too swiftly."

Maeve feigned indifference, despite a perplexing instinct to defend August. "Oh, it's all right. Perhaps I was too held up in so small a thing. After all, there are other cottages at Middle Lake. Perhaps, someday, we'll find ourselves there still."

"Ah, maybe. Especially with the Fenians …" Maeve crooked her head to the side. "Well, things might just work out for us, is all."

"Of course it will. I'm sure of it."

His fingers ran through his hair as he took off his cap by the rim and scratched his scalp. When he looked up, he found Maeve dangerously closing in on him.

"What are you doing?"

She reached him and rolled up on her toes to try to meet his lips. "May not I kiss my husband-to-be?"

Not waiting for an answer, she made the attempt, and succeeded. The small peck was followed by another, deeper and longer. On the third visit, Owen brought his lips down to meet hers, his hands flowing over her shoulders to frame her properly. A churn of guilt seeded deep within, both because of what she was about to do and what she had done, but Maeve fought the desire to pull back. Every gesture buried her deeper in her conflict: not wanting to proceed, yet believing that her submission to Owen was the reaffirming, soul-saving action she must take. When a fourth kiss ended, she found herself pressed against him fully, his arms around her and holding her tightly.

Owen hesitated, wariness in his features.

"Not drunk this time, are you?" he joked, leaning in and kissing the tip of her nose. "Do you know what you're trying to do here?"

A playful smile lit up her face. "Perfectly well. Our wedding is such a short time away. We don't have to wait… if we don't want."

He turned his hand over and, with the backside, ran it over her cheek. Maeve's insides lurched, the action so reminding her of August.

"Why do you tempt me? I can wait."

She answered by pressing her lips to his, boldly sucking his bottom lip as she drew back, fighting a hankering to bite down and violently end the campaign.

Swallowing hard, she mustered up a lie. "But I cannot."

He moved without delay. One moment she was standing pressed against him, the next Maeve found herself swept off her feet, being carried to her room. She had thought having her own little space with an actual bed quite a luxury when she had first moved into the flat. Now she cursed the damned thing's existence.

Owen's mouth didn't stop moving as he carried her, either. With Maeve's hands laced behind his neck, he caressed her lips with his. When Maeve felt her body meet the mattress, she flattened out. Immediately, she was pressed into the quilting by the mass that was Owen's hard, muscled body, made firm by laborious work with hammer and iron. She gasped; having held his hand and even embraced him, she still had never realized how strapping his occupation had made him. He was almost as solid a weight over her as August.

August.

As Owen's hands began to work at her clothing, she thought of how swiftly August had done the same two nights prior. But with him, it had been different. With August, she had felt aflame, as though she would be consumed in brimstone if her clothing hadn't been removed at that very moment. Now, every small bit of flesh revealed felt as though it were scarred and desecrated, as though Owen found only ruin where August had discovered wealth.

His breath was raspy and hot as he kissed down her collar bone. "Wanted you for so long. Since the moment I saw you."

She opened her mouth, but knew anything said in response would be a lie. She hadn't wanted him that way. Ever. She appreciated his looks only in the way one admired any beautiful thing set by God on the green Earth.

"Maeve, did you hear me?"

"Aye."

He gave a small chuckle as he pulled back the lapel of her blouse and undid her lacings. Damn that she had worn the one which laced in the front. A moment later, her back arched involuntarily as Owen's mouth came down, causing the titillated peak to perk instantly.

She hadn't realized she had moaned until Owen's devilish gaze met hers. What surprised her more was not that she found the sensation enjoyable, but rather that she had found it familiar. As Owen's efforts widened, revealing the twin mound on the other side and giving it equal due, Maeve closed her eyes and thought of…

August.

Invoking the memory of his touch, his mouth, his eyes, his smell, she imagined it was August moving over her, driven by lust and carnal hunger. She allowed the delusion to overcome her, and when Owen spoke again, she had convinced herself it was August's voice she heard.

"I want you. Now. Let me take you."

Her fingers ran through his hair. B*londe hair? But August's hair is black, isn't it?*, she thought

It didn't matter. He was here. He was here, they were not drunk, and he wanted her. And Lord help her, she wanted him twice as much.

Maeve felt her head nod, granting permission. Oddly, he made no movement to remove her skirt, only reaching under instead, easing her knickers down and then off. The intruding garment was tossed away as her legs unfolded and fell to the side, inviting him to enter.

And he did. Perhaps his passion was simply too consuming that he hadn't wanted to wait for her to be nude? It didn't matter. August was in her, and she was in heaven.

His tempo wasn't the measured, intoxicating pace as before, but a feverish pounding that made the oak frame of the bed tap out a marching cadence against the wall. She found it consuming: so rough, so driven, so animalistic, quickly bringing her to that wonderful apex he had driven her to thrice before.

"Like that," Maeve commanded, and her words brought her reward. The endorsement enticed her lover, made him work into her harder.

It shouldn't be possible to feel this good, she thought. Lord, she finally understood why this was meant to be kept within marriage. She knew the act could leave her with child, and oh, she would have quite a brood on her hands if she had been free to engage in this bliss at will.

"Maeve, it's coming. I'm going to… I should pull –"

"No!" She weaved her hands behind and dug her fingers into his backside, bringing the push and pull of their bodies into dizzying proximity.

"But I'll –"

"I want it!" Maeve yelled. "I want you. I love you. I love you… I …. I…. Oh…"

She could feel both their bodies beginning to tremble, to shudder, to wash over the edge of that magnanimous sensation.

With a feral growl, she heard her name called aloud. She gave into the pull, allowed herself to be swept away in unison, and called out his name in a licentious echo.

As his form slumped atop her, she thought it odd that his arms should be corded so tightly. She was limp, utterly spent and floating ten feet off the bed. He was eerily poised, as though ready to strike.

"What … did you say?"

The chill in his voice reminded her of the ache that had been in her dear da's voice when he had been delivered the news that Sine had died. More than hopeless, it sounded bitter, as though God himself had just smote him.

"Your… name?" Maeve questioned, perplexed.

Owen backed away, locking her gaze into his. She had never seen him so crimson, so glistening, even when working at the anvil.

"My name?" Owen bit back. "My name!?"

"Yes, I said… Oh God!"

No, she had not said his name. She had not said Owen at all.

"I said…"

"You said…"

"August," they both confirmed together.

Owen was across the room in the blink of an eye, his pants hanging loosely off his hips as he paced fiercely. Pulling his fingers through his hair, he danced on the edge of brutality, his nostrils flaring, his eyes bulged and red.

"I trusted you!" he finally screamed at her, collapsing on the floor next to the bed where Maeve sat trying to conceal her shame and her flesh with the pillow. "I heard rumors, but you assured me! You swore to me it was just talk. I believed you. I believed everything you told me. I said, 'No, not my Maeve. She would never do something so heinous, so ugly. So traitorous.' What have you done?"

Her voice was barely a whisper. "What I thought was necessary. The cottage. He was going to –"

"You laid with him, didn't you?" Looking down at the purity retained by the quilt where they had just been, she knew she couldn't deny it. "When? How many times?"

"Twice, two nights ago."

"Two nights ago!?" he repeated, leaping back to his feet. "You lost your cottage more than two months ago. Why now? For the bakery? Was that the deal? Whore yourself to him and get a tidy income on the side? A way out of marrying me, maybe?"

"No! I swear. It was… a mistake. I still want to marry you. After the pub, we were both so drunk."

"I was three times as bloody drunk as either of you, and I managed to make it home without mounting anyone!"

Maeve didn't know if it was seconds, minutes, or hours that passed as she sat burning in her shame. Owen slid against a wall, white as snow and just as cold.

Finally, he muttered, "Why are you marrying me?"

"Because you are a good man," she answered without hesitation.

"And you are a good woman." He swallowed hard. "Or, you were."

"Will you still marry me, Owen?"

She felt miserable, and even she knew she was asking for a mercy not due her. Owen took several deep breaths, thinking quietly. She knew whatever his answer, she was to suffer from it no matter.

"Aye, I'll still marry you," he declared. "With one condition."

Seeing her chance at redemption, she leapt. "Anything."

"Give him back his damned bakery."

A look of confusion came over her, her eyes darting about the room.

"Move in with me. Tonight."

"But… The town will talk. They'll say –"

"You didn't care what they would say when you opened your legs to him."

The dagger burned as it plunged into her heart. He was right. Absolutely right and she had no cause to deny it.

He continued, "Seems as you don't care what's said of you and Grayson, you shouldn't care what's said of you and me. Surely you'd rather them click their tongues about you living with me than curse you knowing you gave your innocence away to an English mutt."

She nodded; they both knew it was the truth.

Owen rose, picking up Maeve's knickers from the floor and throwing them at her with a sigh. "Go to him. Tell him that I know what he did, so that he knows I'll strike him down dead in the street if ever he even dares speak to you again."

She surrendered. It was an escape from the horrid situation she had created. And it was better than she deserved. She knew better than to argue.

What had she lost, after all? August had never been hers.

"All right, Owen. I will."

24 The Cracking Mirror

It was night when Maeve reached Middle Lake. Westward wind nipped her ankles, blowing under her skirt and through her, making her skin numb. But the pain. The horrible, twisting pain for what she had just done and for what she was about to do… The wind couldn't numb her far enough down to rid her of that.

Shepherd's Bluff stood cloaked in darkness, every window empty of light. For a moment she hoped he wasn't home, but her instincts told her better. Almost like the Almighty was still toying with her, she found the servant's door unlocked. In the silence of the night, she allowed her feet to carry her through the kitchen and up the stairs to August's door. Looking left and right, relief filled Maeve when the halls were empty. It was past eight; the staff would be in the servants' wing, Caroline would be in her room, and August would be…

Well, she didn't rightly know. The realization made her cognizant of just how little she knew of this man she had nearly destroyed her life over. During the time she had stayed at Shepherd's Bluff, if August was not in his study, and if he was not sleeping, then he somehow found a way to be with her. Never alone, of course; he had been cautious always to have someone else with them.

Goodness, had she really been so blind? Even as a host, the efforts he expended to spend time with her now seemed extreme in retrospect. When she was in a quandary, he sought to ease her. When she was in pain, he made means to comfort. When she was happy, it was nearly always because he was around. He loved her. It hadn't come from nowhere; it had been building for weeks, months maybe.

Slowly, she clenched her fist and raised it to the door. With a deep sigh, she rapped twice.

"Go away, Caroline."

Trembling, Maeve took the latch in her hand and pushed. August sat in his chair by the hearth, staring into the fire, his head held on the points of his fingertips, .

"I've told you, I don't wish to discuss it anymore. We set out for Cork on the morrow."

Maeve gasped. "You're leaving?"

August shot out of his seat. For a moment, he lingered by the chair, assessing her from afar.

"August, I… I came to say…"

"I love you."

"It doesn't matter."

"I know."

Maeve studied the fire in the silence, and August studied Maeve. Without the clock measuring their visit, each moment became timeless. Finally, Maeve turned toward the door.

"Owen knows," she said simply, little trace of regret in her tone. It was what it was. "You needn't leave. We'll go. Our lives our simpler than yours; it will be easier for us. I don't think Owen will tell anyone. That is, I'm pretty certain."

"I'm not leaving because of you, I have to… I have business in Norwich which requires my attention."

Her shoulders dropped, thinking herself foolish for supposing everything August did was her cause. "Oh well, all the same."

"Come with me."

"Do not mock me."

He smiled and crossed the room, taking her in his arms though her body remained stiff beneath his embrace.

"I'm not jesting. I supposed you regretted what we'd done, given the way you acted the next morning. But now, you're here. You're here, and I can see in your eyes how much you're hurting, trying to tell me good bye. You love me, Maeve, and you know I love you. I need you. Come. Come with me to Norwich."

"To be your whore?"

"To be my lover."

She scoffed, trying to free herself from his hold. "I'm going to be Owen's wife. Wife. I cannot live in shame and sin."

"No, but you'll live in regret and despair," August stated, releasing her. "What can he give you that I cannot? Moreover, can he give you anything the likes that I can? In Norwich, you'll have fine clothes and furnishings, servants to wait on you, comforts beyond your imagination."

"And be a social outcast and branded sinner. For certain, Owen can't give me castles and gowns and diamonds, but with him, I can hold my head high when I walk down the street. Remember, I wanted it all. You can't give that to me. Not here. Not in Norwich. Not anywhere."

Grabbing Maeve's arm, August spun her around. "He can't give you it all, either."

"Meaning?"

With a knowing smirk, August declared, "You don't love him. How can he possibly make you happy?"

"Happiness in marriage? Do you know how rare that is?"

Again, he grinned. "Your parents had it."

"And your parents did not."

He released her and sunk back, his smile faltering.

Maeve huffed. "I'm sorry. I didn't mean to say something so cruel. Let's just… make an end of it. I must go. He's waiting for me."

"Guinevere, Maeve."

"What?"

Looking up, his eyes brimming with tears, August locked his gaze to hers. In that moment, he looked ever so the boy she had played with years before, innocent and trusting and hers.

"Guinevere loved Lancelot, but she kept her marriage vows to Arthur, and it ended up destroying everyone involved. It was only after years of the pain and emptiness and torture that Guinevere realized it didn't matter how closely she kept to her duties, she would never be complete without Lancelot. You'll never be complete without me, and I… I never can serve my conscious knowing that I let you slip through my fingers."

She found her hand in his as he raised it to his lips. Her knees were shaking as she looked into his eyes and saw the veracity of every word. How dare he use their childhood comforts at this moment. How dare he twist her heart, wringing from it the truth which flowed in the weight of his gaze.

"I have to go."

"But be back before morning, darling. Our coach comes at dawn."

Owen's teeth gnashed. In a harsh tone that sounded like he was invoking a curse, he hissed, "Grayson."

Maeve saw no point in denying it. "He is returning to England, and has asked …" Her voice cracked as the airiness dried her throat. She swallowed hard, trying to make her voice audible. "I will go with him. I love him."

Owen's countenance shifted yet again, consumed with devastation. Somehow, in this small room, they all had become something bigger. Owen was Ireland, August was England, and Maeve the horrid reality between the two. Her last piece of courage nearly broke as a tear rolled down Owen's cheek and he fell to his knees, his body shuddering from the pressure of withholding his sobs.

"Does… *my* love mean nothing to you, then?"

Maeve looked away and raised her hand to her mouth, biting her finger to feel a physical manifestation and some measure of what her heart was being forced to endure.

Some time passed, neither speaking, until at last in a voice filled with grief and sorrow, Owen asked, "Will you marry him?"

She shook her head in denial. She loved August, of that there was no doubt. But Maeve also had no doubt that while words could move hearts and pledges change fate, an official union between she and August could never be.

Owen let out another unsteady sigh. "Does he love you?"

She nodded, holding back her own tears. "He has told me so. I think…" Her mind traced back their history, even back to their youth. "I think he always has."

"Good," Owen concluded. Maeve's head cocked into a curious pose. He gave her a half smile and rose shakily to his feet. "You're about to go through hell, and I'm sorry there's nothing to be done for it. Take comfort in each other, because you sure won't find it anywhere else."

Three steps brought them face to face again. In a way most gentle and sincere, Owen leaned in and kissed her forehead. Maeve's eyes fluttered closed, and she felt unable at last to hold back the rain of tears that had threatened.

"I do love you, Maeve," he whispered as he leaned his forehead into hers. "Change your mind, I will not hesitate. Pure as snow or black as night, I'll always be yours."

"Take care of Da, Owen." How could she face him, tell him of what was to become of her? Running off to England to be the kept woman of the man who had destroyed the home her mother, his wife, had birthed her and died in? She wouldn't insult him by appearing to look for acceptance where none would be found. "August will… I will send money. Tell him I'm sorry. Tell him… it is my place."

She felt numb as she closed the flat door. Pressing on, Maeve caught sight nearby of a familiar carriage. Its presence did not surprise her. She suspected he might follow. She knew he wouldn't risk letting her go so easily.

As August reached out, offering his hand, Maeve also heard the anguished cries in desperation from the building behind her. She collapsed, August barely snatching her arms before she fell like a dog into the street.

With a shimmy and shift, the horses neighed and the carriage pulled away, closing out Maeve's old life. August's arm circled around her as the carriage passed the gates of the cemetery. He drew her close as her tears came on now in full force and without damper. August leaned over and kissed the top of Maeve's head, smoothing her sticky, dampened hair.

"Time will see this right," he muttered, kissing her once again. "Maeve, this will come to pass. Everything will be set right."

As they rolled out of Killarney, Maeve looked up into August's loving gaze. His comforting smile brought the tears under control.

"Please, tell me I've not just doomed my soul for nothing. I have just forever branded myself a Jezebel in the eyes of all Killarney," she said. "If I'm to burn in hellfire for this, so be it, but let your love burn twice as hot until then. Tell me it's not in vain. Tell me you love me, and will love me forever."

Now, he turned his frame and placed both his hands on her cheeks, pulling her toward him and kissing her chastely.

"I swear to you, Maeve O'Connor, I love you, and I will do everything in my power to make you happy and comfort you. I will always treasure you, and I will never leave your side."

She smiled up to him, feeling no doubt in the honesty and sincerity of his pledge. "I love you, August, and always shall. I swear, I will be yours forever."

25 | To England

Even as the ample sun tried to warm Caroline's skin, the wind whipped over the surface of the water and hit the side of the boat like a sheet of ice. She pulled her coat tighter, nudged her hat down over her ears. Jefferson, wanting to be ever the protector, even from the forces of nature, wrapped his arms around her from behind and pulled her into his chest.

"We should get you below deck," he whispered into her ear. "Your cheeks are whiter than June lilies."

Caroline smiled. The care and love evident in his words warmed her more than all the layers of clothing.

"At least up here I can warm in the sunlight," she replied. "Please do not misunderstand my concern, but why again did you and August feel it so necessary to return to England now, when we do not wed until spring?"

Jefferson had been quite insistent on taking up residence in Norwich post haste, though his reasoning failed to inform. Barely four months had passed since the day they had first chanced upon each other in the Killarney market. That they would be wed soon contented her, so she felt no temptation to chance his ire to learn his true motivation.

August had been only too eager to give his blessing when Jefferson asked. The transformation in her brother surprised Caroline to no end. She had fretted that August would demand a proper society pairing, perhaps with a duke or an earl, if one should have become available, but Jefferson had no aristocratic lineage on which to stand. All he had was a heart full of devotion and tenderness. Miraculously, that had proven enough in August's eyes.

When Caroline had learned, however, what had happened between Maeve and August, it all made more sense.

"You miss England," Jefferson noted in brief, which indeed was true, then added teasingly, "True, Mrs. Schand?"

The flutter of Caroline's heart dulled quickly when she looked aft and saw poor Maeve, green-faced and lacking sea legs. The ship had listed starboard and port for hours since leaving from Cork. A fortnight stay in the port city had given August enough time to finish the business of the family's holdings via courier to Woodrow, and gave Maeve chance to stock up on clothing, none of which she seemed to have brought with her from Killarney.

August was at her side, continuing his attempts to ease her, plying her with tea and warm blankets. Neither had seemed to help much.

Excusing herself from Jefferson's company, Caroline crossed deck. August cast his sister a desperate plea with his eyes. Maeve was half slung over the side of the ship, between bouts of retching. August had his arm securely hooked around her waist, keeping her from falling overboard.

"Caroline," he said in a broken tone, "what to do? Perhaps we should have booked passage to Southampton and made the rest of the way by land?"

Caroline sat by Maeve, wrapping her arm about her and coaxing her back. August drew the half-filled mug of now cold tea to her lips. Maeve sniffed it once and looked as though she might need to return to hanging over the side.

"What is that?" Caroline asked, nodding at the mug.

"Earl Grey."

One of the porters chanced by, and Caroline called to him. "Sir, is there any other tea aboard? Chamomile, perhaps?"

He nodded his head vigorously and answered in thick Cockney tones. "I b'lieve so, ma'am. I think the Capt's gotta stash a'mint in 'is pantry."

Caroline smiled warmly, and the gesture was quickly reflected in the young man's face.

"Would you be so kind as to take our companion below deck, allow her to lay down a bit, and ask the Captain if she might have a bit of his mint tea?"

Maeve looked up and gave a slight grimace.

"Ah coors, ma'am. Up ya go now, lass!"

Taking both of Maeve's hands, he yanked, turning soon thereafter and draping her arm over his shoulders. August eyed her with great concern as the pair disappeared below deck, before sighing deeply. Caroline felt a pang of guilt for the question she knew she must ask.

Deciding the best route was a direct one, she looked at August squarely and laid it out.

"Is she ill because she is with child?"

August rolled his eyes and scoffed. "Heavens no."

"Don't disparage me for asking." She shifted about. "You may not have reason to believe so of your dear little sister, but I am not wholly without knowledge of the goings on between men and women." She glanced to Jefferson across the deck, giving him a smile and a wave. "The walls at the inn in Cork may have been thick, but some portion of your caterwauling came through."

August looked maliciously at Jefferson for a moment before his expression softened.

"Fine. Yes, Maeve and I are well known to each other. But no, she is not with child. There was evidence before we left Cork."

"What if that should change?" Caroline returned flatly. "What if you discover at some time in the future she is with child? What would you do then?"

The corner of his mouth curled, breaking finally into a full, brimming smile. "I would love them both with a passion not befitting the bounds of this earth. I would love them beyond my mortal coil, and even beyond death itself."

Angling her eyes, her expression begged suggestion. "This is how you would love your child?"

Confusion passed before understanding swallowed his features. "I see what you're driving at."

"It is an interesting situation in which you find yourself, August," she continued, laying a hand on his knee. "I cannot say I envy you. I have been curious since you announced that Maeve would accompany us to Norwich if you had discussed with her what she is likely to find there."

August grumbled beneath his breath. "The topic has not yet arisen"

Caroline said nothing further, but gave him a stern look not unlike that of a disappointed mother at her petulant child. He squirmed under the intensity of his sister's gaze. With a huff, August rose to his feet, took off his gloves, first left then right, and slapped the leather over his hand.

"Fine, yes," he conceded. "I will talk with her."

At August's exit below deck, Jefferson made way to Caroline again. He pulled her beside him, tracing the outer edge of her earlobe that poked out from under her hat with his fingertip.

"Problems, my peach?"

She grinned, feeling the comfort of his embrace. "August has told Maeve nothing of Norwich."

"Noth… Nothing at all?"

Jefferson's wide eyes told Caroline that he was just as disappointed and surprised as she.

"When does he intend to tell her? We'll be there in only a few hours."

"I hope he's telling her now, though poor dear. She's so sick. Nevertheless, he's assured me that she isn't expecting."

"Well, that is a blessing," Jefferson concurred. He leaned over and kissed Caroline's forehead. "Don't fret, angel. Somehow, all this will find a way to work out. I know it seems impossible now, but just give it time."

Caroline had seen enough of the way love filled the room whenever August and Maeve were together the last few weeks and, if she thought back further, in those days when Maeve had stayed to Shepherd's Bluff, to know that Jefferson was right. Yet she couldn't shake the feeling that this could never be. On Maeve's side, she had been ostracized in Ireland. She had tried to send word to her father in Killarney. He refused to acknowledge her. August and Caroline had already lost both mother and father, but they would certainly be subjected to the same level of public scrutiny once back at Norwich, and Maeve would be burned by it as well, no doubt. Even if she loved August one-tenth the amount he loved her, Caroline didn't know how much more Maeve could endure in the pursuit of that love.

She sighed and relaxed deeper into Jefferson's hold. "I hope you are right. Still, I cannot fathom how August plans to balance the two."

26 The Roost

~Boston, MA~
Late September, 1872

"What did you mean I was named after my father?"

Blessed Mary, don't children hear everything?

The child's big blue eyes, too large for one so small, looked up through the black curls brushing over her face in the autumnal breeze. Maeve hesitated, wondering if she ignored it perhaps Augusta would not insist. She curled her fingers around the child's and pulled her more insistently toward the flat.

"Ma, my father was named Augusta?"

Maeve couldn't help but to give a laugh. "No, Goosie. Your father's name was August. Not exactly the same, but close."

"If I was a boy, would you have named me Maevibald?"

"No, I imagine you would have been named…" Maeve stopped herself short. Augusta noticed the abrupt cut off and turned a familiar grin. "I probably would have named you Aurora, after my da," Maeve quickly recovered.

The lass seemed satisfied with the response as Maeve turned the corner of Federal and Congress towards the old wood warehouse remade to house Irish. A few of Augusta's playmates passed. Augusta giggled and waved, her dark, woolen cloak batting about in the wind.

After a quiet contemplation, she spoke very matter-of-factly. "Your da is dead."

Maeve nodded slowly. "Yes."

"Somebody shot him."

Silence acknowledged it as so.

Augusta stopped completely. "Is *my* father dead?"

Maeve bit her bottom lip, hesitating and deliberately plotting what to say. She had never lied to the child, but had found remarkable ways to stretch, pass over, and avoid the truth. She had become the master of saying much without saying anything at all.

But Augusta was catching on to the game. Perhaps even sharper than her intellectual father, she had learned to be direct with her questions.

Maeve relented to her sincere, innocent gaze. "No, Goosie, he's alive," she sighed. "Only, he and I… Well, after you were born…"

"Did you have a row?" She blinked twice, her eyes soft and patient.

"Something of that sort, yes, dear. We reached a … juncture that we could not cross, and he did something which hurt me very, very much."

"Will I ever see him again?"

"I'm not certain." She paused. "I hope so."

Maeve was thankful that she hadn't asked further after her father. In earnest, she didn't know what she would say if she did.

Did you love him?

Yes, of course.

Then, why did you leave him?

Because I love you too, mo chroi, *and I had to keep my promise.*

But how would such a wee darling understand the truth without thinking the circumstances were her making?

The next morning, a scattering of snow greeted them. Augusta squealed, wanting to run downstairs and toss about in it before it would surely melt away with the sun. As they walked back up the North streets, Maeve watched the wee one giggle and play, sweeping her mitten-covered hand over the top of anything within reach and sending snow flying.

"Mornin' to you, Maeve." Tara peeked out from her stoop, expecting their arrival. She had a woolen blanket at the ready and quickly swept crimson-cheeked Augusta into its warmth.

"Morning, Tara. She's a tad bit stirred today. Sorry if she gives you any trouble."

Tara laughed and kissed Augusta's nose. "Goosie be trouble? Ne'er mention the idea."

She turned the child around to face Maeve as she leaned over and kissed her on the nose tenderly.

"Be a good lass, now. All right?"

"I shall be nothing but honey and sunshine."

Maeve pulled back. Augusta's inflection had been a curious particularity, but had leaned more Irish. In that moment, however, she sounded perfectly English, and so very much like her father. So… appropriate.

"Yes," she sighed in distraction. "Won't be long today. The snow might slow business."

Maeve heard the echo of Augusta's giggle as she walked back down the stairs. Tara had minded Augusta since they'd come to Boston. She had known Owen's father years before. Now she watched Augusta every day while Maeve worked, supporting to some degree all three of them. Tara was an angel to Augusta, a strong protector and loyal nana. It was a fine trade.

Maeve walked hurriedly the remaining distance as the melting snow began to seep through her clothes. For once, she felt herself longing to arrive at the bakery early. On a chilly day like this one, the heat of the ovens and the smell of the warm bread would be a Godsend.

It seemed she was not wholly alone in this sentiment. To her surprise – and frankly, her dismay – the bakery storefront was nearly filled to capacity. Even at mid-morning, the number of eager customers was impressive.

"Sarah?" Maeve called out as she made her way through the small crowd of a dozen or so. "How goes it?"

A mousy, rust-haired girl barely sixteen gave a sigh far too hefty for her own modest size. "It's like we're selling tickets to Heaven this morning, Mrs. Murphy," she returned over the crowd. "Sam's already put third rounds through the ovens, and they're still not slowing down."

Maeve nodded as she took off her overcoat, ducked behind the counter, and tied a white shop apron around her waist and back. For three straight hours she couldn't find time to draw breath. Finally, as afternoon settled in, the tide subsided. Sarah and Sam were given permission to leave as Maeve stayed behind alone in case any mid-afternoon customers wandered in.

She sat for a moment on a stool out of open view, but still with an ear on the front door. Sure enough, some short time later, the store door opened.

"Good afternoon," she said as she emerged from the back room. "What can I get… for…"

Her voice trailed off as she squinted and tried to make out the nature of the omen that had just entered her bakery.

"Owen?"

He nodded, snowflakes falling off his white-flecked hat, as though he wasn't a ghost of her past returning to haunt her.

"Maeve," he said in greeting.

Whether it was a smile or grimace that met her as she stared into his face, Maeve wasn't certain. He seemed to be making up his mind as to whether or not he was happy to see her too. They stared at each other without word or waver. Owen seemed just as uncertain as how to proceed with their reunion after nearly three years as she.

Finally, Maeve broke the silence. "What are you doing here?"

"Something's happened."

Her heart sank in morbid anticipation. Her mouth went dry. "Has someone… died?"

He shuffled a bit, looking with great concentration at his feet. "No. Saints be praised, no. What I mean to say is, something's happened to me."

"What?"

"They know," he stated ominously, and though there was no more than that, Maeve understood in a moment who they were and what they had discovered. "I'm not sure how. They came looking for me."

Her own heartbeat drowned everything else from her ability to hear. She felt weak in the knees as sweat broke across her brow.

"How much do they know?" she heard herself ask, though it seemed as though it was coming from somewhere else in the room.

He gave a small shrug before he answered in a quaking voice tinged with regret. "All of it."

She was nearly in tears. "Then why are you here?"

The words had barely escaped her lips when the door opened again, and two blue-swathed bizzies, night sticks in hand and scowls on their faces, eyed her warily.

"I'm sorry, Maeve," Owen said sincerely. The air was quickly becoming thinner and thinner. "I hadn't a choice; if I agreed to take them to you, they said they'd let me go. They know all about the Fenians, the ones who got away like me. Luckily, I had a bigger fish for them."

"Is this her?" one of the bizzies growled.

"Yeah," Owen offered. "This is Maeve O'Connor."

Before Maeve could reckon the turn of events, one bizzie had her arms behind her back while the other was slipping something cold and metallic around her wrists.

"Come along, now. Don't give us a fight," he demanded.

Her thoughts ran to Augusta. She felt her stomach drop to the floor, wondering what would become of the tender little girl she loved with all her heart. Where would she go? Who would take care of her?

In a startling moment of realization, Maeve knew who. Owen had arranged this, which meant *he* knew and was likely on his way to Boston, if not already here.

The bizzie pushed her through the door of her own bakery, and a myriad of passersby turned in shock and horror.

"Maeve O'Connor," the other bizzie declared, making sure, she was certain that a good number of people were within earshot to bear witness. "You're being taken into custody and charged with the kidnapping of Augusta Grayson."

27 Revelations and Relations

~Norwich, England~
January 1867

Maeve tried to take ease as the coach swayed side to side and traveled the road from Yarmouth to Norwich. She was so thankful for one night's rest at the inn portside so that she could recover from the ship. Her inability to spontaneously sprout sea legs was a great embarrassment. She longed to have August beside her in the night to hold as she had in Cork. Instead, Caroline was her bedfellow. She realized she should have anticipated as much, given that they were now within the peripheral vision of English society.

The proximity indeed made her wonder just how August planned to explain her presence. Would he pass her off as a servant? Caroline's maid? Further, would she care? Within the confines of Meadowlark, she hoped that August would still be August, and that Lord Grayson would not reappear. Outside of Meadowlark, she understood that appearances would have to be maintained.

Seated across from her, August looked more anxious than a plump goose on Christmas morning. Maeve parted her lips to ask after him for the third time in the last hour, but he silenced her before she had a chance.

"Please," he begged, tilting his head to the side.

"I'm not trying to be a bother, August," she tried to assure him. "You should know that I don't care what a cackle of old English hens say. Same as the Killarney chickens with better dresses. I can endure."

He looked amused by her declaration, leaning his head over on his bunched fist and hiding his smirk from view, his elbow crooked to allow the arm to support. His grin evaporated after a few moments when his face again resumed a nervous demeanor.

"You amaze me. You have so much faith in me. I hope… I hope I prove worthy of the sacrifice."

The words were eerily similar to a declaration she had made just a short time ago to Owen. The thought made a chill rush down her frame.

Brushing aside the momentary anxiety, Maeve thanked the saints that Jefferson had suggested two smaller coaches be taken to Norwich rather than a shared larger one. Within the confines of theirs, the curtains drawn so no one could see in and the sounds of the horse's steady *clap clomp clap clomp* preventing any muted sounds of their conversation from being overheard by the driver, Maeve felt at ease to take what actions – and make which sounds – she so willed.

She moved near to August, who seemed at first apprehensive, then relaxed. Letting out a sigh as he put his arm about her, he pulled her close to his side and kissed her on the forehead.

"How did someone like me capture your affections?"

She crooked her neck so that she could look up into his green eyes, like they were a little piece of Ireland given to her whenever she so desired. "I still wonder at how someone of my birth could ever hope to win the love of an English lord."

August leaned in and kissed her, as though this was a counter to her question and she had been a fool for asking it.

"We are all equal in the sight of God. It is only in the eyes of man that we find the faults of this world within."

The warmth of his words washed over her, through her, around her. August took Maeve's hand in his own, raising it slowly to his lips and placing the most tender, heart-felt kiss, never taking away his gaze. He then leaned over again and met her lips chastely at first, before slowly pushing the kiss, marking his every movement with passion.

"*Mo chroi*, I need to…"

His lips found hers again, then trailed down over her jaw. His arms circled round, drawing Maeve's body flush to his as well as could be done while seated.

A ragged breath broke the strength of her voice. "You need to…?"

He paused as his mouth hovered over her neck. "*Tá grá agam duit*, Maeve."

Maeve's mouth curled into an unfettered smile. He had told her he loved her, but never in Irish. "I love you. So much."

Without further hesitation, August moved his hands to her hips and pulled Maeve unto his lap so that she found herself straddling him. She wondered if she should resist. But after all, they were alone, and the cadence of the horses outside would cover up any utterances from within.

Which was a lucky bit of fate. She had learned from the last few weeks of their frequent indulgences that laying with August often led to an inability to subdue her moans and screams. The pleasure, far beyond any thrill she could have anticipated, made her overlook that very dangerous reality of to what such frequent rendezvous could lead.

But now and then, the question would occur to her: how it had come to pass that August and she could have indulged in each other's company so frequently without conceiving? She concluded that the Almighty really did answer prayers. Yet Maeve was surprised to find herself slightly bereft. A tug in her heart wondered if perhaps she might like to discover that she was carrying August's child.

Not another thought could be spared on idle daydreaming for now, however, as August fisted her hair and pulled her face nigh to his. His lips crashed against hers with abandon and Maeve found herself giving way to instinct as he pulled the fabric of her skirt and petticoat from underneath, allowing the pulsating portion of her person to align to his with no more than the fabric of his pants and the thin cotton of her knickers between. August's expression was partly shock and partly thrill. Maeve knew this was hardly the most appropriate place for an interlude, but she couldn't scrape together enough wits to care.

The pale skin of Maeve's knees and thighs revealed a sacred path. His hand traipsed back down the flesh slowly, achingly tantalizing Maeve's senses with want, with need. He moved his hands back up again, this time underneath the fabric to find the hem of the knickers she wore. August looped his fingers down over the waistline and pulled with all his might, shearing the garment in two.

Hardly wanting to sit in wait, Maeve mirrored his actions, grasping at the waist line of his pants and pulling suggestively. He lifted himself off the bench as she held onto his shoulders to keep from falling, then lowered them just enough to let his erection free.

"To make love to you in England..." he breathed, letting his finger fall tantalizingly across her thigh. "I've dreamed of having you in so many ways… In so many places…"

Maeve gasped, as he renewed his efforts with his mouth on her neck, hands full of her posterior, pulling her closer. She had supposed the act would begin to become familiar, dull, but every time held just as much, if not more, of a thrill. It reminded her of the first time she had tasted chocolate and how the mixture of sweet and bitter overwhelmed her senses. Subsequent tastings never brought the thrill of discovery that the first encounter had, but each occasion was just as pleasing.

Maeve lifted herself and came down unto him slowly, savoring the sensation of his filling her. August's hands planted on her hips as he began coaxing her frame in an enticing cycle of wax and wane. Though at first content to let only her body navigate, he soon began thrusting upward with each pass that he guided down. The duality of push and pull drove him deeper into her than ever she recalled. Their eyes locked as he uttered "I love you" like a benediction.

Weaving her fingers through his hair as she rode out the crest of her climax, Maeve pulled his face into her breasts. She successfully subdued most of her screams of pleasure as thc ebbing tide was met by a new crashing wave: August's arrival to the shores of ecstasy.

They stayed joined above and below for some time. Eventually, the carriage slowed and Maeve began to take note of the sounds of street life outside their private paradise. August shifted to the right and opened the flap of the curtain only enough to peer outside.

"We're coming into Norwich now, Maeve." He placed the lightest peck on her chin before allowing her to fall back to the other side of the carriage. He pulled his pants back up and examined warily the shorn pieces of cotton sitting on the cushion next to him. "I'm sorry about that."

"I am not."

It was delightful to see him smile back, though quickly his mood seemed to darken and his brow creased under the weight of his apparent worry.

"August, you can't keep whatever it is eating at you from me."

He looked up as though he was a child caught kicking the chickens. Before he could make an excuse, Maeve narrowed her eyes and stared him down. With a sigh, his body relaxed against the bench, resolved to share whatever woe he had been carrying.

"I have been remiss," he offered. "I've kept something from you that I should have made known long ago."

She tried to quell the sudden pull of her stomach and show him only confidence. "Whatever it is, I assure you, I'll understand."

He melted at her words. "Bless God and all his creation, I hope that is true." He swallowed hard before straightening himself and smoothing out his coat and pants. "I love you. I know I have said this before, but I will say it once more that you may have no doubt. I love you: beyond rich, beyond poor, beyond lord and peasant, Anglican and Catholic, Irish and English. Beyond any measure of time or wealth or ruin, I love you. No greater truth has ever been spoken. But there is a truth. A horrid, unavoidable, undeniable truth – a burden so heavy as I do not know that I could bear it should it cause you slight. What I mean to say is –"

"Meadowlark!"

The carriage made a hard stop, Maeve's body jolting and eyes fluttering as the door of the coach opened. August grimaced, looking as though he were trying to decide whether or not to continue unabated. His decision was made for him by Caroline, who tentatively poked her head into the carriage expectantly.

"I don't know about you," she uttered with a half-smile, though somewhat warily, as though she had somewhat expected to open the door to find a lion ready to strike, "but I could stand with a strong cup of tea."

Maeve nodded and August muttered something under his breath. The coachman presented his hand as she descended. August hesitated but at last emerged and fell in step behind Caroline, with whom Maeve locked arms to be led in fair parade step toward the entry of a veritable palace.

If she had been impressed by Shepherd's Bluff in Killarney, she was in awe of Meadowlark. The differences were striking; it was more refined, built of stately grey, square-cut stone. Truly an impressive sight, it appeared more a fortress than a house.

"Now, Maeve, don't you worry about a thing," Caroline said as she rubbed a gloved hand over hers. "Just remember, such arrangements aren't so unusual. In fact, just a generation or two ago, they were considered commonplace."

"Jesus, Mary, and Joseph!" Maeve exclaimed as she turned with a disbelieving frown. "First August, now you. Whatever are the two of you going on about?"

Caroline's smile evaporated in a cloud of bitter rage. She snapped her whole body in August's direction. "You didn't tell her!"

Defensively, August's hands flew out. "I was on edge of doing so, but you interrupted."

Caroline took no comfort in his assurance. "Oh, August, how could you! This is so uncouth!"

"Please!" Maeve shouted over their escalating battle as she stared down both of the Grayson siblings.

"August?"

The voice was sweet, feminine and full of joy. It came from behind, from the doorway of the house, Maeve realized a moment later when she turned back and looked up at the woman who had just emerged. She was a beauty like those in the paintings August kept at Killarney, complete with hair soft as pale, red roses and crimson lips. She wore a fine dress, delicately pink, though not too detailed. A knitted shawl was pulled taut around her shoulders to defend against chill, though Maeve was certain she was trembling nonetheless. And her eyes! How they startled, like the still, azure blue of Middle Lake in the crisp of winter.

Then Maeve's insides lurched as her eyes lowered down the redhead's frame and took in the view of her swollen belly.

August stepped forward and offered his hands to the gravid woman and lovingly kissed her cheek. He turned and spoke, though the pounding of Maeve's heart in her ears drowned out his voice. His words haunted as she swirled into blackness.

"Maeve, may I present Amelia Grayson."

Her mind reeled, attempting to find a piece of reason that would allow for another Grayson, one heretofore unknown. A sister-in-law? But then, August had no brother. Nor another sister, at least none of which she had ever heard. A cousin, perhaps? Yes, that could… must be it. Amelia must be August's cousin.

Feeling the sense of woe leave her, Maeve gave a respectful nod of her head. "Miss Grayson," she greeted. "How do you do?"

It was then that the coachman, perhaps sensing Maeve' faux pax, approached and whispered to her. "Pardon, Miss, but you'd do well to address Lady Grayson properly."

But that was impossible, she thought. August's mother had been Lady Grayson, and she was dead. There would only be another Lady Grayson if August was… That was, if Amelia was August's…

Maeve's vision blurred, then clouded over.

"Dear Lord, August!" Lady Grayson shouted. "August! August, quickly, catch her!"

27 Our Lady of Mercy

The multihued glare blinded. A small cushion sat behind her head. Other than the dizziness of disorientation, she was comfortable, laying on a bed, or perhaps a sofa. The fire crackled across the room, and the delicate smell of lavender permeated her senses.

"She's coming to!"

August's voice was an equal balance of joy and relief. He sat beside her, leaned over, a smile beaming. As her eyes labored to adjust, Maeve again reveled in just how beautiful he was; his ebony hair was tousled and his eyes looked weary and red. He had been crying, but why?

She smiled back, growing more curious with each moment, a sense of unease bubbling up within.

"Did I swoon?"

A delicate and melodious English woman spoke in reply. "Yes, she'll be fine now. Truly, August, under the circumstances, I wouldn't be so –"

"Ow! Good Lord!"

August landed on the floor with a thud as Maeve's clenched fist made contact with that no-longer-so-beautiful face. Her temples pounded as she sat up much too quickly and recalled arriving to Meadowlark only to find …

"Lady Grayson," Maeve hissed, sitting up and folding her arms over her chest as she took in the astonished face of a woman seeing her husband flat on the floor.

She looked past the blanched wife and took in her surroundings. It was a parlor, its pomp and décor not so unlike that of Shepherd's Bluff in temperament, but multiplied in multitudes. She had apparently been deposited on a burgundy chaise, and a matching sofa was across the way on which the English Lady sat eying the Irish lass warily.

Amelia gave Maeve a quick nod before resuming her contemplative study. Finally, she muttered meekly, "It's very nice to meet you, Miss O'Connor, though I'm certain you do not think the same."

"Hardly seems it," August agreed as he finally collected himself off the floor. He looked to Maeve with the most sympathetic and pained expression she had ever witnessed on him. For a moment, her love for him overrode her rage, and Maeve felt herself weaken. Then, foolishly he added, "Though one could hardly blame her," and her fury raged anew.

"You damnable bastard!" Maeve yelled. "Is this what you meant? Is this why you couldn't give me my all!? Not because I'm poor and you're rich, or I'm Irish and you're English, but because you're already married!? May you burn in hell, August Grayson."

"*Mo chroí*," he invoked, "I've tried to tell you so many times, but all I could think was that you would leave me if you knew."

Her eyes flashed down. "Or worse!"

August reached for her, and despite Maeve's best efforts to try and stay civilized, her foot flew out from under her skirt and cracked into his shin. Doubling over, hopping on one foot and nursing the afflicted limb with his hands, he babbled incoherently, and she wondered as to where she should wallop him next.

"August!" Amelia broke in.

He turned to her, brow furrowed like a puppy who had been abashed.

"Perhaps Miss O'Connor would understand best if I explained everything to her. In any course, I don't believe I'm as likely to suffer as many blows."

August looked unsure. "I don't think she's in a mood to talk, Mel."

Amelia scoffed and grunted as she slowly rolled herself off the sofa, her defined bump becoming more pronounced under her loose-fitted dress.

"She's giving you no less than you deserve, and you well know it. It is a fault most grievous you have shown with disregard to Miss O'Connor. You went to Ireland in part to prove to yourself that you were not your father, and proved only that you are too truly his progeny."

August's face turned bright red as he struggled to keep himself contained. He hissed back at her through gritted teeth, "This is nothing like that; I never wooed her with false promises of acceptance. I made it clear that we could never be together as man and wife."

"Yes, August," she concurred. "That may be true, but nor did you tell her why. Now, let me try to make good this mess that you've created. Jefferson is seeing to Caroline in the library. Perhaps you may be of assistance there."

With a great huff, he bobbed his head quickly in a show of deference to his wife. Then he looked to Maeve once again, as though that mere look offered every apology for his misdeeds, and pleaded that she should consider thoroughly the argument about to be set before her, before leaving the room.

Amelia sauntered across the way, giving Maeve a full sweep of her eyes from tip to toe, and circling about in careful observance.

"August failed to convey to me the greatness of your beauty," she said simply. "You are, indeed, quite lovely."

Maeve couldn't determine if she aimed to demean her by sarcasm or was being sincere. In any case, she did not appreciate being sized as though she were a purchased rug.

"I'm glad I meet the lady's approval," she returned gruffly. "I did not know her husband had spoken of me. He did me no equal favor."

"Hmm, you must have spent much time together. You speak like him. Yes, August wrote me of you, and I've known of you for far longer, though I had no idea you were coming with him to Norwich until I received a message this morning. Luckily, I've had time to make arrangements for you, though now I wonder if you'll want to sleep in the same suite with him or not."

Maeve could barely believe what she was hearing. "The sa… You planned that August and I should…" She looked around the room and then back to where Amelia stood. "I admit that I am fairly confused."

"Good heavens, I simply cannot stand anymore," she answered despite the inquiry. "Maeve – may I call you Maeve? – won't you please sit? This may take some time to explain."

She worked with as much effort to sit as she had to stand. Fearing no more the truth of the moment, Maeve asked the simple question which had been most pressing to her sense of ease.

"Is it… August's?"

Amelia smiled and smoothed her hand over her tummy. "Yes, the child is August's. But let's not get ahead. Well, you clearly knew nothing of me. I am surprised Caroline did not tell you, but I assure you she is quite beside herself at the moment. She trusted August, but didn't see it her place to try to explain. Tell me how much do you know of Emmanuel and Eliza Grayson?"

Maeve was thoroughly confused. "August's father and mother?" Amelia nodded. "Emmanuel was a right disagreeable man, but I know August loved his mother dearly, but she died when he was young."

"More than that," Amelia added. "His mother was Irish as well, you know. August's grandfather, Ezekiel, purchased the land at Middle Lake from Eliza's family. He took August's father, then a young man, to survey it. It was on that journey that he met Eliza. She was from Belfast, and Anglican, though Ezekiel ultimately did not object to the union. August's father loved her dearly in the early days, I've heard. He was convinced that their love would endure, and that even though she was Irish, his society would come to accept her."

"They didn't though, did they?" Maeve asked with a bit of snipe in her tone. She was trying not to hate, trying not to loathe and despise Amelia, who – given their odd introduction – was being more than hospitable. "In English eyes, difference between an Irish Catholic and an Irish Protestant is like the difference between a dirty rat and a clean one."

"Indeed," Amelia said simply. "Well, Eliza eventually couldn't take it any more, and after Caroline was born, she decided that she was going back to Ireland. That's when August's father had the house at Middle Lake built, a last ditch effort to appease her, my mother supposed. Secretly, I think he was planning on stashing her there, out of the way. But it was the famine, and finding Irish labor strong enough to carry out such a project was difficult. Eliza tried to keep up hope. She even taught August to speak Irish. But this all went on at the height of the anti-Irish movement, and Eliza and Emmanuel came down on opposite sides. When it became clear that Eliza wasn't much longer for the world, however, he took her home to die. Caroline was left her behind; she was so young. But August went along. And that is where August met you."

"Aye, that part I know," Maeve interrupted, feeling her temper receding. She recalled the day Eliza had died, the day August ran into the forest.

The day they first had kissed.

Amelia looked at a now-beaming Maeve knowingly. The smug expression struck Maeve's nerve anew, and she quickly vanquished the grin from her face.

"He never forgot you, Maeve."

All the air had left the room, leaving Maeve gasping.

"August and I have known each other since we were children," Amelia continued. "He has dreamt of you from time to time. You may not believe it, but there was a time when I was quite jealous of you."

"Jealous? Of me?" Such a thing hardly seemed possible, and nary of use. After all, Amelia had wed the man Maeve loved, and was carrying his child to boot.

Amelia leaned in. "For my part. But I wasn't the only one who knew of you. August's father knew it too. And after watching Eliza go through such torment, he swore that no son of his would ever make the same mistake. He spent years trying to make August hate the Irish, but it didn't take. August was one of the most desired bachelors in Norwich, in all of England. But he never entertained a romance with another, much to Emmanuel's frustration. Even when wed, it was still your voice I heard him call in his sleep.."

"But then, why would he…" Maeve couldn't fathom why August would put such stock in his father's wishes. Then she realized that while he may not care of his own affair, there was still one for whom his socially-unacceptable actions could have had malicious impact. "Caroline."

Amelia seemed pleased at the quick summation. "Precisely, Caroline. If August should have acted out, Caroline would have been marred by association. August's father knew that once he passed, and after Caroline had wed, there would be no way to hold August back from finding you. So he gave August a choice. Marry someone 'acceptable,' or he'd disinherit Caroline. Then Emmanuel decided to foolproof his plan by making it binding. August would not inherit his estate, and Caroline her portion, unless we produced a child."

Maeve's eyes caught her furrowed brow, before Amelia sighed and added, "The doctor confirmed the pregnancy the day after Emmanuel died."

Maeve sat in silence for some minutes and turned over all that she had heard. As it all began to sink in, she felt her anxiety ease a good deal. Still, one thing was missing, one critical piece of information.

"But why did *you* do this?" Maeve swallowed hard. "Do you love him?"

She smiled sweetly. "In my way, but not as you do. One reason August and I have always been close is because our fathers were born of the same litter. Like August, I too fell in love with someone who … Well, it never could have been."

"He did not fight for you?" Maeve asked apprehensively.

"No, he wasn't as strong as that. He ceded to my father's threats," Amelia answered with great sadness. "It crushed me. So when my father told me I would wed August whether I wished it or not, I couldn't find it in my heart to care. I often think August agreed because of that, in part. I was so broken, so wounded, he could not bear to reject our engagement when our fathers announced it without first consulting us. August understood too that the engagement ended the maligning of my character at the rumors, mostly true, of course, of my affair with a servant."

It was then that Maeve realized that her and Amelia's fortunes had both been milked from the same cow. Amelia was the cream, and Maeve was the whey, both swirling in the same pail. They were both bound to the same man, yet distanced from him in different ways.

August's intentions or the nature of his marriage were not the sole misjudgment for which he must be held to account, however. He had provided a falsehood so scathing, Maeve wasn't certain forgiveness would ever be possible.

"I want you to read something," Amelia said, pulling Maeve from her thoughts.

She pointed to a wooden box on the table next to the chaise. Maeve pulled it to her lap and opened it.

"The one on top. Read it. That is the last post I received from August from Ireland. You might be interested in what it says."

"Irish can't read," Maeve countered.

Amelia smirked. "But you can." She folded her hands and set them atop her belly. "August taught you."

Atop a stack of envelopes lay one of ivory tone, its lettering distinctively in fine blank ink and made out to Lady Amelia Grayson, Meadowlark, Norwich, England. Maeve turned to her questioningly, but Amelia gave an insistent nod. Delicately, as if she were handling something sacrosanct, Maeve removed the folded pages from within and set the envelope aside.

"Dear Amelia,

I hope that this letter finds you in good spirits and good health. I am sad to say that I cannot render the same unto you, as I find myself in dire need of your consult and good judgment. I was very taken aback to learn of the engagement of Miss O'Connor to one of the blacksmiths of Killarney. Of his nature and good character, I have heard from the townspeople no fault or slight that would lead me to believe he is anything less than honorable, faithful, and a man of good intent. I do not doubt that he would spend his life in the pursuit of her welfare and comfort. However, I cannot deny that I find myself hating this man, and consequently cursing his very name and wishing him ill. Upon reflection, I understand that the reason I detest him so is that he was to take away forever my darling Maeve. Though she turned me away when I presented her the bakery (as you know, Mel, I did so only in the honest hope that by it she may find the funds necessary to provide for her father and herself without feeling obliged to marry). I had hoped that time would see her heart soften yet to mine.

What I must admit to you now is shameful. On the very night that Miss O'Connor and the blacksmith announced their engagement, I escorted her back to her flat from a celebration at the pub. My intent, I assure you, was only to ensure her safe deliverance. We had both imbibed, and surely were not in our clear senses. I will not inscribe details, but you have said to me before that you should not fault me if I should love another, so long as the matter was kept silent. I gave myself to her in full. In the heat of passion, I declared my love, and asked her to renounce her fiancé. I fear that my selfish desire for her has damned her to a life of bitterness and shame.

I am a man lost. I know that I should feel aggrieved and remorseful for leading her to this fate, and yet I find myself too euphoric in her presence that I find I do not care what fare she pays to walk this road with me. But what now? How can I honor her and keep her? I know she deserves better than what I can provide. I am in desperate need of your counsel.

I am en route to Cork, on my way home. Return post to the Lancer Inn, where I shall stay a fortnight before sailing for Yarmouth.

A."

Maeve let the letter drop to her lap and stared blankly at the fire. "What advice did you give?"

"She told me to keep you, by whatever means possible."

Maeve gasped as she heard August's voice, and wondered how long he had been standing and watching. Perhaps the whole time. Maybe he had only gone around the corner, wary of what words would flow between the two women.

Maeve, for one, had certainly not expected that Amelia supported her husband in his efforts to win a mistress' heart.

August continued as he strode into the room, each step equally measured and cautious. "She told me that she had endured the pain of losing her love, and that if you loved me as much as I loved you, you would forgive me if, in the end, we were still together. Maeve, please forgive me. I love you, and I never wanted to hurt you. I had to – "

"Not that I suggested keeping my existence a secret," Amelia interjected under her breath.

"But, August," Maeve countered, "a child. How can this work?"

He stopped in his place and looked to Amelia with pleading eyes.

"Maeve, take heed not to push too hard, too quickly," she answered. "You may be surprised the extent to which arrangements just as these are made in many of England's most noble homes. August has always sworn to me that if my love should ever return, he would make similar accommodation. There are ways. But now I am tired and must rest."

"Of course, Mel," August agreed, helping her to her feet. Had Maeve been pressed to tell the truth, it was a tender moment to witness. But as the lord and lady smiled at each other, a spike of guilt and shame warred with an overpowering sense of possession and jealousy. "Maeve, perhaps you could…"

Whatever her feelings, it was not right to jeopardize the unborn child's welfare because of them. Maeve circled an arm around Amelia as August led the way toward the staircase. They guided her slowly and left her reclined on her bed on the second floor. Maeve left as Amelia and August talked in hush tones a short space. Despite that she felt hardly better than August for doing so, Maeve lingered outside and listened.

"I can see even in the way you look at her, you love her dearly."

"More than I ever thought possible. But can she still love me? Only once before has she looked at me with so much hate: the first time we encountered each other when I returned to Killarney."

Maeve heard a soft, endearing giggle. "And yet, you won her heart. You will again. Besides, you did not see what I did."

Maeve could almost picture August's head tilted.

"When she remembered you, she smiled. The same smile you gave when you saw her wake. This may not be ideal, but when have you ever conformed to the path laid before you? She'll come around. You'll see."

"Rest now. We'll speak more after."

"Of course."

He closed the door softly behind him and stood, staring into emptiness before cautiously speaking.

"I'll … show you to your room."

Maeve nodded as he turned and led her down the darkening hall. Some ways on, he turned into another corridor and opened a maple door to a room decorated in a style even she recognized as dated.

"This was my mother's room, after my father turned her out from his," he informed her.

As she passed through the door and surveyed from left to right, Maeve was not too surprised to see a small Comtoise clock. It appeared dead, not a single tick or tock echoing from its mechanical housing.

"Maeve, I –"

"No." She cut him off, halting his attempt to embrace her and pushing him away. "I need time. Too many thoughts now to make sense of them all."

"As much time as you need, my love." Tentatively, he closed the space between them and took her hands into his, raising them slowly to his lips and pressing the most tender of kisses. "If you should ask for forever, then I will be here waiting until the day after forever ends."

His eyes were so stark, so sincere, so true. "I love you, Maeve."

She withdrew slowly her hands from his, determined to keep her heart from melting.

Tears did not stop that night. She hated everyone, and loved everyone. But of those for whom she felt grief, felt some horrid fault of hearts wounded and dreams desecrated, no other's grief did she understand better than that of poor Owen Murphy.

29 The Arraignment

~Boston, MA~
October 1872

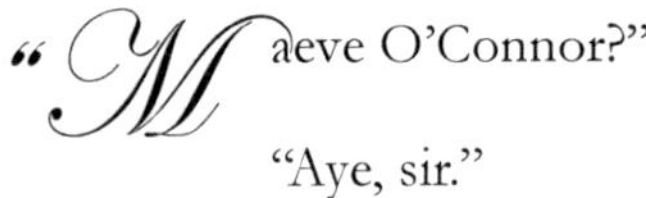aeve O’Connor?”

“Aye, sir.”

“From Killarney?”

“Aye.”

Judge Donegal looked over the stack of papers, his bifocals resting at the end of his nose. At the second confirmation, he leaned over and continued in very hushed tones, “Any relation to Rory O’Connor?”

“My father, sir.”

A grimace flitted across his face as he sat back. “Read about him in the papers. Died with honor, he did. A mercy he didn’t live to see what you’ve sunk to.”

Maeve felt the teardrops tease the corners of her eyes.

The Boston courtroom teamed. The fact that the trial garnered so much attention was beyond belief, but then Tara had told her on a visit to the jail that the papers were heralding the case as a warning to mother’s everywhere: don’t trust anyone, least of all the Irish. “The Nefarious Nanny of Norwich,” that’s what the newsies barked when they tried to hock their papers. In public, Maeve was accused of everything from bribery to arson to murder.

A month had passed since the arrest as the horridness of her reputation grew. Maeve put little faith in the trial; she understood without delusion that she would be condemned for the one crime of which she actually was guilty: kidnapping.

Only her concern for Augusta kept her grasping at fraying threads of hope. Tara had kept the child before their location was discovered. Despite Maeve's treatment by the Anglican-sympathetic press, the Irish of Boston held tight and kept the bizzies occupied on a wild goose chase for a few days. After, she was left with a well-to-do merchant family, acquaintances of Judge Donegal. That was, until a member of her "real family" could arrive to take her.

But now, as the trial loomed before her and she found herself standing before justice, Maeve felt all courage evaporate as the severity of the likely punishment weighed upon her.

"Maeve O'Connor," Donegal continued in a loud booming voice that filled the room. "You are charged with the kidnapping of Augusta Amelia Grayson from the house of her father, Lord August Grayson, Norwich, England, on or about April 18, 1870. How do you plead?"

"Not guilty, sir," Maeve proclaimed through a faltering tone. Her heart knew otherwise, but for Augusta's sake, she would stand firm.

Donegal scribbled his notes before looking up. "Very well. Miss O'Connor, it is acknowledged and recorded that you have claimed innocence. So that you may prepare your defense, this court will recess for three days and resume session Thursday morning at nine o'clock."

The gavel pounded thrice. The only kindness the bailiff paid Maeve was not overly manhandling her as he led her from the courtroom, a sea of eyes following, some sympathetic, some incredulous, some accusatory.

Maeve expected to be thrown immediately back in to her cell, but was surprised when instead she was guided to a small sitting room on the second floor of the court. Her representative, a docile man with wire-rim glasses and a combed-over head of graying brown hair, followed wordlessly. Maeve had come not to expect much assistance from Mr. Kroner. He had said as much on their first meeting that, as she did not deny being guilty in private, he wouldn't "make an ass" of himself by attempting to argue her innocence, but act only in as much capacity as necessary to maintain her right to counsel.

In other words, insofar as preparing a defense, Maeve was on her own.

Mr. Kroner closed the door as the bailiff exited. He eyed her with a disdain often reserved for street walkers.

"Well, that's that," he stated indifferently. "Wondering why we're waiting here, O'Connor?" Maeve looked up at him with loathing. "You have a visitor who wishes to see you in private."

"I told you, I have nothing more to say to Owen Murphy."

Owen had made several foolhardy attempts to visit since she'd been in jail. He even found someone to write a letter, begging her forgiveness, claiming he regretted turning her in. She had ripped it to pieces and refused to face him.

Kroner's mouth curled into a malicious sneer. "Not Murphy."

He turned away with a spring in his step as he pulled the door open and called out into the hall. "Sir, she's ready for you. The judge asks I limit your visit to five minutes. If you like, I can have the bailiff inform you when –"

"Don't bother," came the voice that sent an instant chill down her spine and made Maeve sit straighter than a man hanging from the gallows. "She and I are quite practiced in measuring time."

August rounded the corner as he peeled one glove and then the other off before slapping them into the palm of his left hand. His eyes, the very ones which had looked at her once so lovingly, were now filled with rage and confusion. It had been less than three years, yet he had aged twice as much in that time. A smattering of gray mixed with his ebony locks, and a wrinkle ran across his forehead.

Kroner closed the door behind him as Maeve fought with her better instinct telling her to look away, not to acknowledge August. With a huff, he sat across from her, his gaze now fixed at the table, as though looking at her instead would cast him over as a pillar of salt. Maeve chanced a glance, however, and was surprised to see his expression shifting: one moment a scowl and the next a quivering lip.

He said nothing, and neither could Maeve conjure any word that might properly convey the swirling of every emotion she had ever felt in his presence compressed into one terrible instant.

"Did I… once, ever… Did I ever pose to you a threat?"

Her voice in answer was barely audible. "Never once."

He nodded briefly, and spoke next through clenched teeth. "In all the times I confessed my love to you, did you once believe I was false? Were you, perhaps, harboring some secret fear of me you were too scared to mention?"

"I have never feared you, August."

He pivoted in his chair, now trapping her line of sight to his own, and leaned over the table. "Was it revenge? Was the life we built together just some sort of façade, concocted so that you might give me a comeuppance? Is that why…" His voice broke and he turned away. "Is that why you stole her? To avenge yourself?"

"No, August."

His Adam's apple bobbed. "Did you truly love me?"

His eyes bore into hers with the weight of the world, as though the sanctity of all humanity and the very key to heaven lay in the beseeched truth of his inquiry.

"I love you still."

His expression softened, and he reached across the table, his fingertips running across the inside of Maeve's wrists delicately.

"God help me, Maeve, I … I don't know…"

He trailed off again, his brow furrowed. Had she not known better, she would have sworn her presence was ripping his heart from his chest. His face screwed up in confusion as he bit his upper lip and winced. Maeve felt herself melt, wanting to do something – anything – to soothe him. Her head lilted sideways and her eyes began to tear.

"August, I'm..."

Her rock of conviction was crumbling. For so many years, actions had been justified – as drastic as they were – certain that what she did had to be done.

She had left, yes, but was there any other way? She had made a vow, and in the service of the vow, all else that she held dear was forsaken.

"I'm so sorry, August," Maeve said sincerely, pulling her hands back into her lap.

The withdrawal was met by his equal retreat as August rose. Maeve chanced to continue, not knowing if perhaps this would be the last occasion on which they might ever speak.

"It was never my intention to hurt you. Or your wife."

He paused at the door, his hand lingering on the handle. He turned his body and spoke over his shoulder.

"Wife? After what you've done, why should I marry any one?"

He left, taking with him the last semblance of righteousness Maeve possessed.

30 | Augusta's Hands

"I'm so sorry, August."

For one passing instant, one brief flicker of time, August forgot all that had happened, and wanted Maeve beside him. But as he watched her hands retreat from his and fall out of view beneath the table, he recalled the place and hour. They were in the Boston courthouse, and Maeve O'Connor was on trial for kidnapping his daughter.

Their Goosie.

Had not Maeve raised Augusta as her own? Had they not been blissful? Within the grounds of Meadowlark, they were a family, no matter the lack of acknowledgement from church and state.

Why did she leave?

The coldness descended upon his heart again as he finding them gone without explanation, without cause, without warning. Yes, she deserved this now. She deserved to be ripped of her liberty and thrown in jail. Not for taking Augusta; Maeve loved her as much as she loved him, if not more. She would never endanger her, no matter the circumstance. No, she deserved this because of what she had done to him. August had loved twice unconditionally: first with the girl who had kissed him by an Irish waterfall, and second with the gift from heaven that was his own flesh and blood. In one fell swoop, Maeve had denied his love twice over.

But her tone, her regret… It sounded so sincere. Perhaps, whatever the reason for her departure, there was a chance she truly loved him still. But did August have it in him to forgive her?

No, absolutely not, and if he stayed in the room any longer, his resolve would break. He could not deny his love for Maeve any more than he could deny his lungs breath. Standing to leave, he vowed not to say another word to her, ever.

And, although it tore at him to do so, he had reason to leave: his second love was nearby, waiting.

August had nearly succeeded in fleeing without falter, his hand on the door knob, when he heard her mutter, "It was never my intention to hurt you. Or your wife."

His body stiffened, and he was relieved she could not see the pain in his twisting expression, could not see how he bit his own bottom lip to keep from speaking. How dare she suppose that he would wed another, that she had meant so little to him.

August took in a slow, deliberate breath and turned that she may hear clearly. "Wife? After what you've done, why should I marry any one?"

Quick steps carried him. He took refuge in the awaiting coach. As soon as the door closed, August drew the curtains as the sting of the tears burned his eyes. Such a swirl of emotions – he loved her; he hated her; he hated her for letting him love her; he hated himself that he could hate her and love her still.

But then a small ounce of reason seeped into the churning seas of August's soul: He loved her. He had always and would always love Maeve. He only hated that she left, hated not knowing what had transpired to make her go, hated that he spent so much time thinking she did not love him as he loved her. But to forgive such a transgression? August hated most that he was left lurching in that contemplation.

Augusta. His darling child, his sweetest angel. She was the reward for all the pain and sacrifice and struggle, perhaps the one tribute of divine grace wrought from Emmanuel's misguided attempts to assure his children's recovery from his own social gaffe. God blessed them with Augusta.

Through his tears, August found his heart racing with anticipation and a smile surfaced across his face. Would she remember him, he wondered. Had Maeve told her anything of him? If so, what? And why did she think he was not with her? Had Maeve told her that he died, or whether she had ever loved him?

So many questions, but today, August just wanted to see her face and hold her in his arms to prove to himself that she was real and not a figment of his imagination. As the coach pulled up in front of the brown-brick row house, his disappointment and hurt momentarily receded, replaced by joy. He practically leapt from the carriage and knocked at the door, not even allowing the coachman opportunity to assist. A few moments later, August was greeted by Mrs. MacDougal and led up the stairs to the nursery.

"We're quite taken with Goosie, Lord Grayson," she said in a thick, Bostonian tone. "She's such a generous child, and so well mannered. Clearly good breeding. Though no great compensation for being separated from her by that vile woman, at least she was miraculously well-minded."

August felt himself instinctively cringe at the defaming of Maeve's character. Defending her seemed the most natural posture to assume, but he could not think of a convincing argument to be made. What did it matter what this woman thought of Maeve, anyhow? Had it ever mattered to him what anyone had ever thought of her?

"Miss O'Connor was always a superb governess" was all he could manage as they rounded the top of the stairs and started down a narrow hall, the floorboards beneath moaning with each step.

They came at last to a white-washed door, and August could hear the sounds of a child singing just beyond. His stomach tied into knots; anxious, quivering knots at the realization that his daughter sat within, only the round matron before him barring entrance.

"Remember," she warned, her eyes stern and her tone certain, "with all the time passed, and considering how young the dear heart was when she last saw you, you may be no more than a stranger to her. Let her warm to you at her own pace. With all she's been through these last few weeks, don't unsettle her by running into the room and scaring her half way to kingdom come by swooping her up like a puppy."

August swallowed his pride and his intent, nodding stiffly. "Yes, of course."

Mrs. MacDougal gave a little half grin and cracked the door. With a slight sweep of her hand, she gestured him forward.

Augusta, the perfect specimen of youthful resilience to the realities of circumstance, sat on the floor, playing. Did this look like a child who had been stolen in the night and kept unwillingly from her ancestral home? Was this the image of a neglected Cosette, bartered away for her own safe keeping only to be met with disdain and indifference? Could this child have possibly suffered a day of depravity in her small number of years?

No, she was happy and perfect, and a bestowment of grace on earth.

The hinges creaked as the door opened wholly. Augusta paused in her tending of a small, porcelain-faced doll to turn around.

"Miss, this is a friend," Mrs. MacDougal said in a light voice. "He's traveled a very long distance to meet you."

Augusta very carefully put her toy on the floor and stood. August was amazed at how tall she was. Last he had seen her, her arms would circle around his leg as she would kiss his knee. Now, her head reached the level of his hip, and her hair was long enough to be neatly pinned in a bun atop her head.

She took a few paces in his direction, a tenuous but not unpleasant look on her face. August schooled his instincts telling him to reach down and take her. Instead, he allowed his daughter to set the pace. She stopped and, to his surprise, curtsied.

"Very nice to meet you, sir. I'm Augusta Murphy."

"God, child!" Mrs. MacDougal scolded, clicking her tongue and shaking her head. "How many times have we told you, your name is…"

"Nothing but a name!" August interjected. His host cowered, and Augusta flinched.

"It's all right," he said as he kneeled down and rubbed his daughter's arms in comfort. "Augusta, do you know of William Shakespeare?"

She shook her head as confusion spread across her face.

"He was an English playwright. He wrote once, 'What's in a name? That which we call a rose by any other name would smell as sweet.' Murphy or not, you are still the same sweet child. It's very nice to meet you. My name is Gus. Do you mind if I sit and play with you for a while?"

Augusta's eyes flashed to Mrs. MacDougal, as though asking permission. The thick woman gave a curt nod, and then shot August a warning glare. August bobbed his head. With a spin of her heel, Mrs. MacDougal exited, closing the door behind her.

He assumed a seat on the floor and studied his daughter. She was so perfect, so divinely perfect. Her eyes were brilliantly blue and big – Amelia's eyes, soft in their expression. Surprisingly, her demeanor was Maeve's. She held herself tall and forthright, and even her smallest mannerisms and the tone of her muddled accent reflected an Irish influence.

August looked for a distraction to stop the tears from coming. He spotted her plaything on the floor and picked it up.

"Does she have a name?"

Augusta ran her fingers over the doll's black, curly locks and pale ivory skin. "Alice."

"Alice? What a fine name. Where did you learn of it?"

"My mother read me the book," she said plainly. "Do you know it?"

August beamed at her. "Yes, I think I do. The one with the rabbit hole, yes? Alice runs away, doesn't she? And has great adventures, before realizing that she misses home very, very much and tries to find her way back. Do you like that book?"

"It's Ma's favorite," Augusta answered, a bit of joy coming into her voice now as she took the doll from him and smoothed out its blue dress. "But it makes her terribly sad too."

"Why?" Honestly, he could not understand.

Augusta shrugged. "I think she wants to go home too. She just doesn't know how. She can't find the way."

His heart ached in earnest. But still, he wondered. "Did your mother tell you where home is?"

She smirked, and as though she were conspiratorially letting him in on a secret, she answered. "It's a beautiful house in a faraway land. Ma says my da was a sort of prince. Did you know he called her Cinderella?"

August's breath hitched, but he refused to worry Augusta by crying; tears could be afforded in solitude. He had only adopted the pet name for Maeve a few months before their disappearance, after they had taken to telling Augusta bedtime stories. During a retelling of the little cinder girl story, Maeve had joked at how similar the tale was to her own fortune. 'Then you must be the prince,' she told him when he held her in his arms.

Did telling Augusta about this endearment mean that she still recalled their happiness?

The child's questioning gaze led August to realize that he had been silent for some time. He smiled, and was overjoyed when the divine gesture was reflected twofold on her face.

"A prince? Wouldn't that make you a princess? Princess Augusta!" he proclaimed with all due pomp as he held hands high in the air in exclamation.

She giggled, and it made him laugh too. "I like you," she said. "You're funny."

Without further delay, she ran to August and threw her arms around his neck, kissing him on the cheek. He could deny it no more. August wrapped his arms around her and held her petite frame close, taking in the scent of her hair, the smoothness of her face pressed against his.

"I've missed you so much, dear one," he muttered as he pressed more kisses unto her chin, her forehead, anywhere. "I thought I might never see you again."

"You are a prince, aren't you?"

He laughed. "Right now, I feel like a king."

"Did you come to rescue my mother?"

The stark comment threw him. August pulled back. Augusta's face was full of hope. He felt his insides roll.

"I came to rescue you, dear heart."

Her face screwed up in confusion. "Rescue me?" she asked, perplexed. "Rescue me from what?"

From what indeed, he wondered. August knew not what to say. The contemplation was cut short as she spoke again.

"You have my hands," she said, running her fingers over his.

Augusta pulled his hands into hers as best she could, though tiny they were and not able to fully encircle her father's. She turned them over several times, examining the length of each finger, the wrinkles of skin over his knuckles, tracing over the crease that fortune tellers in London called "the life line." Then she splayed her fingers wide and held her hand next to his. For so young a child, August marveled at the realization on her face; he could almost see the thoughts running through her mind as she passed from disbelief to amusement to stark comprehension.

"My ma says I have my father's hands. Are you…"

He didn't have to say anything. The truth was there to be seen, even by a child. August felt pride swell within as his daughter found him out for who he was. She squealed as her arms tried to wrap about him.

"Oh, it is you! You've come! You've come for us at last, to take us back to your castle!"

Images of father and daughter sitting in the gardens of Meadowlark flashed through his mind – beautiful, but incomplete. Then the vision shifted, and August saw his daughter sitting in Maeve's lap, with him seated on the ground behind them, his arms circling around Maeve's waist, and only in the possibility of that vision would he be content.

August felt warmth unlike any he had ever known. It was folly to suppose, however, that the wounds between them could be so easily mended. He needed to know so much; so very much was still a mystery. At the very least, how had his daughter come to be called Augusta Murphy? Maeve left Owen and Killarney years ago. Was it really so beyond belief that August may have gotten his just desserts, that the intervening force of providence had delivered her back into Murphy's arms, that perhaps they had even wed? But if Owen loved Maeve one-one thousandth of how much August had, how could he have betrayed her? Allowed her to move to the Americas alone, and with a small child in tow?

August needed answers. He knew he would believe whatever Maeve may offer – truth or lie. He was too willing, too eager to believe anything that would allow forgiveness without further delay, to just pick up and carry on.

If she loved him, why would she leave? The question kept nagging at him. August needed to hear it from *him*. He needed to hear the words from the Fenian Furrier of Killarney.

Three days passed in bliss as father and daughter reacquainted. Caroline and Jefferson arrived, little Charles at their side. Augusta delighted in her cousin's company, even when the three-year-old climbed onto her lap and pulled at her hair. Jefferson canvassed town, using his few contacts amongst the Irish to track down Owen. Finally one night they found him, half drunk, seated at the bar of a Quincy pub.

"Another whiskey!" he shouted to the barman as August sauntered up from behind and sat down several stools away. Owen didn't notice his presence, for which August was glad. He wanted to observe him first, aided by the dim light offered in the pub.

"Must be a woman," August said in perfectly toned Irish, and luckily the alcohol and false tongue didn't rouse suspicion as Owen turned and took in the partially-lit profile.

"Aye, that is part of it," he answered back groggily. "And that I'm a right bastard who'll burn in hell, and won't the whiskey make my burning easier for the devil?"

August played along, desperate to learn what loose lips may betray. "Here to drink your guilt away, then? Tussle some tart?"

"Worse. Took a mother from her child for my own selfish ends," he spat back. "Somewhere in Boston, there's a girl who doesn't know what became of her ma. Doesn't know she's in jail because of me, because of what I convinced her to do."

It hardly answered his question, but August couldn't think of how to broach the subject without rousing suspicion. Instead, he decided to play sympathetic.

"I'm sure it's not that bad. Everyone's on their own card, in the end."

Owen turned to him, a rue smile on his face. "Not her, sir. Wasn't her idea to go so far, to leave him forever. I convinced her," he assured, poking himself in the chest with his thumb. "Told her it was best for the child. But how could it be? That child lost her ma and… Hey, don't I… Do I know you?"

"Do you know the funny thing about this, Murphy?" August no longer felt need to continue the ruse. "The last time you and I sat in a pub, it didn't end so well for you either. I have a feeling that history is about to repeat."

August leapt from the stool and seized Owen by the collar, lapels twisting in his hands as he pushed him back over the bar, sending the whiskey glass shattering on the floor.

"If you knew where Maeve was, why the hell didn't you tell me? Everyone in Killarney knew I would have done anything to find them. I could have found her out on my own and kept this tragedy from happening."

"Calmer headers and cooler manners can solve this, now!"

But August's ire would not yield. "You have taken away the love of my life!" he bellowed. "You've denied my daughter the only mother she has ever known."

"She made me promise not to tell you!" Owen pled. "Turning Maeve in was the only card I had to play when the redcoats came for me, so I took it. Not like you would marry her. Not like I ever would have let her linger in shame the way you did."

August snarled, and before he knew it, the meeting of his fist to Owen's face had set them both back a step.

"You're right," August growled. "You never would have. Nor would you have ever loved her the way I did. The way I…" His voice broke as he struggled, wondering if he could admit it to himself, let alone Murphy. "The way I do. Just tell me one thing. Did you marry her?"

Owen's head sunk in shame, muttering, "No, she wouldn't have me. Still loved you too much, even after what you did."

His words stuck like a poker into August's heart. "What? What did I do? Why did she leave?"

Owen's half-smile was mocking, even as a stream of blood dripped from his nose and over his lips. He understood as clearly as August did; what August was really asking was, 'Why did she come to you?'

He gave a low chuckle. "Tell me, Grayson, what wouldn't you do for the woman you loved? Rather," he leaned forward and spoke in a leading tone, "what didn't you do?"

31 | A Posteriori

~Norwich, England~
March 1867

Women never ceased to amaze August. That his wife and his lover would somehow form so tight a bond was unfathomable. In the weeks that followed the odd return to Meadowlark, the generous nature of both those fair creatures overrode whatever discontent they had felt with him. In passing one day, Caroline mentioned that she was even somewhat jealous of Maeve's kinship with her. Amelia was quite curious of Ireland, the land her husband had pined for and dreamed of for so long, and took advantage of Maeve's vivid descriptions. At the same time, Maeve tried to decipher August's past and what kind of man he truly was by querying Amelia. In coming to know more of August from each other, they came to know even more so about themselves.

Though often the air was tense and the mood pensive when all three were together, the two ladies passed most days in languid repose and in each other's company. August, of course, had matters of business to which he needed to attend, and Caroline had been in a tizzy of wedding planning.

The circumstances being what they were, often the men of Meadowlark found themselves sanctioned to the library or stables, particularly when matters of a matrimonial nature were on the slate. Caroline had always been a superstitious soul, and not only did she think it would bring bad fortune for Jefferson to chance a look at her wedding gown before the blessed day, but also that his seeing anything *inappropriate* would rain disaster upon their good fortune. August scoffed at the notion, of course, asking why not make the journey when one's already read the map.

"Caroline, by your admission, he's already seen the most precious thing you could reveal to him," August snickered at her one night as all lounged, individually occupied, in the sitting room.

Amelia rolled her eyes. "Tut tut, August. It's hardly gentlemanly to say such things of your little sister."

Caroline's cheeks stained red, but always his equal, she wasn't about to stand down. "I am sorry that not all of us wish to be such prudes to wait for our wedding night as did you, dear brother."

Maeve, quietly reading next to the fire place, smacked her book shut and shot up.

"Well, I'll be off to bed, then. Caroline, Amelia, Jefferson." She turned only a burning gaze to August before spinning on heel and marching from the room.

August ground his teeth in frustration, and Caroline's accompanying look indeed conveyed some sense of apology and regret. She had been conflicted about which way to advise Maeve. Surely, as August's sister, she wanted to see her brother happy, but she loved Maeve and Amelia nearly as much. Still, she had never actively sought to rally one way or the other, choosing instead to stay uninvolved in the matter. Reminding the present company, however, that he and Amelia had consecrated their marriage as recently as within the last year was hardly aligned with that neutral posture.

August put aside his correspondence, took one of the lamps from atop the fireplace mantel, and pursued Maeve. He squeezed Caroline's shoulder in passing to let her know he held no ill feelings. He caught Maeve at the top of the stairs as she turned down the hall toward her room.

"Maeve, please wait…"

Her eyes were afire and if it had been possible, August was certain he could have burst into flames from that look alone.

"Why must you constantly remind me of my shame?"

"Your… Your shame? If anyone should feel ashamed, it's me," he pled in tones mixed with embarrassment and abhorrence.

In the light of the lamp's glow, August saw her face soften. He knew better than to let go the opportunity.

"Rest assured, I am not proud of what I've done. To know that I've caused you such pain and torment, to know that you trusted me and, perhaps, hoped for that which I knew fair well I could not give you… Well, I know I am not worthy of you. I have never been and could never be. But I cannot change what has happened. I cannot undo –"

"How many times?"

Her question came out of the blue and took him off guard. August cocked his head to the side.

"How many times have you lain with Amelia?"

Should he answer? Was it really any of Maeve's affair to know, no matter her place in his heart? Would she hate him more if she knew the truth?

"The occasions were few."

Maeve nodded, but the look on her face was hardly affirming. "Mel said you laid with her every night after you were married until you were certain she was with child, at least for two months."

Dryness parched his throat. "She… She told you? I was only trying not to hurt your feelings. I didn't mean to –"

"Did you like being with her?"

Her eyes sharpened, a warning not to be so imprecise again. August decided it would be of no use to try. Clearly anything she was asking now was solely for verification.

"Yes, I did." His tone was sincere but remorseful. August lowered his eyes, staring into dark nothingness beyond reach of the lantern's light.

She seemed somewhat assured. "There, that's the truth. Now, tell me truly, and don't be trying my patience with beating around the bush. After your child is born, and sufficient time is passed, will you lay with her again?"

His eyes widened in horror and shot up to her most stern of expressions. Was this what she feared? Was this what tormented her?

"Never," he pledged. "Maeve, it was necessary, and I will not deny that I enjoyed her. Amelia is beautiful. But that pleasure was only skin deep, and the action only a means to an end. There was no purpose in my intent other than to have her taken with child. And Mel was conflicted as well in liking it, which you will have known if you've discussed this with her."

Maeve seemed as though she was debating acceptance or disgust. "And yet you continued to bed her."

"If we failed to produce a child quickly, Caroline would have been disinherited," he reminded her. "There is not benevolence without bane to be found in this. We are all victims of our best intent."

From her distracted expression, he could see that the thoughts were turning over in her mind.

"Then you and Amelia…"

"Wife and husband, as deemed by the church and law and, as need be, in the eyes of English men," he answered. "But in my heart and at the gates of Heaven or Hell, I am yours completely."

A smile fluttered across her face.

"August…"

He held the lantern high to better illuminate the space between their bodies.

"I don't know if I can… This is all… How can we possibly…"

With his finger pressed to her lips, August quelled her rambling. "It is what it is. The only decision you need to make is, are you willing to let it become what it may?"

Her lips pulled into an uncertain smile as his hand dropped away. She came into his arms like a benediction, a cleansing of his soul. She did not kiss him, and yet August felt himself burn in her proximity. Her scent filled his lungs in fullness as she settled her head against his shoulder. A tremble registered against him, and with silent heaves, August realized she was weeping.

"There, now," August cooed, stroking her hair. "You'll make me much aggrieved if you should forgive me."

She gave a small chuckle without pulling herself away. "Don't you want my forgiveness?"

His fingers pulled under her chin, drawing her eyes up to meet his. "I said I would wait until the day after forever for you. Take me into your heart, and does that mean forever has come to pass? It simply will not do, as I intend to spend forever with you."

Her lips, wet with tears and red from excitement, quivered.

"Then I shall never forgive you."

"Bloody Hell, August, kiss the girl already!"

Amelia's voice rang from the bottom of the stairs where she and Caroline stood expectantly.

The lovers grinned.

Their kiss, their promise, and love renewed. August was hers, and she was his, and so it would be until the fates turned them to soil.

33 | Reverence

Morning light cascaded over Maeve's form, enhancing her graceful figure, naked and soft. August pulled himself to her side and threw his arm around her. Not waking, she stretched nonetheless and shifted closer. Silently, August prayed that his father somehow knew from beyond death's gates that he had not won. He had Maeve, and had still followed through with the cursed requirements of Emmanuel's last wishes.

Both their heads perked up when the first tick echoed through the room. It was an impossible thing; the clock had not worked since before Eliza had died. It sounded again, then again, and August heard Maeve give a low chuckle. She rolled over, circling her arms around his neck.

"I don't recall exactly where we left off, Lord Grayson. Was it eleven minutes I owed you next?"

The steady cadence of the clock's rebirth marched in time with his heart. August lowered his mouth to hers.

"For a start," he teased as he sought her kiss, moving his lips against hers in a build of mounting need and desire. "We can do so much in eleven minutes, but if we're lucky, we'll lose track of the time, and do far more still."

"One can hope," she purred as he moved his mouth to her neck. "August?"

"Hmm."

"Why did you …" She gasped as he lowered his mouth over her collarbone, then lower. "Ungh, I missed that a bit."

August smiled, but didn't let her see, moving his lips instead to the other side to pay equal homage.

"August, stop a moment, I want to ask you something sincerely."

In frustration, he bit his bottom lip as he pulled back. She smiled and placed her hand over his cheek in comfort. August's eyebrows arched in reflection of the curiosity now welling within.

"Why did you go through the ruse? If you wanted to open the mine on the land under our cottage, why didn't you just compensate us and move us out? Or even just kick us out? It was your right."

This was the question he had been dreading many a long night. He only wondered now if she would believe him. With a sigh, he began.

"Growing up, my father had been so crass, and when my mother died, he seemed to somehow blame it on the fact that she was Irish. He treated you horridly that day when you brought me back home, and I was an even larger ass for acting the same way, feeling for a moment that my father's approval was more desirable your friendship. The moment haunted me for years. I don't know… I remembered seeing the few above-ground spikes in the hills near your house, and I knew the land was rich with copper. But I also knew how much your cottage meant to you and you'd hate me when I took it from you, no matter what compensation I gave you. And when you found me in the stable that day, my mind twisted."

August paused and looked up at her. Maeve's gaze seemed to say she trusted his veracity, but still hadn't decided if the intent was credible.

He continued. "I still wanted you so badly. But I knew it was too late; I was married, and later I found you were engaged. I never thought you'd accept the arrangement, much less carry on with it. When I kissed you that first day –"

"Five seconds," she interrupted.

August smiled. "Yes, five of the most glorious seconds of my life. But even then, I was certain you wouldn't come back. But you did. And did again. Our lines started getting blurred. I knew I couldn't give you what you deserved, and sometimes I didn't care. I'd try to keep our roles firm, but every movement you made and every word you'd say would soften me. Even as the time increased, I rationalized I'd be doing right by you in the end. Opening the mine meant helping Killarney, and helping Killarney was helping you. But then I got to thinking: from my perspective, the agreement you made with me wasn't so different from the agreement you made with Owen. You didn't really have a choice on either count. I wanted you to, Maeve. I wanted you to have freedom to choose, and I prayed you would choose to be with me… for the right reasons."

"So you gave me the bakery," she concluded, a dawn of understanding coming over. "You really didn't mean to make me look a kept woman, did you?"

"Not in the least. I thought, since Rory would be living with you too, how could anyone say I was keeping you there just to have access? And if that rumor spread, who could argue you were more accessible to me while stationed at the bakery than you had been way out at Middle Lake? Besides, no one would associate Rory with such a heinous arrangement, given his reputation."

"His reputation as an occasional drunk?" Maeve joked.

But August was sincere in his response. "No, his reputation as a Fenian."

She crooked his head at him. "You mean my father is part of the Brotherhood?"

"Part of it? He's one of the principles. And how could such a Fenian allow his only daughter to be sneaking about with an Englishman for something as petty as money?"

Maeve's tears came suddenly. "He must hate me now, I know it. I'm as good as dead to him."

Immediately, August wrapped her in his embrace. "Shhh, there now," he cooed, smoothing down her hair. "He'll forgive you. A father's heart never can sever from his daughter. It is only the son whom he holds in contempt for daring to be the man he once dreamed of being."

She looked at him, perplexed.

"Trust me, on this I speak with authority."

"But your father created this whole situation. And Caroline –"

"My father," August interrupted, cutting her off, "did what he thought best for Caroline. I think Amelia is wrong on that matter. You see, in our society, Caroline would never have been able to find what my father considered a suitable match if her rebellious older brother had gone out and wed a peasant. The fact that Caroline is marrying a commoner – and a Yank, nonetheless – is just one final comeuppance for his misguided efforts. But if Caroline had wanted to marry someone of nobility, I would have wanted that for her. My father's intents, though ill-construed, were driven by love."

"And if you have a daughter?" Maeve wondered.

August could see where that conversation would take them, and refused to be mired down again in malady so soon after reclaiming Maeve's heart.

"We shall deal with everything as it arises."

The knock on the door drew both of their attentions. As the staff was likely aware August was in Maeve's room, he wasn't surprised.

"Yes, what is it?" he called out.

A very elderly gentlemen's voice, which August recognized as that of one of the staff, returned answer. "Apologies, sir, but you have a very insistent caller. He claims he's on errand from Ireland." Maeve and August's eyes went wide. "A Mr. Woodrow."

Ease overcame August. "It's only my barrister from Killarney." He rolled over and kissed her before rising from the bed. "Still, I wonder what the devil he's doing here. Get dressed, darling. I want to take you out today, show you the town."

"Out?" She seemed sincerely confused. "However will we…"

He winked at her as he went to her closet and pulled out a uniform he had had the servants prepare and place there just the day before. "Congratulations on your employment, Miss O'Connor. After an exhausting search," he tossed the black taffeta over her naked body, "we have selected you to be the head nanny for the Grayson baby. Unless you'd prefer being a chamber maid."

Maeve sat up and held the dreaded, unflattering garb against her frame. "I suppose it's better than being sent to the kitchen to bake the bread."

Downstairs, a dressed and hastily tidied August found an agitated and disheveled Woodrow in the foyer. "I'd offer you breakfast, but you look like you've already been fairly scrambled."

Woodrow gave a little yelp at the sudden appearance of his employer, as though he feared to be in his presence. August could see the nature of this visit was far from social. The man was a white as a winter morn, and frozen nearly as solid.

"Goodness, Woodrow, what has happened? Here, sit down."

He motioned to the nearby sofa as August took seat on the chaise and waited.

"M… m… m… Morning, sir. I c… c… come with ter… t… t… terrible news."

Suddenly concerned, August leaned in, his voice rising. "Terrible news? What is it, the mine? Is there a set back?"

"Please, I will t… t… tell you in full, but, please, don't interrupt." Woodrow closed his eyes, forcing his breath to slow and his voice to steady. "Several days ago, I received a visit from Mr. O'Keefe, who resigned his position as middle man."

"Did he say why?"

"Yes, sir, and that is part of this whole mess," Woodrow continued. "He was leaving with his family for the Americas, and as he left my office, he advised me to leave Killarney as well. I didn't think much of it – people in departure from any one place often ease themselves of the experience by casting the place in dark colors. Makes the place they're off to seem brighter, more hopeful. But there was such immediacy to his words, as though he was telling me not to leave any time, but right then, that very hour. Still, I went on with the day, and it wasn't but the very next day that the shots rang out."

August knew too well, though he had hoped Rory's efforts to keep violence from bubbling over would have worked.. "The rebels."

"Yes, that so-called Brotherhood of theirs. Well, the rebellion was quickly squashed. The police seemed to have been tipped off before of their intentions and were ready and waiting for the Irishmen to make themselves known."

So, Rory did go through with turning on his own, August confirmed inwardly.

Woodrow continued. "But I regret the whole affair did result in some damage… and some casualties."

A shaky hand extended across the distance, offering August an envelope. August took it quickly and pulled out the contents, a clipping from the previous day's Killarney broadsheets.

With the rendering of this item, Woodrow's tension began to ebb. "I hope you don't begrudge me for coming unannounced, Lord Grayson, but I thought it proper to deliver the information in person. She should know."

Stunned and shaken, August blinked rapidly, hoping the words on the paper would rearrange themselves into something less horrid. "No, it was very good of you to make the effort. Please, if you'll excuse me."

In later years, August would try to recall walking up the stairs that day, the clipping in his hand weighing two tons. He would try to remember the agony of arriving at Maeve's door, only to open it to find his Irish lover examining herself in her mirror, taking in her appearance as she donned the nanny frock. He would try to summon the taste of ironic bitterness on his tongue as he brought this woman whom he adored and had promised to protect, the dark wave of despair that was typed into a passing sentence on the page Woodrow had delivered.

He would never remember this. Years later, the only moment of that day that remained in his memories was Maeve's face, stricken white before she fainted, having learned that, as the paper reported, "The first of the rebels to fall in the square upon charging the English Guard was a former groundskeeper from Middle Lake, Rory O'Connor."

33 | *Augusta*

Maeve and August jolted as Caroline burst into their room without warning, greatly distressed. August noticed the look of utter terror on his sister's face, and knew at once some calamity was afoot.

The excitement was the first flutter of activity in quite some time. For nearly a week, Maeve had barely spoken or eaten. She sat in her room, never emerging but for the most necessary of tasks. August stayed often with her, leaving only when necessary to see to business or household duties. He knew she needed time, needed comfort, and that was what he was there for.

"Caroline, what is it?"

"Amelia," she gasped back. "The baby! It's time!"

Not a moment later, a horrid, piercing scream echoed through the house. Caroline turned without pause and ran back from the room, saying, "August, get the doctor. Jefferson is readying your horse even now."

August leapt from bed. "I shall. Stay with Maeve while I…"

But Maeve was already on her feet and dressing as August wrapped a throw about his shoulders.

"Maeve." August tried to hold her back, but she continued unfettered. "Darling, it's all right. You don't have to –"

"What about the midwife?" Maeve interrupted, focusing on Caroline and ignoring August's coddling.

"She wasn't expecting Amelia to break for another few weeks. She's away."

Of all the cursed luck.

Maeve had dressed in blinding speed and rushed past August in a blur. Caroline followed and August ran to the stables a few minutes later, his pulse racing for speed with his feet. Jefferson was already mounted and waiting.

"I never let a man go alone into battle," he declared.

When they arrived back to Meadowlark not an hour later, Jefferson and August shepherded Dr. Stone into the house without delay. Amelia's screams had grown more intense, the depth of her pain clearly evident in the shrillness of her woe. Jefferson and August kept constant vigil near the door, but neither was permitted entry. August could hear the murmur of Caroline or Maeve passing along reassuring words. Amelia pleaded, pleaded with God and the Heavenly host, pleaded with anyone who might offer an end to her agony.

With every cry, August cursed his father all the more and spat upon his memory. It was his doing that had the poor creature begging for the graces of the merciful creator as she struggled and strived to bring forth the contractual child demanded.

As afternoon passed away, her pleas became mottled and soft. Amelia wept silently, though if it was because the pain was less or that her voice had simply left her from the strain, August knew not.

Finally, after a day of endless agony, a silence descended upon the house. The slightest of rustles came from inside the room. August put his ear to the door and heard only a soft uttering. He couldn't even distinguish which of the three women he loved – each in her own way – was speaking.

Frustrated, he gnashed his teeth and decided he'd had enough of keeping a gentleman's proper place. He needed to be inside, and had nearly reached the doorknob when, unexpectedly, it turned and the door opened.

Out stepped Stone, his face flushed and his clothes covered in a mess of fluid August didn't want to know the more of.

"The child is born," he said. "A girl, Lord Grayson, and very healthy."

His heart leapt despite itself and more than that, August's whole body smiled in a wave of unparalleled euphoria.

"I am… a father."

As though it had not been real until that moment, he grinned. He had a daughter. His daughter lay inside, just beyond the doors, just out of view. He made again for the room, but as he did, Stone held out an arm to stop him.

"However…"

"Yes, Amelia – how is she?"

The doctor's eyes dropped to the floor. He spoke with such caution that August felt his stomach turn.

"She went peacefully, in the end."

"Peacefully?"

What? What did he mean, she went peacefully? "Oh, no."

Caroline's bloodshot eyes met August's panicked expression as he burst through the door and found the heart-wrenching scene: There, lying in a bed of what had been pure white sheets, in a wholesome dressing gown now stained with blood, was Amelia, eyes closed, skin ghostly. A covering had been placed over her, but August could see the smattering of red specks seeping through. The blood was as fresh as her death.

To the right, Caroline prostrated herself, her arms still outstretched, holding Amelia's hand. August watched in anguish as he saw the tears stream down his sister's angelic face and the words "I'm so sorry" mouthed without sound despite the rapture of her body's quaking.

To Amelia's left, Maeve held a similar repose, though her eyes were dry. It was not from lack of sorrow; August knew her better than that. Rather, he deemed it to be shock, disbelief. She clutched tightly in front of her a blanket with one hand, her other arm beneath it for warmth, he assumed. The knuckles of her exposed hands were nearly white from wringing.

Jefferson was at August's side in a moment. When he saw Caroline's crumpled form, however, he dove to her, taking her in his arms as he tried to offer comfort. August slowly paced alongside Maeve before falling to his knees and reaching out to stroke Amelia's cheek, the skin already pale, her warmth fading.

Maeve's voice was that of a stranger's when she spoke, rough and broken and stained by despair. "So much death, August."

"Maeve..."

She cut him off. "But she saw her before she passed. She kissed her daughter."

Suddenly, August's mind returned to the moment. There was a baby, but where? August's eyes darted across the room, searching out for some evidence of the child, his child.

The slightest whine came from under Maeve's blanket.

He looked down and saw the revelation of the as-yet unwashed product of his and Amelia's union, blissfully sleeping in Maeve's arms.

"Augusta," Maeve held the swaddled infant out to his instinctively awaiting embrace. "Her mother asked that she be named after you."

34 Uncouth Men

~Boston, MA~
November 1872

The blond, dimple-faced boy giggled heartily as his playmate, his fair-skinned, blue-eyed cousin, tickled his feet. Charles screamed and squealed and hollered like a jack rabbit in a jamboree as Augusta rolled him onto his back and attacked his stomach.

"Stop it, Goosie, that hurts!" Jefferson's son begged with perfect British inflection.

His mother, the sweetest English flower, laughed in time and looked over at the children rolling on the floor. Caroline only took a moment away from her stitching to click her tongue playfully.

"I'll stop tickling you when you stop laughing!" Augusta pledged in her mottled tone, part Irish, part British, part uniquely Augusta. "Or I'll sing to you, if you'd like."

Charles wormed out from under her and sprang up. "Oh, yes, do!"

August looked up from the small writing desk across the room, his face beaming as he gazed at his daughter. "Do you know any songs, Goosie?"

"Ever so many!" she squealed with pride and wrapped her dainty little hand around her chin in contemplation. "Now, what would you like to hear?"

Caroline smiled warmly. "Well, it is getting awfully late. Perhaps you can undo the tizzy you've gotten him in by singing a lullaby. Do you know any lullabies?"

Charles looked at his mother askew. "What's a la-la-bee?"

August abandoned his feverish notations and went to the children's side. He took Augusta upon one knee and Charles on the other. "A lullaby is the most wonderful innovation in the history of parents and children. You see, it is a song one sings to put children to sleep."

Charles looked up detestably at his uncle, his curls bouncing to and fro with each bitter word he spat back. "I don't want to sleep! I want to play with Goosie."

"Now, now," Augusta cooed, "we'll play tomorrow. What can I sing? Oh! I know."

Jefferson watched as Augusta's angel face lit up and her delicate voice took off in song:

Hush, the waves are rolling in,
White with foam, white with foam;
Father toils amid the dew,
But baby sleeps at home.

"Oh, my! August?"

In a whirl, Caroline had leapt from her seat and was, despite her humble personage, bracing August from falling back on the carpet. His face was positively pale as cotton. Jefferson hastened to help, taking over the lion's share of the burden.

"I'm fine." August spoke more to Augusta than the adults as her face had glossed over in concern. Straightening his shirt, he made as though nothing had happened. "That's lovely, Augusta."

In her relief, she smiled widely. "Ma sings it to me at bed time."

August returned her warm expression. "Your Aunt Caroline probably cannot recall that our mother did too. Do you mind if I sing with you?"

She shook her head, and they resumed together:

Hush! the winds roar hoarse and deep-On they come, on they come!

Brother seeks the wandering sheep, but baby sleeps at home.
Hush! the rain sweeps o'er the knowes, Where they roam, where they roam;
Sister goes to seek the cows, but baby sleeps at home

He leaned over and kissed the bridge of her nose. Augusta closed her eyes and threw her arms around his neck.

"When are we getting Ma and going home, Father?"

Seeing the confusion on August's face, Jefferson cleared his throat as he leaned over and lifted Charles off the floor. "I think it's time for bed now, children. Caroline, would you?"

He gave his wife a meaningful glance, and she immediately understood.

"Of course," she said as Charles' small frame slacked from her embrace. "Come on, poppets. Let us settle you down."

With a small peck on the cheek, Augusta kissed her father before exiting with her aunt. August looked to Jefferson with a smirk.

"I know what you want to say, so just hold your tongue."

"It's not right," Jefferson chastised, undeterred, taking a seat in the arm chair nearby. "You can't drag out poor Goosie's expectations like this. She thinks somehow you and Maeve are going to find a way to overcome everything. You must tell her the truth. Tell her that Maeve is not her mother and that she will not be with her again."

"I spoke to the Judge, you know."

He stated it so matter-of-factly that it took a moment for Jefferson to be taken aback in shock. "No, I was not aware."

August shrugged. "I tried to get him to drop the charges, but the bastard demanded that I swear on the Holy Book Maeve had permission to take Goosie. I could lie to him, but never to spite the Lord."

Jefferson slumped back in the chair, his thoughts shooting off in a million different directions.

"Are you saying that you'd actually… That despite everything, you'd take Maeve back? My God, man, she stole your child."

His green eyes nearly turned black in their hostility. "You know it wasn't like that. Maeve had a reason. And for all the torment I put her through and expectations I made? I don't know, perhaps it was my due."

"Landing another fist on you might have been more merciful."

August shrugged again as his eyes turned to the fire, pulling his attentions wholly inward. In the years Jefferson had known his brother-in-law, never had he been more distant as in recent days. Caroline was beside herself with concern, although in front of the children she displayed no less than utter poise and placidness. In private, she kept replaying everything in her head, trying to decipher if there had been signs missed. Maeve and Caroline had been as close as sisters. That even she could not gather what had driven Maeve to such desperate measures had been taxing on August. If it had been another lover, he may have handled it better. At least then he could place fault. As there was no evidence to suggest that, he took the error to be totally his own.

The conversation he'd had with the informant only seemed to reinforce that.

"If only Murphy would share a little more insight," Jefferson mused as he, too, became mesmerized by the fire.

Jefferson had been only too happy to help August find Owen. As the issues at hand were between the two of them, however, he had remained out of sight otherwise. Jefferson didn't want any of Murphy's grudges against him to deter August's efforts in learning the truth.

But he wondered now if maybe that's what was needed. Maybe if Owen saw that all the cards were on the table, he'd be more forthcoming. Maybe it was time for Jefferson to step in, though he knew he opened himself up to public scrutiny by doing so if his vindictiveness extended to all the Graysons and not only August.

He sat up with a sense of determination, slapping his palms against the arms of the chair. August jolted, turning to Jefferson with a concerned look.

"Tomorrow, I'll go with you to the courthouse and talk with Murphy. You did say he attends most days, did you not?"

"Yes, I did," August answered confusedly. "Why do you think he'll talk to you when he won't talk to me?"

Smirking, he answered in no uncertain way. "One thing I've learned as a soldier: To win the war, you must use the right balance of force and fortitude. I think I know how to get the blacksmith to talk."

Caroline handed her husband his hat as he looked in the mirror, adjusting the deep purple cravat.

"Anxious, darling?"

"I've done nothing wrong."

"But perhaps when August learns…."

His mind turned back through the years, to his and Caroline's whirlwind romance. Jefferson had come to Killarney with a firm goal and purpose, and that purpose was certainly not to fall in love with his intended enemy. He shuddered to think that his activities, had he not chanced upon Caroline in the marketplace that day, could have very well ended her life had he not convinced her to return to England. Of course, how could he ever had known that vacating his once-lofty role leading the Killarney Fenians wouldn't have the slightest effect on its ultimate short comings?

Fate did not depend on the whims of a few, though so often it formulated the misfortunes of the many.

"He won't," Jefferson answered, effectively cutting her off. He chuckled lowly, and said, barely audible, "It is a far, far better thing that I do…" Caroline gave him a coy smirk. "I'll find a way to speak with Owen alone. But don't think wrongly of my intent, darling. I am a man who does not shirk from his past. I only worry that August, should he learn that you have kept these things secret, will think the lesser of you."

"My loyalty lies with my husband first."

Jefferson looked to his bride and delighted in the pink flush of her cheeks. He did not doubt her sincerity, not in the slightest.

"Yes, well, despite that, August needs you now and we should not circumvent the bond the two of you share. You are a great comfort to him."

August rounded the corner just then, lingering in the open doorway as Jefferson leaned over and kissed his Caroline softly.

"I love you. Now let me see what I can do to resolve this."

August was silent all the way to the courthouse, staring blankly out the window of the coach. Jefferson did not endeavor to engage him. Since August had been reunited with his daughter, the silent living death in which he had kept himself for years had lifted. When he was with her, he smiled once more, laughed once more. But the moment he left her side, his darkness returned. An attempt to rouse him from this state often resulted in harsh words or rounds of sarcastic bickering.

Across the street from the courthouse steps, Jefferson saw Murphy entering the building. Making some excuse to August, Jefferson strode away, following Owen through the crowded halls.

He caught him up, and in as delicate a manner as possible, positioned himself behind the Irishman, leaning slightly over his shoulder as he spoke deftly, else someone overhear.

"You and I, sir, need to converse in private."

Owen's breath caught in his throat and Jefferson swore he heard him take a nervous gulp of air. Still, as he turned, Owen's manner was collected and cool.

"Aye, if you like."

Jefferson leaned his head to the side in a vague directional gesture. Owen walked casually the path indicated. They wove through halls and vestibules for minutes, until at last Jefferson believed they were alone.

Without further hesitation, his hands slapped against Owen's shoulders, pinning him to the wall.

"I want you to know, Murphy," Jefferson began in a tone both firm and gravelly, "I have killed men before with my bare hands, and I have the ability to do so without leaving any indication of my involvement."

"Jesus, Mary, and Joseph! What are you playing at?"

Utter rage filled him, and almost without thinking, Jefferson's hands pulled away from Owen's shoulders and circled his throat, squeezing just below his woolen scarf where no marks would show above the collar. Owen gagged.

"I will let go my hands and allow you to breathe. You, in turn, will wisely use this breath to answer one question and one question only. Answer me falsely, and it will be your last breath. Do you understand?" Owen nodded vigorously, though his eyes were tearing over. "Good." Jefferson released his throat. "Tell me, why did Maeve take Augusta and run off to America?"

"Be… cause," he spluttered, doubling over, "because of what she promised the bastard's wife."

"What did she promise to Amelia!?"

"I don't know!" he almost screamed. Jefferson violently whipped his head left and right to make sure no one shared the hall and the conversation. "She wouldn't tell me. She only said she had to keep her promise."

He was telling the truth, that much was certain. But what was also certain was that he was still holding something back. Jefferson could tell by the tension apparent in his eyes.

"And?"

"And… whatever it was, it wasn't enough. She still wanted to go back to him, even after everything." Owen straightened, a smug smile crossing his face. "Aye, but I saw through the mess. I convinced her that she would only be hurt again, and if she really wanted to protect the child, she had to leave. For good."

"And you…what? Brought her to America? Only later to turn her into the police?"

The supposition struck a nerve, and Owen's fair-skinned face flushed red.

"It's as much your fault, you know! If you had done what you promised, Rory O'Connor might even still be alive. If you hadn't had him spying on Grayson, he never would have come up with that hare-brained idea to shoot himself in the foot."

Jefferson grounded his teeth. "Which he did only when you panicked because Maeve was trying to convince you to let them move in with you and away from Middle Lake. You told Rory he had to do something that would distract August, make him feel too guilty to throw them out."

"Does it matter?" Owen spit back. "But God only knows if Maeve would have fallen for Grayson if she had never stayed at his house. And if you had been there during the uprising instead of turning tail, Rory might have never been killed that day. Maeve would be with me. I hope your trollop was worth a good man's life and a good woman's name!"

Owen doubled over again as Jefferson's fist connected with his stomach. As he groaned and grimaced, Jefferson leaned close and growled into his ear. "No one has ever loved Maeve as August. And I hasten to say that until your involvement, Maeve had loved August just as much. And if you ever insult my wife's honor again, I will see you six feet un –"

"Jefferson?"

August's voice echoed up the corridor. Jefferson tensed. August's face twisted in confusion, trying to decipher the scene before him. Owen took advantage of the break to flee. As August approached, Jefferson tried to shake off the nerves that had overtaken him.

"What's going on? Did you learn anything?"

He shook his head. "He said only that Maeve said something about a promise to Amelia. Does that mean anything to you?"

"Not a thing," August answered woefully. Then his eyes narrowed. "Did you… You said, 'Owen.' Did you… Do you know Owen Murphy?"

Jefferson made his answer brief while keeping to the truth.

"I had encountered him in Killarney. Shall we…?"

He motioned with his hands up the hall.

"Yes, court will be convening soon. Let us."

August spent the next several hours biting his finger in frustration, staring squarely at the back of Maeve's head from his seat in the crowded galley. Maeve's gaze never drifted beyond the edge of the table before her. When alas she was asked if she wished to speak in her own defense, she declined. August let out a sigh of regret in the wake of her only words:

"No, sir, I cannot add to anything."

The judge made no attempt to coax her into changing her mind. "Very well.

If you will not speak in your defense, does the defense rest?"

Maeve's counsel consented, and the court recessed.

"Come on, August, let's go back to the children."

August remained still. Around them, others rose and exited. August's chest heaved as he sighed deeply, catching Maeve's eyes for the slightest of moments as she was led from the room, sweeping past.

"They're going to convict her, you know."

Jefferson placed his hand on his shoulder in an attempt to comfort him. "Yes, I think you're right."

His face was stone, cold. "I cannot bear it. Something must be done. I just keep thinking, if only we knew why she left. Then we could make sense of this all, find a way…"

"I've been considering that. I think there is someone who might be able to fill in that missing piece. Come, August. Let's go home."

35 | Geall mé

"Come away from the window, poppet."

Augusta did not stir. Her body and attentions remained fixed on the street below, as though keeping her eyes set firmly on the front gate would somehow bring her father home faster. Charles, on the other hand, was thoroughly enthralled with his bilboquet, again and again batting around the handle and almost catching the ball in the cup.

"Goosie? Did you hear me?"

She woefully nodded and backed from the window. "Yes, Aunt Caroline."

With all the sorrows of the world, the slumped shoulders of the child shrugged as she planted her petite frame in the chair opposite her cousin. Augusta and Caroline gave a jolt as Charles squealed. They cast glances at him only to discover that his efforts had finally paid off; the wooden ball rested comfortably in the cup.

"Very good, Charles."

"Aunt Caroline?" Augusta piped up. Her adoring relation gave her a quick smile before returning to her embroidery work. "Why does Uncle Jefferson talk so funny?"

"Funny? What do you mean?"

Augusta shifted in her uncertainty, squirming as she tried to work out a rewording. "The way he says things, his words sound all crooked."

Caroline suppressed a laugh. In the early days of their courting, she recalled having similar thoughts. "Well, Uncle Jefferson is from America, where that's just the way things are pronounced."

"But Boston is in America, and the people here don't talk like him," she countered in her determination.

"Jefferson is from the south, which is very far away. Ireland and England are closer to each other than Boston and Georgia, and yet the people speak the same language very differently," Caroline volleyed, and without thinking added, "Just look at your mother and father."

Augusta's body became a positive bolt of lightning in a storm. She alighted from her chair and crossed the distance of the room in a flash. Her eyes were as bright as the fire burning on the hearth.

"You knew my mother too, didn't you?"

Caroline's bottom lip bore the brunt of her self-betrayal. August had asked his sister specifically not to mention Maeve to Augusta. While he was not denying the child a smattering of information, he wanted to play gatekeeper to that knowledge. As he was yet uncertain what the future held, he didn't want to make illusions of Maeve – either positively or negatively – that at some point would need to be shattered. Caroline had respected that request, seeing the importance of presenting a unified front.

Still, the child had asked, and Caroline didn't see the harm in a simple answer to a simple inquiry.

"Yes, I knew Maeve," she answered, laying aside the needlework and setting her hands in her lap.

Augusta smiled and leaned in closely, asking in a conspiratorial whisper, "Did you know my *other* mother too?"

Caroline's very breath stilled. "Your… other mother?"

She nodded. "Amelia. Ma said she was very pretty and very, very kind."

Words seemed to tumble from Caroline's mouth in a time without context. "You… you know about Amelia? You know that Maeve isn't your… isn't your… That she…"

Augusta was positively affronted. "Yes, Ma told me," she all but barked – to the extent that a child could. Then her face brightened again at the realization that she had found a new fount of information. "Oh, Aunt Caroline, will you tell me about her? I ask Ma questions but it always makes her so sad and she says she didn't know her all that long anyhow. Tell me about my mother!"

Taken aback and gasping, Caroline tried to take a hold of the situation. "I… I, I, I… wouldn't know where to start. Besides, your father has asked me not to speak with you about Amel –"

"Caroline!"

August's unannounced and shocking rebuke cut Caroline off. Both Augusta and she spun on the spot to find him and Jefferson gaping from their place at the door. Augusta's attentions were diverted away as she ran into her father's arms as he bent to meet her.

"Father!" she squealed. "Did you see Ma? Is she coming home?"

Though guilty of no fault, Caroline felt obliged to defend herself. "August, I swear, she brought it up herself."

The joy drained from his eyes as he turned again and set Augusta on the floor.

"We mustn't confuse Goosie. I trusted you to keep what you knew to yourself."

Jefferson interceded before either was able to carry on. "Let's focus on the matter before us." He bent over to their niece. "Sugar, may I ask you to take Charles and let us alone for a while?"

"But I want to stay with Da!" she objected with a whine and stomp of her foot.

Jefferson laid his hand against her cheek. "Only a few minutes. I promise."

"All right," she conceded, arms crossed to show that while she was going along with the compromise, she clearly was not happy with it. "Come on, Charlie. Let's go."

Charles, ever eager to spend time alone with Augusta – in what Caroline anticipated to include all sorts of foul play – jumped up from the carpet. The children exited the room in due process, each kissed atop their heads by doting fathers as they passed through the door. Jefferson closed the door behind them, and both he and August took seats on the chairs adjacent to the fair seamstress.

August's face was white, his eyes shallow. "I'm sorry. I didn't mean to snap at you."

She leaned over and squeezed his knee. "These times must be very difficult for you."

"Do you remember the day Amelia died?"

August presented the question so nonchalantly that Caroline was taken aback.

"Yes," she answered in a tone laced with venom. How dare he make her relive the pain? "Vividly. I was in the room when it happened."

He pressed on. "Did she know she was dying, or did she just slip away?"

Caroline gnashed her teeth and shot daggers at him. Had she not told him well enough and a thousand times that she had no desire to discuss that day? She laced her arms over her chest and fumed with utmost resolve.

August's eyes beseeched her. "Please, Caroline. This is utterly important."

Sensing that he was taking no comfort in the subject either, she softened. "The doctor said she had only a short time, though he said so only to Maeve and me, not to Mel."

"But might she have heard?" Jefferson interjected.

His entry into the conversation drew his wife's suspicions. "I… I suppose so. What is this all about?"

August groaned in frustration, rising and crossing to the very same window at which his daughter so often kept vigil. Caroline wondered if he, like she, hoped his attendance would bring the missing piece of his heart back through the gate.

"Caroline, my love," Jefferson cooed, falling on his knees and holding both his sweetheart's hands in his own. "August needs to figure out why Maeve left. I know if you ever left me, and I… Well, I'd just be beside myself with grief, but I'd want to know why you did it, for my own peace of mind."

Caroline shook her head. "But I already told you, I don't know why she left."

Jefferson acknowledged her repeated declaration with a nod. "I know, but from what we're able to gather, whatever prompted Maeve to take Augusta had something to do with a promise she made Amelia. August feels fairly confident that it must have been regarding something Amelia felt he couldn't handle. They were such constant companions up until the day Goosie was born that he thinks it unlikely she would have kept something from him otherwise."

Caroline concurred; it followed reason.

Jefferson continued, "August and I were discussing it, and we feel that if Amelia had known that she was dying, she might have asked something of either you or Maeve. Perhaps something regarding Goosie? Tell us, please. Did Maeve make any promises to Amelia before she died? Did Amelia ask anything of her?"

Closing her eyes to concentrate fully, Caroline tried to recall the horrific day. All she could remember at first was the blood. There had been so much, and it seemed with every raspy breath Amelia had grown weaker. The labor had come on quickly in the early hours of dawn. Amelia had been brave beyond measure. It was only in the last hours that Caroline began to realize something was wrong. The pain was growing beyond her tolerance, though Caroline knew well that pain was inherent to the process. But it was as though Amelia had begun to lose determination, as though she knew something was not going as it should. The doctor saved the baby, but said there was nothing to do for the mother.

"She was very weak at the end," Caroline began. "She was babbling, incoherently. Every few minutes, the pain would wrack her. She… asked Maeve if she regretted falling in love with August. Maeve said she would have preferred the situation had been less trying, but that she loved him despite her best efforts to do otherwise."

Caroline looked deeply into Jefferson's eyes, feeling oddly relieved to at last pass along even these few details.

"She asked me if I was happy, though I had married a commoner and foreigner," Caroline continued, "and I told her yes, you made me very happy."

Jefferson smiled. "As do you, my love. More so with each day and each hour."

She blushed in the reflection of his twinkling blue eyes. August, however, sensed her reticence to continue.

"Was there anything else?" he prompted.

She turned to him with a sour expression. "Do you not think I have thought of this before? Amelia said she wanted the baby named after you. Maeve and I told her Augusta was a lovely name. Then she began mumbling. That's when the doctor told Maeve and me that she would pass soon. I collapsed, but Maeve stayed strong. She knelt beside her and held her hand. Even then, Mel was still more concerned for others than herself, and said that she prayed her daughter would never suffer the way she had. Then she was gone."

With the flicker of memories long kept at bay, Caroline played the moment over in her mind. She had been consumed by tears at that point, but something vague and distant surfaced in the recollections.

"I think Maeve may have prayed? She muttered something about God'll have me?"

"God?" August suddenly perked up. He seemed confused, his brow furrowed in contemplation. "No, if she was praying something from the liturgy, it would have been in Latin. Besides, Mel wasn't Catholic. Or, did she…" He spluttered for a moment. "Caroline, is there any chance she might have said *geall me*?"

The sound of the foreign words rang like a remembered tune in Caroline's ears. As though blowing dust away from a neglected book, its invocation crossed the years and she recognized it at once.

"Yes, I think she did. What does it mean?"

August snapped his finger as he made for the door. "It's Irish!" he exclaimed as he turned the handle. "It means 'I promise.' Caroline dear sister, thank you. Thank you so very much. Jefferson, come with me?"

Jefferson hesitated. "Of course, but where? Why? Goosie is waiting for –"

August smiled. "I know why Maeve left. I was such a damned fool not to have realized it before. We're going to need to pay a visit to Murphy again. The task before us will require the aid of a blacksmith and a true Fenian."

36 From the Outside Looking In

~Norwich, England~
April 1870

One eye cracked ever so slightly as she lifted her head and looked back over her shoulder at the lustful gaze devouring her frame.

"For the love of Mary, not yet, August." Her head surrendered back to the pillow, though she counted herself lucky that he couldn't see the playful smile dancing across her face. "Let me sleep a bit more."

"Maeve… church. Caroline will be here soon. If Goosie's not ready…"

He trailed off and she groaned, knowing the threat was true. Caroline doted on her niece, and even though she now had a child of her own, was appalled if Augusta didn't exemplify the height of fashion whenever the family made its way into town.

"Fine," Maeve huffed, rolling up slowly on the heel of her hands and stretching her back in the process, looking much like a newly awoken kitty. August's eyes grew dark as she arched before him. From his side of the bed, he fisted the neck of her nightdress and pulled her over him. She clicked her tongue in disapproval. "As you said: church. We mustn't miss Easter service."

He gave a coy smile, indicating with the movement of his eye the pronounced bump in the smoothness of the sheet that covered them. "Or we can stay in and read some verses."

Maeve rolled from the bed. His hand traveled with her languidly, giving a half-hearted effort to pull her back.

"That is positively sacrilegious."

"Positively sacrilegious?" he mimicked. "You almost sound English."

She smiled as she threw a shawl over her shoulders. The morning was crisp, though sun streamed in through the partially pulled curtain.

"Well, after three years, it was just a matter of course, I suppose."

His finger traced vague patterns on the bed.

"Do you miss Ireland?" He sat up, his look more concerned and sincere than Maeve had noted from him in a long while. "Do you wish to go back? If you wanted to, we could make arrangements to stay at Shepherd's Bluff in a matter of –"

"No," she said by way of cutting him short. "There's… there's nothing left for me in Killarney now. Da's gone. Patty has moved to America."

"Well, there's always Owen Murphy."

She smiled at his jest. "Yes, I suppose I could always try climbing that tree again. Would you consent? May I take my leave?"

Not answering in words, he instead crawled across the bed and attempted again to divert Maeve's focus. August mumbled as her lips met his. "Never. I shall never let you leave me, least of all for Murphy."

His hands encircled her, pulling Maeve to him. He offered kisses in praise, and she accepted more than willingly. Had there not been a knock upon the chamber door, she may very well have allowed his attempts to unclothe her person continue.

As it was, he grimaced in his frustration. "Later, my love."

"Of course, my lord." Maeve turned toward the door as she stood and tied a sleeping gown around herself. "Enter!"

"See, they're still in bed."

Caroline's voice was full of I-told-you-so as she entered the room, little Charles in her arms. He looked exquisitely dapper in his best navy blue suit.

"Good Easter, sister," August said, welcoming her. "Where is Mr. Caroline?"

Charles giggled as he caught sight of Maeve, stretching out his arms in childish glee. Never one to deny, Maeve took the dimpled babe in her arms and spun him around. The jollity was quickly ended, when August snatched him for himself. Charles was all too equally taken with August to complain. His uncle tossed him high into the air, catching him just in time to give him the proper dosage of fright mixed with fun.

"I declare," Caroline sighed, clicking her tongue in mock disapproval, "sometimes I wonder if you'll enchant my own child out from under me. Jefferson is seeing to the coach." She held her hands out to Maeve. "Happy Easter, Maeve." She leaned in and kissed her cheeks. Her eyes then took inventory of the room, and she turned a curious glance back to Maeve. "Where is Goosie?"

"Still asleep, I would wager."

But of course, at that very moment, the door opened even further and a pair of angelic blue eyes resting on cherub-cherry cheeks peeked around the edge. August would not wait for her. Without letting go Charles, he made for the door and scooped up Augusta in the opposite arm. He spun the two around, singing songs to them. Between August and the children, it was difficult to ascertain who took more joy from the frolicking.

Maeve dressed before making her way down to breakfast. It was an odd arrangement in such a traditional, aristocratic home, but one to which the staff had all become accustomed. After all, Maeve was staff, even if all in the household knew that her persona as the Irish nanny to Lord Grayson's only child was only for appearance's sake. Within the walls of Meadowlark, it was understood that she was the lady of the house, but so kindly and egalitarian a lady that none of the staff engaged in malice of thought or action to demean her character at large.

And so they had lived quite happily this way. Until the previous Christmas. August still saw to obligations outside the home, as required to keep up his commercial endeavors and provide for the household and the estate. He had taken on Jefferson as an associate, and found in him a most agreeable colleague.

In late December, August and Jefferson had been invited to a Christmas ball at the home of one of their more profitable clients, a merchant of

French origin, Monsieur Jacques Prideux. It was made clear by both way of the invitation that children were to attend as well. August was all too proud to have occasion to present his striking child to society. As a widower, Monsieur Prideux had suggested to August that "the nanny" come as well, to keep watch on Augusta.

Maeve was hesitant. Certainly she had any number of instances ventured out of Meadowlark with the Graysons, but acting the nanny during an outing to take a stroll up the lane or even a trip to sea for a week was only natural. To a Christmas Ball, however? As Rory had been fond of saying, that was a beer of a different brew. It was not a mere trip to market or the park. It was a gala on the scale of which Maeve personally had never witnessed.

Arriving appropriately attired for one of her outward profession, she felt like a house cat strutting amongst lions. While those in attendance were not unkind, outside of August and Jefferson (Caroline deemed Charles too young and stayed behind), she found hardly a friendly face among them. August was kept most of the evening seeing to business, or that is, the business of making himself known in the crowd. As a separate playroom had been prepared for the younger children and Augusta seemed well occupied and entertained among her peers, Maeve gave herself permission to take a few moment's rest in the chilly night air on the back veranda of Beau Visage, Monsieur Prideux's marble-encased manor.

She did not hear him approach.

"Mademoiselle O'Connor?" Prideux asked, jarring Maeve from her reverie.

She jolted.

"I am sorry, I did not wish to disturb. Only, I saw you standing alone. I hope nothing is wrong?"

Maeve caught her breath, her hand stationed firmly over her chest to calm her heart.

"Of course, Mr. Prideux. I'm fine. I'm sorry if I distracted you from your guests."

"You did not." His head cocked forward, trying to study her more closely. "Is the party… not…?"

Shaking her head vigorously, Maeve answered. "It is quite a gay affair, sir.

Only, I found myself a little out of place. I needed a moment without feeling like a reed amongst the roses." As though a hot poker had entered her chest, Maeve immediately felt the burn of remorse. "I'm sorry. It was not my intention to insult."

"Can I share something with you? I know exactly how you feel." He leaned in closer still, and all but whispered to her. "Truth told, I am the son of a Greek sailor and a French whore. Not quite the caliber of those inside, either."

Blinking several times in disbelief, Maeve tried to gauge if he was jesting; she concluded he wasn't. Yet she hadn't the words to respond, not knowing what to say.

Luckily, he chose to continue. "This party, it is for them a chance to show off their baubles and gowns and compare the size of their… assets. I take no pleasure from it. How is it you say, it is only 'good business.'"

"Of course," Maeve responded with a smile. "And the children are quite taken with it as well. Thank you, sir. It is nice to know that I'm not the only one of humble stock."

"Your parents?"

"Before they died, my mother was a seamstress and cloth maker, and my father was groundskeeper at Shepherd's Bluff, the Grayson's estate."

"But," he began, seeming to stumble for words, "you are so young to be without them. Can I ask how they died?"

The hurt had long since dulled, so it was no more than a retelling of facts. "My mother was taken by consumption when I was sixteen. My father was killed during the Fenian revolt a few years ago."

Prideux grew somber. "My sympathies. It must have been very hard for you. And now–" To Maeve's unease, he reached out his pasty hand and traced a long, bony finger over her chilled flesh, looking out from heavy-lidded eyes, " –you are forced to play governess to a British bastard's child."

Maeve snapped back her hand, her face burning and her teeth gnashing. "Lord Grayson is a fine man, and I have not been forced to do anything. I love Augusta as though she were my own."

His dismissive smirk was accompanied by a pitying gaze. "Of course you do. She is a sweet child. But when she grows and starts to bark orders at you like so many English mutts, you'll feel differently. For some one of your particular… qualities –" His hand reached up and stroked her cheek, coming to rest on her neck, long fingers wrapping around and taking firm grip as his other hand planted itself on her waist. "– I am certain I could find better employment for you in my household. Perhaps even one of an extremely domestic bent."

"Sir, you will remove your hands. If you don't, I will –"

"Scream?" He gave a mischievous smirk. "You might, but all I need say is that I caught one of the nannies trying to escape with my valuables." He reached into his pocket and quickly flashed to her a golden chain, an exceptional emerald dangling from it. "As an Irish woman and a servant, they'd be all too ready to believe. Please consider, I am prepared to make any service you perform very well compensated."

Loosening from her neck, his hand moved down the front of her collar and hesitated over her breast. Panic overtook Maeve as she attempted to pull away. Prideux snapped up her wrists and forced himself upon her, planting his vile mouth on hers. Struggling, she broke free of the intrusion and screamed.

"You limey bastard!"

The Frenchman flew from Maeve as she fell to the ground. The echo of fist upon jaw met her ears. Looking up, Maeve witnessed August moving swiftly, Jefferson quickly approaching, and Prideux doubled over in pain as a knee plowed into his stomach.

"I caught her stealing!" he cried.

Maeve heard Jefferson break in. "Maeve is no more a thief than you are a cotton gin! August, see to Maeve. I'll take care of this vile disgrace."

With hesitance, August backed away and rushed to Maeve's side. The commotion had drawn party-goers who were quickly filing out on to the veranda to watch. August's arms were around her, pulling her up, before Maeve could even reason fully what had happened.

"Are you hurt?"

Maeve shook her head but could not speak. August pulled her to his chest, and unthinkingly planted the witnessed kiss that all took to the rumor mill, grinding the finest flour of falsehoods.

August found himself a slandered man. No one questioned his concern; a gentleman would aid any lady in distress, even a servant. But to kiss her? What of that? Compassion for the fellow man did not reach the rosy-hued lip of the lord to the lady.

And lesser still to the hired help.

Caroline reported back to Meadowlark that all manner of talk had spread. August remained unconcerned, reassuring Maeve that despite her worries, it was just a passing fancy among the clucking hens, and that another bag of feed would soon occupy their small brains and smaller worlds. It would be forgotten, he claimed, in a fortnight. But the rumor proved too persistent, and when invitations to Augusta's tea - a fashion for the children of the wealthy- were sent to several prominent families in the community, more than a few came back denied.

Caroline and Maeve discussed at great length, but August held firm; he did not believe the matter required any attention or action. Jefferson finally convinced him otherwise. It was determined that if they had nothing to hide, then appearing in public in proper roles could dispel the rumors. Maeve would attend Easter service sitting in the Grayson pew at Norwich Church.

Only they did have something, not to hide, per se, but something they did not wish to expose to public scrutiny.

"Are you certain you want to go through with this?" August said as they all sat to breakfast.

Augusta was wholly consumed with a piece of toast, her feet dangling back and forth from her chair. Maeve drew her gaze from the child and looked into August's concerned expression.

"I'll not have Goosie losing face on my account. It won't require much, only that you treat me with utter indifference for a few hours. And that you remember to call me Miss O'Connor."

He smiled warmly and rubbed the top of her hand. "Then you must remember to call me Lord Grayson."

"I have some experience with that." She smirked.

"Joos!" Augusta wailed, her arms striving to reach the tumbler just beyond her reach. "Da, I wan' joos."

August lifted the wooden mug and moved it closer. "It really is a magnificent dress you fashioned for her, Caroline," he said upon closer examination of the garment. "Quite exquisite. And it took you only one day, you say?"

Caroline positively beamed at the compliment. "It is a talent of mine, though I had rather hoped I might have opportunity to employ the craft soon at Meadowlark."

Cheeks as red as embers burned brightly. "Caroline!" August spat. "You and I have said our piece on this, and I'll speak no more of it."

Maeve's head lashed left and right. August huffed and Caroline sighed.

"Of course. It was not my intention to upset you."

Maeve gave the siblings a sideways glance. "Whatever are you two going on about?"

His tension melting, August chuckled. "Did I not tell you?"

Caroline nodded, a timid blush in her cheeks. "You're right. She does sound English anymore."

"Jesus, Mary, and Joseph, whatever are you two croackin' about?"

Jefferson, seated at the end of the table, cleared his throat. "Shouldn't we go?"

August wiped his mouth before throwing his napkin on the table. "Yes, quite right. We'll be late."

Confused, Maeve refocused as she glanced at the clock and realized their time was up. A short carriage ride away, she steeled her nerves and prepared to play the role expected. All would be well as long as she kept her wits about her. And didn't look directly into August's eyes. As certain as rain, Maeve knew that would be her undoing, as even now, a simple glance was enough for him to pull her to any whim or fancy.

The first part of the service passed with relative ease, even with the sideward glances from every corner as they sat at the family pew, the second from the front. After the initial interest, the ruse settled in. Eyes focused forward as the somewhat stoic nature with which August treated Maeve fooled the lot. He was a little *too* convincing, Maeve thought, as even she began to wonder if she had slighted him in some manner.

As the second part of the service began, and Rev. Rathmore began the sermon, Maeve felt a pang of anxiety weave its way into her soul. Rathmore spoke of the importance of faith in the resurrection, of the ability to rise above one's sins and lead a proper, moral, and Christian life. The Bible showed all men could ascend above their station or equally fall from it, he preached. And when he quoted Proverbs 6:20, "My son, keep your father's commands and do not forsake your mother's teachings," Maeve was certain that his eyes were fixed steadfastly on August.

August, to his credit, did not flinch.

Shortly before the end of the sermon, Maeve looked and noticed an unfamiliar face in the front pew opposite. About her same age, the lady's grace was unparalleled. High, crimson-hued check bones were framed by delicate blonde curls. The fashion looked Parisian, augmented by a diamond broach on her lapel large enough that Maeve was certain a good Irish Catholic priest would have called it a vanity to wear in the house of the Lord.

"Caroline?" Maeve whispered as the organist began to play. "Who is that woman there?"

Caroline looked over her hymnal. "Duchess Alexandra Hannover."

"Alexandra?" Maeve repeated. The name wasn't familiar, despite that she was familiar with the names of most the aristocracy. "Is she new to Norwich?"

"Alex? Just returned, actually. Her husband, the duke, passed a few years ago. Now that she's mourned properly, she's come back home to… find his replacement, I suspect." She paused before adding, "She once fancied August. Everyone fancied August, though."

As the service dragged into the second hour, Caroline was blessed to have little Charles fall asleep on his father's shoulder. Augusta, however, was not so easily sidetracked, and fidgeted terribly. Maeve could see August's conflict; he wished so to reach out and calm her, but as they were mocking innocence, it would be the servant's job to keep the child quiet. Augusta, however, wasn't having it, and began to whimper. More than anything, she wanted her father. Cradling the child to her side, Maeve leaned in, feeling each eyeball in the church move with her.

“Lord Grayson?” she asked with a volume slightly higher than necessary. Perhaps some nearby would hear the formality in her voice, she thought. August did not turn, only leaned slightly in. “I think perhaps I should take Miss Grayson out?”

“Yes, quite right,” he answered quickly, waving his hand at her dismissively.

Maeve nodded her head in compliance and rose to leave, Augusta clutched in her arms. The service was nearly over, and it was unlikely there would be need to return, if fortune should favor. But as she stepped cautiously into the aisle, Augusta began to wail woefully.

“Daddy!” she cried, her arms stretching out. “I want Daddy!”

Several sympathetic gazes met Maeve’s. She was surprised. The little ruse must have worked, she hoped.

“Not now, Goosie. He’ll be along soon.”

The child screamed, every bit of air in her wee lungs fully utilized. “No, I wanna stay with Da. Let me go!”

“Please, poppet, he’ll come shortly. Church is almost over.”

The tempest of tantrum would not be quelled, and as every single eye, every ear observed young Miss Grayson, she gave yet another twist and pull. “Let me go, Ma! Let me go to Da!”

Ma. Da.

Not knowing what else to do, Maeve ran down the aisle, passing in her flight under the stained glass window depicting Eve’s banishment from Eden.

“I can’t go back, Caroline,” Maeve told the pleading woman a short time later.

She had fled to possibly the worst place: August’s coach. Not so unlike the day she had told Owen of her intention to leave, Maeve felt like Persephone becoming the consort of Hades.

"Maybe this all happened for the best," Caroline tried to counsel. "After all, there's been whisperings of it for years – it's better to just get it out there. Perhaps now August won't have any excuses."

"Excuses?" Maeve pondered. "Excuses for what?"

She could see Caroline cross herself in frustration. "It has been three years since Amelia died. It is proper for a gentleman to wait one year before considering marriage after losing his wife. It is commendable to wait two. I have advised August that, going on three years, it looks simply silly, and is to Goosie's disadvantage."

"What do you mean? August means to marry?"

Confused and unsure, Maeve's mind filled with terror at the notion that her August might even consider it. He hadn't discussed it with her, but of course, why would he? No doubt he would anticipate Maeve's taking exception to another Lady Grayson.

Caroline's nervous smile faltered. "Alas, no. He insists that the idea of marrying only to satisfy some social conditioning is laughable."

That relieved her somewhat. "Got a lick of sense about him still, then."

Caroline was dumbfounded. "You don't seem to understand. I am aggrieved that he's of this mind-set. It was my hope that he marry *you.*"

Nervous giggling erupted without delay, but Caroline was sincere. Suddenly, Maeve recalled the remarks at breakfast, of having hoped to have occasion for clothing for use at Meadowlark. It occurred to Maeve now that she was referring to a wedding gown.

For her.

"Well, that's just silly," Maeve spluttered dismissively. "August and I can't… I mean, he's a lord, and I'm a… It would never be acceptable to –"

No half-uttered excuses dissuaded Caroline. "Honestly, why not?"

"He's nobility and I'm Irish." Could she not understand? "There may be a quell amongst the Irish at the moment, but I am still… unacceptable."

"I married Jefferson," she countered, as though that very argument should solve the dilemma. "Maeve, August is afraid and conflicted. He knows what you two are doing is abhorrent in certain eyes. As a mistress, however, they expect you to be just a passing fancy. But if he marries you, I suspect he's afraid you'll end up hating him for the role you will be expected to play. With your heritage, the hens will never think you worthy and never accept you no matter how you may excel. No doubt that we all have elected to lead our lives the ways we think best, but that doesn't free us from the judgment of others."

Maeve looked at Caroline sternly, finally understanding.

Caroline continued, more sheepishly, "I think that August doesn't want to see you crumble as did our mother."

Maeve's brow furrowed. "What is it you think?"

"Me?" She grinned defiantly. "I want to see my sister, Maeve Grayson, make the chickens of Norwich choke on their own rotten eggs."

"Maeve Grayson," she repeated like an Amen to the longest prayer of her life. It sounded right, proper even.

"He won't ask you," Caroline added, stroking the now slumbering Augusta's hair. "You and I have hardly been traditional in our relationships with the less fair sex. Let's keep to that, shall we?"

Maeve cocked her head.

"You know Rathmore can not appear as though he's condoning adultery of so generous a patron of the church as August. Go now. Ask Rathmore to give his blessing for you to be wed. Once he sees that Rathmore agrees, I don't think August will be likely to resist."

It was all happening too fast to comprehend. "You're suggesting that I go ask August to marry me?"

"Do you think he would deny you?"

The sly smirk on Maeve's face served as answer.

"Then go. After all, I don't want my niece to grow up without a mother."

After kissing Caroline's cheek, Maeve rushed from the coach. Caroline was right. This was right.

She was going to marry August.

Whispers clocked her in silent accusation as she passed through the thinning congregation. She paid them no mind. Nothing would deter her from her errand. Maeve all but ran through the church. Outside the Reverend's closed door, she hesitated, steeling herself for one last moment before committing to the task.

She reached for the handle.

Then heard another woman's voice, and stopped.

"Really, August, it is fortunate that I've arrived to Norwich when I did," it said, following the shuffling feet inside the room. "It is an utter mess you've made of yourself. You should be thankful I'm so understanding of your plight as to offer my assistance."

"Alex, it was always my intention to marry," Maeve heard August say. *The Duchess,* she thought as her teeth ached from the pressure. "Of course, you're right. I've never been so embarrassed in all my life. The look on Maeve's face… It was…"

"Embarrassing, just like you said," the Duchess concurred, causing Maeve's stomach to twist.

She had embarrassed August? Didn't he consider how she felt?

"Well, August, you know what must be done."

"I have to agree," Rathmore added. "The Duchess is most correct. And I must say, offering you her hand is a blessing you should not take lightly. Your child needs a proper mother, not a nanny."

August grumbled. "Yes, of course, you're both right. Thank you. I'll announce our engagement tomorrow. But I'm woefully unprepared. I don't even have a proper ring to offer."

"We'll ride into London tonight and select something that will be divine," the Duchess offered, and Maeve wanted to gouge out her eyes. "I have exquisite taste, August. You needn't worry."

"But Maeve –" he protested.

"Don't worry about Maeve." She cut him off. "Really, I'm sure she's expecting it. After the trick you tried to pull today, she'll know you had to do something to keep Augusta's good name."

He sighed deeply. "I hope so. Best to wait to tell her tomorrow."

Maeve's hand fell. More precisely, her whole body suddenly felt as though it were stitched together and was threatening to spill out at the seams. Her heart – moments before flying on the tides of ecstasy – broke. She fell back to the street and to the coach, using the last of her strength to put on a brave, disingenuous mask of ease, so that she might escape Caroline's company.

"You can take comfort, Caroline," she told her would-have-been sister as she stepped into the coach. "Rathmore was able to sway August easily."

Caroline heard what she wanted to hear. She transferred the sleeping child into Maeve's arms and blew a kiss before closing the door. Not wanting to give August a chance to join them, and knowing from what she overheard that he would not in any event, she asked the driver to take Augusta and her back to Meadowlark.

August was to be wed, for certain, to someone who could be a "proper mother" and keep Augusta socially acceptable.

Not a poor Irish nanny.

Amelia would have been devastated if she knew. But Maeve would keep her promise. She would not allow him the opportunity. Not to her Augusta.

37 From the Inside Looking Out

Augusta's voice rang to the rafters, "Ma" echoing in a seemingly endless loop. August turned to Maeve, and was shocked by her crimson flush. They might have stood a chance if only the Irish lass had remained dismissive or, better yet, had chastised her charge for the mistake. Under the pressure of so many watchful eyes, Maeve panicked. With a scurry only achievable by one fearing for her life, she fled.

Every eye of Norwich society turned immediately to August. The time had long since passed since he cared what the ninnies thought of him; Caroline was long since wed and that concern had weakened. What they thought of Maeve, however, concerned him a great deal. If he had carried on an affair with any other "proper" lady of British society, it would have been frowned upon, but dismissed as a gentleman's dalliance. Even if the matter had just involved Maeve, it likely would have been seen as tawdry but no less abhorrent for a man of his status and particular marital situation. Or rather, lack of marital situation.

But what had just happened was so much worse. His young daughter had just called her "nanny" Ma in front of the whole of slew of them. Their eyes demanded explanation. More so, some had condemned him with the weight of their stares alone.

August turned to Caroline and found a smile both perplexing and oddly comforting; the very warmth of that expression told August things could not be nearly as bad as they seemed. He gave a small dismissive laugh, thinking that a cavalier attitude would serve to confuse, and turned back, seating himself without further deliberation.

The next twenty minutes found August motionless, his eyes transfixed on Reverend Rathmore. When at last the service concluded, he arose. The only errand on his mind was finding out Maeve, letting her know it was alright. August was a little surprised, however, when he felt a hand on his shoulder.

"A word in private, Lord Grayson?"

Rathmore's face displayed both concern and urgency. August noticed his eyes darting around and followed them, taking in the multiple queues forming flanks down the aisles. It was then that August realized Rathmore's protective intentions.

He remained calm and coolly turned to his sister. "Caroline, would you mind tracking down Miss O'Connor and letting her know I've been detained, but that I will see to her shortly? Please also let her know that I am not upset with her for… Goosie's outburst."

Caroline nodded gently, not wishing to wake Charles, who still kept silent in his father's arms. Jefferson passed without a word, only giving a reassuring smile.

A few minutes later, August found himself seated across from the clergyman in the silence of his chambers. He kept office in a small annex at the side of the church. They had successfully sequestered themselves without having been accosted. Rathmore was quiet, contemplative. Finally, after nearly all August's patience had left him, he spoke.

"The Bible says, 'Let he who is without sin cast the first stone,'" he mused. "I'm not about to attempt to call you out. I think you know perfectly well the church's position on adultery."

A sharp intake of air prefaced his retort. "I think the church knows perfectly well my family's generosity," August boldly declared.

To August's surprise, Rathmore's face lit up. "I have offended you. It was not my intention."

Giving him a less than kind glare, August asked, "What precisely was your intention?"

"Everybody knows," Rathmore stated succinctly, with a dismissive wave of his hand. "Your relationship with Miss O'Connor has been presumed for quite some time. Within Meadowlark, few care how you carry on. However, once you brought that into public at Prideux's –"

"He was trying to manhandle her!" August broke in. "I was… concerned. She looked so frightened, and I just wanted to assure her that all would be well."

"Wanted to assure her?" The Reverend leaned forward, one eyebrow cocked. "Lord Grayson…August," his gaze narrowed suspiciously, "how long have you been in love with Miss O'Connor?"

August could not bring himself to lie to a man of God. Nor did he wish to. He tired of the denial, of Maeve playing a part to keep by his side only for the sake of saving him the scandal.

"Since I first saw her when I was hardly more than a child," August admitted, and found himself jovial despite the gravity of the moment. "She was meant for me, as though God had crafted us, the one for the other. But we are from two different worlds. She and I could never…"

"Why ever not, August?"

The familiar voice of his past jolted him. He had not heard the door open, or the lady walk in. Both Rathmore and he turned to see the impressive visage of…

"Duchess Hannover." Rathmore completed August's thought. He gave a slight nod of his head in welcome. "I apologize, but we did not hear you come in."

Alexandra had always been catty, and August still recalled vividly her headstrong fashion and presumption to know best of other's affairs. It puzzled him that Amelia, so genteel and compassionate in nature, had been such a confidante of hers.

"As I intended it," she returned, a smug smile gracing her face as she turned and closed the door gently behind her. "Please, gentlemen, don't let my presence deter you."

Rathmore shifted uncomfortably. "Duchess, if you seek counsel, might I offer to make an appointment another time? Lord Grayson and I are…"

Alexandra removed her silken gloves and slapped them in a flustered manner into her left hand. "If women left all concerns to men, there would be a great slighting in the matters of the sexes," she huffed. "Now, August, you just said that you love this O'Cabbage woman, did you not?"

"O'Connor," he corrected, though wondering what business it was of the Duchess' to meddle. "And yes, with all my heart. But I don't see why you –"

"Amelia was my dearest friend," she said, cutting him off. "Perhaps the closest I have ever had, though that may not count toward much. She and I continued writing to each other, even after your marriage. Were you aware of that?"

"Not in the slightest."

Alexandra grinned amusedly. "Yes, well no doubt she recalled your distaste for my company. Mel wrote me about your O'Connor, told me you seemed quite taken with her. Oh, she did not mention her by name, but you look to that Irishwoman the way Mel described, I can only assume it is her. And I can see it. In the very air that sparked between the two of you despite your best efforts, I can see it."

August stared at Alexandra, unable to believe that Amelia had shared so intimate a confession. Then again, he mused, Amelia must have been very alone during his time in Ireland. Was it not possible she would have reached out to her bosom friend, a woman who, like herself, had agreed to a match benefiting her social role but leaving her heart bereft? And, perhaps, in the echo of bitter choices, a champion for romance?

The Duchess continued. "I miss my friend, and I know you two treasured each other as well, in your way. Mel and I always understood you were not like us. You were not meant to live your life in the service of your title. In memory of my friend, please, do what is right and marry Miss O'Connor."

He could scarcely believe his ears. The two in conjunction were telling him everything he longed to hear, and nothing to which he could stand to listen.

"I cannot," he proclaimed, shaking his head in denial. "I would not do that to her. The way it would change her, what would be expected of her... And I don't think she'd…."

"You actually think she'd deny your proposal?" Alexandra posited, a clear tone of chide and disbelief inking into her words. "Fine, do not ask her. Tell her. Tell her you are marrying her. Of course, I will be willing to lend my hand to the effort, as far as gossip is concerned. If the Duchess of Hannover accepts you, what can the ninnies of Norwich argue in defense? Really, August, it is fortunate that I've arrived to Norwich when I did. It is an utter mess you've made of yourself. You should be thankful I'm so understanding of your plight as to offer my assistance."

"Alex, it was always my intention to marry." And he did hold that as a distant dream to be fulfilled someday – when Augusta was grown and wed, when her place in society could no longer be jeopardized by her father's questionable relations. But not now.

Still, August grew desperate to free Maeve from the prison in which his decisions and life had trapped her. In that moment, he knew it was useless. He couldn't cause her the grief any longer. For all the things she had given him, the least he could do was offer her legitimacy.

The wisdom of following the sage, though unsolicited advice of the Reverend and the Duchess was suddenly all too clear.

"Of course, you're right. I've never been so embarrassed in all my life. The look on Maeve's face… It was…"

"Embarrassing, just like you said," Alexandra concurred, and August felt his stomach twist into a knot.

Oh God, how would Maeve ever forgive him?

"Well, August, you know what must be done."

"I have to agree," Rathmore interjected. "The Duchess is most correct. And I must say, offering you her hand is a blessing you should not at all take lightly. Your child needs a proper mother, not a nanny."

Maeve had never been just a nanny, but how could they understand that? But that had not been what the Reverend intended.

"Yes, of course," August finally returned. "You're both right. Thank you. I'll announce our engagement tomorrow. But I'm woefully unprepared. I don't even have a proper ring to offer."

"We'll ride into London tonight and select something that will be divine," Alexandra offered. "I have exquisite taste, August. You needn't worry."

"But Maeve…" he protested.

She was a simple woman, and likely anything a duchess selected would be far too excessive for her tastes. It would be likely to overwhelm her, and perhaps she'd realize the mistake in becoming the next Lady Grayson.

"Don't worry about Maeve," Alexandra insisted, seemingly reading his thoughts. "Really, August, I'm sure she's expecting it. After the trick you tried to pull today, she'll know you had to do something to ensure Augusta's good name."

"I hope so."

He wanted to go to his love. They had been so certain that marriage would be impractical, it had never been brought up as anything more than a passing *imagine if...*

But Maeve needed to know that he was sincere, that August wanted this not only to legitimize Augusta's place in society or shield himself from further gossip. He was doing it because he wanted *her*.

Yes, she would need a ring. Something simple. Something sincere. Something…

Something completely Maeve.

He sighed, knowing truth for truth and acknowledging its name.

"Best just to wait to tell her tomorrow."

38 | The Pursuit of Happiness

The years had brought her beauty to full blossom, her cheeks still rose red and her skin as milky as Owen's every memory could recall. But she was sad, manifested in the loss of her glow.

Still, it was Maeve.

"Jesus, Mary, and Joseph, can it really be?"

Nary could the blacksmith believe the love that had slipped through his fingers three years before was at his door. The very door she had closed behind her, never looking back, as he cursed her name to the Heavens. Maeve's scent, floral and feminine and full, hit him, and Owen knew. This was no ghost of his ain true love; this was she for whom his heart had starved.

"Owen," she said softly, simply.

Of course she was at a loss for words. Though she avoided his gaze, it was all too apparent that she stumbled for what to say, some place to go beyond the mere invocation of a name. His hand reached for her, brushing delicately along her cheek, confirming to his still-doubting mind that she stood before him once more.

So entranced momentarily had he been with her visage that he hadn't seen that on to which she held, nothing less than the tender limb of a weary child with radiant blue eyes and raven locks.

The child, hardly more than a toddler, looked warily past the blacksmith and into the flat. Dripping with beauty, Owen instinctively wanted to pick her up and pinch her cheeks, but the question of exactly who she was cut him to the quick.

Had Maeve… Had she bore…

"No, Owen, she's not yours," Maeve stated quickly, and he thought he heard shame in her words. "Nor mine. At least, not by blood."

Gulping, the anger that threatened to rise and overtake him was quelled.

"Grayson's." Owen spat it out through gritted teeth; an understanding, not a question.

Maeve nodded, wise enough not to deny what was so evident. "Her mother passed during the birth."

Gnashing his teeth further, he pulled back his hand in disgust. "So now you're not only his whore, but you're also his child's slave. And this is what you left me for?"

She looked neither offended nor apologetic, choosing to remain silent instead.

"What do you want? Why are you here?"

She guided her ward in and closed the door behind her, not bothering to wait for an invitation. She took little time to make herself at ease as she knelt in front of the child and began unbuttoning her opulent cloak.

"I didn't know what else to do, so we came in with the post last night. No one saw us."

The words were fast, as though trying to convince herself of her own lie. Dismissive. Suddenly, the thought crossed Owen's mind.

"What the hell did he do to you?" the blacksmith demanded, anger rising red with the flush of his cheeks. The child trembled and flinched, but Owen's rage was too well justified to be so easily tamed. "Did he hurt you? Did he hit you?"

"Never!" Maeve gasped as she stood and started taking off her cloak. "He just… Whatever we had, it's over."

"What sand!" Owen barked, trying nonetheless to dampen his tone as he could see the child shake with fear. "What sand have you, Maeve O'Connor, to show up on my doorstep after leaving me with your broken promises and your broken house! And with the bastard's child!? Your father would turn over in his grave if he could see the sorry excuse of a daughter you've become."

Legendary Irish rage showed itself as her rosy cheeks flushed crimson and her brown eyes stormed. "How dare you! I'll remind you that I got into the crazy situation by trying to protect my father!"

Oh, but this girl still knew no bounds when it came to driving him mad. Owen pulled her to the only window the little flat could boast and pointed out, over the rooftops of the surrounding buildings, to the cemetery.

"And yet, there he lies – cold, dead, and forgotten. Slain by English arms. And here you stand, clothed in his enemy's best governess gown."

The slap she landed broke the child's resolve as the little one began to cry full out. Maeve's body shrank with guilt as she hastened to her side.

"There, there now, Goosie. I'm sorry, love. Mummy just got a little angry. I promise, it won't happen again."

"Mummy?"

Maeve grimaced at Owen. "The only she has ever – or will ever – know. Now, Mr. Murphy…," She grabbed the child's cloak and hand, and began moving toward the door, "if we're not welcome, we will most certainly –"

Panic sobered him. "No, Maeve, don't go!"

Owen knew in the moment he saw her turn that, no matter how determined he told himself to be, he couldn't deny truth. He knew to the very reaches of his soul that he could not stand to see her go a second time. Even if he didn't own her heart, even if it would kill him in the end and make him neighbors with Rory, he needed to keep her.

Owen sighed, letting out all his frustration with a shrug. "Just… tell me. What do you need?"

"A place to hide for a few weeks," she said plainly, "until I figure out what to do."

The blacksmith looked around the one-room flat, knowing the one thing for which she asked, he could not give her. Perhaps her, but not her and a child, and in the midst of town.

"This won't do," he said, motioning to the wider room. Owen looked the child, her tears drying over-reddened cheeks. "Too small, and too dirty for your *leanaí.*"

Then a thought, brief but strong and persistent as a bull, crossed his mind. "But I think I might know a place."

"Maeve?"

Owen knew she was there; he could see the wispy but ever-present smoke emanating from the chimney, rising towards the darkening sky. Maeve was reckless this way, burning fires all times of the day. Anyone who may have made their way from the overgrown and unkempt path to Shepherd's Bluff would see clearly that squatters had taken up in the middleman's abandoned cottage.

Still, Maeve cooked. She could not weep, she could not go to market, she could not sew, but she could cook. And by cooking whatever meager scrap the blacksmith was able to bring her from town in the evening or find in the forest at morn, she kept herself occupied so as not to dwell.

So as not to think of him.

In the two weeks since she had arrived, Owen still hadn't figured out exactly what it was that had happened in England. It was obvious he wasn't the pull. She had been searching for a sympathetic friend, despite his initial reticence. For now, if that was what she needed, that was what Owen would be.

Maybe, just maybe, if enough time passed, and he allowed her some space, her heart would find its way back to him as well.

"Back here, Owen!"

In the bedroom, he found her sitting next to the child, the sleeping figure's chest keeping a slow rhythm of rise and fall.

Owen mused at the image before him, thinking that, but for the lack of such fine, ebony hair in either of their families, this may have been the reception he had come home to every day. Though, in his fantasies, there was more than one child: two strapping boys, and one tender lass.

"She really is quite lovely, isn't she?"

Maeve beamed in her pride, as though she had something to do with the fact. "Yes, she's beautiful. She looks so very much like her fa…"

Her words died as the memory was resurrected. How many times had Owen witnessed since her return the way her body would seize up at the mere recollection of Grayson? Maeve had settled into the temporary arrangement with a mellow spirit outwardly that still surprised him. Still, whenever the English bastard entered her mind, her face clouded over in sorrow and her brow became heavy with doubt.

Crossing the threshold, Owen took her hand and led her out of the bed chamber. He closed the door and guided Maeve to a chair next to the hearth, pushing her down and kneeling before her.

"You have to tell me what happened," he began, his voice firm. "What made you leave? Can't it…" Owen couldn't even believe he was making the suggestion, but every unspoken whisper in the air told him she loved Grayson still. "Can't it be mended somehow?"

Maeve shook her head vehemently. "No. He didn't do anything to me, and that is exactly why I left – he didn't do anything to me. He loved me, protected me, cherished me, but always as though I was a secret plaything he kept hidden in his closet. I let it go for so long; I didn't mind because I knew every moment he loved me. But he didn't love me enough to…" She trailed off, her eyes filling with tears.

"Go on," Owen encouraged. "Not enough to…"

Letting out a shaky sigh, she let go the tension. "Well, not enough to give me anything more than nothing."

What she said next threw the unsuspecting blacksmith for a loop.

"We have to go back."

He nearly choked on his own tongue.

"Go back?" Owen stammered, shooting to his feet. "You can't be serious!"

"No matter his offense, it was wrong for me to take Goosie from her father."

"But, Maeve!" he protested further, pacing. "I have seen you with this child. She loves you, as true as her own mother you were."

"It's still wrong. She asks about August constantly. Caroline and Jefferson as well. I can't keep finding excuses. I can't keep lying to her, Owen. If August wants me to…" A throaty gulp swallowed more than tears. "If he wants me just as her nanny, then at least I don't lose Augusta too. At least I can still make good my promise to Amelia for her daughter –"

"What in the hell do you care about Amelia Grayson? Was she ready to step aside so you could take her place?" She would not answer. "Think about this for a moment. Grayson loved you. As much as it pains me to say that, it must be true. Took you from the only home you'd ever known and all the others you have ever loved. And then he… did whatever he's done. What makes you think he won't d his own daughter the same?"

"Don't be silly. August would never do that to Goosie."

"Really?" Licking his lips, Owen dared her. "Then why is she here, Maeve? What were you protecting her from? Can you still protect her from it if you take her back now?"

"No, no I couldn't."

Realization dawned on her face, and he could see he had won. Maeve looked… blank. Owen mused that this was good; finally, she would have a fresh perspective not clouded over with her unfounded feelings for the English dog.

Her empty eyes turned to him. "What do I do, Owen? I can't raise her hiding out in a middleman's cottage, and least of all at Middle Lake. He'll come here eventually, looking for me. I have to go… somewhere. And soon."

Owen smiled, knowing well that this was the time to tell her, to make her believe this was right.

"I know," he said, taking her hand in his and kissing it. She flinched for a moment, as though she might pull back, before allowing him to run his fingers over hers. "Don't worry, I have a plan. But we'll need some money."

His eyes tracked to the corner of the room and the few items of clothing and small bag that Maeve had brought with her from England.

"How much do you think we can get for your things?"

"Unkie Owen!" the child squealed, bouncing up and down. "Houses! Houses!"

Maeve smiled, stroking the child's hair into place. "Yes, Goosie, houses. Ever so many. Jesus, Mary, and Joseph, how many! It's just like London, isn't it, sweet?"

Owen grimaced. "Aye, and just like London, they hate Irish here too."

Maeve rolled her eyes. "This be the man who convinced me this would be a fresh start?"

He loved that her few weeks in Ireland had cleared her voice of the English overtones.

"Are you rescuing me from the lion's den just to throw me back to the wolves?"

With a small chuckle, he shook his head. "No wolves here, Maeve. Just overfed fat cats."

Castle Garden was stuffed to the rafters with every vagrant and riffraff from Europe and beyond. Augusta held Maeve's hand, overwhelmed at the clutter of the clueless as they queued for processing in the steamy interior of the old military fort. For hours they waited. With each passing moment, Owen's body and tolerance grew wearier. When he heard the child yelp as some passing brute knocked her down, reminding Owen that he was likely to be tossed right back on to a departing ship if got started was the only way he calmed enough not to duck the oaf.

"I meant nothing, I didn't see her," the offender pleaded.

"Be lucky she didn't break anything!" Owen barked back, shaking his fist. Maeve pulled Augusta, shaken but unhurt, back to her feet as Owen leaned over to inspect her. "Are you okay, Goosie?"

Maeve's shocked eyes shot to him. "What did you say?"

"Are you okay, Goosie?" a confused Owen repeated.

Maeve's mouth broke into a broad, beaming smile. "Owen Murphy, do you know that's the first time you have ever called her by name?"

Owen retraced his memory and realized she was right. He had only thought of Augusta as Grayson's child. Now a little pocket of his heart was expanding to embrace her.

"Guess so," he returned, holding his hand out to Maeve. She took it readily, running her fingers in little circles over the back of his hand. As their eyes locked, he swore a spark of their former infatuation passed between them. He knew Maeve had never loved him, even before Grayson swept her away, but there had been a camaraderie, a suggestion that one day she might.

"Next!"

The shouting officer brought Owen to attention.

"Remember, just let me do the talking." He leaned over to Maeve and whispered.

"We haven't all day, now. NEXT!"

Sheepishly, Owen approached the table, Maeve and Augusta following closely.

"Port of Origin?"

"Cork."

"Town of Origin?" The officer looked up over half-moon spectacles, his eyes focusing on the Irishman expectantly.

"Killarney."

He made a few quick scribbles. "Names?"

"Murphy – Owen, Maeve, and Augusta," he answered, pointing to each in turn.

"Murphy, Owen. Wife, Maeve and daughter –" The officer eyed the child warily, noting no doubt that she did not look particularly like either her mother or father, "Augusta?"

Owen smiled and shook his head. "No, Maeve is my brother's widow, sir. And little Goosie here is theirs. A great tragedy when her da died. A different sort of man from me, took after me mother's side. Not a bit of –"

"All right, all right," the officer grumbled dismissively, his pen scratching hard over the paper, venting his frustration. "Enough. Just give me what I ask for and no more, cotton? Murphy, Owen, the suffering widow, Maeve, and daughter, Augusta."

Several other bits of information were collected before a physical inspection. Augusta giggled when they thumbed through her hair, looking for bugs. Owen unabashedly smiled at the thought of Grayson's child being treated like a true Irish commoner. Some part of him thought it served justice.

Finally cleared, Owen took Maeve by the hand, who in turn took Augusta. Outside of Castle Garden, Maeve's eyes scanned the crowd.

"Are you certain they'll be here?"

Owen shrugged. "He's always been trustworthy, I wouldn't expect him to –"

"Wouldn't expect me to what, Murphy?"

A great shadow cast over them, engulfing Owen whole, as Maeve spun on heel and took in the grinning mug of –

"Patrick O'Keefe!" she exclaimed, throwing her arms around his muscular frame. He picked her up clear off the ground. "Praise be, I never thought I'd see you again. Where is Patty?"

"Back at the flat," he answered as he set her down. "Clare and Pat are spiteful today. Owen." He greeted the blacksmith, giving a quick tap on the shoulder. "Good of you to finally bring our Maeve back to us. And hello to you, little lass."

Bending over, Patrick took little Augusta's hand in his bear-like paw and shook it all playfully and wild.

"I suppose you must be Miss Augusta. Jumping Jehoshaphat, but aren't you a sweet little thing?"

Augusta seemed confused, flashing her eyes to Maeve. "Am I, Mummy?"

Maeve grinned. "Sweeter than honey, *mo chroi.*"

As Patrick and Owen saw to loading the trunks on the cart, Maeve and Augusta settled right behind the driver's bench. The neighborhood of Five Points where Patrick and Patty had a small flat made Owen feel they were descending slowly in to Hell. He wondered how Patrick and Patty had tolerated living in such cramped spaces and squalor after having lived their lives at verdant Middle Lake, and despaired to think Maeve, having been wooed by the opulence of British society, might take one look at this way of life and turn tail towards Britannia.

As the cart swung from side to side, hitting every bump to ever dot the streets of New York City, Owen could see Maeve's face turning greener. Poor girl, he thought. She had become so accustomed to comfort. He almost growled at the recollection that it was not him, but Grayson who had provided her with that.

"Leaving in two days?"

Patty gawked at Owen and Maeve in disbelief, as though they had told her that in two days, Maeve's head would fall off and Owen's skin would turn purple.

"I cannot stay in New York," Maeve declared as she threw the dish rag over her shoulder and turned away from the stack of drying plates. "August knows too many people with business here. There's too much chance someone will recognize us."

Patty was incredulous. "I assure you, none of August's people are likely to stray down to Five Points. You've been here less than a month. Besides," she added, "we'll be heading west soon. I expected you would come with us."

As far as the Irish in Five Points, the O'Keefes were better off than most. Patrick had a natural ability to move men to his will, both by brain and by brawn. He was a strapping worker too, and had quickly gained a commanding position on the docks. It gave him enough income that he and Patty had been able to keep a three-room flat for only the children and themselves, instead of piling up two families to a room the way so many others did. Jobs were ample in America, and a hardworking man could always find a way to earn an honest loaf of bread. But bread at the end of the day didn't make a nice pillow, and the wages of the Irish were often too low to do anything other than overcrowd the small tenements.

Maeve turned as she sat next to Owen on the O'Keefes' settee. He fought the temptation to scoot closer, perhaps even allow his fingertip accidentally to brush against hers, but hastened himself to act slowly. The greatest torture came after dark, when Maeve and he would make a bed on the sitting room floor to sleep. How often would Owen lay awake, staring at the way the moonlight from the one window fell over her, dreaming that it was their marital bed instead of an old quilt spread over the dusty mat, remembering the feel of her body under his…

Maeve sighed, her shoulders slumping. "No, Patty. I won't go west. I want to stay east."

"Want to stay somewhere where you can go back easily if you change your mind," Patrick grumbled as he fidgeted with the table across the room, trying to locate the source of an irritating squeak.

Maeve made no response, and as such, Owen considered that Patrick might have hit the nail on the head. It hadn't occurred to him that that was the reason she had convinced him to accompany her to Boston. Still, Owen was certain she had gained enough distance now. Since they had left Ireland, Maeve had made very little mention of Grayson. Even Augusta was asking less often after her father.

Closing her eyes, Maeve collected herself upright and pronounced in a very certain voice, "I am not going back, Patrick. I simply don't want to go to the wilds of the west and try to help raise civilization from scratch. Boston will be good for Goosie. And for me."

Owen glanced to the child already asleep on the floor for the night, wondering what Maeve's true intents were for her.

And for him.

Maeve's eyes narrowed on Owen as she leaned against the back of the newly purchased chair. It had eaten up the last money they had managed to raise selling her things in Ireland, but the house now felt like a home rather than some random flat in South Boston.

Her vague question still lingered in the air. Owen looked away from the window where he sat whittling a piece of wood he'd pick up off the stack by the fireplace.

"Why what, Maeve?"

"Why have you done all this for us? After the horrible thing I did to you?"

She crossed the room, taking slow, deliberate steps as she folded her arms over her chest, waiting for a reply.

Turning attention back to the half-shaped block of wood, he shrugged. "You well know why. Don't make me say it."

"I want to hear it," she returned a playfully as she laid her hand on his knife, stilling his work. With begging eyes, she added, "Please, Owen?"

Running his fingers through his hair, Owen knew he couldn't hide it anymore. He rose, standing proudly and without shame before declaring, "Because I love you, Maeve O'Connor."

Rather than seem surprised or taken aback, she instead began to weep. Instinctively, Owen moved to comfort her, wrapping his arms around her and pulling her close, laying her sobbing frame against his chest.

"I don't… deserve… you," Maeve muttered between heaves of her chest and the flow of her tears. "After… everything… how can you? How could anybody love me?"

She doubted her own value again, and he inwardly acknowledged his own contribution to her belief. Owen had spent weeks demeaning Grayson's treatment of her, questioning his feelings. Of course, Maeve would turn it around and think that instead of calling out Grayson, Owen was questioning her own. She thought she wasn't worthy of a Lord. And now, perhaps, she even thought she wasn't worthy of a lowly blacksmith.

Her hair grew wet from weeping as Owen smoothed his hand over her cheek. "Maeve, when you give your heart to someone, it's theirs to do with what they please, no matter the cost." He leaned closer, and whispered into her ear, "Like you for him, that's how I feel for you. Is that so hard to believe?"

Her eyes looked up, red and wet and all too pitiful. A smile lingered on lips unkissed for far too long. Owen couldn't breathe, could not think of anything but the taste of her, like a childhood memory resurfacing.

Slowly, he pulled her chin up and lowered his lips to hers, reliving every promise made when their hearts were young and their way untried.

He expected her to pull back, to retreat, but praised the heavenly host when instead she rolled up on her toes to bring them closer together. Her hands found anchor on his neck as his hands slowly descended down her back. All the passion and yearning suppressed doubled back on him as Owen held her.

"Maeve, I love you."

Hot breath fell across his ear as he turned his attention to her neck, tasting flesh for which he had hungered for years. Barely had Owen's mouth pulled back to the underside of her chin when he felt Maeve stiffen in his grasp. Fearing some pain had been caused her, Owen distanced their bodies to take in the horrified expression she wore.

"I cannot."

Unrequited flames of love and lust flared into anger. "Still, Maeve!? Still, you keep yourself for him?"

Her hand clutched her stomach as she turned. "Like you said, I love him... no matter the cost."

"Don't!"

It was so simple a solution, why couldn't she see it? All Maeve needed was to stop loving Grayson, and start loving *him.* Start loving him, and he would make her happy. Owen laughed at his own conflicting demands. She would perhaps never love him as she loved the English bastard, but Owen was willing to love her enough for the two of them.

"Maeve, marry me."

Bulging eyes evidenced her surprise. "What?"

He pulled her shaking figure back, determined to make her see the truth. "You love him? Fine. But I'm the one here now. I have crossed an ocean in pursuit of your happiness all because I love you. I've given up my home, my business, all because I love you. And I will make you the happiest wife in all of these United States, all because I love you. Please, see reason. I'll always take care of you – and Goosie – as though she were my own, our own. Please, Maeve, just… say yes."

He could see the debate behind her eyes. "But we've told everyone I am your brother's widow. Won't it look quite the scandal?"

He grinned at her. "Is that the best excuse you have? We'll move. That's one beautiful thing about this country. There's so damn much of it."

He kissed her firmly on the mouth, thinking they were sealing the agreement. Instead, she spoke into his lips.

"I cannot marry you, Owen, even still."

Stilling his efforts, he closed his eyes and drew away his lips, letting out a lengthy, frustrated sigh.

She continued, "But I can show you my appreciation for all you have done for us…"

A strange lurch overcame him as his body shook. Maeve's hands sank to his hips before slowly trailing down over the front of his pants.

"Maeve, what are you doing?"

He could see plainly her reluctance and disgust with her own actions. "It's the only repayment I can offer you."

Nothing short of a growl escaped his throat as Owen recalled himself, remembering that Augusta was asleep in the next room. "Don't you dare, Maeve O'Connor!" he spat, pushing her roughly back into the chair. "Don't you try to pay me off the same way you paid him! Don't you try to make me into him to relieve your guilt. I'll have your hand, or I'll take none of you."

She cried, tears stinging her eyes. "Ask any price of me, but my hand and my heart I cannot pay. Both are purchased in full."

Barely able to realize his own actions, his hand drew back, prepared to strike sense in to her. Maeve winced as, instead of his palm across her check, he grabbed her wrist, forcing her right hand up to the level of her eyes.

"I don't see Grayson's ring on this finger." He threw the appendage back at her. "And now I know it will never wear mine."

As Owen crashed through the door of the flat and rounded the bottom of the stairs, he swore he heard her call for him. For a moment, he paused, thinking he had been rash and that he should go back before his pride got the better of him.

He considered the same the next morning as he awoke curled in a ball on the steps of the Old Courthouse. And he considered it thrice as he signed with Captain Jeremiah Burgess' crew bound for Cork.

But after that, he would think no more that she might someday be his. Maeve was Grayson's, clear as the day was long.

Rory had understood that too. He had never gone after Maeve, knowing her heart had been claimed for good. Finally, Owen had learned the same. No wonder Rory had been so quick to sacrifice his life in the uprising; the English had already stole him of the one thing that made his life worth living.

39 | Common Ground

November 9, 1872

Maeve awoke with a start. She didn't know if she shivered because the night was cold, or if the warmth of human kindness had abandoned her. She tried to pull the thin throw tighter around her trembling shoulders. The brick walls of the jail did little to keep away the chill, though crossing her arms and rubbing vigorously helped some. As she began to pace, trying to warm, the approach of loud voices, brash and bawdy, and the jingling of keys met her ears.

Another prisoner. The first in some time who would share the wing of the jail, in fact.

No sooner had Maeve made the conclusion than her eyes squinted from the light that accompanied the entrance of the three men to the holding area, her home since the day Owen had led justice to her door.

"All right, you," one of the officers barked at the poor sot being manhandled in the direction of the empty cell next to hers, "keep your head down and your mouth shut and you might make it 'til morning."

Maeve could hear him struggle against their efforts. "For the love of Jesus, I didn't do a thing," he contested.

Maeve recognized the accent at once – perfectly County Kerry. A vague momentary thrill flashed through her that she might actually know this man. After the weeks, she was thrilled with the notion of having anyone to talk to outside of court. It was fortunate that he should be put here in the same wing of the jail. Still, arrests heated up when the temperatures went down and all manner of cheap spirits were employed in lieu of expensive clothing to keep away the chill. Perhaps the other areas of the jail were occupied.

The second officer must have thrown him pretty hard into his cell before locking the door with a metallic clank. Maeve heard his body fall to the floor with a grunt, and felt an instant sense of unease for his welfare.

The begrudging voice of the authority ground out, "Now, I'm going to go have a little chat with your victim. Keep your yap shut, and remember your manners." A reddened face curved around the wall as the officer sneered at Maeve. "There's a… lady present."

With that, the officers commended each other on a good "roughin' up of another damned pick-pocketin' Patrick" and left, locking the door behind them, leaving Maeve and the new arrival to uncomfortable silence.

She heard his body sliding against the floor as, she assumed, he scooted his back up the wall.

"Well, go on with it," he invoked at last, speaking Irish.

"With what?" Maeve asked innocently, surprised he had correctly assumed she was a fellow countryman.

"Telling me what you're in for," he returned, as though it were the most obvious thing in the world. "Isn't that how this works? We compare stories and then complain about our sorry lot in life?"

"I guess." His bluntness would have surprised her in any other venue. "Kidnapping. And you're a thief."

He scoffed. "So they say. Are you guilty?"

"In a manner of speaking. You're not?"

"Sure, but they'd be hard pressed for proof."

"What did you steal?"

He laughed lowly, "Time." And even though it was in mock of her, the giddiness gave her restless spirit a temporary reprieve. "What do you mean by, 'in a manner of speaking?'"

Why hold back? Her trial was all but over, and Maeve was sure to be convicted. What fate held for her beyond that, who knew?

"I stole a child from her father's home," she admitted in as matter-of-factly a tone as possible, before clarifying, "but I like to think it was at her mother's request."

He clicked his tongue disapprovingly. "Now that's a convenient defense. How did you manage to pry a child out of its mother's arms, let alone with permission?"

Maeve had never told her story to anyone, never once revealed the promises made in the shadow of Amelia's deathbed. It had seemed almost sacred at the time, like a nun taking vestments and a vow of silence. Amelia died to give Augusta life, to ensure August's place, and Maeve lived on to ensure that sacrifice was not in vain.

With a deep sigh, she proceeded with the confessional. "Her mother was my lover's wife and died during the birth. I just… became her mother after that. It was an odd set of circumstance, but we all just made the best of what was what."

"The father… You loved him?" he asked, sounding genuinely curious.

She didn't have to qualify that answer in the slightest. "To a fault. But I was so naive in those days. I thought if I loved him enough, and if we both loved his daughter, that we could just go on living in our perfect little secret. He was a noble, see, and me? Well, I'm nothing so special as to not end up here. I told myself just having him was enough."

He was silent for a few minutes, and Maeve had thought he might have fallen asleep. Or passed out. The smell of alcohol coming off him wasn't so strong as to be overwhelming, but it did snake around the corner of the cell, nonetheless.

But instead, he almost frightened her to death when his voice came across the darkness, a little more inquisitive and softer than before. "And your secret became known?" With a scoffing chuckle, he added, "What happened, did the mistress become the missed? Take off with another lass, did he? Or did you finally come to your senses and took his kid for revenge? Hell hath no fury and the such."

He could not have possibly understood the pain so vulgar a suggestion induced.

"The former," she said bitterly from behind clenched teeth. Taking a deep breath, she attempted to ease the sudden tension racking her body. "Without my knowledge, he arranged to wed another. I suppose he meant well. She could certainly give our… *his* daughter better opportunities than a poor Irish nanny could."

"Wait a fine moment!" he exclaimed. "If he was making all these dealings behind your back, how did you come into the know?"

"I heard him agree in front of a reverend to take her hand."

"Is that so?" He scoffed. "Bloody English. Doesn't even have the decency to betray you to your face."

"Seemingly not," Maeve agreed with a snide grimace. "Not sure he would've. He'd kept things from me before. Big things. Besides, I'd made a vow to the mother – on her deathbed, no less – I'd never let Goosie endure that … façade. The way I saw it, me staying while he married that… woman… would have broken that promise. So yes, I took her and left before I would allow him to make a fool of me and a justification of her. Then, of course, he didn't marry."

"So surely your conclusion was correct."

Maeve's brow furrowed as she marveled at the way his thoughts so perfectly aligned with her own. "I suppose after I took his child away, there wasn't a purpose for it anymore."

"But you still love him."

Were her emotions so inherently ingrained into her tone?

"Yes, but does it matter?"

"Women!"

As the echo of his *hmph* echoed, Maeve felt a universal insult at his interjection on behalf of her sex. "What does that mean?"

"You always assume you're the only ones who make sacrifices." She could hear his body shift toward the front of his cell, his voice becoming clearer. "You say you took the child to protect her from her father's giving into society. But did you ever consider that he was doing the same to you?"

Maeve sat thoroughly confused. "I don't follow."

"You say he was a widower. Well, why didn't he marry you if you were so happy together?"

Even from a drunken Killarney sot, it was a ridiculous suggestion. "He was a lord."

"Aye, and wouldn't a lord think long and hard about asking such a compromise of an Irish peasant?" His voice slipped into English. "Would have put you in a precarious position, subject you to the scrutiny of his demeaning and demonstrative class."

An impossible and fantastical sense of familiarity filled her, but she couldn't make herself believe the farcical notion of whom the "thief" might be was true. "I'm not –"

"Isn't it possible he always intended to marry you, but was afraid the consequences that would bring for you?"

"But he never made any mention of mar –"

He wouldn't allow her to make a proper retort. "Might he not have been seeing out a vow he himself made to never again put the women he loved through the inquisition and rejection of his kind?"

"I never said there were other…"

But there were. Amelia, Eliza, Caroline… all victims of the wrath of the English and their expectations. But how did he…

"And then, perhaps, just perhaps," and his voice softened again, his lilt shifting east, ringing with a pure essence of Britannia, "after voices of reason had finally talked him down from his sacrificial altar where he had put his own happiness and best interest up for slaughter by denying his love's own freedom to decide that fate –"

"It was hardly a choice; there'd have been consequences no matter my deci –"

"IF!" he interjected, an urgency for her understanding creeping into his tone that Maeve just couldn't fathom. "If, perchance, he had decided to sacrifice his all for you to prove how he treasured you, only for you to misunderstand the nature of the very proposal he was to make… Might not he have suffered from the realization that it was his own shortsightedness that cost your happiness? Despite that he has suffered in his loneliness and concern for his daughter and his intended, is it not possible that he understands how the thing it cost him was the thing he promised to honor and value the most?"

Her head pounded in the contemplation. Was it possible? Could it really be him? Dry words whispered past a parched heart. "What did he value most?"

His voice was eerily close as he gained every inch of distance not forbidden to him.

"Your time."

"August?"

"Yes."

Her breath reclaimed its grace, but Maeve's heart refused to forgive the fault in the air between them.

"But you… The Duchess…"

Tears slipped from the corner of her eyes and blazed a heated path down her face as he answered. "Perish the thought. It was the Duchess who was intervening on your behalf. I wanted to marry you, but was too frightened." He paused, sounding on the verge of tears himself. "I still want to marry you, Maeve."

She wanted so desperately to believe, to know that her beloved sat just on the other side of this cold brick wall, wanted to look into his eyes and remind him of her heart's unfathomable love for him.

"I don't… How are you… Why did you get… Are you going to…"

Too many questions to be answered, but Maeve couldn't calm her racing mind long enough to focus. She heard him laugh, amused at her perplexed state.

"All will be well soon. "

Again, a twist of agony writhed within her. "Oh, August, I'm so sorry."

"Me, too."

Lord in Heaven, had she really misunderstood? Had she invited this torturous existence because she had jumped to false conclusions? Suddenly, the punishment seemed all too fair a fate. Maeve thought it was just that she sat imprisoned. She should be given no reprieve, for what she had done was unconscionable.

She struggled to speak, let alone make sense. "You were going to ask me… to marry you?"

"I never meant for you to misunderstand. And if that's what you promised Amelia, knowing what you believed to be true," he exhaled slowly, as if letting go his own regret, "if you thought that I was marrying Alexandra, then I understand why you took Goosie. I suppose it's my punishment. I took three years of your life from you, and you've denied me three years of mine. But Maeve…"

She could picture his face pressed against the bars of his cell.

"I don't want to live without you and Goosie anymore. Time has stolen too much from us already."

Tears as hot as coals fell down her face like ash. She had never dreamed the day would come again when August wooed her with honeyed words.

"I… thought…" Maeve sniffled. "I thought… you were… marrying …"

She mumbled, willing some divine force to intercede and magically erase the last three years. Maeve wanted him to tell her it had never happened, as though she had just fallen asleep on that Easter night and had an awful dream.

"Never," he declared. "Maeve, I love you far too much to ever do such a thing."

The reality of their circumstances, however, did not elude her. "Fat bit of good that will do. Yes, you're here. *In jail.* What could we do now?"

"Well, quite simply, we're going to break out."

Of course the knowledge of the workings of a prison were woefully lacking in the British aristocracy.

"You're here to get me out?" she repeated back sarcastically. "To get me out, by being thrown in?"

It was precisely at that moment that Maeve heard the approaching of foot-falls and the cursing voice coming out the outer corridor.

"….just want to eye him down, see what kind of man does this."

The voice was all at once familiar, its Dixie drawl all too indicative of the owner: Jefferson Schand.

"Here we go, Maeve," August whispered quickly. "Don't say a thing."

The door opened at the far end of the room and the steps moved to the front of August's cell.

"This is him, the ungodly cur," Jefferson spat vehemently. "This is the man, if we can call him that, who accosted me in the street and attempted to steal my bill fold."

August's voice rang back with scorn, invoking the false Irish tones of his cover. "Did not, you stupid thumper. I've no need of your money."

"Officer Hume, give me five minutes. Five minutes with the dog and let me have vengeance. Damned Irish! Let me give a good lesson."

The accompanying officer cleared his throat and shuffled in place. "Yes, sir, as you wanted. Put him back here especially because no one would witness it."

Jefferson's face peeked around the wall. He winked. "What about this one? Will she say a word?"

The policeman sneered as he too eyed Maeve. "Not if she knows what's good for her. She'll be sent to the reaper soon enough, as it is."

Both men pulled back as Maeve heard the rustling of paper.

Money. Jefferson was paying off the officer to get time alone with August under the auspices of delivering a little un-civil justice.

"Leave him alive and just a little… wiser, gentlemen" the officer cautioned.

Metallic clacking followed as the gate to August's cell slowly creaked open. Maeve, always a careful examiner of words, wondered at the plurality of "gentlemen." She tried to crane her neck to see who else had come in, but her view was regulated by the angle of their position.

"Don't break anything. I don't want the hassle."

Jefferson chuckled. "Don't worry, he'll heal. In time."

Lone footsteps paced back up the hall, followed by a cracking of the door and subsequent latching of the lock. In her cell, Maeve began to piece together the basics of their idea, but still couldn't conceive how it would work. August's cell might be open, and Jefferson may be here, but how were they planning to get…

"Maeve!"

She jolted as the voice called out to her and a most unexpected face came into view. Maeve's took shelter against the back wall as her nerves jumped to full attention.

"Owen!"

He made to hush her, his eyes darting to the door to assure that the outburst wasn't bringing any attention from the outside.

"Owen, what in the name of Kingdom Come are you doing here?"

His smile almost unnerved her with its vague self-assuredness.

"Doing what I should have done a long time ago," he declared as he fished out from his pocket some scrap of cloth. His hands worked with alarming speed unrolling it, before he leaned against the bars of the cell. A scratch and tinkle of metal upon metal confused her, until a moment later when, to her shock and amazement, the lock of her cell disengaged, and the gate swung on its hinges.

Owen, wearing a smirk of confidence, took two steps in, backing Maeve into a corner. "Now, take off your clothes."

As August rounded the corner, he was distressed by the look on Maeve's face, her expression one of utter confusion and misunderstanding. If there had been time, August could have expounded upon the events leading to this moment at great length: how Murphy and he had agreed to set aside everything and focus on freeing her from jail; how Jefferson's military experience allowed them to craft the covert mission with the best chance of success; how a hurried stop at their temporary residence had alerted Caroline, who had aided the effort by letting out hems and waistlines of the necessary clothing to better allow the interchange of attire.

And how it was all for her.

If there was one thing of which August was certain, it was that he could not live with himself if any ill befell her again. His foolhardy decisions had already cost her too much: her father, her friends, her home.

"Maeve, quickly!" Owen insisted as he began to peel off the clothes August had exchanged with him only an hour before. In wearing the fine dress of the aristocracy, if August had not known better himself, he would have sworn the Irishman to be any well-bred gentlemen on the street.

August came to the sudden realization that he stood motionless, gaping at his Maeve, her face full of doubt. Owen snapped his fingers with an echoing click at his face, bringing August from his reverie.

"Grayson, we haven't time for tea. Jefferson, how's it coming?"

The blacksmith was right. With a nod, August too began to peel off the outer layer of his garments, Owen's commoner garb, and hand them to Jefferson.

"What…?"

As Maeve looked at all three disrobing, August saw understanding begin to dawn in her tear-drought eyes.

In rushed words, he tried to explain. "Murphy will dress as you, Jefferson as the pickpocket and they'll both stay behind in the jail. In the meantime, you and I will escape disguised as the victimized two gentlemen."

"Escape?" she repeated, but still made no motion to comply. "But if you help me escape, you'll be an accomplice."

No longer could he let his or her heart doubt the veracity of his dedication. In this hour, at this moment, the clock was ticking away, every second pulling an opportunity to flee. She needed to know, to trust that he would protect her, and that he was sincere. She needed to trust that he was prepared to lose everything he ever had to gain back the only thing that would ever matter.

Without further hesitation, August closed the distance between them and crushed her body to his, pushing her head to his shoulder.

"I'm sorry. I'm sorry. I'm sorry…"

His apologies became his breath, the steady ebb and flow by which he maintained life. Maeve's face heated against the thin cotton of Owen's borrowed shirt, but the tears had stopped. Her frame shook.

"August, you cannot do this."

He pulled away and looked longingly into her eyes, begging with his gaze for explanation.

"Goosie!" she cried suddenly. Her brow hardened as she stiffened in his arms. "I could even go to gallows with my head held high, but only if I know that Augusta will be all right. If you are caught…"

He took her face between his hands, running his thumb over her cheeks. "Don't you dare, Maeve O'Connor. Everything you have done, you have done for Goosie or me. Don't you think for a second that I'm about to let all that be for nothing." A gentle kiss on her lips broke her tension. She pulled away, eyes closed, breathing easy. "Our daughter needs us both."

The momentary comfort was brought to an end when a pile of clothes landed on the back of August's head, and he turned to see Murphy's impatient scowl, the Irishman standing in nothing but his undergarments.

"For the love of Mary, will you two get on with it?"

At last, Maeve complied. Tossing aside her wrap, she pulled her frock over her head. Luckily, despite the difference in her feminine frame and the blacksmith's sturdy physique, the loose cut of prison attire allowed Owen to don the woman's garb without too odd an outcome. With a quick bend, he retrieved the woolen, gray wrap and threw it over his head, hiding and absence of long chestnut hair.

Jefferson and August had also finished their exchange of clothes when Jefferson retrieved the set-aside lantern and held it aloft. What beheld August's eyes as he turned stopped him at the quick: Maeve was staring at Murphy, eyes wide and watering, as he leaned patiently against the back wall of her cell, waiting for the gate to seal him in. Owen returned a sheepish smile, beaming right back at her. Realizing they both needed this moment, August placed his hand on the small of Maeve's back, now covered by coat tails, and nudged her forward.

Leaning in, August whispered into her ear. "It's all right. I understand."

One measured step, then a second, and with two more purposeful strides, she reached the blacksmith and wrapped her arms around his neck. Owen bent over and returned the gesture, placing the most tender of kisses on her cheek.

"*Tá mo chroí istigh ionat*," he said to her, inhaling deeply her scent as she all but cut off his breathing with her grasp.

"I will remember you for this always, Owen." Maeve turned her head and returned his chaste kiss.

Though the scene might have driven August to the edge of mad jealousy before, he felt nothing in its wake but gratitude.

With one more lung full, Owen exhaled and kind-heartedly eased Maeve away. "Go now, before it's too late."

"Yes, Hume is likely to return any moment to assure that we haven't seriously injured the prisoner," Jefferson agreed. "You two should make haste."

Taking Maeve's hand in his own, August led her out of the cell. Her eyes remained fixed on Owen. Jefferson made to close the gate, but Owen stepped forward, wrapping his hands around the bars and pressing his face through the cracks as the lock clicked into place.

"Grayson!"

August looked away from Maeve, trying to help her gather her hair into the crown of the tall black hat.

Owen smiled at August for perhaps the first time. "You make sure you remember that she chose you above all. Don't you ever make her regret that again."

He acknowledged the demand with a gracious nod. "I shan't. Never again. I swear."

The agreement was sealed in a silent gaze. Finally, Owen broke the moment.

"You should get in, Jefferson. Keep to the shadows if you can."

"This is ridiculous!" Maeve barked suddenly. "Even if I hide my hair in this hat, they're going to notice that two blonds walked in and two brownies are walking out. "

"It was dark, he'll just suppose he didn't see us well enough," August tried to assure her.

"And what about the fact that I'm a whole head shorter than all of you?"

"Jefferson made sure to slouch when he was coming in."

"And my body is so much smaller than –"

"*Mo chroi!*" August snapped, cutting her off abruptly. She jolted, but only eyed him with curiosity. "Did Guinevere dissuade Lancelot with all the why-nots? Are you so opposed to being swept off your feet and made deliriously happy?"

"No, I suppose not," she playfully returned, her cheeks blushing over.

And though her skin was covered in the grime of her imprisonment, though her face was now streaked with lines left by tears, her smile was the most beautiful thing in all creation. Even after all, August could see in that smile that she loved him.

He pulled her close without thought of consequence or circumstance. The rim of her hat pushed against his forehead as he lowered his lips. It fell to the side and to the floor. As Maeve's hair spilled down over her shoulders and his lips caressed hers, August felt her body go stiff. In the distance, outside the jail and from the tower of the adjacent court house, the ringing of a clock echoed through the night.

He pulled away only long enough to take in her terrified and rigid shock before looking over his shoulder.

Hume held the lantern high overhead, illuminating the entire scene all too well: August, hands on Maeve; Maeve, dressed in a man's long-tail coat and wrapped in another "man's" arms; Owen, scowling like a billy goat behind bars; and Jefferson, still outside the cell and dressed in a poor man's garb, holding their own lantern aloft.

August was certain, though he did not look himself, calculations of courses of action were screwing Jefferson's appearance as the strategist nature overtook his sister's husband.

Hume came back from his wordless shock. "What the… bloody…hell?"

A revolver was drawn. A lantern was thrown. Maeve screamed. Glass shattered. A figure shot past August. A struggle ensued. Another lantern clanked against the floor. More shattering glass. The sound of a scuffle. Jefferson's fist flew. Hume ducked. Everything went black.

Then, light.

Terrifying, consuming, scorching, flickering light.

The woolly wood planks of the floor creaked as the oil of the lanterns flowed between the cracks, creating a myriad of pathways for the fire to follow. A small swirl of flame burgeoned into a chasm of blaze. The wood all around – dry, old and worn, framed inside the brick of the exterior walls – glowed briefly before any realized what had happened.

Hume did not waver. He waylaid into Jefferson full force, landing a fist in his stomach, causing the Captain to double over. Looking smug, the officer didn't respect the fortitude of his opponent.

Jefferson gave one fury-filled glance as he looked up. The flames reflected in his eyes, adding to the veil of tyranny August feared had been many a Union soldier's last view of this blessed world.

"Go." Jefferson growled the order clearly. "August, get away. NOW!"

Wisely, August hesitated no more. Grabbing Maeve's hand and pulling her through the door, he heard Jefferson's body slam into Hume's as the latter shrieked in agony.

Maeve's feet were swift and her tongue still as August maneuvered them down the stairs and through the outer gate which, thankfully, Hume hadn't opportunity to lock behind him. A gaggle of busies eyed them suspiciously as they emerged into their presence.

"Fire!" August yelled to distract them from the woman dressed in men's clothing hooked under his arm. "In the cells. Quickly!"

All jumped as August moved with determination in the opposite direction, for the door leading to the street. Behind them, he could hear the already-frantic police scramble. As Maeve and August plunged into the bitterly cold Boston night, a pang of anxiety overtook him. There was no need to worry about Jefferson; his skills in defense and escape were no doubt sufficient. As they ducked and scurried through the darkened Boston streets, August's mind replayed the image of his final backward glance: Murphy, oddly serene in the flickering firelight, the shadow of the bars intersecting his face.

August couldn't think about that now. It was only a matter of time before the fire would be put out and all would realize the truth: the Norwich Nanny had escaped. August felt Maeve tremble as they fled, trying to gain distance enough to reach the wharf where Caroline was stationed.

"August!"

He turned to see what alarmed her. On the far end of the street, three police pointed in their direction, turning to pursue.

"This way!"

He coaxed Maeve through an alleyway and into the recesses of a landing dock. It wasn't far now. He could hear the lapping of water.

The police paused at the end of the alley as August tilted his head forward to observe while trapping Maeve against the wall with his arm. Their pursuers made a few paces up the alley. August held his breath and gave every prayer that their sight would not pierce the blanket of the shadows over him and Maeve.

"They're over there!" someone shouted from beyond August's scope of vision. He tensed and gasped, as did Maeve.

Instead, the officer, now just some ten feet away, whirled in a different direction and ran off. Easing his frame, August realized only too late that another took his place, stalking up the alley.

The clop-clop of his footfall kept time with the tap-tap of the night stick to his hand, at the ready. His pace was measured, deliberate, as if he all but knew they were there but refusing to pounce on his prey before he was good and ready.

In that moment, everything became clear. August knew what he had to do, and he knew what it would cost him. He knew that it would kill him, as well. Still, he would not see Maeve taken back into custody. He would not see her suffer anymore.

Gently pulling Maeve closer, August whispered so that, by the grace of God, only she could hear.

"When I make for him, you run. Meet Caroline at the wharf. She's waiting there with Goosie."

He could taste her tears on the breeze. "No, not without you."

Shuddering with resolve, August pulled her hand to his lips and pressed a silent kiss to her fingers.

"Maeve, I'm sorry. For… Well, for not doing what I should have done."

"August, don't…"

"No time to argue. Take our daughter and be safe. I love you, Maeve. I love you."

As though words alone would be enough to see her through the years of loneliness that would follow. The book was written, and his sacrifice would be the seal. What a bittersweet tragedy, made whole only in a final scene in which the two women August loved most in the world–his Maeve and his Augusta–were safe and together.

"On three. One…"

Maeve vehemently shook her head, her eyes wide. "No."

In the meeting of their gazes, he nearly renounced his intentions.

"You must. Two…"

"I can't." Her tiny fists beat into his chest. "I can't leave you."

"Maeve, please." He stilled her fists and kissed them, taking one longing look at her, knowing very well it was the last. "Three!"

Leaping into the light, throwing his fist at the perplexed officer, August felt a surge of comfort as he heard Maeve's feet begin to carry her swiftly up the alley.

What hit his ears next, however, made him cringe.

"What in the Sam Hill, August!?"

Maeve stopped abruptly.

"Jefferson?" August gasped as a flood of conflicting emotions overtook him. He pulled up his brother and embraced him in relief. "What the Dickens…"

Jefferson glanced at the night stick clutched threateningly in his own hand. "Sorry to scare you." He shrugged as August's eyes ran the length of him, taking in the garb of a police uniform in the pale moonlight. "Figured I could change clothes one more time tonight. August, the fire's spreading. Half of Boston is awake, trying to figure out what all the chaos is. Let's see if we can use it to our advantage and get you gone. No timc to waste."

Jefferson led them to the edge of the alley, peeking cautiously around the corner. He raised his hand to still them, before his fingers flexed and they followed him back into the street. In the far distance, the commotion consumed the soundscape: bells, whistles, the pounding of hooves over cobble-stoned streets.

"I fear looking back," Maeve gasped as the wharf came into sight around the next corner.

"Don't, just don't," Jefferson returned.

August saw Caroline's petite frame lower from the driver's bench and land gracefully on the street.

"Maeve!" She ran forth. "Maeve, how I worried."

"I've missed you! Oh, Caro!"

The reunion made his heart clench, but not so much as a moment later, when the tarp of the cart peeled to the side and an angelic pair of blue eyes framed by ebony hair peeked out.

"Ma?" Augusta asked, rubbing the sleep from her eyes. "Ma? Are you here?"

August leapt forward and pulled the beloved child down, but was hardly able to keep a grasp as Maeve claimed her into her embrace. The common stock of blood–or lack thereof–was forgotten. August felt his own heart weep as he pulled both of the girls–his girls–into his embrace and knew, unequivocally, that bloodlines mattered not. This was his family.

And this family would never be separated again.

A raspy, little sound drew his attention to Augusta's face, and her scrunched up expression.

"Ma, you smell horrible!" she squealed.

Maeve only laughed. "Isn't it the Lord's honest truth, Goosie? I can't deny it."

Maeve caught August's eye, and he couldn't help but laugh as well.

"From the mouths of babes," Caroline mused, eying them approvingly.

An hour later, through the haze of the burning fire, the cart pulled to a stop atop Beacon Hill. All, save Augusta and Charles sleeping in the back, leapt down and took in the sight with awe.

Boston burned.

Plumes of smoke wafted skyward, pushed by the inferno erupting from the rooftops below. A smoked-over moon hung low in the sky, as though unable to turn from the horrific scene. The smell – the unmistakable scent of ash and cinder – enveloped them.

"Owen!" Maeve cried.

Jefferson's head hung low. "I tried, but by the time I had Hume's uniform, the fire was too intense. I wanted to, Maeve. I tried. I just… couldn't."

A sadness struck August, as though he had lost someone very dear. Looking to his brother-by-marriage. Defeated again, August suspected that guilt consumed him, knowing the successful escape had caused the blacksmith his life.

August recalled something he had said to Maeve, once so long ago: *"There is not benevolence without bane to be found in this. We are all victims of our best intent."*

Again, he recalled the blacksmith's serenity in that last glance. Was it because of the guilt he felt that he was so prepared to die? Or had Owen loved Maeve so fervently that the sacrifice was the only way he had to show it? August had the honor of Maeve's love for so long, and squandered it in a misunderstanding of nobility and honor. How noble and honorable was he now, embracing the reverie of having his love beside him at the cost of the life of a man of true honor?

"August?" Caroline asked as she witnessed the destruction of her brother's resolve. "Why are you crying?"

"I don't deserve her," he answered tearfully, speaking to his sister but looking at Maeve. "I'm not good enough for her."

Maeve hastened to him, bringing her hands up to his face. "Don't you dare!" she rebuked. "I made a promise to your dying wife, and you made a promise to my dying friend. And we are going to stick to those promises. I'm going to love Goosie and keep her safe, and you're going to do the same for me. We're going to make good our word so that their deaths don't count for nothing."

As Maeve's eyes locked into his, and August saw the power of her conviction, he realized this is what it meant to be noble, to go forward with grace and humility, to see through the promise of the sacrifices of others, lest they be in vain. To do anything less than allow himself to love Maeve with all his heart would be a disgrace to the memories of all those whose valor and surrender had delivered them to that moment.

Owen. Amelia. Rory. Even Eliza.

His mother, Eliza, who gave up her home, her family, and her identity to love Emmanuel, who in turn never embraced her sacrifice but spurned it in needless worry over the impressions of others.

August would not be his father. He would not spurn Maeve's sacrifice. Not one moment longer.

He realized, this was it – the very thing that even Owen Murphy could see that he had withheld from her. It was the one thing he had never given her, and the only thing she had ever needed. In essence, his surrender. August had always made the decisions for her, decided what she could and could not be in his life.

"Maeve," August gasped, lowering his forehead to hers. "I'm so sorry. I should have… Maeve, marry me. Have mercy on the wretch that I am and marry me."

He felt her smile as his lips sought hers. It was his sacrifice. August offered her his heart, though he knew it unworthy, and Maeve could destroy it now with a single word. The decision was hers.

I surrender.

"Yes, August. Yes."

The Boston Globe

Monday November 11, 1872

BOTH VICTIM AND PERPETRATOR OF GRAYSON KIDNAPPING ASSUMED DEAD IN WAKE OF FIRE

From our remote office, Cambridge-Damage from the fire that swept through our city is still being assessed. In some areas, cinders still glow. It will be many weeks, if not months, before we can fully gauge the breadth of the destruction.

Reports of casualties are rising, though not as many as first feared. Many remain without shelter. We pray any able in coming winter months to open their homes to those left without will do so, in the name of Christian charity.

Hundreds of buildings are lost, it is our sad duty to report. The courthouse was damaged, but may be recoverable. Many of our brave citizens ignored danger and were able to secure the Old North Church from harm, however. Also a victim of the inferno was the city jailhouse, where two extremely burned bodies have been found. It is believed one of these was that of Maeve O'Connor, the infamous Norwich Nanny, housed there pending conviction. In an odd twist, it is believed that the other body was that of Lord August Grayson, coincidently visiting the jail at the time the fire broke out. This suspicion is further credited by the report of Mrs. Caroline Schand, Lord Grayson's sister, that her brother has not been seen since the fire.

"We are overcome with grief," she told The Globe last evening. "We believe that my brother has perished. We cannot abide to stay and be reminded of our pain. My husband and I are returning to England with our son and our niece, to mourn privately."

Mrs. Schand further thanks the people of Boston for their kind wishes and sympathies.

In Perpetua

~Oregon~
Spring 1878

"Riordan!"

Patrick O'Keefe's booming voice was the only one that could ever compete with the ferocious crack and groan of a shorn redwood falling to earth. August let the axe rest where it had landed in a tree he'd been at for the last few hours, and turned around to take in the mammoth figure of the foreman.

"Yes, sir?" he asked back in his perfected, false Irish brogue.

"Quitting time," he grumbled, cigar-gnawing not forsaken, then added with a curt smile. "Get home to your wife."

August looked around, only noticing now that in his complete concentration on the work, the sky had begun to darken.

"Yes, sir!" he exclaimed, peeling off the gloves and fetching his lunch pail off the forest floor.

Instinctively, the fingers massaged the rough spots on his hands, once so soft and warm. Five years of arduous work had done away with that. The life he and Maeve had made was not an easy one, but it was one where their labors and not their laity determined their fate.

Sometimes, as he held her in his arms at night and paid homage to their love with long, tender strokes, August wondered if the coarseness of his palms vexed her. If it did, Maeve never breathed a word. Truth be told, time and fortune had left each with wear. She was still just as beautiful to his eyes, if not more so, but gone was the soft, supple lass of Killarney. What remained, however, was more precious still: the love of his life, the light of his heart, the adopted mother of his child, and the reason he drew breath each morning.

"Good night, Curtis!" August called as he paced towards the road. He knew Patrick would be waiting as always, so they could walk together.

Curtis threw his gloves aside, calling out his goodbye as August passed. "Night, Paul. See ya in the mornin', eh?"

August heard Patrick chuckle as he came into view, leaning against the side of the rest building.

"What?"

"Paul Riordan," he mocked. "Do you ever get used to it?"

"Do you ever get used to Patty making jokes about you whacking your log all day?"

He clicked his tongue in rebuke. "Watch it there, *Riordan.* Remember, I am your boss and I won't hesitate to fire your English arse." He chuckled, a full-bellied, echoing laugh, at his own jest. "And then I would be whacking my own log. Patty would turn me out."

They sauntered on another half hour to the settlement where both their homes sat. As his cabin came into view, Patrick asked, "Maeve hasn't caught on, has she?"

"*Mary,*" he reminded Patrick lest some wayward passerby hear the faux pas, "hasn't a clue. Thanks to your help, of course. I can't wait to see the look on her face. Goosie's staying with you tonight, eh?"

Patrick threw his brawny arm around August and squeezed his shoulder, nearly causing the Englishman to squeal. "Aye, and she's welcome to. Patty feeds that lass right: good crisp bacon and warm brown bread. Not that wet muck of dough that gets passed as bread at the Riordans."

"We'll return the favor, of course," he continued as Patrick let go of his shoulder, the muscle burning in the wake. "If you and Patty ever need a quiet evening, we'll take your lot in."

"All five of them?" he asked with a coaxing smile. "Well, now I just think you're trying to get a promotion from me."

Goosie was sitting on the front porch when August came into the yard. She jumped up and darted across the distance when she caught sight of him at the gate. Patrick's cottage was a quarter-mile back up the road, where he had turned off.

"Da!"

August twirled her around as best he could in his arms; she was so tall and slender now that the task was becoming nearly impossible.

"What's all this commotion about? Just me, same as always."

"All the commotion? It's your anniversary. It's so romantic! Ma has been at it all day, singing and cooking, and cooking and singing. There's enough food in there to feed an army."

"Is that what she's giving me for our anniversary, I wonder? An army?" August scratched his chin in false contemplation. "Well, that would make dragging the logs to the shore easier on the horses."

Augusta gave her father a poke in the shoulder. "Think you're quite the joker, don't you, Da?"

"Well, he better not try to pull any jests on me tonight, if he values his life." Maeve walked out on the porch, rubbing a kitchen rag over her hands. Her eyes twinkled as she met August's stare.

Patty stepped around Maeve and out on to the porch, a bundle of white pulled to her chest.

"Evening, Mrs. O'Keefe." He tipped his cap to her.

"Mr. Riordan," she said with a kindly nod, winking. "Little Brie here will be waking up wanting to eat soon, as will Patrick, no doubt. I should be going. Goosie, all ready?"

"Yes, Mrs. O'Keefe," Augusta answered, dangling a sack in front of her. "I'll come home after mass, Ma?"

"Yes, please do," Maeve confirmed. The wind blew through the trees then, and Maeve pulled her wrap closer around her. "Make sure you keep warm tonight. There's an awful chill in the air."

"Good night, Da." Rolling up on her toes, Augusta swept her long locks aside and planted a kiss on August's cheek, which he returned.

"Good night, my dear. And good night to you, Mrs. O'Keefe."

August turned and watched them exit through the gate. Patty's one arm kept the baby well-secured, while the other circled around his daughter's shoulder.

"Oh, and Patty!" he yelled. She paused, her gaze focusing on August, curious. "Tell Patrick I'll have the rest of the money to him next week."

Patty smiled. "We know you're good for it. Whenever you get to it."

He swore he heard her add under her breath, "Just, please, don't be trying to barter any exchanges with him."

Maeve was smirking when August turned back to her.

"Money?" she queried. "For what?"'

Stepping up onto the porch, August took his wife into his arms and kissed her with the passion that had been building the whole day. "A man of good upbringing delivers his wife a present on their anniversary. I like to believe myself a man of at least adequate upbringing. Patrick helped forward the funds on my behalf."

The scents coming from the cabin tempted him: squash, potatoes, carrots. Maeve must have made one of her famous stews.

And of course, bread.

But the temptation he wanted to give into now was the one in his arms. Maeve's scent set his heart afire, and August wanted nothing more than to draw every possible pleasure from her. His mouth trailed down her jaw and then to her neck. They remained on the porch, her quickening breath sending clouds of condensation into the night air.

"Uh-uh." She reprimanded him with a sideways glance as she pulled back. "We have plenty of time for that tonight, *mo chroí*. I've spent the last two hours putting up with all of Patty's primping and prepping and you will behold it with the proper attention it's due."

"Really? Well, step inside our home and let me see, Mrs. Riordan."

For so many years, August had secretly held fantasies of the day when he could call her Mrs. Grayson, or even Lady Grayson. But this was better. There had already been one Lady Grayson as his wife. Despite the nature of that union, he never wanted Maeve to believe that she was somehow a second-hand replacement for the mother Augusta had lost or the wife he had. Maeve was an act of grace unto herself. They knew from the Boston newspapers that they were both presumed dead, and to ensure that their names did not tip anyone off of the fallacy, they had selected Riordan in homage to Eliza.

It hurt to know that one of the bodies assumed to be theirs was Owen; the other must have been Hume's. Caroline and Jefferson had returned almost immediately to England as Maeve, Augusta, and he had fled west. Caroline ignited a rumor that Augusta had boarded ship with them, but took ill and died a sea, where she was buried. The Grayson title passed then to young Charles, though Jefferson and Caroline assumed control of the family's estate. Caroline wrote to August with great amusement when Woodrow read from August's will, "In the event that I am without male heir at the time of my death, and should I still remain unwed, I bequeath my entire estate to my nephew, Charles Schand, with the condition that in his adulthood he be permitted to marry whomsoever he wishes without condition."

Caroline promised to make it so.

Maeve was right, Patty had gone to great lengths. His wife's hair had been extensively curled and clipped into cascading ringlets the trailed down over her shoulders. Truth be told, it was quite regal. Maeve looked like a queen, and August felt humbled in her presence.

"With beauty such as this, you deserve a gown of oriental silk and fine pearls," he mused as he twirled one of her locks around his finger. "If only I could still give you those things…"

"Now, what use would oriental silk be here?" She blushed, causing him almost to give into the temptation to pull her to their bed that very moment. "Besides, pearls against my ivory skin? Gold would be a better choice."

Beaming, he nodded in agreement. "Gold it is then. Whenever you desire." He reached out, tracing a finger down her neck, then over her breast. "Seems unfair to show up the gold like that, though."

Her mouth twisted into a devious, knowing grin.

August made love to his wife on the floor in front their fireplace, just as he had the first time, absent the ticking clock. That clock, which had measured each of their stolen moments mockingly. Now they were free to embrace, to kiss, to love without measure and in every measure.

After they had redressed, August led his Maeve outside, telling her they would stroll by the river. The night was cold, despite the mildness of the day. Even as they languidly meandered, his arm around her to help keep her warm, snowflakes intermittently floated down from above. At a bend in the river, with the moon knitting a soft glow that weaved through the forest canopy, making it look as though fairies danced to and fro, he led her off to a rarely-used path.

"Where are we about?"

August smirked. "I want to give you your present now." He pressed her forward with more haste.

"Way back here? August, it's cold and I'm… not… St. Peter, is it really?"

"Every plank and every thatch."

"The cottage!"

Maeve ran to the front door, reaching out a hand to make certain it wasn't a mirage. As her fingers made contact with the worn wood of the front door, she felt faint.

"How is this possible?"

"You didn't think I had actually destroyed it, did you? No, I had it carefully disassembled and stored. It was my intention to rebuild it elsewhere, after the Fenians had their little uprising done. But then, well… You know, fate just didn't favor it."

Tears burned down her cheek. "But here? In Oregon? It must have been so costly."

"Pricier to find some lads to put it together who wouldn't let the cat out of the bag." August grinned as he recalled asking Patrick for the help, both in finding such men, and for good measure, paying them on his behalf so they wouldn't know precisely whom the building was meant. After initial disbelief, Patrick had agreed. He thought it proper, he added, that after having taken Maeve's cottage from her, giving it back was the least August could do. It would be the first time the English gave the Irish back their homes willingly, he had joked.

August reached out and opened the door, coaxing her inside. “You forget that Caroline has mineral rights to a rather productive copper mine. The gift is from her too. And Jefferson, of course.”

Everything was perfect; it looked just as it did the day she had left it years ago, right down to the proper chairs and broom by the hearth.

A mug, distinctly missing a chip, was on the table.

“August,” she said happily, “I have a present for you too.”

“Oh?”

“Well, I mean to say, I will, but it won’t be here for … another five or six months.”

“Six months?” He laughed. “Did you send off for something in a catalog?”

She giggled. “No, I didn’t send for something.” Her hands reached for his, and when he gave them into her grasp, she pushed them gently against the little bump of her stomach firmly. “It’s actually something you’ve given me. I’m hoping, a son.”

Realization like thunder struck. A child was under his hands. Their child.

“You’re… expecting?”

It couldn’t be possible. After all the time of thinking Maeve was barren, and having resigned to that fact, she was carrying a child.

Which they would raise together, here, in her cottage. Maeve would have her all.

She turned and threw her arms around his neck, pulling his lips to hers. August wanted to respond, but was frozen in shock. Maeve mistook the silence. He saw that same fret curl its way around her heart, and she pulled back in anxious vexation.

“I thought you’d be happy. I know we never said we’d have children, but we didn’t think I could and--”

Melting, August pulled her back to him and wrapped his arms about her, kissing her feverishly.

"Maeve, nothing sweeter has ever been said," he assured her. "I just don't understand. Why now? After so long? How?"

"Love the Lord, and He will return the love two-fold." She smiled against his lips, though he was confused. "Perhaps He just thought we needed time, August."

August didn't care that they had just lain together an hour before, he wanted her now. Again. He wanted to show his wife–the mother of his child, his *children*–the extent of his happiness.

"Speaking of time, I think you owe me twenty-two minutes tonight, Miss O'Connor," he teased.

Maeve blushed. "But Lord Grayson," she quipped in a playful, seductive tone, "I did not come last night. Surely, per our agreement, my time should be doubled."

"Jesus, Mary, and Joseph, you're right! In fact, you've missed quite a few nights. Your debt must be up to hours now."

Maeve began giggling again.

"What is it, darling?"

"Just thinking what a silly arrangement it was. Do you realize that it wouldn't have been long before my debt to you would have grown into days, then weeks and so on?"

Of this, August needed her to be without doubt, to know in no uncertain terms the veracity of his love. He stooped and gently, slowly, tenderly pulled her hand to his lips and pressed a kiss to her trembling, pulsating wrist.

"If our arrangement had gone on and on until we were spending all eternity together, it still wouldn't have been long enough. I loved you from the day you found me at the river. I refuse to declare silly any moment. This," he ran his hand over the life – his child – growing within her, "this is our forever. Every day, I love you more. *Mo Maeve, mo chroi.* My heart."

ABOUT THE AUTHOR

Killian McRae considers herself a fan of history. Hence, many of her fictional works are packaged in historical wrappers as she tugs and twists the edges of the truth to ponder the inevitable "What if?"

Born and raised in rural Michigan, Killian later attended the University of Michigan where she took a tour of majors, making stops in Operatic Performance, International Business, and Elementary Education before finally obtaining a degree in Near Eastern history, with a focus on Ancient Egypt and Turkic Empires.

She is currently a member of the Stanford Writing program, as well as a PRO member of the Romance Writers of America.

Killian lives in the San Francisco Bay area with her husband , two children, and a tiny dog who thinks he's a cat.

ACKNOWLEDGEMENTS

A Love by Any Measure has occupied a three-year span of my life, and gone through many rewrites, redrafts, and regrets. However, it also documented a transition in which, after years of self-doubt and self-effacement, the encouragement of others brought me to see my own value and embrace my own passion for writing.

I'd like to thank the dedicated pre-readers who patted me on my shoulder while kicking me in the rear, when needed. They didn't hold back, for better or worse. The hardest thing to be in this world is honest. I am in their debt.

To Lo: *Measure* is a book, but Lo is its spine. In the first drafts, she kept me focused and in tune with the characters, becoming their advocate against my wild expectations. She is a beautiful person and a talented writer, and one of the best critique partners ever.

To the readers: Thank you for sharing with me how this story has touched you, and giving me encouragement in the times when I felt I couldn't go on.

To my children: your patience with me is amazing. You set the bar pretty darn high.

To Tiffany and Nina: You may think the part you've played is very small, but the effect one has on a person's life isn't measured in words or in minutes, it's measured by impact. You two are the Himalayas.

To my husband, who doesn't always agree with my writing, but tries to support me anyway.

CPSIA information can be obtained at www.ICGtesting.com
Printed in the USA
BVOW032038081011

273139BV00001B/9/P

9 780983 979708